S

OLD SINS

By Aline Templeton

OLD SINS

ALINE TEMPLETON

Allison & Busby Limited
11 Wardour Mews
London W1F 8AN
allisonandbusby.com

First published in Great Britain by Allison & Busby in 2021.
This paperback edition published by Allison & Busby in 2022.

A CIP catalogue record for this book is available from
the British Library.

10 9 8 7 6 5 4 3 2 1

ISBN 978-0-7490-2728-5

For my friend Jenny Mayhew, who introduced me to tea and cocktails

'OLD SINS CAST LONG SHADOWS.'

English proverb

CHAPTER ONE

FEBRUARY 2020

That night, the Inverbeg Inn was busy as usual. On Saturdays there was almost a ritual gathering to keep the little pub in business, so the craic was always good and it drew in custom too from half-a-dozen of the little townships round about. With the nearest police station only open 9 till 5, Tuesday and Thursday, it was the old-fashioned rules that applied: you were reckoned fit to drive if you could keep the car in a straight line and turn a corner when you got to one. Though admittedly, there were quite a lot of those.

Flora Maitland always made a point of coming. The well-worn path back up to the croft might be rugged terrain, particularly in February, but as her father had always said, she was sure-footed as a mountain goat. So even at seventy she saw no reason to curtail her pleasures and she always made an evening of it to justify the effort.

She looked forward to Saturday. She'd no regrets about leaving London; here in the peace and the silence, tired at night after hard physical work, she was sleeping as she hadn't slept for years, deeply and peacefully, but she had to admit that getting any kind of stimulating conversation out of a sheep was a bit of a challenge, so she relished the company. The natives were friendly and there was always a changing group of workers from the rewilding project on the Auchinglass Estate – young folk, often. She always got on well with the young who seemed to realise that her grey hair and wrinkles were just a clever disguise so that no one would ask the rebellious seventeen-year-old inside for ID.

Tonight she was propping up the bar in the centre of a group of them arguing with a fellow-crofter Angus Mackenzie, her neighbour and friend, about bringing the wolf back to Scotland. He was not, to put it mildly, in favour.

'They'd threaten my livelihood, that's what they'd do. They're not daft – are you really saying that when they got a bit peckish they'd go after red deer? You've maybe noticed they're the ones that run like the wind and have antlers, but you still think your pals wouldn't pick up a few lamb chops on the hoof instead when they were up for a takeaway? Oh, it's dead romantic, right enough – the grey ghosts, slinking through the trees with only the golden eyes glowing and giving a wee howl or two for effect. Just don't try telling me this is to save the trees.'

'But you'd get compensation,' one lad argued. 'And at least it would help keep the deer numbers down to give the saplings we're planting a chance.'

Flora's eyes glinted with mischief. 'But there's always the traditional way,' she said provocatively, raising an imaginary shotgun to her shoulders. 'Healthy food and local employment—'

One of the girls, very young, with green-streaked hair and piercings, obligingly rose to the bait. 'No!' she protested. 'That's just barbaric, killing beautiful animals for sport!'

Flora was just about to say, 'And the wolves' methods are more humane?' when she caught sight of a group coming in.

Flora froze mid-word, feeling the blood draining from her face. Banquo's ghost, she found herself thinking wildly: her moral failure appearing before her, like an apparition in human form. Immediate and present danger. She had to escape . . .

'Are you all right?' one boy said anxiously. 'You've gone awful white.'

'Oh, sorry – didn't meant to be rude,' the girl mumbled.

'No, no, it's nothing. My fault.' She turned hastily. 'Actually, I've been feeling a bit fluey. I'd probably be sensible to get on home.'

There was a finger of Scotch left in her glass. She downed it for Dutch courage, then with a brief, too-bright smile, slipped through as they stood aside to let her pass. She was aware of the concerned looks and the little buzz of conversation behind her as she reached the side door and stepped outside, zipping up her jacket.

It was bitterly cold after the cosy fug of the pub, a crystal-clear night with the ground, even at ten o'clock, already glinting with frost. The light from the windows fell in golden patches on the forecourt and there were lights in the car park but beyond that, nothing but blackness.

It took her eyes a few moments to adapt. It was the dark of the moon but the stars were showing bright – millions and millions of stars covering the sky that seemed like a bowl upturned over her head, wheeling, whirling, pressing in on her so that Flora staggered for a moment, feeling dizzy.

Panic, she told herself, stopping to take deep breaths of the icy air. She had to stop this at once, start thinking rationally. She'd a good brain; she'd made her living on that. She switched on her torch and set off up the rough path.

Flora was pretty certain she couldn't have been recognised. She'd turned away instantly while the group was still making their way in, and surely a grey-haired elderly lady in a tired-looking green padded jacket wouldn't be easy to identify as the defiantly hennaed, professionally immaculate manager she'd been.

She'd known someone could come looking for her, of course. She'd had the sense of trouble coming, though that wasn't what had prompted her to end her long and financially successful career. At the beginning, when she was young and wild, the business, with its historical overtones of outwitting a greedy state, had seemed edgy and defiant and romantic – oh yes! Romantic above all. Now it was different, hideously different, and she just couldn't live any longer with that sick feeling of disgust at what she'd allowed herself to become. With some skill, she'd managed to bow out gracefully into retirement without alarming the bosses, making the shameful decision to keep silent.

But when she heard an investigation had indeed begun, she'd realised her own peril. She had no illusions: doing the right thing, handing herself in to the authorities and throwing herself on the mercy of the court when it came to complicity, would be signing her death warrant. She must simply disappear.

Her father had just died and the croft he'd inherited from his father was hers now. She'd never talked about her background and there was only one person she'd ever told about her childhood, idyllic in retrospect. Perfect. She was ready for a quiet life; she reverted to her maiden name, stopped dying her hair and moved in. It was certainly rugged compared to what she'd been used to but in some strange way it felt as if she was sloughing off the dead skin of the past and emerging clean. She'd barely left the place since.

Surely they couldn't have known, she told herself, as she followed the cliff path up to the croft house. If the bosses had known, she wouldn't be here now, she'd be at the bottom of the bay there in a sack with a stone tied to her ankles. Coincidence, that's all, she told herself. Just a passing visitor. I can lie low, keep out of the way for a bit.

She'd never liked coincidences, though. Mostly, when you looked into it, they were no such thing. What could be the connection? Then it hit her.

The present owner had been there for a while. But before that . . . Remembering how she'd got involved in the first place, Flora shuddered. She must be mad; she'd actually chosen to hide in plain view.

So danger had come from the direction she hadn't thought of, deadly danger. She'd have to leave tomorrow, first thing. She'd phone Angus, ask him to check on the sheep until she could sell up. The sooner she got home to prepare the better, and she tried to speed up – she wasn't quite such a brisk walker these days and the gradient was taxing.

The windless night was very still. She was used to the silence here, the sort of silence that was oddly unbroken by the gentle swishing of the waves below or the sudden cry of a startled bird, but tonight it almost seemed oppressive, as if it was waiting for something to shatter it. Nerves again, she told herself, but she did look back over her shoulder.

She could see the lights of the pub below, and more lights further along on the other side coming from the sprawl of the salmon farm. A few of her ewes were sleeping on the turf nearby, their fleeces a light patch against the darker outline of scrubby gorse bushes and as she looked lower down, one started up suddenly, as they so often did – did they have bad dreams? That woke her neighbour and they bundled off in the direction classified as 'away' in their woolly brains.

There was no other sign of movement and Flora hurried on, a bit breathless now, round the final turn in the road that skirted the drop down to the beach before the croft house came into view. It was only then she felt the sudden rush of movement behind her, heard pounding footsteps, heavy breathing.

She tried to spin round, but a blow in the small of her back knocked her off her feet. As she struggled to get up, her flailing legs were pinioned in a strong grip and she was pushed across the turf, across the rough grass, small stones grazing her face, right out over the edge. She scrabbled desperately, breaking her nails as she frantically fought for purchase on the frozen ground, but only dislodged one of the little stones that fell with her as she crashed head first down, down, down to the rocky shore.

'That ewe – I'm a fool,' was her last conscious thought.

They were standing waiting in the church hall where tea and sandwiches were waiting after the crematorium service, brief and basic in accordance with Flora Maitland's wishes. Her brother, his wife and their daughter had formed a sort of receiving line ready to greet the other mourners when they came straggling in.

'Always said she drank too much. Catches up with you sooner or later,' William Maitland muttered. He was a big man, balding and paunchy, and his mouth was set in the downward curve it usually took when he mentioned his sister.

'You might at least try to sound sorry,' his daughter said, giving him a look of dislike. Plump and pouting, her hair was a harsh shade of blonde that did her no favours and the black eyeliner flick was clumsily applied. 'You never saw her the worse for wear. She could drink anyone under the table.'

'That's not really an accomplishment, you know, Danielle,' her mother Moira said gently, and William added, 'Typical! I know you thought we'd a down on Flora but that's exactly what made us feel she was a bad influence. Encouraging you to go the same way she did.'

Danielle glowered. 'So what's wrong with that? Flora was dead cool. And she was the only person who really got me, who knew how I felt. And it wasn't just that you had a down on her for – you were pissed off that your father left the croft to her, not to you.'

William gave an unconvincing laugh. 'Don't know where you got that idea from. It's more or less a bothy. Anyway, here's people coming now.'

There were thirty or forty in the congregation, mostly older people from the farming community. The Maitlands had an appointment with Flora's solicitor in Lochinver later that morning and William wasn't encouraging when they lingered as they offered their condolences.

There was one exception. Danielle, standing awkwardly a little behind her parents barely listening to what was said, noticed that his attitude changed when a tall man in a smart suit came up. He made the usual noises, then said quietly, 'This isn't the time, but you know my position and you've got my contact number. Let me know when you're ready to talk.'

'Of course, of course,' William said cordially. 'Once we've got the details straightened out . . .'

'Danielle?' She turned. An elderly man with a shock of fluffy white hair was standing at her shoulder. 'I'm Angus – Angus Mackenzie. Flora was my very good friend. I'm going to miss her a lot.'

There was no mistaking his sincerity and her face softened. 'I'm going to miss her ever so much too. She was just, like, the greatest aunt ever. We'd some brilliant laughs. And it's Danni – I really, really hate Danielle.'

He smiled at her. 'Danni, then. She told me all about you, you know.'

'Did she? We used to have the best times together when she was still in London – went to all these really cool places.

16

It's so awful – I can't believe she's gone. I can't believe she was drunk, either. I've seen her drink plenty, and she never showed it, even a tiny bit.'

Angus looked at her, suddenly serious. 'To be honest, I can't believe it, either,' he said, his voice flat. 'I saw her that night. She was on her first drink, then something upset her and she left suddenly. There was no reason for her even to be near the edge of the cliff. I said that to the police, you know, but they weren't interested. I tried to suggest to your father that he could maybe take it up with them, but—'

'Danielle!' William Maitland called sharply, 'Get your coat. We'll be leaving shortly for that appointment.' It was said loudly enough to prompt people to start finishing their drinks hastily, but Danni scowled.

'I'm talking to Angus,' she said defiantly.

'I'm sure he'll excuse you,' her father said and Angus, with a polite nod, went on his way.

She waited until they got into the car to drive across to Lochinver before she started. 'Dad, he thinks there's something funny about Flora's accident. He says he told you that, so what are you going to do?'

Even from the back seat in the car she could see red blotches appear on his neck. 'For God's sake, Danielle! Some old boy who's probably senile thinks there's something "funny" about my sister's death – what do you think I'm going to do? Absolutely bloody nothing, that's what. Look, I spoke to the police, I read their report. They're satisfied, and so am I. End of. Got it?'

Danni subsided. There wasn't a lot she could do. They hadn't paid any attention to Angus and they wouldn't to her

17

either. It wasn't as if there was anything to say except that it wasn't like the Flora she knew to do something seriously dumb like staggering off a cliff. But of course she hadn't actually seen her since she left London to come and live up here in the back of beyond and she was pretty old now – she could have got doddery. And what would be the point, anyway? Even supposing they did find out that it wasn't an accident, Flora would still be dead.

The Lochinver solicitor's office was in a bungalow looking across to the busy harbour, with the Sugar Loaf top of Suilven looming up behind it. Flora had used her father's lawyer, Donald Mackay, who was waiting for the Maitlands with three chairs set out opposite him.

He remembered William Maitland, a big, blustering man who had been openly outraged that his father had left his meagre estate to his sister, with the exception of the 'bairn's part' that Scots law obliged him to pay his other child. He'd tried to argue that the old man had lost it and didn't know what he was doing but Mackay had given him a very dusty answer. Maitland Senior had certainly been as sharp as a tack in summing-up his children: 'He's a great, fat, greedy sumph. She's maybe not always just kept to the rules, but I've aye had a weakness for a black sheep.'

Flora Reith, slim, sophisticated, with dark red hair and bright red nails, had sat in perfect calm, letting her brother rant on and leave, and then proceeded to deal with all the arrangements in a slickly professional way. When, sometime later, she'd come in to make her will Mackay had hardly recognised her in the grey-haired woman with roughened hands and broken nails who had gone back to her maiden name.

She'd laughed openly at his confusion. 'I'm just a shepherdess now,' she said. 'Weather-beaten, exhausted, losing money and a stone heavier but I'm perfectly happy.'

The size of her estate had come as a surprise to him. Whatever it was she'd done that hadn't obeyed the rules had obviously been profitable.

When he saw the Maitlands' car draw up outside he went to meet them. As they shook hands and he murmured, 'Sorry for your loss,' William's smile was distinctly forced.

Moira made appropriate noises as the daughter hung back, looking sulky. He smiled at her, going to shake her hand. 'You must be Danielle. I've heard a lot about you.'

William stiffened. 'I hate to think what that might have been,' he said sharply. 'I wouldn't believe it all – my sister was inclined to exaggerate.'

A very unwelcome suspicion was obviously already forming in his mind as Mackay led them through to his office, so obviously that he might as well have spoken it out loud: Flora couldn't have – could she?

Once they were seated, Mackay opened the file lying on his desk and said, 'I'll give you the terms in detail, of course, but I should say at the start that it's actually a very simple will. There's a couple of other bequests, one to a neighbour on condition that he takes on her flock of sheep, but the rest is to come to you, Danielle.'

Of the three gasps that followed the announcement, the loudest was Danielle's. Looking stunned, she said, 'She left it to me?'

William's face had turned an ugly purplish-grey. 'You mean my father's croft, that he inherited from his father and his father before that – I'm being bypassed again?'

'Yes, Mr Maitland. And this time there can certainly be no question about competence. Your sister was very clear about what she wanted.'

'But for God's sake, the girl's barely twenty! All she's done is waste her life on a series of short-term jobs – trying to "find herself", for any favour! What money there was would come to her in the end, of course, when she was old enough to appreciate it – not now, surely not now! We could put it in a trust—'

'Mr Maitland, I have no authority to do any such thing and nor, I'm afraid, do you.'

William got to his feet, pushing his chair back so roughly that it toppled. Moira, glancing nervously from her husband to her daughter, got up too, then bent down to set her husband's chair back on its legs.

'I'm not sitting here to listen while my sister gives me the finger from beyond the grave. She's been a bad lot all along, Flora, and her precious niece is all set to go the same way. Giving her tainted money will just send her to hell in a handcart even faster.'

Moira put a restraining hand on her husband's arm. 'William,' she quavered.

'Don't "William" me!' He strode across the room, then paused at the door to address his daughter.

'We're leaving for Glasgow now. You can come with us or you can make your own way back. You're a woman of property now.' He flung the door open and marched out.

Moira was looking anguished. 'He doesn't really mean it,' she said to her daughter. 'You know the way he flies off the handle. We'll sort it out later – just come now.' She waited for a moment, but when Danni didn't move, she followed him.

The girl had sat, still and silent, since she'd heard the news. Mackay looked at her over the top of his glasses. 'Are you all right?'

'Oh, me? I'm fine. But if he doesn't calm down, he'll give himself a heart attack.'

Mackay looked at her with interest. This girl with her pierced eyebrow and heavy-handed make-up seemed to have inherited her aunt's sangfroid along with her estate. She was going on, 'Do I get anything right now?'

No comment on her sudden good fortune, no gratitude to her aunt – just straight to the point. He shook his head. 'I'm afraid not. The estate has to go to probate, as it's called, while all the details are sorted out. It could be some months, I'm afraid.'

Danni's face fell. 'Oh. I should maybe have gone with them. Haven't got the money to get back to Glasgow.'

She was, when it came right down to it, little more than a child. 'Look, I'll tell you what,' he said. 'I'll lend you what you need on the office account and claim it back later. And if you like, I'll take you up just to have a look at the croft house before you go home.'

'Can't see me exactly wanting to live there, but it'd be kind of cool to have my own house, even if it's just a bothy, like Dad said.'

'I'll explain the formal details more fully about what happens now. But your aunt said I was to give you this before anything else.' He took an envelope from the file and handed it to her.

Danni took it, frowning, and opened it. The letter inside was short.

You were a great pal, kid. Have a good time with all this – you know you want to! But I've a wee bit of a conscience about some of the things I've done and about some of the things I taught you were OK. You're like me – there's a bit of the devil in us both, so think how it's all going to end up before you start doing stuff or one day you'll start hearing a funny flapping sound. That's chickens coming home to roost. They always do.

Be careful. Be safe. Have a great life.
Your wicked aunt Flora.

Mackay watched her as she read it. He had no idea what it said, but Danni gave a little grimace, then folded it up and put it back into the envelope.

'Can we go now?' she said.

Admittedly, it was quite exciting when the lawyer guy gave her the key and waited in the car while she went to unlock the door to the croft house – her house – but it was pouring with rain and the sky was grey and the sea was grey too and there was a wind that cut right through you. She shivered, wondering how the aunt she'd known, who'd actually taken her clubbing as well as to some seriously fancy restaurants, could bear to live in this awful bleak place miles from anywhere She must have changed a lot.

It wasn't a bothy, just a wee stone house. She unlocked the door and pushed it open. The first thing she thought was that nothing could be less like Flora's flat in Putney – all minimalism and modern furniture. Apart from anything else, she must have got, like, really, really messy – there were papers lying all over the floor and drawers left open and cupboards not shut. The furniture here looked as if it had been in the place for a hundred years and not new even then. It was dark, too, with just these small windows in great thick walls.

As they'd driven to Inverbeg she'd had a picture of it in her head. She wasn't expecting a big house, but she'd seen pictures of posh holiday homes with great kitchens and wet rooms and stuff and Flora had always liked the best. What she'd expected certainly wasn't this dreary wee hovel. It was a crushing disappointment – dark, fusty and unwelcoming. In fact, not just unwelcoming, downright hostile, as if she shouldn't be here. She felt the house didn't even want her to go inside and look around. With a shiver that had nothing to do with the cold she locked it up again and went back to the car.

Mr Mackay looked surprised to see her back so quickly. 'Seen all you want to see?'

She pulled a face. 'Yeah. It's in a bit of a mess.'

'Oh, that's right, I remember the assistant who came out to shut it up said it was very untidy. If you plan to come up and stay until you sell it, I can arrange for someone to do a clean-up.'

'Right.' She sat silent, chewing her lip as he drove her back to Lochinver to get a bus. She'd been high at the start and of course once everything got straightened out, she'd have a great time. But right now, she just felt depressed. She'd have to go home and get a hard time from her father – and the house had got to her, somehow. Living out here had changed Flora in some weird way and she'd better be careful it didn't do something to her too.

CHAPTER TWO

OCTOBER 2020

It was still dark at 5.30 a.m. when Kelso Strang tiptoed through the silent house, holding his boots in his hand and leaving by the little-used front door instead of the mud room, where the two black labs would express their delight at this early visitor with their customary exuberance and wake the household. It wasn't actually raining so far – good – but the forecast wasn't great – bad – when you were planning to go up a mountain.

Ranald Sinclair, his host, had tried to dissuade him the night before. 'They're talking about a squall coming in later. You know how vicious it can get and even once you're off the mountain it's a long walk back to the car with sunset around half-past five just now. Tomorrow could be better.'

But Kelso didn't want to wait. 'With the way the weather changes around here, it could just as easily be worse, Ran,' he pointed out. 'And I've done Suilven before. If time's running out, I can stop off in the Suileag bothy and do the last stretch in the morning, but if I waited till tomorrow I couldn't – I'll have to make a prompt start on Sunday to get back to the treadmill on Monday.'

'I suppose that's right,' Ranald conceded. 'Just make sure you've got all the gear, then. Dead embarrassing for a DCI to be calling out the Mountain Rescue. They'd never let you forget it.'

'Trust me,' Kelso had said, but he checked it all carefully as he packed. What he hadn't said was that he'd made provision for a night in the bothy whatever happened.

As he drove off on the single-track road towards Lochinver he reflected on the past two days. Since his wife's death in a traffic accident three years before he hadn't taken a holiday. Running the Serious Rural Crime Squad – set up after the creation of the unitary force Police Scotland to be despatched to deal with any major crime in an area where there was no longer a functioning CID – had kept him busy and the idea of holidaying on his own hadn't appealed. But recently his boss, Detective Chief Superintendent Jane Borthwick, had started muttering about him taking some of the accrued leave.

'People who start believing that they are so indispensable that they can't take a holiday become a problem sooner or later,' she said darkly. 'For goodness' sake, Kelso, take a break. I need you here, doing the job.'

He was always respectful of her rank, but they'd been working together for a long time now and he risked saying, 'It's almost like I'm indispensable, isn't it?'

JB had raised an eyebrow but smiled. 'Cheeky sod. I saw that coming before the words were out of my mouth. Even so, Kelso – take a break.'

So he'd given it some thought. He'd done a lot of hill-walking in his youth and now he felt the pull of the mountains again. He'd missed that – the wild beauty, the freedom, the physical challenge, that feeling when you reached the peak that you were standing on the top of the world. Yes, it was too long since he'd done it.

And he had a standing invitation from a mate from his army days who, as it happened, was now running a fish farm not far from dramatic Suilven, which wasn't too demanding even when you hadn't climbed for a while.

Ranald Sinclair and his wife Harriet had been trying to persuade him to come for a visit ever since Alexa had died but he'd kept all his old friends at arm's length, making work his excuse for baulking at being the lone man among the friends who'd known them as a couple. Ranald, though, had been posted abroad at one stage and their wives had only met briefly, so there would be no emotionally demanding reminiscences to deal with. The invitation was immediately renewed when he asked.

And the Sinclairs' welcome had certainly been warm. They had a charming place, an old fishing lodge with views out over the bay that had a chintzy, Country Living vibe and a dark blue Aga in the farmhouse kitchen that made it the hub of the house.

Hattie's food might be old-fashioned in style, not featuring a lot of quinoa and couscous, but it certainly tasted good after a day in the open air. She was a typical army brat, cheerful, adaptable, and having cut her teeth as a chalet girl many years before, she was now offering ready-meals for the pods on the Auchinglass Estate that accommodated the workers on their rewilding project and tourists as well in season.

An idyllic life, Kelso had thought, if you didn't mind the pervasive smell from the fish tanks, just round the corner from the house. At least, he had thought that at first, before he picked up on the toxic atmosphere in the marriage.

They didn't have kids. Given what he knew of them, it was hard to believe that this had been a lifestyle choice – more likely a private sorrow – and Hattie treated the black labs like furry children, which infuriated her husband.

'They're gun dogs. Cost me a fortune to get them trained and you're ruining them,' Ranald had snapped when she laughed at the way they frolicked round Kelso when he arrived. Not the first time he'd said that, clearly.

It wasn't so much of a problem during the day, when Kelso and Ranald were mainly outdoors, but in the evening when they'd all had a bit to drink – and Ranald was nothing if not a generous host – it had been excruciating, as everything either of them said was immediately sniped at by the other. When at last it was late enough for Kelso to yawn, talk about too much fresh air and retire, he was exhausted with the effort of not being drawn into taking one side or the other.

So much anger, in them both! After the first night, Kelso had tried to draw Ranald into confiding as they walked round the premises, but all he wanted to talk about were his plans for development, thwarted on one side by the Auchinglass Estate and by the croft on the other, owned according to Ranald by 'a thrawn old besom' who'd got a bit drunk and fallen from a coastal path earlier in the year.

'Belongs to the niece now. Doesn't look the type to settle away out here in what's just a but and ben – thought she'd just appear to wind everything up and then be off, but now she's started hanging round with the rougher element working at the estate and doesn't want to sell at the moment – or not to me, anyway. If she doesn't, it's a real problem. We're overstretched at the moment, but I can't afford another man without expanding.'

They had reached the end of the shingle beach, and he pointed to the top of a cliff face.

'Her land begins there, with access across the main road and even a couple of barns. I could build a processing unit, maybe a smokehouse, and cut out the middleman – just now I do the work and he takes the profits. The big worry is that I'm sure Sean Reynolds is talking to her. He sees Auchinglass as his little kingdom, rewilding, all the rest of that crap. It'll be wolves before you know it, and beavers, for God's sake – so far we've been spared that but you can imagine what that would do.

'He's been leaning on me, trying to buy me out. I told him he could shove it, of course. But he seems to be loaded and he could outbid me if she starts playing us off against each other.'

He couldn't leave the subject alone and as a topic of conversation it palled. It wasn't until they were walking past some wooden outbuildings that Ranald broke off. 'Now, out there in the bay – you see? That's the farm.' He pointed to an area of netted cages out on the sea loch. 'And here, these are the pools.'

The two pools, like huge rubber tyres with railings round them, were close in to shore and held a mass of the great silver fish, writhing as they competed for the brown pellets a man in yellow oilskins and boots was throwing in.

'We've a refrigerated van coming tomorrow, so these'll be taken out then,' Ranald explained, and went on to explain at great length about the technicalities.

As Kelso made suitable noises and avoided saying that they reminded him of battery hens, he laid his plans, thankful he was only staying for three more nights. He'd spend a day on Suilven and it looked as if there might be a bit of weather coming in that would give him the excuse to camp out in the bothy; at this time of year the route wouldn't be dangerous if you were well prepared. A quick visit to the little convenience store at the Inverbeg Inn had given him all he needed.

Now, as he reached the car park, a mile from Lochinver on the Glencanisp Lodge road, and got out, he switched on his headlamp, picked up his backpack and strode out into the darkness with a huge sense of liberation.

'Kelso must have left very quietly this morning,' Harriet Sinclair said. 'The girls didn't make a sound.'

'Just as well. I wouldn't have been amused if the *dogs* had barked,' Ranald said. 'He told me he was aiming for five-thirty.'

She was standing beside the Aga, holding a frying pan. 'Do you want a bacon butty?'

He shook his head. 'Had too much to eat last night.' He patted his flat stomach; he'd kept his army posture and the physical nature of the job had kept him fit. As Hattie shrugged and put the bacon on anyway, he raised his eyebrows pointedly.

She flared up. 'Oh, don't start on that! I didn't drink as much as you did last night.'

'If you say so.' He went over to the coffee machine, peering out of the window as he did so. 'It's looking all right at the moment for Kelso, though there's clouds building out there now. He should be well into the climb – a shame if it closed in so he didn't get the views.'

'How long will it take him? I did it once, but I can't remember.'

Filling his cup, Ranald gave her a disparaging look. 'No wonder – it was hardly yesterday. Eight hours or so, other things being equal.'

Hattie flushed as she made her sandwich defiantly and sat down at the table. The dogs, lying in baskets by the Aga, moved as one to sit by her chair. 'Will he make it back for supper, do you think?'

He didn't sit down. 'How would I know what the weather's going to do? Anyway, I'll take this through to the office. I can't bear to sit and watch you – those dogs are drooling.'

Hattie's eyes filled with tears. She should be used to humiliation by now – it had become the common currency of their marriage. Perhaps it would be less painful if she could learn to submit, but she'd been brought up to give as good as she got and at the start that had been all right: then she'd been able to make him back off, and the sparring had been a sort of game. Even after they came here, when there was so much to do together to get themselves set up, they'd still been close and could apologise when it went too far and make it up again in bed.

Then the kids that this place would be so perfect for hadn't appeared. They'd gone through all the hoops until, as Ranald put it, they'd discovered it was 'his fault'. She'd choked back her own distress to support him but the bitterness went deep and there was no way he would even discuss the subject after that, as if the disappointment had been all his. It was then that their quarrelling had become a destructive habit and recently it had got worse, much worse.

She bit into her sandwich, thick-sliced bread, greasy with the melting butter, warm and delicious. Perhaps she had let herself go a bit, but when you spent all day working in the kitchen it wasn't easy. Anyway, around here there weren't a lot of women in the 'nothing tastes as good as skinny feels' camp.

One of the dogs nudged her knee, in a gentle, reminding sort of way and Hattie looked down at the wet patch its mouth had left on her jeans.

'Juno!' she said reproachfully. 'Just wait, all right? Look at Jax – she's being polite, so she's getting hers first.' She divided the last bit between them.

She hadn't been allowed to choose their names. Ranald said he had to be able to call his dogs without explaining why they had the sort of silly name that she'd want to saddle them with and she hadn't fought it; mostly she just called them 'sweetie' or 'darling' anyway. And yes, she was fully aware of what she was doing. They were her only consolation.

Ranald hadn't been so blatantly rude when Kelso

was there but, even so, she at least had noticed how uncomfortable he was with their endless bickering. She hadn't known him very well, and his wife hardly at all, but he had an easy way with him that was very charming – quite good-looking too, even if the scar on his face had been a bit of a shock. Plastic surgery was brilliant nowadays, so presumably he either didn't care or felt it made some sort of statement.

She wasn't actually expecting him back for supper. She'd seen him returning after his visit to the store with a little camping stove and he'd come to the kitchen to tell her he might well take shelter in the bothy if darkness closed in.

'So don't cater for me, anyway. If I come back starving maybe I can raid the fridge for bread and cheese.'

'I can do better than that,' she had said, smiling. 'There's the microwave and there's dozens of meals for one in the freezer, so you can even have a choice.'

'You're very kind. And you're a brilliant cook – your customers are very lucky. Are you happy, being constantly tied to a hot stove?'

He looked as if he was genuinely interested. Hattie suddenly became aware that her cheeks were flushed from the heat of the cooker and her forehead was sweaty. She mopped it awkwardly with the back of her hand.

'Oh well, it's all right. I've always enjoyed cooking and it's a good little business now. The tourist season's pretty much over, of course, but the land clearing and tree-planting at the estate is year-round. They've a minimal labouring workforce and some longer-term volunteers but mostly it's a mixture of kids who come for a week or a fortnight to volunteer – they're OK with the stuff they can get in the store, but there's older people who like to have something a bit more special. Usually at the end of the week once the M&S supplies they've brought with them have finished.'

Kelso had pulled a face. 'Not very fair to local shops, but I suppose you can't stop them. Those won't be as good as your food, anyway.'

He'd smiled and gone off and she went back to the salmon wellington she was making – that was always in demand and of course it was cheap to do too. She got lots of compliments from her customers but when was the last time she'd been complimented on what she put on her own table? The most she ever got from Ranald now was a grunt that could be interpreted as satisfaction – unless he didn't like it. He was ready enough to comment then.

She brushed the puff pastry with beaten egg and put it into the oven, then made herself a coffee with just a sliver of the lemon drizzle cake she'd made earlier and sat down with a sigh.

Could they go on like this? The thing was, Hattie couldn't see an alternative. If she walked out on Ranald, she'd have to give up a lifestyle she enjoyed – her business, her lovely house, friends that she'd made. He'd probably insist on keeping the girls; he'd paid a lot for them, after all, and that would break Hattie's heart.

No, there was a saying in her family, 'Grit your teeth, tilt your chin and get on with it.' She'd just have to grow a thicker skin. Anyway, when it came right down to it, she still loved him in a weird way. When she didn't hate him.

* * *

Kelso Strang was making good progress and the weather so far had held up, though he could already see signs that it was starting to close in. He'd been keeping up a steady, swinging pace and now he began pressing on up through the zigzags of the gully, hoping before it did to reach the ridge between the two peaks – the spire of Meall Mheadonach and Caisteal Liath, the rounded summit that gives Suilven its 'Sugar Loaf' name.

He stopped as he emerged on to it, gasping in the keen fresh air that felt like swallowing icy water, breathless not only from the climb but also from the awe-inspiring view stretching out below him, almost as if he had soared like one of the golden eagles who hunted here. Below him the rivers and the lochs made a tapestry with colours that changed with the light as clouds veiled the sun. Looking south, he could see the rocky crest of Stac Pollaidh; Canisp to the north was barely distinguishable now as the squall came sweeping in.

The sky had an ominous purple tinge and the wind was strengthening all the time. He'd have to step on it to get to the top. He was protected to some degree as he went along the side of the drystone dyke but when he rounded the corner he staggered against its brutal force. He was bent double by the time he reached the cairn on the top of Caisteal Liath, and yes, it felt just as he remembered – as if you were straddling the world, freed from the bonds of earth.

He didn't linger, though. By the minute the wind gusts were getting violent enough to blow him off that exposed summit; the views were being blotted out before his eyes and there was the promise of snow in the sleety rain, now falling fast. No chance of Meall Mheadonach now. He checked the Mountain Weather app on his phone and it was still forecasting a squall that would pass in an hour or so.

As Kelso started the descent, he was looking for shelter where he could sit it out even as he pushed on. He'd only need a cranny angled away from the wind; he had another couple of layers and a rain cover in his backpack as well as a hip flask and a bag of flapjacks Hattie had pressed on him yesterday. The weather might not be ideal, but the exhilaration of the climb had still left him on a high that would see him through till the weather changed.

'He's not going to make it back now,' Ranald Sinclair said, looking out of the window. It was fully dark. 'We may as well eat – no point in waiting any longer. The weather must have cost him at least a couple of hours.'

'You don't think you should phone his mobile and check he's all right?' Hattie suggested. 'You never know, with weather like that.'

He gave her a look of contempt. 'No, I don't. He's a big boy, he can look after himself. He said he'd go to the bothy if it got late.'

'Yes, he said that to me as well.' She sipped her gin and tonic, her second; he was on his third Scotch. Maybe it was Dutch courage that made her say, 'I think he fancied the idea of getting away from us, to be honest.'

'What the hell do you mean by that?'

'You didn't notice that he found the way we speak to each other embarrassing?'

Ranald went red. 'For God's sake, he's been married himself! Everyone has little tiffs.'

'"Little tiffs" is what we used to have. Now it's getting downright nasty. Something's wrong, Ranald. What is it?'

He glared at her, his eyes bulging. 'I can't believe you're making a drama out of this. Nothing's wrong, except that I have a wife who's got so touchy that she bristles at every word I say.'

Hattie sighed. 'Yes, I suppose I do. But I'm touchy because it makes me so unhappy. If Kelso's not coming back, let's take the chance to talk about it properly over supper—'

'Talk about what?' He had worked himself up into a rage now. 'If you think I'm going to sit here all evening while you list all my failings as a husband, you can think again. Suddenly I'm not hungry any more. I'm going along to the pub.'

As he got to his feet the two dogs, stretched out asleep in front of the sitting-room stove, sat up, ears pricked, then, as he stormed out, lay down again. Hattie bent forward, her head in her hands.

That hadn't been her best idea, had it?

As he got lower down the mountain, the snow stopped and the weather had cleared by the time he reached the turn-off to the Suileag bothy but he didn't hesitate. Not wanting to set off on the long hike back in gathering darkness was all the excuse he needed.

It had been a good day. He'd hardly seen a soul since he set out – a group on the lower slopes, a couple he waved at across a valley. JB had been right, as she so often was: he felt the better for the break and there was something about the majesty of the mountains that put mundane concerns into perspective.

The bothy was primitive enough – bare walls, plank floor, a couple of rough tables and a sleeping platform, with a fireplace that was no more than a space left in the wall with a chimney above. There was no one else there, luckily, though there was food litter in one corner that someone had been too lazy to carry down with them. But on the other hand, some public-spirited soul had left dry wood stacked in a lean-to outside to make a fire.

Kelso got it going, unrolled his sleeping bag and spread it on the platform, then set up his little stove. Decanting two cans of baked beans with sausages into his metal mess tin and heating them up, he didn't even feel wistful about the no doubt delicious meal he was missing at the Sinclairs'. After fresh air and exercise anything tasted wonderful and with the last of Hattie's flapjacks and a chocolate bar he was well satisfied.

He always carried a book. There was still a little left in the hip flask so he sat down on the platform with that, to read by the light of the fire and a small camping lamp. It was no good, though; even Sebastian Faulks couldn't stop his eyes from closing and although it was ridiculously early he gave up the struggle and crashed out.

It got cold as the night wore on and the fire went out. Kelso woke up, shivering, and looked at his watch; it was well after midnight, so he'd already had a few hours' sleep. When he didn't drop off again, he got up to fetch some more wood and coax the embers back into life.

It was icy cold when he opened the door, cold and very

clear with all the stars out so that he could make his way round the side of the building by their pale, eerie light. Looking down there was only darkness, apart from the steel-grey glint of starlight reflected in a loch below.

He paused, just listening to the silence. It was at that moment he heard it, and in an instinctive, age-old reflex, the hairs rose on the back of his neck. It was faint and far off but unmistakable if once you have heard it – the howl of a wolf.

CHAPTER THREE

DC Livvy Murray was in a thoroughly bad mood coming off the night shift – late, of course, because by the time they'd managed to get a social worker out to pick up the kids it was way past eight o'clock in the morning. She couldn't leave till then because, while the man who'd been beating their mother up was on his way to the nick with the lucky PC who could go off duty once he'd checked him in, she was meant to get a statement from the mother who was so drunk she couldn't speak and certainly couldn't be left alone with the children.

It was what was known as a 'sticky hoose' too, where the carpet was so filthy that it stuck to the soles of your shoes as you walked. The room stank, not just from the filthy nappies abandoned on the floor but from the messes made by the ratty little dog that bared its teeth and growled at her every time she moved.

The children, two and one, weren't difficult, poor mites; they had sat, or slept, in front of the TV with dummies in their mouths and blank expressions. Murray suspected that this was all they ever did. The vests they were wearing were grey with dirt and their nappies were soiled; since their mother was sunk in a slack-jawed stupor she'd changed them herself. She'd had a hunt round for clean clothes but there didn't seem to be any.

By the time blessed relief came, Murray was stinking herself. She'd have to go back to Fettes Avenue to clock out, but when she got home what she was wearing would go straight in the bin – every experienced DC wears cheap clothes – and she would stand under a hot shower with the strongest-scented soap she possessed until she couldn't smell the place any more. Then bed – her eyes were sore and gritty with tiredness.

It was bad luck that as she was at last on her way off duty, Detective Inspector Rachel French appeared, coming from the other direction. DI French was looking like she always did – smart, together, assured. It was easy to look like that when you were tall and slim and had the sort of great hair that always looked as if you'd just come from the hairdresser. And she was a graduate who'd been fast-tracked to inspector in a couple of years. And she was competent and well-respected.

Of course she couldn't help being everything Murray would have liked to be, and wasn't. She told herself regularly that French hadn't done it out of spite, just to make Murray feel inadequate, but it didn't work. And of course it was sod's law she would appear when Murray was at her worst – smelly and dishevelled and unhappy anyway with her newly dyed black hair.

French stopped, making a sympathetic grimace. 'Oh dear – tough night, was it?'

'You could say.'

'Getting off now, though? That's good.' She hesitated, then said, 'I heard the result. Don't let it stop you going for it again – you're good, Livvy.'

'Thanks, ma'am,' she muttered. Having to sound grateful was the worst bit.

'I know DCI Strang thinks very highly of you too. And it'll be easier next time, trust me.' French smiled and went on.

Murray knew it was childish to stick her tongue out at French's retreating back, but the painful humiliation of having failed the sergeant's exam was bad enough without knowing that French and Strang had been having pally chats about her behind her back. Strang had spoken to her, of course, and been encouraging while delicately suggesting a more dedicated approach next time might pay off; somehow that was easier to take than French's attempts at confidence-boosting. She knew he was right.

And she was ambitious still. It was just she'd never had the habit of studying, and now she'd found a great social life here in Edinburgh – and a guy who was sort of almost a boyfriend – it was hard to turn down a night round the pub with mates in favour of a night on her own staring at a book that might have been deliberately written to bore the pants off you.

Murray gave a huge yawn. She wasn't going to think about it now. She was going to think about buying a bacon and egg roll on her way home and hoping she wouldn't fall asleep on her feet like a horse before she won through to her bed.

* * *

DI French, too, pulled a face DC Murray couldn't see as she walked away. She had the depressing feeling that this had done more harm than good, but what the hell was she supposed to do?

Murray was one of her constables. If she hadn't said anything about the sergeant's exams, that would have been a black mark too, just something else for Livvy Murray to hold against her. The woman was the personification of the Scots motto 'Wha daur meddle wi' me?' with additional spikes and a cherry on top, but if she couldn't manage to win her over, it would be her failure – and she hated failing. She had too much baggage from her childhood with a father who took any failure on her part as a personal insult.

She was only a few weeks into the post and she was still uncertain, trying to feel her way. It had run fairly smoothly with the rest of the guys so far; much of the time was spent at her desk while they did the grunt work, but she felt it was good leadership to get to know them and Murray seemed to be the only one who'd resented her attempts.

Oh, she hadn't been insubordinate or anything – the police force is a very hierarchical set-up – but at briefings she could sense a sort of flat resistance from Murray to what she was saying. It didn't help with team building.

DCI Kelso Strang had been something of a mentor to her. With his responsibilities for the SRCS he was only peripherally involved in team politics and had previously been a source of good objective advice when she'd been very new and a bit shaky. She buzzed to ask if he'd time to see her.

In the broom cupboard he called his office, French edged herself on to the chair in the corner and said, 'I was just wanting to pick your brains about a problem I'm having with one of my constables.'

He looked at her with a slight smile. 'Let me guess. Livvy Murray.'

French looked surprised. 'I wasn't sure you'd even know who she was.'

'Oh, I know Livvy, all right. And what's more, I should tell you that JB is something of a fan.'

That was enough to give her a hollow feeling in her stomach. 'JB is?'

'I know! But she believes she has potential. It's a long story – I won't bore you with it. But I've worked with Livvy on three SRCS homicides now and apart from occasions when she's gone off at a tangent and I could cheerfully have killed her, I've been impressed. She has original ideas, if you charge her with her a task she'll go at it like a terrier shaking a rat to death, and she's a learner too. I've great respect for how far she's got with sheer determination – I don't know the background details, but I think she'd a difficult start in life without the chance to learn about mental discipline.

'She's keen to get on, though, and failing her sergeant's exams will be a big blow, even if I'm not convinced she took the work seriously enough. I'd happily bet on her next time round, but she'll be really hurting meantime.'

'Well, I can certainly make allowances for her,' French said with a sigh. 'The trouble is, I'm not sure she's prepared to make allowances for me.'

Strang pulled a face. 'Mmm. Her problem is that you look as if you've got everything absolutely sorted – yes, I know it doesn't feel like that to you, but that'll be how she sees it. It's all about a fundamental lack of confidence.'

'Right,' she said slowly.

But when she'd seen Murray coming in from what had obviously been the night-shift from hell, she had tried. She'd got nowhere and that wasn't a comfortable thought now she knew Detective Chief Superintendent Jane Borthwick might be taking a special interest in her protegée.

At first, she thought the knocking at the door was the pounding in her own head. Danni Maitland opened bleary eyes. Her mouth was gritty, her tongue sticking to the roof of her mouth, her lips were dry. The clock on her bedside table said nine-thirty – who the hell could be coming to the cottage at this hour?

The knocking started again. Whoever it was didn't seem to be prepared to go away and come back later, so groaning and swearing she swung herself upright. The room swung round her too; she let it settle for a moment as her stomach heaved, then moved gingerly. She'd been feeling clammy and sweaty but now it was freezing cold. She grabbed up the jacket she'd tossed onto the floor when she came in the night before and struggled out into the living room, muttering, 'All right, all right, I'm coming!'

When she opened the door, she winced under the assault of the strong, fierce light of a clear frosty morning. Shivering, she looked at the man who stood on the doorstep – Sean Reynolds, the man from the big house on the Auchinglass Estate.

Despite the weather, he wasn't wearing a jacket, just a white linen shirt open at the neck, with buttons that struggled to meet the buttonholes on the other side across his broad chest. He had short, dark, curly hair and with his cheeks rosy from the cold he had an air of robust health that, given her own enfeebled state, looked positively aggressive.

'I'm sorry,' he said, not very convincingly. 'Were you asleep?'

'What does it look like?'

'Terrible waste on a glorious morning like this.' He turned, shielding his eyes against the low sun to look out over the shore where little white-tipped waves were curling gently to the bay beyond, a benevolent blue under a clear sky.

'If you've got me out of bed to tell me it's a lovely day,' Danni began, 'I—'

'No, no,' he said hastily. 'Wanted a chat. Can I come in?' He was halfway across the threshold already.

'Can't stop you, I suppose.' She followed him in, shut the door and switched on the electric fire in the fireplace, huddling over it ostentatiously.

She knew the room was a mess and he didn't bother to conceal his distaste as he looked at the discarded clothing and dirty dishes, the cigarette burns on the coffee table, the overflowing bin. He coughed, as if the fug from last night's cigarettes was catching his throat.

'You don't have to stay if you don't like it,' she said flatly.

He didn't reply, only going across to the battered leather sofa and shifting an empty frozen pizza box so that he could sit down. He looked up at her, standing there awkwardly in her purple pyjama bottoms and grey T-shirt with a parka jacket draped over her shoulders, then patted the sofa beside him.

'Come on and sit down, Danni.'

She didn't want to. In the first place, she didn't want to move away from the fire; in the second, she felt it would put her at a disadvantage, but she found she was doing it anyway. A sort of raw energy radiated from the man and he spoke with such confidence that somehow she couldn't argue.

Sean was looking round. 'It's still pretty much how it was when the old boy was here, isn't it – I talked to him a couple of times. More bookshelves and stuff, and the kitchen looks better.'

'She put in a new shower room, but that was all.' At the mention of the shower, Danni shifted uneasily, aware of the smell of dried sweat. 'Look, what is this about?' As if she didn't know.

'You know what it is,' he said, 'but I think we need to talk some more. You're not staying here for ever, are you? I guess you've a job somewhere? You'll have to get back to it.'

It gave her enormous satisfaction to say airily, 'Nuh – gave it up. I can do what I like now.'

Surprise showed on his face, then disappointment. 'I see. Your aunt – well off, was she?'

'She'd done all right. So I can take my time, OK?'

Sean leant forward, his elbows on his knees, reaching out towards her with his hands spread wide. The back of his hands were covered in fine black hairs but the palms

47

were cracked and calloused with ingrained lines across the palms – so he knew about hard work, even if he had got money coming out of his ears.

'When we talked last time, I assumed you'd just be wanting to get rid of the place as soon as you could. I know Ranald Sinclair is after it as well and I said we'd top whatever he offered. What I didn't do was explain properly why we need it.

'Surely you wouldn't want to see him developing more of those disgusting polluting fishnets. You're young – you know what state the planet's in. It's your world we've mucked up and now we have to save it. Well – you've heard of Greta Thunberg?'

He used the name as if it was the clinching argument but she looked at him with cold eyes. Yes, she'd heard her.

'She's a hypocrite,' she said. 'Bet the vegetables she eats got to the shops in a lorry – and if she really cared that much about the planet she'd have stayed at home and Skyped instead of going to all those conferences.'

To her satisfaction, Sean looked gobsmacked. 'I-I can't believe you said that! You're young – surely she speaks for your generation?'

Danni shrugged. 'Nuh. Only the posh kids. And the celebs who'll just do what they want anyway, like Harry and Meghan.'

She watched him coolly as he struggled to work out what to say next. From the look on his face, he'd have liked to lose his temper with her for saying such dreadful things – ooh, naughty Danni! – but he needed to keep her sweet if she was ever going to agree to sell to him. Having power was a new experience but she was enjoying it.

'Look,' he said at last, 'I hear what you're saying. I'm not preaching about all the things people shouldn't do – I'm looking at it a different way. You know we're planting all these trees . . .'

'Well – yeah.' If she'd forgotten that, the headache she was struggling with would have reminded her. She wouldn't still be around if it wasn't for the guys who were working on his project. Apart from them this place was pants and she'd have been out of here long ago.

'Right. So that's at least something we've been able to do to help. But the thing I really want above everything else, why we need as much land as we can possibly get our hands on, is to restore this place to what it was like before men came in and spoilt it.' He was leaning towards her, his eyes alive with enthusiasm as he went on, 'Scotland was really a sort of paradise for wildlife at one time and with enough vision we can make them thrive here again – red squirrels, pine martens, wildcats, wolves even—'

'Wolves?' It was her turn to be astonished. 'What would you want wolves for? They're dangerous.'

Sean flushed. 'That's the sort of thing they say, but it's crap. People all over Europe live alongside wolves and they belonged here until we came on to their territory and wiped them out. They're reclusive animals – you wouldn't know they're there, mostly.'

The man was completely barking. 'Until they got hungry.'

This time he showed his temper. 'That's fatuous,' he snarled. 'OK, they might take a sheep or two, but—'

Danni gave an enormous yawn and stood up. 'Don't see it, to be honest. Look, do you mind . . .'

Sean got up immediately. 'Sorry, sorry. Just don't make any hasty decisions, will you? And remember, if it's a question of money . . .'

The way he said it had a little flick of contempt – as if there was something wrong with caring about money instead of caring about wolves – wolves, FFS! She said stiffly, 'I heard what you said. You can't bounce me into anything.'

'No, of course not. Thanks for talking to me, anyway.'

He smiled, but she could just about hear the gritted teeth. He'd planned to sweet-talk her, expecting her to fall for it, but he'd failed. He was well pissed off, and really quite scarily angry – just like Ranald Sinclair when she'd told him the same. She'd never quite realised what fun it was to have money. Cheers, Flora!

There'd been a big argument at home about how she was going to spend it. Her dad was so angry he couldn't speak about it without going radge and even her mum, who usually avoided any sort of argument, had lectured her about it.

'It's a nice wee nest egg, Danielle, and you'll get a good bit for the croft to take you on to the property ladder. Flora would be pleased to know she'd given you such a good start in life.'

Danni had only given her a sideways look and said nothing. She hadn't told them about her aunt's letter; Flora had wanted her to have fun with it, not to go soft on her and set out on a life like her mum's. She'd bought herself a jazzy little yellow Honda that was her pride and joy and gone off to Inverbeg.

But no way was this permanent. With a can of Irn Bru for her hangover, she sat down to think about what she was going to do next. 'When you're on top, go for the jugular,' Flora had always told her. 'If you don't, the wheel'll turn and you'll be on the bottom, ground into the mud.'

Danni was on top at the moment. She was going to play Sinclair off against Reynolds and turn the screw until their eyes watered. OK. That worked. But when?

Inverbeg must be about the dreariest place in the universe and she still couldn't get her mind round the cool, glamorous Flora she knew being able to stand it, with only the boring locals for company – and sheep, huh? The only way Danni could hack it was by spending the morning in bed and going to the pub whenever it opened. There was a guy she fancied and a couple of others she was having a bit of fun with, but one of them had got kind of intense lately.

And tbh, the house was sort of spooking her. The weather was getting colder every day and even when she switched on every heater in the place it didn't shift that creepy smell of bare stone and old smoke from peat fires; it seemed to reach out to cling to you whenever you opened the front door. And every time she came back to it, she found herself thinking about Flora's death. Head injuries, they'd said, and she kept having a vision of Flora spreadeagled there on the beach with her skull smashed in. Danni shuddered, thinking about it now.

She needed to get out of here, soon. And then she'd go off travelling. Australia, maybe? They'd great beaches there, and she kind of liked the cute wildlife. Better than wolves, anyway.

* * *

Setting off from the bothy at first light, Kelso Strang had made good time on the long walk to his car and arrived just as Ranald Sinclair was walking from his office back to the house looking for coffee.

'Oh, there you are! Did you manage to make it to the top?' he said, opening the door to the mudroom and ushering him in. 'That's Kelso now,' he called through to Hattie in the kitchen.

'I'll make the coffee,' she called back as Kelso hung up his jacket and kicked off his walking boots. Whenever Ranald opened the kitchen door the dogs came romping through, eager to do their duty as greeters.

'Down!' Ranald snapped, and the two labs, giving him a wary glance, subsided to the floor immediately, catching Kelso off-balance with his hand outstretched to pat them. He followed Ranald, saying, 'Managed Caisteal Liath, but I'd to get off it pretty sharpish – the wind was savage, and I didn't even try for Meall Meadhonach. I'd a great day, though – bit of a blow in the middle, but it settled after that. Hi, Hattie.'

'Good to see you, Kelso. We were thinking about you when the rain came on here. Were you all right in the bothy? You're probably starving – what can I get you?'

'Always Hattie's first thought, food,' Ranald said unkindly. 'Don't rush him! Let him decide what he wants to do – probably wants to change out of the clothes he's been sleeping in and have a shower.'

Hattie looked crestfallen. Trying to lighten the atmosphere, Kelso said, 'Is that a hint, Ranald? I tell you what, you stay downwind of me, I'll grab a cup of coffee and a piece of toast or something, and then I'll go up and get respectable.'

'Whatever suits.' Ranald sounded a little stiff. 'Liberty Hall.' The dogs, subdued, had come through behind him and when he said 'Basket!' they trotted across to lie by the Aga. The men sat down at the table with mugs of coffee and Hattie started frying bacon for a butty.

'I tell you what was seriously weird,' Kelso said. 'I can't get this out of my head. I woke up cold in the bothy in the early hours and went out for some wood to get the fire going again and I heard a wolf howling – a long way away, but definitely a wolf. Does someone keep them around here?'

Ranald shook his head. 'A wolf? Naah. There's some big dogs around – that's probably what you heard. And up a mountain, middle of the night – no wonder it seemed weird.'

'Not a dog.' Kelso was definite. 'I was on an exercise in Dalmatia once and we heard them at night – the most eerie thing you could imagine. Suddenly you're primitive man and the sound goes straight through to chill your spine.'

Hattie turned. 'Do you know, I heard someone talking about that in the shop. There was a rumour going round that one of the crofters saw a sheep being mauled and he swore it was a wolf that was doing it when he scared it off.'

'Dog, most like,' Ranald said. 'Difficult to tell, with some of the new breeds you see nowadays.'

'They were all saying it must be to do with Sean Reynolds. He's got a thing about bringing them back – maybe he's got one even before they're allowed,' she went on, and suddenly Ranald was interested.

'Hang on – I suppose that could be right. The man's trying to buy up all the land round here and then he'll start pulling strings to get a licence to enclose and bring in wolves and suddenly it all makes sense. With Scotland's "right to roam" nonsense there's no right to privacy if you've got a bit of land. You can't stop people going anywhere they like – we've actually had oiks walking right past here and peering in our front windows. But they're all dead nuts about reintroducing wildlife and if you were able to keep wolves, you'd be allowed to fence off the whole lot in case boy scouts started wandering around and getting eaten. Job done.'

Kelso was fascinated. 'I'd never have thought of it like that. It seems an elaborate way to get privacy, but . . .'

'He's certainly obsessed about wolves,' Hattie said as she set down the sandwich, to appreciative noises from Kelso. 'Stand still long enough and he'll start telling you more than you really want to know about them. You can see for yourself tonight – I expect we'll be going along to the pub and Sean's always there on a Saturday.'

As Kelso finished his breakfast and went off to shower, his spirits lifted at the thought of being spared another evening of listening to the Sinclairs sniping at each other. It's strange how relationships change as you move on; he'd have said Ranald was a good mate, but now he realised they had merely been brothers-in-arms, which was a very different thing.

Ranald had been an army man through and through; for Kelso, taking a short-term commission had merely been a sop to his father, Major General Sir Roderick – a wasted gesture that hadn't worked, since he'd never been forgiven for leaving when it finished – and their life-experience had been vastly different since.

Now Kelso realised he really didn't like the man at all. Ranald had been a good officer, well liked by his men, but perhaps he'd carried the authoritarian attitude on into private life. The way he was treating Hattie was nothing short of bullying and their marriage was falling apart before his eyes, hard to watch when there was nothing you could do. As an outsider he couldn't hope to understand the internal dynamics of other people's relationships.

But perhaps tonight he would get a chance to talk to Hattie on her own. When you lived in a place like this confiding in your friends was dangerous if you didn't want your private problems to become common knowledge, and being able to let off steam to Kelso, whom she would most likely never see again, might help.

CHAPTER FOUR

Sean Reynolds' displeasure was written on his face as he came back into Auchinglass House. The cleaner was hoovering the parquet flooring in the hall and she hastily switched it off and moved the machine out of his way.

He didn't thank her. 'Where's my wife?' was all he said.

'She's in the sitting room with your mum.' She gave him a jaundiced look as he strode off.

The sitting room was flooded with light on this bright sunny morning. Though the house's Victorian ancestry showed in the pitch pine doors and windows and the ecclesiastical-style fireplace where a log fire was burning, the decor and furnishings were emphatically modern, employing neutral shades with clever highlights of colour.

Maia Reynolds glanced up as he came in, then looked down, her light brown hair swinging forward around her face.

She said, 'Shirley and I are just having a coffee. Do you want one? I'll get you a mug.'

'Fine,' he said, sitting down as she got up and went out.

His mother Shirley gave him a searching look. She was sitting in her 'riser' chair, her tripod walking-stick beside her, her gnarled and twisted hands evidence of the arthritis that was crippling her, but there was nothing wrong with the sharp mind behind the bright brown, hooded eyes.

Sean's thick, dark brows were drawn into a straight line and his cheeks were flushed with temper.

'Didn't go your way, then?' Shirley said in her gravelly, ginny voice.

She viewed her son as a duck would if playing mum to a fluffy chick – well disposed, but baffled. There was a sort of naivety about his romantic idealism and his fanatical devotion to his rewilding cause and his wolves that, as a cynical pragmatist, she found hard to understand. It was engaging, though, and even admirable in its way, and she was loyally prepared to go along with him and read the books he put into her hands and listen while he talked about his precious wolves the way a lover might talk about his mistress.

Sean grunted. 'Mmm. Lippy little bitch! She's playing games with me.'

'No more reasonable than the aunt, then?'

'I explained to her what it was all about and she just sneered. I couldn't believe it – she's young, and it's her world we're trying to save. She should be impassioned! She really has no right to think like that. And where do people get these stupid ideas about wolves from? It completely stops them listening to reason.'

'Something to do with those films with Russians in troikas in snow and a wolf pack gaining on them?' Shirley suggested drily.

'That's just so much nonsense – you know that!' he protested.

'Yes, but they don't.'

'For heaven's sake! They wouldn't even notice if there were, say, a pair on the estate.' He shifted a little uncomfortably under her sceptical gaze. 'Anyway, you're all for it too, aren't you?'

'Oh, I'm all for it. But we still need just a bit more land to meet the requirements.'

'Oh, tell me about it! How do I dislodge her? Come up with something.'

Shirley might have been a stay-at-home wife and mother but she had a good business head. She gave a moment's thought to Sean's problem, then said, 'Maia says she's having a fine time playing off Ben Linton against Joe Dundas. So, sack the pair of them and she'd probably leave. The wee posh laddies who volunteer for a week won't interest her.'

He sighed. 'Yeah, logically speaking that's fine and I haven't a problem with brutal when it's necessary. But I need them both. Maia says Ben's got the admin running now like a Rolls Royce and Joe's a hard grafter who knows his stuff – not a lot of them about.'

'You can never afford to lose key workers, right enough.' Then she gave a throaty laugh. 'But maybe just sack them both then re-employ them quickly whenever she's gone?'

She made Sean laugh too. She'd always been able to do that, with her acerbic take on things and she knew he enjoyed her company, especially with Maia being so quiet.

She got on perfectly well with her daughter-in-law; it was almost impossible to dislike someone who was so polite and thoughtful and who never expressed a strong opinion. She could understand why Sean had married Maia – she had a sort of elusive quality that was quite compelling. It was just that she couldn't understand why Maia had married Sean.

But she was resigned to never finding out, and if there was a tiny part of her that had felt rebuked by him choosing a wife so unlike Shirley herself – still noisy, still opinionated and still doggedly raven-haired – she'd got over it. She was lucky to have a daughter-in-law who didn't mind her husband's closeness to his mother.

By the time Maia came back with a mug for him, he was asking Shirley's advice about changing suppliers for the plastic sleeves that protected the young trees from the attention of the ever-growing population of red deer. She poured coffee from the pot, topped up her own mug and Shirley's and with a small sigh sat down again.

Inverbeg Inn was a long, low, whitewashed building, which had once been a row of four cottages, with a garden terrace at the back where there were tables for use on the rare occasions when it wasn't raining and the midges weren't out.

The store at one end was what used to be known as a 'johnnie-a'-thing', where the limited stock was tailored to what might be needed between visits to the Spar in Lochinver or the Tesco in Ullapool, with a good freezer section. The owners, a cheerful Polish couple, had bought it after it had been shuttered up and decaying for two years and the community had responded with gratitude, arranging a rota of volunteer helpers to make sure the Novaks didn't burn themselves out and leave.

Expecting a quiet little local, Kelso was astonished by the crowd. They had lingered over dinner – an excellent game pie – so the car park was almost full when they arrived and as he opened the door to let Hattie go in front of him, the noise was like a wall of sound. It was a comparatively small space, with perhaps fifty, sixty people crammed in, and the low ceiling didn't help; everyone had to shout to make themselves heard.

The most surprising thing was the age range of the drinkers – from kids who might well be there with forged ID, to the senior citizens who looked as if they'd been steadily pickling themselves for years. Some kind of informal apartheid appeared to be operating: a sort of student-type party going on at one end; in the middle, tables seating couples and small groups; propping up the bar a gathering that looked like the regulars he'd expected, mainly older single men with the weather-beaten complexion that goes with a life on the land.

As they made their way in, both Hattie and Ranald were hailed by friends and paused to speak to them while Kelso made his way directly to the bar. The three people serving were all being kept busy and he turned to speak to Hattie as she reached him.

'I'm setting up a slate, so there'll be no arguments – you've been feeding me for days. Tanqueray and tonic for you and the Macallan for Ranald, is that right?' he said.

'That's far too kind,' Hattie said. 'It's been a pleasure to have you. But it'll be a long evening – better make that Gordon's and Famous Grouse or you'll be bankrupt.'

'Think I can take the hit,' he said. 'As long as I can persuade someone to set it up.'

She bent closer to him to murmur, 'That man there – the

60

one with curly dark hair – that's Sean Reynolds. It must be his turn on the voluntary rota tonight.'

Kelso looked at him with interest. It was hot in the room; the man's cheeks were flushed and there was sweat on his forehead as he pulled the pints. He had a strong face, wide across the cheekbones, with a very square jaw. He looked the sort you'd be wise not to question if he'd decided you'd had enough to drink.

Now the other man was coming over. 'Hi Kasper!' Hattie said. 'This is our house guest, Kelso. He wants to set up a slate for us, so be nice to him.'

Kasper was a big man, broad-shouldered and loose-limbed, with an easy manner. 'Am I not nice to everybody, Hattie? Especially if they are buying drinks!'

He took the order and Kelso looked round. 'Where's Ranald?' he said, a moment before he spotted him standing on the far side of the room, talking to a woman. She was small and slight and pale, with delicate features and straight, light brown hair that skimmed her shoulders. Ranald was stooping over to talk to her and she was looking up at him with a slight smile; it was natural enough, given the acoustic problems, but something about the expression on Ranald's face made Kelso look at them sharply and his heart sank. Oh dear. That would explain quite a lot.

Hattie glanced over her shoulder. 'Oh, he's over there, talking to Maia. She's Sean's wife – quite reserved, but very nice. Oh, hello, Angus, I didn't see you there.' She broke off to speak to the older man on her other side.

Was Hattie as oblivious as she seemed? Kelso thought she was, probably; he assessed her as a very straightforward person and he was pretty sure he'd have known if she was putting on an act. His eyes went to Maia's husband; he was probably too busy with his barman duties to have noticed anything – and what he himself had noticed might in any case be one-sided.

Maia's face was inscrutable.

Hattie was saying, 'Angus, I'd like you to meet our friend Kelso Strang. He and Ran were in the army together and now he's ever such a high-powered police officer, so you'll have to behave yourself.'

Kelso cringed inwardly. He hated that sort of joke and he hated being marked out as a police officer in social settings; the reaction was often hostile and even if it wasn't he was usually forced on the defensive over some story about bumbling coppers that had nothing to do with him.

Angus Mackenzie, to be fair, took neither approach. 'How interesting,' he said. 'That must be quite a challenging job. I'd like—'

Hattie interrupted. 'Kelso, Kasper's bringing the drinks now. Shall I make a move on that table where the people are leaving?'

'You do that. I'll bring them over. Thanks, Kasper.' He turned back to Angus, but someone had claimed his attention on the other side.

She had secured the table, but before she could sit down she was accosted by two women at the next one and with an apologetic grimace to Kelso went over to speak to them as he brought the drinks and sat down.

Ranald noticed him arriving and raised a hand in greeting.

'Sorry – just coming.' He put an arm round Maia's shoulders and ushered her over to the table. 'Maia, this is Kelso – old buddy of mine from army days. Maia's pretty much our next-door neighbour, Kelso – that's her husband, helping out behind the bar tonight.'

Kelso stood up politely. 'Do join us. Can I get you a drink?'

She smiled a little careful smile that didn't reach her eyes. 'No thank you. I must get back – my mother-in-law's at home and I don't like to leave her alone for too long.' Somehow she slipped away through the crowd without anyone having to move aside for her.

Ranald picked up his glass from the table saying, 'Sláinte!' then, when he'd sipped it said, 'That's very kind! They don't give it away in here.'

'Least I can do,' Kelso said, sitting down again. 'I've had a great break. But I'm interested by your neighbours. You said Sean Reynolds had all this money – where has it come from?'

Ranald gave a short, bitter laugh. 'Well, the story is he had an Internet company that got bought up by one of the big operators. I don't exactly know about that, but what I can tell you is he gets tens of thousands in subsidies from the Scottish government every year for this rewilding nonsense. And now he has all those pods filled with saving-the-planet types who come for a week or a fortnight and pay handsomely for the privilege of labouring for him. Nice work if you can get it.'

He broke off. 'Oh, I've just seen one of the local councillors – I'm needing a word with him. Would you mind . . .'

'No, of course not.'

Ranald went off to one of the other tables, leaving Kelso to pursue one of his favourite activities – people-watching.

Shirley Reynolds was watching a recording of Masterchef and pressed the remote to pause it when her daughter-in-law came in.

'Good evening? Any gossip?'

Maia smiled. 'Nothing much to report. Usual crowd, usual gossip.'

Shirley suppressed a sigh. She was quite sure if she'd been there she'd have managed to glean something interesting, and she felt like a dog whose nose tells him his owner is cooking something delicious but he knows he's not going to share it. Sean was only a little better than Maia; she'd have to rely on Ishbel the cleaner when she came in on Monday to catch up with the news.

'You shouldn't worry about coming back for me, you know,' she said. 'I'm quite happy here with my programme.'

'It's not a sacrifice, honestly. Are they any good?' Maia sat down and looked at the TV and Shirley clicked it back on. The end was just coming up and as John Torode decreed that one contestant should leave, Shirley tutted. 'You're wrong there, John. He's better than that girl that was making eyes at you.'

Just as she switched off there was a knock on the door and Ben Linton opened it tentatively.

'Hello – hope I'm not interrupting your programme.'

'No, no,' Shirley assured him. 'It's just finished. Come and sit down.' She liked Ben; quite a serious-minded young man, much what any mother would hope her son would be – well-mannered, nice, neat hair, smartly turned-out and prepared to carry on an interesting conversation, unlike some people she could name.

'Did they send the right one home?' he asked, smiling.

Shirley snorted. 'Fell for the pretty girl, like they usually do, poor saps. Not at the pub tonight?'

For some reason he looked uncomfortable. 'Just back from there,' he said.

Shirley gave him a quizzical look. 'Much going on?'

'Not much,' he said, disappointingly. 'Maia, I'm going to pop into the office. A couple of the girls who were sharing a pod have fallen out and aren't far from the hair-pulling stage. There's empty ones at the moment and I thought it might be good PR just to let them split up and use another, if that's OK?'

'Of course. Oh dear!' Maia shook her head. 'Those girls! They do make each other so miserable.'

'Not just each other, I hear,' Shirley said slyly. 'How's your friend – Danni, isn't it?'

She enjoyed seeing the young man turn pink. 'Oh – Danni? She's fine. Thanks, Maia – I'll go and leave a note for the staff to have it ready.' He left.

'Oh, that's a pity – he seems to have taken fright,' Shirley said. 'This Danni doesn't sound the right sort of person for him, anyway.'

'No, I'm sure she isn't,' Maia agreed. 'She's not doing either of those boys any good.' She hesitated, as if she was making her mind up about something, then said, 'Actually, Shirley, I'd value your opinion about Ben.'

Shirley was surprised. 'Yes, of course,' she said. This wasn't like Maia.

'You know we're looking to expand the business. I decided to let him have a look at the books, and he's come up with some pretty good suggestions. I've actually been wondering if we should invite him to make a third on the Auchinglass board along with Sean and me. He's making a name for himself around here and we don't want him getting restless and being poached by someone else – landowners are always on the lookout for a good factor and none of them would scruple to pinch him. He could handle it if something came up when my parents need me in London – you remember that time I'd to come rushing back to deal with a grant application that had to be returned at a moment's notice.'

'Oh yes!' Shirley said. 'That was a right hassle. The girl who was doing the books at the time hadn't a clue and neither did Sean.'

'It would be a big step, though,' Maia said. And she was, Shirley noticed, definitely looking quite nervous. 'Antony Stanton – you know?'

Shirley nodded. He was a big wheel in Maia's dad's business and he'd stayed once or twice on his way north. Very London, she'd thought, and it wasn't a compliment.

'Well, he's coming up for some fishing near Scourie next week, so if he came here first, he could check Ben out. But he doesn't know him, you do, and you're a good judge of character. Would he be loyal, do you think?'

Shirley was flattered. She was used to Sean consulting her, but it was Maia who ran all the business and she'd always dealt with any problems in her usual quiet, competent way. The only time Shirley had offered advice unasked – when they were discussing sending nine-year-old Oliver off to prep school – it had been politely ignored. But right enough, Maia's father was getting very old now and Maia might have to spend more time in London than she did at present.

'It's a big decision, but he seems a nice, reliable young man to me, and it would certainly be useful to have another good practical brain involved,' she said thoughtfully. 'He's very competent that way, isn't he? Sean's certainly got the vision thing but you can't look to him for business input.' Then she paused. 'I've just been wondering of late – you don't think he could be doing something really stupid, do you?'

When Maia didn't reply immediately she hurried on, 'No, that's not fair. I shouldn't ask my daughter-in-law to be rude about her husband to his mother's face. And, of course, we both know he could be, don't we?'

But Maia just looked back at her with that small, enigmatic smile.

Hattie was still talking to her friends, but Kelso didn't mind; he was watching a little drama unfolding at the farther end of the room.

At the centre of it was a young woman, early twenties probably, who looked as if she'd had quite a lot to drink already. She had a pierced eyebrow and was wearing a tight purple minidress over black leggings, a style that didn't flatter her well-padded frame; her arms were folded across her chest, displaying a butterfly tattoo in blues and reds just above the wrist. There were two men standing beside her, one a red-haired lad in heavy jeans with a lumberjack shirt and hiking boots, the other, fair-haired, blue-eyed, in chinos with a white T-shirt and a casual jacket.

Again, the body language said it all. There was aggression there and some of the group who looked quite a bit younger had started drawing away awkwardly, as if they hadn't really noticed anything, but in case there was something they wanted to make sure they weren't involved.

Kelso's instinct kicked in – go over, talk them down, defuse the situation before the trouble started. He fought it down. He'd do it if the need arose, but he was on holiday, dammit.

To his relief, before that moment came Kasper was striding across and the men drew apart. 'You two again!' he was saying. 'One more problem, you are banned.' Then he turned to the girl. 'And I know who makes this happen. You are as bad. You be careful.'

The men, Kelso noticed with interest, looked abashed. The woman didn't. She was wearing the dumb insolence expression familiar to every police officer as she said, 'Yeah, sure.'

With a final warning glare, Kasper walked back to the bar, shaking his head. The one wearing smart casuals said something to the girl and then left.

'Sorry, sorry, sorry!' Hattie arrived at the table in a fluster of apologies and sat down opposite him. 'You know how it is – they started talking about a charity coffee morning for repairs to the community hall that we're arranging and it was hard to get away.'

'Don't apologise,' Kelso said. 'I've been enjoying the cabaret. Who is the truculent young woman with the pierced eyebrow?'

Hattie turned her head to look. 'Who? Oh, Danni Maitland. Of course. As they say, that one would cause trouble in an empty house. She's in here most nights, I think, and her favourite hobby is playing the men off against each other. The two she's with at the moment are permanent workers on the estate – Joe Dundas is a local, but the sharp-looking guy, Ben Linton, is a sort of factor or accountant, I think. The others are all Sean's young eco-warriors – come for a week or two, looks good on their CV. But since Danni came they have a party every night, which I suppose is good for business. But the locals are starting to get fed up with it so it's making Kasper and Zofia a bit stressed.'

'Where did she come from?'

'Not sure. She inherited the croft Ranald was talking about, the one Sean will be trying for as well, if she decides to sell.'

'Right. Have to say, it looks as if she's settled in all right, anyway. How's your drink?' He picked up the glasses and went to order. The man Hattie had spoken to before – Angus, was it? – was locked in conversation with Sean Reynolds – a conversation, Kelso was casually interested to note, that had a distinct edge to it.

Angus's face was flushed; though he wasn't showing other signs of being the worse for wear, Kelso judged it was only because he was a hardened drinker. He'd probably been at it since early evening and now he was getting belligerent.

'I'm going to report it,' he was saying. 'You can't do

that. It's against the law.'

'You'll only make a fool of yourself.' Sean Reynolds' voice was terse. 'Of course there isn't. One day, sure – but when it happens it's all going to be above board.'

Angus was stubborn. 'I know what I saw. And your kind thinks they're above the law. At least when it's legal we'll get compensation. I'll be sending you the bill – the poor beast had to be put down.'

'If you think I'd fork out for someone's dog being out of control, you've got another think coming, fast.' Seeing Kelso, Sean turned. 'Sorry to keep you waiting. What can I get you?'

Kelso gave his order. He wanted to ask Angus some more about what had happened – could this be the explanation for the haunting cry he'd heard? – but he hesitated. Hattie was waiting for him by herself at the table and it could be his chance to be a listening ear, if she wanted one. However, just as he brought the drinks across Ranald appeared from the farther end and joined them.

'Sorry, I've been neglecting you,' he said. 'It was a useful bit of business, though. Well, what do you think of our local? It's not quite what you would expect for a sleepy wee place like this, eh?'

'No,' Kelso agreed. 'There's obviously quite a lot going on, one way and another.' He said it deliberately looking pointedly at Ranald, hoping he might show some sign of consciousness and then consider backing off the fragrant Mrs Reynolds, but it went unnoticed. Not a very sensitive person, Ranald Sinclair.

'Well, you know what small towns are like,' he said.

'Always something happening.'

No, Kelso didn't know what small towns were like. He'd had a peripatetic childhood, never in one place for long, and then he'd lived in a city. The only time he came across small towns was in the course of his work when the SRCS had been summoned and the place was in crisis. It was an education for him to see how many tensions could be seething under the surface in a small town that was just going about ordinary life.

He went on with his people-watching as he chatted to his hosts and saw Danni being led out of the door on to the terrace by Lumberjack Shirt.

'You didn't mean that, did you?' Joe Dundas said, a hint of desperation in his tone.

Danni looked at him coolly. 'Mean what? You said you wanted me to come out and you'd give me a fag. I didn't come so you could start interrogating me.'

'I'm not interrogating you! I just asked a simple question. I want to know what you meant, all right?'

'Ciggie first. Where is it? Come on!'

'OK, I don't have any. I only keep them for you, and I didn't finish in time to get to the shop before it shut.'

'Well, buy some over the bar, then,' she said impatiently.

'Kasper doesn't keep them, except in the shop.'

She turned. 'Not much point in being out here, then, is there? And I'm getting cold.'

He put his hand on her arm to detain her, then lifted it as she said, outraged, 'I beg your pardon?'

'Sorry. Look, wait for a minute. You said I was a

71

roughneck and Linton laughed.'

'It was a joke, all right? Now, can I go back in?'

'No. I just got the feeling you'd been sneering at me behind my back. If that's how it is, I'm not interested.'

She gave him a long, indifferent look. 'Fine by me.'

Joe stared back at her, his face a mask of misery. 'Do you really mean that?'

'Stop asking me if I really mean that. I don't know what I mean. I just want to have a good time and the way the two of you are going on is getting me in trouble.'

'Tell him to back off, then. You know he's mucking you about – he's nothing but a slimeball. He's only interested because you've got a bit of money.'

Danni bridled. 'Oh really? I'm so unattractive that no one could fancy me for myself? And where does that leave you?'

'I'm not like that! I-I think you're brilliant. I've been trying to tell you that ever since I met you. I'm serious, Danni, and I thought you fancied me, a bit. It's driving me daft, the way you let him keep coming between us all the time.'

Her arms were folded. 'Maybe it never crossed your mind that you may be serious but I'm not? Do you really think I would settle for getting stuck in a dump like this? I'm getting bored already and there's a great big world out there.'

'You're not planning to leave, are you?' he said, alarm in his voice.

Danni shrugged. 'When it suits me.'

His head went down. Then he looked up, gazing into

her face as he moved towards her. 'I'm going to make you care,' he said.

Alarmed by his intensity she eyed him warily, unsure what he was going to do. He was a big man, tall and strong, but when he pulled her into his arms it was clear he was only going to kiss her and she had no alternative but to let him. Then he released her looking, great sumph, as if he thought that might have changed her mind.

She swung her arm back and slapped his face as hard as she could. She had a heavy dress ring on one finger that left a bloody mark across his left cheek.

'Oh, you really have blown it now!' she said. 'I'm never going to speak to you again and if you come near me, I'll tell the police.'

She went back into the pub and slammed the door.

CHAPTER FIVE

At the slamming of the door, heads turned in the pub. Danni, her face stormy, marched across to the coat hooks in the corner, snatched her parka and went out of the other door. There was a stir of discreet amusement that became a small but hurtful ripple of laughter when the door opened again and Joe Dundas, with a red face and a cut on his left cheekbone, came in to fetch his own coat, not looking to left or to right.

Hattie, a kindly soul, was dismayed. 'Oh dear! Poor boy! She really is a nasty bit of work. And I notice Ben Linton's vanished. Quite honestly, he'd be better to keep away from her altogether.'

'If she'd just vanish I'd be happier,' Ranald said. 'Though of course it wouldn't solve the problem of me getting hold of the property and not Sean.'

He looked as if he was going to start the old story up again. Kelso had been hoping he might get an excuse to ask Angus Mackenzie a bit more about his quarrel with

Reynolds, but it didn't look as if he was going to get the opportunity. Rather than gritting his teeth and preparing to listen, he looked at his watch.

'I hate to break up the party but I'm going to have to make an early start in the morning. If you wouldn't mind . . . ?'

Ranald rose. 'Me too. All right, Hattie?'

They all got up and he was walking past the bar when Angus Mackenzie reached out to grab his arm. He was showing more sign of his evening's entertainment, but he was still perfectly coherent and stable on his feet.

'Hope I'm not taking advantage,' he said, 'but could I have a word with you?'

Hattie stopped. 'Angus, Kelso's got to be up early tomorrow. I'm just going to drag him away.'

'Oh well,' Angus said, polite but crestfallen.

'No, no,' Kelso said hastily. 'It's fine. You go on Hattie – won't be long.'

Hattie drew him aside to whisper, 'Bit lit up tonight, I think. Are you sure?'

'Don't worry. See you shortly, I hope.'

'We won't lock the door.'

Kelso turned back to Angus. 'There's a table free over there. Why don't we sit down and have a chat?'

High on the adrenaline from her outburst, Danni Maitland set off briskly up the track to the cottage. It powered her for the first bit but after that it was steeper; she was seriously unfit and progress got slower and slower.

It was very, very dark, the sort of dark where it felt like someone had put a blanket over your head and you wanted to put up your hand to push it away. Up till now the weather had always cleared at night and with moonlight and starlight you could at least see where you were going, but the heavy cloud cover tonight meant that she could barely see the ground under her feet as light from the pub dwindled. A tussock of grass brought her to her knees, swearing.

And she'd forgotten to bring a torch, FFS. How dumb could she be? That meant either she'd have to stumble on a bit more slowly, staring at her feet, unless she wanted to go back down to the pub to borrow one – embarrassing in itself, after the exit she'd made – and then have to start the climb all over again. She stumbled on.

It had been a rotten evening, anyway. Of course Danni wasn't interested in Joe – like she would be! – but she'd been using him to try to keep Ben interested. She fancied Ben – he was well fit and quite classy with it, but she'd no idea where she was with him. She'd once or twice been kind of worried he maybe saw her like she saw Joe – the way he'd said, earlier tonight, that he expected she'd move on soon, like he was cool with that. Not like Joe, gawping at her like a codfish when she said she would leave.

He'd a good job on the estate, Ben – management, not a labourer, like Joe – and for a wee while she'd even reckoned she could get used to the place and the weather, because he was quite sexy, but even if he did fancy her, Danni wasn't sure that would make up for everything else. Like not being able to pop out to the shops on a Saturday.

She was sweaty and breathless now, reaching the steepest part of the path, the part where it skirted the edge of the cliff where Flora had fallen. It always creeped her out, this bit; she'd even dreamt last night she was falling off it herself, and she shuddered now, looking back over her shoulder, though of course she knew there couldn't be anyone there.

But could she be sure? How would she know if there was someone just coming up silently behind her in the darkness, stalking her step by step, like someone could have stalked Flora? Joe, maybe, angry at what she'd done to him . . . ? Giving a little gasp of fright she forced herself into a staggering run to reach the cottage.

She never locked the door – nothing inside worth stealing – but once over the doorstep she locked it now and leant against the wall panting for breath, nerves twanging like strings being plucked. Then she bent to peer out of one of the low windows. She couldn't see any movement, but then it was pitch-dark. Deathly quiet too. A seagull squawked suddenly and she almost jumped out of her skin.

It was really getting to her now. No way could she go on like this. Face it – Ben Linton wasn't a good bet, so the sooner she got out the better. She could go and tell the lawyer on Monday to get things moving, and then all she had to do was decide between Ranald and Sean.

And that would take, like, a nanosecond. She couldn't care less what they did with the place; choosing the top bid was a no-brainer, and she could spend tomorrow on the Internet, looking up places to see in Australia.

When Angus Mackenzie joined him at the table the conversation didn't take quite the turn Kelso had expected. Having heard him say to Reynolds that something was 'against the law', he'd assumed he would be hearing a complaint in the hope that it would be passed on, backed by pressure from 'ever such a high-powered police officer', as Hattie had termed him. That was what people usually did, in these circumstances.

He was wrong, though. The man who was sitting opposite him with tears in his eyes and his hands trembling, wasn't talking about his sheep. His faded blue eyes were bloodshot and he was admittedly far from sober but nor, Kelso judged, was this just the maudlin stage of drunkenness. Something was distressing him and he took out a handkerchief to blow his nose.

'I'm sorry – excuse me. It's hard for me to talk about it but it could be this is my only chance. You probably know about what happened to Flora Maitland?'

It took Kelso a moment to remember who she was. Hattie had indeed mentioned her but only in passing, and he probably couldn't have come up with the name if challenged. 'She had an accident, is that right? A fall from a cliff path?'

'Accident? Oh, that's what they said. They said she was drunk, staggered off the path close to the house. They said she was tottery because she was old and drunk with it – well, not in those words,' he admitted, seeing Kelso's look of astonishment. 'But that was what they meant. I told them they were wrong. I told them I knew Flora better than anyone—' His voice broke and he bowed his head. 'Sorry.'

'She was your good friend,' Kelso said gently. 'It must have been very upsetting.'

His head snapped up and he glared at Kelso. 'Not just upsetting – wickedly wrong!' he said fiercely. 'Flora was up and down these hills day after day with her flock, no bother. She was fit and she could certainly walk me into the ground. And drunk? I tell you, she'd the hardest head of anyone I know – man or woman. Whatever she drank, she never showed it. I'm a lightweight, compared to her.' He paused. 'I know you think I'm a bit on the go tonight, and you're right. I quite often am on a Saturday night, since Flora went. But it doesn't mean that what I say isn't the truth.

'And that night, she was still on her first drink. I was there beside her, in a group talking to some of the kids from the estate project. We were arguing about their bloody wolves and she was laughing and then suddenly she wasn't. She went white; it looked as if she'd seen something that scared the life out of her, but when I turned to look, I couldn't see anything out of the ordinary. She said she didn't feel well and just finished her glass and went. That was the last I saw of her.'

'And you told the police officers this?'

The laugh Angus gave him was bitter. 'Oh yes, I told them. I told a couple of different ones, more than once, and they patted me on the head and sent me away. I told her brother what I thought, thinking the family might have had more clout, but nothing's happened. The niece,' – he shrugged – 'I don't see her doing anything.'

'Right,' Kelso said slowly. 'What you're saying is that you believe someone killed Flora, is that right? So of course I have to ask you why you think anyone might have wanted to harm her.' Immediately, he sensed Angus's withdrawal; for the first time he was looking shifty.

'Why? Um, well, I couldn't say, of course. She'd – she'd had an interesting life, I think. Not that I would know, really.'

Which meant he did know something. Kelso could press him, of course, but there wasn't any point until he'd some idea of what this was all about. He said merely, 'So what are you expecting me to do about it?'

'I don't know you, so I'm not expecting anything. But Hattie said you're very senior and I felt there was just a chance you might ask some questions, get them to open the case to look at it again.'

So Kelso had been wrong about what Angus Mackenzie was going to talk about, but he'd been right that it was the usual motive. He shaped his response carefully. 'It doesn't work like that, but give me your contact anyway. What I can say is I'll try to see the report and if there was something I could legitimately ask about, I will. I'm afraid that's all I can promise.'

'Thank you.' Angus got to his feet. 'Thank you, on Flora's behalf. She's entitled to justice. I'm sorry to have kept you.'

'Wait a moment,' Kelso said. 'Tell me about the argument you were having with Sean Reynolds. Something about sheep-worrying?'

He sat down again. 'Sheep-worrying? Oh, it's not just the sheep that's worried. It's the rest of us. The man's obsessed with this rewilding stuff. He's got the ear of the environment lobby and the government's in their pocket. Oh, it'll happen eventually, bears and lynx too, no doubt. But the bastard's jumped the gun – I know he's got wolves up there. I saw one attacking one of my gimmers with my own eyes – and don't tell me I don't know the difference between a dog and a wolf! It held its ground, too, even threatening me – I'd a crook in my hand, luckily, and when I slashed at it and my own dog started barking it ran off.

'There's been rumours among the farming community for a while about mauled carcasses. Oh, everyone goes on about how we'd get compensation once the wolves came back, as if it was just a question of money. But I spend night after night slogging through the lambing season and it isn't so I have ewes permanently terrified with wolves prowling around and then getting torn apart.'

'I can see that,' Kelso said. 'I'm asking you because I heard a wolf howling myself late one night. I'd have to point out, though, that it's possible that someone quite legally keeps one that's enclosed – and I suppose it might just have escaped that time you saw it.'

Angus listened with an ironic smile. 'Aye, that'll be right. Believe it, if you like. But if you ask me, it won't be just the one. There'll be a pair around somewhere, making lots of wee wolf babies. If Sean wants to get them established, he'll be doing what that lot with the beavers did – release pairs into the wild while it's still illegal. And then you get all the daft city folk that like cute furry animals saying you can't be cruel and get rid of them now they're there. For some reason, woolly animals don't matter the same way. I guess it's happening, whether we want it or not.'

'Have you reported it to the police?'

'The police?' He gave a short laugh. 'Oh, you mean the ones that drift in to Lochinver a couple of times a week? If they won't do anything when they're told someone's been murdered, they're not really likely to do much about a savaged sheep.

'Anyway, thanks for hearing me out. Sorry I kept you from your bed.' He touched a finger to his forehead and walked out.

He probably hadn't been all that drunk, Kelso reflected. Emotional, certainly, and he definitely wasn't going to pass any breathalyser test, but his mind was perfectly clear.

He was thinking about it as he walked along to the Sinclairs' house. If there really were wolves roaming free it was a serious issue. Oh, he knew the theory all right – timid, retiring species, scared of people – but even so, it was a ludicrously dangerous, and arrogant, thing to do without taking any account of the risks. Angus Mackenzie was right, though; there wasn't really anything for the police to take action on – even if an ever-so-high-powered officer mentioned he'd heard howling.

The light was on in the kitchen when he reached the house and he put his head round the door, just to say goodnight; he wasn't planning to settle down again. But when he looked in Hattie was by herself with the dogs, who trotted across to welcome him.

'Oh, I'm glad he didn't keep you too long. Ran's gone to bed. Would you like a cup of tea or anything?'

Kelso hesitated. He was ready for bed himself and he'd have to be on his way by six in the morning. On the other hand, he'd wanted to give Hattie the chance to confide in him, if she cared to take it.

'Well – if you're having one yourself . . .' he said.

'Kettle's on the stove. I quite often sit on for a bit with the girls when they've been left all evening – you get a bit lonely, don't you, poor old things? But how did you get on with Angus?'

He sat down at the table. 'I liked him. Salt-of-the-earth type. But tell me, what do you know about Flora Maitland?'

'Flora? I knew her to say hello to in passing, but not much more than that. She came a few years ago after old Willie Maitland died. She was in the pub propping up the bar most Saturdays.'

'Did she often seem to get drunk?'

'Drunk?' Hattie paused to think as she warmed the pot. 'Not that I ever noticed.' Then she stopped. 'But of course! So that's why he wanted to speak to you! They said that was how she came to fall off the cliff, didn't they? And I remember Angus was very upset about it, wouldn't believe it could possibly have happened unless someone shoved her. Oh dear, I'm sorry if he was seizing the chance to bend your ear about it – how tiresome for you. I'm sorry.'

'Don't apologise. I was interested. He was very emphatic that it hadn't been an accident at all, and he knew she'd been murdered, but he was evasive when I asked him why she should have been.'

Hattie brought the mugs and sat down. 'I don't know much about her, really, but there were always a few pursed lips among the older locals when she was mentioned. I suspect she might have had a bit of a rackety past. Not that that means much, probably; they're still fairly traditional around here.'

'Right,' Kelso said. 'He was quite convinced, too, that Sean Reynolds has let wolves loose on the estate.'

'And you heard that howl!' she exclaimed. 'Oh, I wouldn't put it past him. He's such an arrogant sod. And he seems to have all the money in the world and it's driving Ran insane. If Sean just goes on bidding up the price for the croft, no way can we match him.'

'It does seem to be getting under Ran's skin.'

'I honestly don't believe he can think about anything else. Oh, apart from my inadequacies as a wife.' Hattie's lip trembled. 'I'm sorry. You've had enough to put up with, listening to us squabbling all the time. You don't want to hear any more about this.'

'I think he's amazingly lucky having a wife like you. If you want to tell me about it, I'll listen.'

'Oh, I shouldn't inflict it on you.'

'Sometimes it helps to talk. Go on.'

It all came pouring out. Her hands gripping her mug so tightly that the knuckles showed white, she said miserably, 'To be truthful, I'm in despair. I just can't think what to do. There's something wrong, but Ran won't even acknowledge it – just walks off whenever I try to get him to explain what it is. Oh, we've always had quarrels, of course – all couples do, don't they?'

'Sure,' Kelso said, though in fact he couldn't remember anything more than a brief tiff in the three years he'd been married.

'After we realised we weren't going to have the kids we'd always wanted, it all got a bit more fraught. But it's only lately he's started treating me as if he almost can't bear to have me around and it really hurts. Has – has he said anything to you?'

Kelso shook his head. 'All he's talked about is needing to get hold of the croft and expanding the fish farm.'

'That's the odd thing – I don't actually see why he's quite so desperate about it. We're doing fine as we are, with what I bring in from catering. He only began talking about it after he heard that Sean Reynolds was interested. He thought he'd stolen a march on him by contacting Flora's brother William whenever she died – they'd more or less agreed the sale – but then of course it turned out she'd left everything to Danni.

'I don't think he got on very well talking to her. He tends to come over a bit army with kids like her – you know, the officer telling the squaddies what's expected of them. But he knows she won't let him have it unless he'll pay top dollar and of course Sean's loaded, and I think Maia's probably got money too. It's absolutely eating him up.

'It almost seems to have become some sort of macho thing, but I can't see why he should feel he has to prove himself against Sean.'

Kelso had a sinking feeling that he knew why, but he didn't feel pointing it out to Ranald's wife would be helpful. 'There's always a tendency to make it a zero-sum game when two men want the same thing,' he said. 'And as I remember it in our army days, Ranald was always the competitive sort. If his squad didn't have the fastest time on the task there was hell to pay.'

'Oh, that was Ran all right!' Hattie laughed, but it was a shaky laugh and there were tears not far behind it. 'Those were such happy times. We were all right, then. Oh, I'm not trying to claim it was ever a match made in heaven, but it worked for us. It's not working now.'

She sighed, but then stood up decisively. 'Oh, listen to me! This is ridiculous. I'm keeping you out of your bed and I know you'll be off at some ungodly hour tomorrow.

Thanks, Kelso.' She bent forward to kiss his cheek and stood up.

'Will you be all right?' he said.

The laugh was more confident this time. 'Course I will. I'll be fine. The old school motto was "Tenez ferme." Which at the time I remember we all interpreted as meaning, "Keep your legs crossed".'

He was laughing as he left the kitchen but he was worried for her. Despite the way she was being treated she still loved Ranald, and as he drove back to Edinburgh on Sunday she was much on his mind. They had a beautiful home and they lived in an incomparably beautiful place, but when you were as isolated as that you had to rely on each other for companionship and support and with Ranald offering little of either, hers was a bleak outlook.

Had he always been a bully? He was certainly acting like one now – and he was clearly infatuated with Maia Reynolds, though there hadn't really been any noticeable sign that she was equally infatuated with him, and on balance Kelso thought it was unlikely. A very cool customer, Maia.

When he got time next day, he would have to fulfil his promise to Angus Mackenzie. He suspected there'd be nothing to investigate: elderly people being unsteady on their feet after a drink or two was hardly a hold-the-front-page story, however much they – or their friends – might protest. But there was something impressive about Angus's steadfast loyalty, especially with Ranald's behaviour leaving such an unpleasant taste in his mouth.

An odd little place, Inverbeg, with some very unhealthy cross-currents swirling about. The sleepy little township that he'd imagined, peopled by decent country folk going about their peaceful rural lives, existed only in his imagination.

He was glad to be returning to the big city. It might be bustling and dirty but it was more peaceful, in its way; you do what you like without anyone even noticing. And if it lacked the drama of the mountains and the seascapes, there was still nothing wrong with the view across the Firth of Forth from the window of his old fisherman's cottage.

The rain came on in Inverbeg shortly before midnight, heavy and persistent. On this windless night it made a sound as soothing as white noise, a gentle hiss as it ran off the roof and fell in a sheet past Danni Maitland's bedroom window.

She was just drifting off to sleep, having spent the day checking out the Visit Australia website. It had looked fabulous and the pictures she had seen and the plans she had been making had started to blur into a dream: Danni in her bikini, a wide, wide beach . . .

Then the world exploded, in a crash that shook the whole building and smashed the bedroom window. Shards crashed on to the floor and as Danni sat bolt upright in the darkness, screaming, her bedroom was transformed by the lurid light from an inferno of red and orange flames outside into a vision of hell.

CHAPTER SIX

The lights started springing out all over the township as Inverbeg startled into wakefulness. The blaze on the hill beside the Maitland croft house was subsiding into sullen, red, sooty flames as the little yellow Honda parked on the hardstanding at one side burnt itself out.

In blind panic, Danni leapt out of bed and ran to the door, heart pounding so that she could scarcely breathe. She didn't even notice her feet were bleeding from the broken glass on the bedroom floor as she wrestled with the locked door then plunged outside and ran to the corner of the house.

Through the teeming rain she peered frantically about her, trying to make sense of what had happened. Oh no! Her car – her lovely yellow car! It was just a twisted mass of metal, the flames still licking greedily around it as they died back. The acrid smell caught at her throat and the smoke was stinging her eyes.

And now she noticed her feet were a mass of blood and gave a shriek of terror. How could they be? What else might have happened to her? She could hardly breathe – she could be dying! What was she to do? Coughing and giving strangled sobs, she huddled her arms around her as she was racked by paroxysms of shivering.

Then below, she saw the lights of a car speeding towards her from the direction of the Auchinglass Estate. Ben! she thought wildly. It was Ben, coming to rescue her. She'd only have to hold on for a few minutes now.

But as it drove round on to the road leading up, she heard a woman's voice calling. 'Danni! Hang on, I'll be with you in a minute.'

In the flickering light she could see a figure below running along the road by the pub and starting up the path through the smoke to the cottage and recognised Hattie Sinclair. She came up more quickly than Danni ever could, though she was out of breath and coughing as she got to the top.

She was wearing an oilskin jacket over jeans and a hoodie and she pulled it off to put round Danni. 'Get that on before you get hypothermia. Oh dear, your poor feet! Did you tread on some glass? Your bedroom window's broken.'

Glass. Oh. 'I-I suppose so,' Danni gulped. 'I didn't know what it was. Just—the bang woke me . . .'

Hattie walked over to look. 'Oh, it's your car! I couldn't think what on earth could have happened when I heard the noise. It must have gone on fire, for some reason, and then exploded. But look, it's burning itself out now, so it's safe enough. This smoke's horrible, though – let's get inside out of the rain and get your feet sorted out. But watch where you tread.'

She put her arm round Danni's shoulder to usher her inside, but Danni hesitated, looking over her shoulder. 'I think that's Ben, coming to rescue me,' she said as an SUV drew up on the road.

But it wasn't Ben who jumped out of it, it was Sean Reynolds, his hair plastered to his head and wearing a zipped fleecy that was already soaked by the deluge.

He stared about him. 'What the hell has happened? You all right, Danni?'

Hattie stepped forward. 'Hello, Sean. I'm just trying to get her inside before she catches her death. You got here quickly.'

'I was working late. When I heard the bang, I just ran out and then went to fetch the car when I saw the fire,' he said, coming in behind them, with a glance over his shoulder at the dwindling flames. 'Doesn't look as if there's anything more to worry about now, and it doesn't look as if there's been any structural damage. The rain's helping to put it out, as well.'

As Danni hobbled in and collapsed onto a chair. Hattie switched on the lights and the heater. 'I'll just get a basin and water to clean your feet, Danni. Sean, if you could find a brush and shovel and clear up the glass in the bedroom it would help.'

Sean didn't look pleased about being given orders, but he went over to the kitchen area, opening cupboards till one yielded up a broom and a dustpan, while Hattie examined Danni's feet and the water in the basin turned red.

The girl was showing signs of shock and when there was a tap on the door and Angus Mackenzie appeared, in gumboots and with a wax jacket over his pyjamas, rain dripping down his face, she said, 'Oh Angus – that's good! Could you make Danni a cup of tea? You probably know where everything is.'

He was looking fairly shocked himself as he went to the stove to fill the kettle. 'That's a terrible thing. You poor lassie! And what's happened to your feet?'

'It's not actually as bad as it looks,' Hattie said. 'The bleeding's more or less stopped but I can see one splinter that's still stuck in, so I'll need tweezers and certainly some disinfectant. Do you have any?'

Danni was still whimpering in pain. 'No. And I haven't bandages or anything. And, anyway, I'm scared. I don't want to stay here alone.'

'Of course not. Look, never mind the tea, Angus. Sean, if you could give us a lift round to our house, you can stay with us, Danni. We'd better call the police too, I suppose.'

'Not much point in that,' Sean said. 'The call will go through to Inverness or Glasgow or somewhere and if you tell them the fire's out they won't do anything.'

'Actually, I'm sure you're right. They never really leap to respond. You'll need to report it for your insurance, Danni, but we can do that tomorrow. Now, I'll just go and forage for night things and a toothbrush for you.'

Sean held out the brush to Angus and stood waiting for Hattie to return. Angus took it, then paused in the doorway to the bedroom.

'I'll phone the glazier first thing in the morning, Danni,' he told her. 'Don't you worry. He'll have the place weatherproof again in no time.'

'I'm not staying here ever again,' she said. 'That's it. It was a nasty creepy place before and I'm really scared now.'

'Bit paranoid, surely? Car fires happen,' Sean said. 'Ah, there you are, Hattie. What a busy little bee you are, getting us all organised.'

Hattie had come back carrying a bundle of clothes and a zip-bag and had a towel over her arm. She crouched back down again and held it out to pat Danni's feet delicately. 'Sorry – I do tend to be a bit bossy after all those years with the army. Can you carry her to the car, Sean? You're stronger than I am.'

'Sure,' he said, swung Danni up and carried her out. Hattie hesitated, but Angus said, 'Off you go. I'll take care of things here. And there'll be others coming to find out what's happened, I've no doubt.' And sure enough, there was another car drawing up on the road already.

'I'll go, then. Thanks, Angus. Danni doesn't need lots of people flocking round.'

Sean had deposited Danni in the back of the car with her feet up and Hattie climbed in beside him while they drove round the road to the Sinclairs' house in silence apart from an occasional small sob from Danni.

As Sean parked at the back of the house the door opened and Ranald stood there in his pyjamas and dressing gown, his hair rumpled.

'Hattie!' he exclaimed as she got out of the car. 'What on earth's been going on? I was asleep – there was a bang.' He peered into the back of the car. 'Is that Danni Maitland?'

'Car went on fire. Cut her feet on some broken glass,' she said briefly. 'Thanks for the lift, Sean. Ranald can carry her in now.'

'Of course,' Ranald said stiffly. 'Lucky you were around, eh Sean?'

Danni edged forward so that he could lift her out and he carried her through the mud room to the kitchen where the two labs trotted forward with tails waving, pleased to have entertainment at this time of night.

He rapped out an order and they retreated, tails between their legs.

'Put her in the chair by the Aga,' Hattie said. 'Danni, before I deal with your poor feet, I'm going to make you a cup of tea and put a slug of brandy in it – that'll make you feel better.'

Danni was still shivering but she managed a weak smile and a thank you. It was a lovely cosy kitchen and with Hattie taking care of everything she was able to fight down the panic that had been threatening to overwhelm her.

'Do you want tea, Ran?' Hattie asked.

'Not really,' he said. 'You must have got there pretty quickly?'

'I ran up the path. I was just watching a programme' – she gestured to the small TV that was still on – 'when I heard the bang and dashed out. The whole sky was lit up at the time – it was almost like a fireball. Terrifying!'

'You could say,' Danni put in with feeling.

'Right,' Ran said and yawned. 'I'll just get back to bed, I think. I'm sure you'll feel better in the morning. We can put in a report to the police to get a number for a claim.'

'Too right, we can.' Danni was reviving in the warmth. 'And they can effing well come out here and examine it properly. Don't see why my car should have suddenly gone on fire like that. And I don't see why Flora should have just fallen off a cliff like that either. I'm certainly not going to sit there saying nothing until something happens to me. I'm going to make them find out what really happened to her.'

Hattie and Ranald looked at each other for a moment. Then Hattie said awkwardly, 'Of course. Now, I'll just go and get the first-aid kit.'

There was a backlog of reports when DCI Kelso Strang went into his office on Monday morning. He'd only had a few days off but he usually cleared his desk before he left each night and it surprised him how much had piled up. It was late morning before he got round to checking phone messages and emails and he hadn't even thought about his promise to Angus Mackenzie.

It came back to him with some force when he read a text message asking him to call Hattie Sinclair urgently. He frowned, and rang at once.

'Hattie? I was going to phone to thank you anyway, but do I gather something's happened?'

'You could say that! Last night at around twelve there was this huge bang and then all these flames. I was still up and I ran out and it was Danni Maitland's car – it had gone on fire and exploded. I ran up there and she was all right – no damage except for cut feet from a broken window. Sean Reynolds arrived just minutes after me and gave us a lift back here. She's staying with us but all she wants now is to pack up and get out.

'The thing is, she's convinced herself that Flora Maitland's death wasn't an accident and that this has been an attempt to kill her too. When the police come to inspect the car, she's going to demand that they reopen that case, but the trouble is they've just said there's no need for them to do anything except record it and the insurance company will do their own investigation, but she's not satisfied with that. She's getting more and more frantic about it and she says she's not leaving until they've come and shown they're taking it seriously. I know this is taking advantage of our friendship, but is there anything you can do?'

'Good gracious,' Kelso said blankly. 'You do live life on the edge out there.'

Hattie groaned. 'Yes, I suppose so. But my personal problem is that with her in the house, Ran is trying to pressure her to commit to selling to him and went off in a sulk when she wouldn't. If the police would just come and have a look . . .'

'The trouble is, they're following standard procedure for a car fire where it's burnt itself out. It happens quite often. But you said it exploded?'

'Oh yes, this incredible bang! Sounded like a bomb going off. It was just lucky it was well away from the house.'

'Certainly was. They won't have detectives based locally – just someone whose remit is basically community policing, but your best bet is to keep up the pressure on him – it's the squeaky wheel that gets the grease. I'm very doubtful that there's anything I can do, but I promised Angus I'd have a look at the Maitland file when I got a moment, so I'll check that out at the same time. Keep me in touch with what's going on at your end.

'And thanks for being such a brilliant hostess. Once my aching muscles recover from the unreasonable demands made on them on the way up Suilven I'm sure all that fresh air will have done me good.'

But Strang was in a very thoughtful mood when he put the phone down. It was an odd little story, that. Cars regularly go on fire – electrical faults are the most common explanation, apart from a carelessly extinguished cigarette butt. Car manufacturers know that they do and build in an incredible level of protection around the fuel tank. Cars on fire almost never explode. Not without a lot of help. And knowledge of what to do.

Off the top of his head, he could think of two people who could have an interest in giving Danni Maitland the sort of scare that would change her mind about settling down in Flora Maitland's cottage and he acknowledged, with a sinking heart, that one of them at least would possess all the knowledge required.

Strang glanced at his watch. It was time for his break and he had a meeting scheduled in the afternoon, but he decided he'd cut lunch. A bit of starvation would do him good after all those lavish meals at Inverbeg.

Hattie Sinclair got up from the table and moved the pan of chicken soup to one side of the Aga hotplate. As Danni was going out, she'd told her they had lunch at half-past twelve but it was one o'clock now and there was still no sign of her.

Ranald had come in as usual, and she'd told him to go ahead while she waited for Danni. He shrugged, had soup and a toasted cheese sandwich, grumbled about some supply problem and then went out again.

At least Hattie wouldn't have to be on tenterhooks about what he'd say next. He'd certainly been very efficient and helpful this morning: he'd gone up to the house first thing, checked that Angus was going to arrange for a glazier and that there was cardboard in the window meantime, collected the insurance papers, called the company and then even made a follow-up call with the police when Danni insisted on it because, she said hysterically, they wouldn't listen to her – not that they'd listened to him either, as he'd told her they wouldn't.

He'd spent quite a bit of time on it, but Ran couldn't disguise the fact that he didn't like her and she clearly didn't like him either. Her offhand 'Thanks' when he'd put himself out so much for her riled him; Hattie could see the angry flush rising in his cheeks and with dismay heard him pretty much suggesting that in gratitude she ought to agree to sell the croft to him. While Hattie had given a sort of inane, covering-up laugh and fluttered that of course he was joking, Danni had said nothing, only giving Ran a long, cold, sideways look.

She'd gone out after that. She hadn't said where she was going and Hattie hadn't liked to ask. Danni could have been meeting one of her young men, or even both, but she had an uncomfortable feeling that she'd probably gone to see Sean to see how much he'd pay.

So there probably wasn't any point in waiting. Hattie made a toastie, warmed up the soup again and ladled some into a bowl, then sat back down with two attentive companions, one on each side.

When she'd talked to Kelso on Saturday night, she'd been thinking things could hardly be worse. How wrong she had been! She'd been worried then, but now she was actively scared.

She wasn't stupid. Both Sean and – oh god! – Ran had wanted to get Danni to leave and last night's events were going to achieve that. The car fire had actually been more dramatic than dangerous, but you couldn't be sure – a sudden gust of wind, say, and burning material could land on the roof and set timbers on fire. She didn't dare to think what she might have found last night if it had.

And now if Danni was being stubborn about not leaving before the police had come, and if even Kelso couldn't do anything about their stubborn refusal, what would happen now?

There was a gentle nudge on her left knee. There were pleading eyes fixed on her face and tails that had begun to twitch hopefully. The toastie was cooling on her plate and she discovered she wasn't hungry after all. For form's sake she scolded Juno for nagging, but then she divided the toastie between them. Ran would have a fit if he knew, but she didn't care.

This was pointless! After fifteen minutes of trying to trace who was dealing with the vehicle fire at Inverbeg, DCI Strang was no further on. There was no point in asking for a name he could discuss it with since the case had no existence except as a number, logged by a civilian assistant in Glasgow.

He gave up and moved on to see what he could access about Flora Maitland. There had at least been a full enquiry but here, too, it was difficult to get a clear picture: it was a good example of what was wrong with the unitary force that had reduced local CIDs to a bare minimum. There were apparently no suspicious features so it hadn't come the way of the SRCS and had been treated as a reportable death, like any other accident. There had been no one team specifically allotted to it and there were a number of different detectives involved, none of them based in the area, as far as he could tell. A report had been made to the Procurator Fiscal and the medical officer had been satisfied enough to sign the death certificate. So, NFA – no further action.

The autopsy report was straightforward. Flora Maitland had died from severe trauma to the head; her other injuries were consistent with a fall down a rock face from a height onto a stony shore. She had fallen face first and there was no evidence that suggested any third-party involvement. Strang noted that some fingernails were broken and had traces of earth underneath them, but she could have fallen and tried to get some purchase on the ground to stop herself going over.

The witness statements, too, supported the accident theory. A couple of them stated that Flora had said she wasn't feeling well; one of them also claimed that she'd quickly swallowed a shot of whisky just before she left in a rush. Others had testified to her presence that night and to her leaving, but with no further detail.

Then there was Angus Mackenzie's statement – statements, in fact, since after the death certificate had been issued he had returned twice to protest against the case being signed off. All echoed what Angus had said to Strang himself – with one small exception. His third statement mentioned 'threats' – unspecified. 'He was unable to say what these threats to Ms Maitland might have been' was the next sentence. Reading between the lines Strang guessed that the questioner had decided this was a story calculated to make the police pursue the investigation further and the final judgement had been that there was nothing left to pursue. That could well be true.

Yet he'd seen for himself Angus's reluctance to provide a motive for Flora's putative killer and he didn't believe this had been simply manipulative. It wasn't only Flora's general fitness and hard-headedness that had left Angus unconvinced; he knew something about her past that made a deliberate execution at least possible.

Certainly, if you wanted to commit murder without leaving any traces, a fall off a cliff was pretty much ideal. Get your unsuspecting victim over the edge with a sudden push, and there would be nothing that couldn't be explained by the fall itself.

If there was someone with an obvious motive – the heir, say – any investigation had only their movements to focus on, and even then it would be hard to prove non-accidental death. Danni Maitland hadn't arrived in Inverbeg until well after her aunt's death. Angus had mentioned a brother too, but he didn't seem to have been around either.

Strang couldn't see grounds for reopening the case, whatever ancient history Angus might be prepared to relate. He didn't think it was unlikely that Flora had just fallen – she'd mentioned feeling ill and a dizzy turn could be enough to have her staggering off the steep path. He'd liked

Angus and admired his determined loyalty, so he would be sorry to disappoint him – and Hattie too, over Danni's car. Not very impressive for an 'ever-so senior' policeman.

He had a fleeting moment of curiosity about what Flora Maitland's 'interesting past' might have comprised and he began a search. According to the Criminal Records Office, she had no previous convictions. No apparent presence on social media – unusual. Very unusual, in this day and age. He frowned – someone deliberately living under the wire? That might be suspicious in itself.

Then he glanced down at the file in front of him. It was headed, in the normal Scottish style, 'Flora Maitland or Reith,' with the maiden name first. That was what she had been using, but she'd been married previously, and when he keyed in 'Flora Reith' she sprang into immediate, vivid, virtual life.

She'd been a striking-looking woman, quite tall and rangy, and she'd taken a lot of trouble with her appearance. She'd changed her hair, in colour and style, on a regular basis: everything from a flaming auburn crop to black shoulder length with a Cleopatra fringe and eye make-up to match. As she got older, she had settled for a glossy hennaed bob – very chic.

There was no privacy restriction on the Facebook page and it was almost exclusively photos with a brief jokey comment. They had often been taken in a club or restaurant, along with some sun-lounger beach shots, and a bottle or a glass usually featured somewhere. As he flipped back through her postings, he found a few of her with a much younger Danni heavily made up to look as if she was

101

eighteen, rather than the fourteen or fifteen he reckoned she would have been, in venues that obviously hadn't a very strict age policy.

It certainly squared with what Angus Mackenzie had muttered about her past, but it didn't so much as hint how the life displayed here had been financed. Kelso had a certain curiosity about that, but he had a lot more immediate demands on his time. The detectives who had investigated Flora's death had decided to NFA it, and on the face of it he couldn't see what else they could have done. Sorry, Angus!

As one last gesture – a homage, really, to loyalty – he went back to the records to see if Flora Reith, her alter ego, did have previous. He had barely typed in the name when a notice flashed up. He stared at it blankly.

There was a DCI in the Met urgently requesting information on whereabouts and feeling fairly stunned, Strang picked up his phone.

Life on the edge in Inverbeg, indeed!

CHAPTER SEVEN

She'd struck lucky with her tasks this morning. Unusually, everyone she needed to talk to had been in when DC Murray called and she'd got back to Fettes Avenue early. She reached the CID room before anyone spotted her and, resisting the temptation to join in the general gossip that was as usual going on, she installed herself at the desk in her favourite corner by the window and behind a large filing cabinet, which obscured the view from the door if someone came in looking for a DC with time on their hands.

Murray fetched out the textbook she was working on for retaking the sergeant's exam and opened it with a sigh, but she didn't focus on it immediately, just sat looking out of the steamy window at the raindrops running down. It was getting close to crunch time: she had a serious decision to make. She'd told Pete, her almost-boyfriend, that she was going to start working for it again and he hadn't been impressed. He'd been complaining it was getting in the way of what he wanted to do, even before the exam when she hadn't actually been studying much at all, and now, though he hadn't spelt it out in so many words, he didn't need to.

She had to choose: the relationship or her career. A guy she liked who maybe would work out to be the right guy, or the ambition that had driven her for the last three years? She knew in her heart the decision wasn't that difficult. She'd had a good time with Pete, but if she was brutally honest she could see it was always all about him, not about her, or even about them. She needed to wave him goodbye and knuckle down to work.

And she could get started right now. With another sigh she started reading the open page that was thick with the yellow highlighting she had made last time. This time she had to remember, not just highlight, and it did seem to be making a bit more sense as she applied herself. She could be making progress at last.

When the door opened, she cowered back in her seat. There were three other detectives in the room to choose from but with dismay and annoyance she heard DI Rachel French saying brusquely, 'I was wanting DC Murray. Does anyone know where she might be?'

Oh, she bloody would turn up just now! Grinding her teeth, Murray closed the book and stepped forward. 'Yes, ma'am. I'm here.'

French was looking a little flustered. 'Oh good. I didn't realise there was a desk in that corner. Livvy, I've got a list of information I need to have tracked down as a matter of urgency. Are you able to get on to it right now?'

'Yes, ma'am,' she said stiffly, coming to take the list French was holding.

'Thanks, Livvy. Type it up and run it off, please. Quick as you can.' She went out.

The list had been scribbled on a sheet of paper and Murray recognised the DCI's untidy scrawl. She bit her lip. Surely if Strang wanted her to do something, he could have summoned her direct? He'd always done that before. In SRCS business, he'd relied on her, treated her like his first assistant, not just a dogsbody. It had meant a lot to her that latterly he would take her into his confidence and even wanted to know her opinion, sometimes. She'd worked hard for that trust, felt she'd earned it.

Had French edged her out? When she'd spoken to her on Saturday morning Murray had realised that the two of them had been discussing her. Now, if a big case came up, would he call on French, not her?

Of course he wouldn't. You wouldn't need to send out a DCI and a DI on the same case, and she was sure Strang liked being hands-on himself. She was just being paranoid. And anyway, she should get on with working through the list. She'd better not make things worse by failing to get the job done by the time French came back.

Strang had asked for details of Flora Maitland or Reith's will. No problem there: niece, Danielle Maitland was the sole heir, apart from a couple of minor bequests. The solicitor's firm was in Lochinver. He'd wanted Flora's brother's address too and with Danielle's cited address being in Glasgow she took a punt on that being her parents' home so checking out William Maitland was quicker than it might have been.

After that it got more labour-intensive. Transco, an import–export company: check on all board members and employees on the list, and it was quite a large company. They were pretty much clean, apart from a few minor offences, which she duly noted. Directors seemed to major in speeding fines and the odd drink-driving ban.

She was just printing off the information, as requested, when DI French came back. She looked as if she was still on edge.

'How are you getting on with that, Livvy?'

'Just finishing up, ma'am.'

'Excellent. I'll wait. DCI Strang's in a hurry for it.'

'Oh, you're obviously busy. Don't worry – I can take it round to him myself.'

French shook her head. 'I'll have to discuss it with him, anyway.' As Murray reluctantly handed over the report, she added, 'Good work, Livvy. The boss was right when he said you were efficient.'

Patronising cow! Murray gave her a smile that did not quite reach her eyes, then went back to her desk – no longer a safe haven, now French knew about it. It had been her own little secret for years but that would be the inspector's first port of call if she suspected Murray was skiving. She was muttering sweary words under her breath as she propped her head on her hands and tried to concentrate on her studying.

DCI Strang had arranged for DI French to fill in at his afternoon meeting and told her what had happened and what he was planning to do. 'I'm going to ask JB if you can cover for SRCS if there's an emergency. I'll only be away for a couple of days. All right?'

He'd have thought she would jump at the challenge, but she looked distinctly taken aback even as she agreed. He didn't have time to consider that now, though, as he hurried to see if Detective Chief Superintendent Borthwick was in her office. If not, he'd have to leave a message, but he'd have liked her blessing before taking off and it would make everything simpler if he could talk it through with her.

She wasn't. But as he was in her office scribbling a message, she came in behind him and stopped, surprised.

'Good gracious, Kelso! I didn't even know you were back from your Highland break. How was it?' She sat down at her desk and waved him to a seat.

'Ah well,' he said, 'thereby hangs a tale! In fact, I was just going to let you know I think I ought to go back there.'

Borthwick's eyebrows, always a feature, rose. 'Good as that, was it? Well, you've certainly got plenty of leave stacked up.' She had spoken lightly but he knew from the wary look in her eye that she understood there was more to it than that – though if she was trying to guess what it might be she wouldn't be even close.

He gave her the background to Flora Maitland's death and explained how it came about that he had taken an interest. 'As far as I could see there was nothing suspicious about the circumstances and nothing wrong with the investigation – they'd done everything by the book and on the evidence available I'd have closed the case myself. Just from idle curiosity I checked out the Internet – no joy with Maitland, which struck me as odd, so I tried under her married name, Flora Reith. No problem there – lots of Facebook stuff. And then, from force of habit, I suppose, I checked for previous – just a slap on the wrist and a fine after being caught by Customs with her car boot full of cases of French wine when she was twenty – but the thing was, the Met had posted that they were looking for her urgently.'

'The Met? Go on, surprise me.'

'They're after a big import–export firm. Plenty of legitimate business but the Met has been convinced for years that this was somehow covering up for the way they were dabbling in the grey market, where goods without the maker's badge are distributed – a grey area, you could say, and inspections over the years haven't managed to turn up evidence of actual wrongdoing.

'It was one thing when it was cigarettes and white goods – there are so many firms at it that quite honestly it isn't worth the cost of a major investigation. But now, according to DCI Jason Dryden, they have strong reason to believe that they have moved on to weapons and illegal migrants.

'Flora seems to have been using her married name, Reith, at that time – no sign of a Mr Reith, though. She was their most senior manager, pretty much running the show for the last forty years, and if anyone knew where the bodies were buried it was her.

'She retired not long before they decided to action a major investigation. So far, it's been a waste of the taxpayer's money but Dryden got his teeth into it and he won't let go – he sounds the terrier-type – and they've been looking for Flora ever since. She'd just disappeared completely, and he was gutted when I told him she was dead – he reacted with some very choice words. His reaction was that they must have got to her first.'

'I see,' Borthwick said. 'So her old friend perhaps wasn't wrong after all?'

Strang grimaced. 'Hard to say. But he may have useful information, and if I talked to him informally I might persuade him to tell me. And I'm getting the address of her lawyer, too; there may be papers he's still holding.

'There's nothing on my desk that I couldn't defer for a couple of days. I could leave now, reach Lochinver tonight, do the interviews in the morning and then drive back via Glasgow to talk to Flora's brother. I don't see that we can justify reopening the case without considerably more to go on – and frankly I don't have high hopes of coming up with anything useful there, but at least if there's pressure from the Met we could tell them we've tried. If I'm lucky, I can do that and be back here tomorrow night. I've asked DI French to pick up if there's a call for SRCS, if that's all right.'

There was a knock on the door. 'Oh, that will be my next appointment,' Borthwick said. 'Come! Yes, carry on, Kelso. Will you get a bed with your friends again?'

He had stood up. 'Er . . . no, I don't think so. There are . . . ramifications. Take too long to go into them – tell you about it some other time. Hello, Steve,' he said to the sergeant who had come in, 'I'm just going.'

'Good hunting,' JB called after him as he went out.

He was glad he didn't have to embark on the story about the car that had mysteriously gone on fire and his professional reluctance to be associated with someone who, if the insurance company inspection raised uncomfortable questions, might be high on their list of suspects.

Insurance companies had much more of a vested interest in apportioning blame than the police force did in these circumstances, and he had a nasty feeling that there might be difficult times ahead for someone.

Hattie filled the crate she had set ready on the kitchen table with ready-meals and carted it out to stash in the boot of the Land Rover. She had an order to fill for the freezer in the Novaks' store but she'd only one delivery to make to the pods today.

The daylight hours were getting fewer now and it was turning much colder. Today the rain was lashing down and there was a wind coming in from the sea that had an edge as cutting as a knife blade. The eco-conscious senior citizens preferred their week saving the planet to be earlier in the year and the youngsters, who were doing it either from idealistic conviction or cynical calculation that it would look good on the CV and were battling on, weren't her best customers.

There was only one elderly couple left now, undaunted by the weather. She liked them; they were perennially cheerful and very appreciative of her cooking, ordering their supper from one day to the next so she could bring it ready for them to eat.

She carried it in – chicken pot pie and a chocolate mousse – while they all agreed about the depressing nature of the forecast and the pair squabbled about their next order, exchanging amiable insults that made her laugh as she left them.

Hattie hadn't laughed much today. She hadn't seen Danni Maitland or heard from her since she'd walked out after breakfast, and she had no idea whether or not she'd be back for supper. It didn't matter much if she didn't appear – she could always use up leftovers – except that Ranald would be infuriated by the lack of courtesy. Everything was feeling so – what was the word? Fragile, that was it. Like a glass bauble that might shatter at any moment.

As she drove away from the pods she'd be passing the driveway to Auchinglass House. She could call in and find out if Danni was there, as she suspected she would be. If at least she knew what the girl's plans were, even if they didn't involve her coming back to the Sinclairs till late at night, she could concoct a story that would fob Ran off. She'd have to listen to him moaning in general but at least there wouldn't be an excuse for a tirade.

When Hattie drew up outside the house, Sean's Discovery wasn't in the car parking area by the stables, just the big BMW. Sean must be out, then. Hattie wasn't sorry; she didn't like him and the situation with Danni made things very awkward now.

It was Maia who answered the door, looking a little surprised; they weren't in the habit of popping in on one another. But she was very welcoming, saying, 'Hattie! For goodness' sake, come in quickly. You're getting soaked!'

The warmth of the hall embraced her as she stepped inside. The panelling here was painted in several subtle shades of cream that made it feel a tranquil haven after the storm raging outside. Hattie was very conscious of her hair in wild disorder and her baggy old jeans and scruffy fleece now she was faced with a smiling hostess whose silky hair was immaculate and whose pale opal sweater was undoubtedly cashmere.

'Have you time for a drink?' Maia said. 'I'm just looking for an excuse myself. Sean's not in yet.'

'That's very kind, but I won't take you up on it. I've got some meals to deliver at the inn for the store and Ran will be expecting me back so he can get tanking into the Scotch – you know what he's like!' She laughed a little awkwardly as Maia smiled politely. 'Actually, I just came to ask whether you'd seen Danni Maitland. She's staying with us at the moment because of the fire, but I haven't seen her all day.'

Maia frowned. 'Fire?' she said. 'Has there been a fire?'

'Oh, didn't Sean tell you? Danni's car exploded outside the Maitland house last night.'

'Exploded? When?'

'Around midnight. You didn't hear it?'

'No. I must have been sound asleep.'

'I hadn't gone to bed, so I dashed up there at once and Sean arrived minutes later. The house was OK apart from broken glass, but Danni had cut her feet and was a bit upset so he gave us a lift back home. I'm surprised he didn't tell you about his good deed.'

'I've hardly seen him today,' Maia said slowly. 'He finished breakfast as I came down and he was preoccupied with some problem up at the harbour – with the weather, the boats bringing in the latest shipment of trees from Scandinavia have been delayed and he went straight out. Danni certainly hasn't been here. I don't really know her except from seeing her in the pub. How is the poor girl, anyway?'

'All right, I suppose. Upset, obviously, and I think she'll be going back to Glasgow soon.'

Maia nodded. 'Not really the type for rural life, I'd guess.'

'Have to agree. Anyway, thanks for your help. I'd better get on.'

Maia held open the door for her, shuddering at the blast of cold air that came in. 'That's winter on its way now, isn't it? Do come back for that drink when you've a bit more time.'

Hattie thanked her and dived back into the shelter of her car. Maia was always very nice whenever she saw her, but she never knew quite what to make of her. No matter how many times they met, she never felt she got to know her any better.

She glanced at her watch as she drove back down the drive under the muttering, groaning trees. Six o'clock – the pub would be open now and it was where Danni had always spent her evenings, so this was her best hope of finding her. Usually, she'd just take the food round to the back door to give to Zofia to put in the shop freezer, but tonight she went into the bar and looked around eagerly.

But Danni wasn't there. It was very quiet; a bit early for the younger group, who, if they'd been working outside in this, would probably be warming up with hot showers. She nodded hello to a couple of the locals and set the crate on the bar.

Kasper came over. 'You're early tonight. What can I get you, Hattie?'

'Nothing thanks, Kasper. Just, could you pass these back to Zofia, please? I wanted to ask you if you'd seen Danni Maitland at all today?'

'Danni? No. Is she all right? I heard she had a bad fright last night.'

'Yes, really scary. But she's OK – I just wondered if she'd be back for supper with us tonight.'

Kasper picked up the crate and swung it down from the counter. 'I'll hurry her along if she comes in, shall I?'

'Oh, not to worry. We'll see her when we see her.'

Hattie went out, her brow furrowed. Where could the girl be? Well, she wasn't her mother – and for all she knew, Danni could be at home waiting for her.

She wasn't, though. Ranald wasn't there either, but she'd just gone through to the sitting room when he appeared, making a beeline for the drinks cupboard and filling a glass with Scotch.

'When are we expecting the cuckoo in the nest to return, then?'

'Not sure. I'm not really reckoning on her being here for supper.'

'Oh right,' Ranald said without much interest. 'If you want ice in your gin, you'll have to get some. Here's the ice bucket.'

Once he'd have had it filled ready for her – or if he hadn't, she'd have complained. She didn't do that now. As she took it from him, she said, 'I was just talking to Maia—'

Ranald froze, glaring at her. 'What were you talking to Maia for? Where did you see her?'

Surprised, Hattie said, 'I just called in at Auchinglass House to see whether Danni had been there talking to Sean, that's all. I thought you might like to know.'

'Well – I suppose so. And had she?'

'No. Maia asked me in for a drink but I had meals to deliver to the pub. She was very nice.'

'She always is.'

His tone had softened and Hattie looked at him sharply. Had she been missing something? With a hollow feeling in the pit of her stomach, she said, before he could notice her reaction, 'The funny thing was, she didn't even know about the fire. You'd have thought Sean would have told her, wouldn't you?'

'I don't think he pays much attention to her. You couldn't expect a yobbo like that to appreciate someone like her.' Then, as if he realised he was saying too much, he went on gruffly, 'Anyway, do you want that gin? I'm not going to stand here holding the bottle all night.'

Feeling sick, Hattie got herself out of the room and with her eyes full of tears blundered down the corridor. This explained a lot. And how could she be surprised, when she'd thought herself how scruffy and dowdy she'd felt by comparison with elegant Maia in her tasteful home? But Maia had always been so friendly – could she be two-faced enough to be carrying on an affair with Hattie's husband at the same time?

She was certainly as cool as the ice cubes Hattie was turning out into the bucket. But would Ranald, her simple soldier, appeal to someone like Maia? That was the big question.

The weather worsened the farther west DCI Strang drove. After Inverness, the windscreen wipers on full had struggled to cope with the relentless sheets of rain, and gusts of wind had left him wrestling with the wheel to keep the car on the road. He'd reckoned on six hours or so when he left Edinburgh just before three o'clock, but it was half-past nine now and he wasn't there yet.

Angie Andrews, the Force Civilian Assistant who ran his arrangements with impeccable efficiency, had already warned the guest house she had found for him that he would be late, made an appointment with Flora Maitland's lawyer the following morning and arranged with William Maitland in Glasgow that he would be available later in the day.

He'd phoned Angus Mackenzie himself when he'd stopped for petrol and a sandwich. He hadn't gone into detail, beyond saying he wanted to ask him more about Flora, but there had been a break in Angus's voice when he said, 'That's – that's wonderful.'

'Don't read too much into this,' Strang said hastily. 'I'm going to be staying in Lochinver. And can I ask you, please, not to mention that to the Sinclairs?'

Angus agreed to an 8.30 meeting, which would give Strang time to interview him before his 9.30 with the solicitor, and he drove on satisfied, thinking about the case.

Livvy Murray's research hadn't thrown up any new lines of enquiry, really. Flora's conviction for smuggling was interesting but she'd managed to keep her nose clean after that – or at least she'd seen to it that none of her later activities had come to the attention of the authorities.

He'd given Rachel French a very sketchy briefing on the situation when he'd asked her to get Murray on to the research, and he'd discussed what Murray had dug up before he left. She'd obviously still been feeling nervous about babysitting SRCS and he'd reassured her that he could return if necessary. It had surprised him; she had such an assured air that he'd assumed she'd take it in her stride.

He'd enjoyed their mentoring sessions. She was interesting and she was good to look at too, with that attractively open face and the wide-set grey eyes; though she seemed quite serious her face lit up when she was amused. She was a bit of a perfectionist, he'd noticed. Her organisation was impressive but even so she overworried about getting things right. It occurred to him to wonder if she'd had a very critical parent – he knew all about that – and whether that might explain it.

Livvy Murray had clearly been winding her up. He could have a word with her, of course, but he rather thought that might make things worse, not better. They each had their hang-ups – well, who didn't? – but they had their strengths too and they could just get on with the job and work through their issues in their own time.

He saw the Lochinver sign with a sigh of relief. The guest house was right on the seafront, easy to find, and it was promising that the sign outside was still illuminated, though swinging wildly in the blasts of wind. His hostess opened the door for him before he reached it and had coffee and sandwiches waiting.

It had been a gruelling journey but at least his time plan was still in place. And with the changeable weather around here, the storm could have blown itself out by morning.

It had become a habit with Hattie to sit up late in the kitchen, half-watching wallpaper TV and enjoying the peace and the quiet company of the dogs, sleeping in their baskets after an energetic day.

Recently, though, the peace had been elusive and tonight she had no defence against her tormenting thoughts. She didn't even notice when Juno started the excited yipping and twitching in her sleep that usually made Hattie laugh and wake her in case she was having a bad dream.

She had cried for a bit for what she'd lost. But not for very long; the milk was spilt now and you just had to get on with mopping it up. And the more she thought about it, the more likely it seemed that Ran's relationship with Maia was a crush rather than an affair. Hattie might not like Sean herself, but he was certainly attractive in a very alpha male way, with a sort of energy and enthusiasm that could be almost magnetic when it suited him to switch it on. She'd even experienced its power herself sometimes when they'd socialised, before the whole property thing came up.

He had the money, too, to give Maia the right sort of life for someone with her style: lovely clothes, child at private school, beautiful house with expensive decor, domestic help. She'd want to risk all that – for Ran? Maia wouldn't strike anyone as a 'world-well-lost-for-love' type.

So that was what Hattie decided to believe. She wouldn't provoke any storms, would play a waiting game and hope that it would pass eventually, like the storm that was rattling the windowpanes right now.

Danni was the other worry. She hadn't returned, hadn't phoned, and Hattie didn't have her number to call. Where could she be, on a night like this? She had no idea what other friends Danni might have, but there was that boy she'd been quarrelling with in the pub – had they maybe made up and she was with him?

There was nothing Hattie could do, anyway. At last the programme finished, she switched off the TV, got up and let the dogs out. They didn't linger – just shot out and came straight back. She peered out into the swirling rain and darkness; unless Danni was going to get a lift from someone, she wouldn't be coming back tonight. But she put the outside light on and didn't lock the door, then left the light on in the kitchen as well.

Ranald must have come up to bed quietly. Now he was asleep, lying on his back and snoring and she nudged him to turn over. She didn't fall asleep immediately herself, trying to listen for a noise that would tell her Danni had returned, but it was hard to tell; the old house was creaking and muttering and the storm was so noisy, rising to the sort of howling peak that should mean it would have blown itself out by the morning.

At last Hattie drifted off. But the storm raged on.

CHAPTER EIGHT

The storm hadn't blown itself out. When Kelso Strang went down to breakfast next morning the wind was still howling and the roaring sea was high with breakers that built up then came crashing onto the shore. The road in front of the guest house had a covering of blown sand and was strewn with stones and great olive-brown roots of seaweed, thick as a man's arm.

There was only one table set for breakfast and as he sat down, Mrs Munro hurried in. She seemed to feel a personal responsibility for the weather. 'Oh, I'm awful sorry about this! It's no sort of welcome for a visitor. I hope it won't give you a scunner to the place.'

Kelso laughed. 'No, no. I've been up this way often enough. Went up Suilven last week, in fact – though I have to admit the weather wasn't great then, either.'

He realised he had made a mistake and piqued her interest. 'Oh really?'

'Yes,' he said, going on quickly, 'I was about to ask you – would it be all right to use the sitting room after this? I've got someone coming to see me at half-past eight.'

'Oh, of course. I'd better get my skates on, then. I could do you smoked haddock with a poached egg if you could fancy that – by the looks of things it'll be the last fish we'll be getting for a while.' She bustled off.

Angus Mackenzie was prompt. Strang saw his car pull up outside just as he finished his toast with Mrs Munro's home-made marmalade, but he punctiliously waited until exactly eight-thirty before ringing the doorbell, by which time Strang had moved through to the sitting room where his hostess had already laid out a tray with coffee and biscuits.

He heard her greet Angus warmly as he came in. He hadn't bargained for that; round here everyone knew everyone else, so it wouldn't be long before it got out who he was and what he might be doing – not that it mattered, particularly, since he'd be back in Edinburgh tonight.

Angus shook his hand with meaningful warmth and, 'Thank you again', was the first thing he said.

As Strang handed him a mug of coffee, he said firmly, 'Let's get this straight. It isn't an official visit, just a chat. As of now, I see no prospect of reopening the case. Yours were the only witness accounts that cast doubt on the accident theory, and they were no more than a statement of what you believed – not evidence. The investigation was done by the book and there was nothing there to justify pursuing it further.'

'I can see that,' Angus said, 'But—'

Strang held up his hand. 'Wait a minute. When we talked on Saturday night, and I asked the obvious question – why on earth would someone want to murder your friend? – you didn't give me a straight answer. I think you said you thought she'd had an "interesting life" but you didn't know. That wasn't true, was it?'

Not a man accustomed to lying, Strang had thought then, and now a red flush came into Angus's cheeks. 'No. I'm sorry – I'm ashamed of that. I just couldn't . . .' His voice trailed off.

'Would I be right in saying that you knew something – or some things, even – about Flora that you considered were shameful, and that you baulked at exposing her to others' scorn?'

His head was bowed. 'Yes,' he muttered. 'Yes, just that.'

'There didn't seem much point in pressing you that night, but circumstances have changed.'

Angus looked up. 'Something's happened?'

'I'm not at liberty to go into that. But I need you to tell me now whatever you know about Flora. Her married name, Reith – is her husband still around?'

He laughed bitterly. 'No. Driving a high-speed smuggling boat, trying to get away from the coastguards, thirty years ago. Flipped it over. Body never recovered. He got what he deserved.' There was vicious satisfaction in his voice.

Forget the husband; follow up on that reaction. Strang changed tack. 'How did you get to know Flora?'

'Oh, the girl next door. I still work the croft where I grew up. She was a tomboy, funny, cheeky, rebellious, brave. I was six years younger. I trailed around after her when she'd let me, which wasn't always. Sometimes she'd dare me to do some daft thing she'd done herself and I did. When I broke my collarbone falling off the roof of the hayshed I

122

was forbidden to see her. I didn't pay any attention – that just made it more exciting.

'But of course she grew up and lost interest in that sort of thing. She was never exactly a raving beauty but she had what used to be called "It" and now she'd discovered boys she'd no use at all for some gawky kid who still wanted to do the sort of things that would ruin her nail varnish.

'She started looking ten years older than me, not six. And the local boys she'd been fooling around with were dumped when that sleekit bastard Piers Reith took an interest.'

'He was . . . ?'

'His father owned Auchinglass House at that time. Didn't live there much, but that last summer Piers was there all the time and they were an item. She didn't want to know me any more. I tried telling her what they said about him – he wasn't to be trusted, he was doing some bad things. That went down about as well as you would expect.'

Angus gave a sigh. 'She went off to London with him. He was nineteen, she was eighteen. I heard later they were married, and I heard too she'd got arrested for smuggling – her mother was black burning ashamed about that. Then I heard about him drowning while he was being chased by the law – it was in the papers.'

Strang digested that. 'So – you never saw her after that?'

'I moved on myself. Got married, but somehow it didn't really work – I suppose she could never match up to Flora. I worked in the Department of Ag and Fish in Edinburgh with a tenant here after my father died, but when I got an early pension I came back, about five years ago. And when Flora retired here . . .'

He paused, looking down at his hands. 'I . . . I suppose it was the happiest day of my life. Not that she was any more interested in me as a partner than she had been all those years ago, but at last she was the girl next door again and we'd sit late over a bottle talking for hours.'

He stopped. Strang let the silence develop, but that trick didn't work this time. At last he said, 'We've reached the problem now, haven't we?'

'Yes. But I suppose – what harm can it do? Flora's gone and I don't care if her family's upset – her brother believed she was trash and the niece she thought the world of didn't even try to find out what really happened. And if it means she gets justice—'

'Wait,' Strang said. 'I won't mislead you. Whatever you tell me, they won't reopen it. The Crown Office would assess the likelihood of a conviction and I can't see a chance here – even if a suspect's been seen standing on the cliff beside a victim, actual proof is problematic. But if they'd reason to think her death was in someone's interest, they might investigate that.'

'I see. Well, thanks for being honest. I don't know what Flora would want. I do know she was permanently afraid – she hid herself away here, didn't go about much, just to the pub and the shops. And I know there were things she had done that she deeply regretted.'

'Did she say what they were?' Strang tried not to sound too interested.

'She talked about getting involved in smuggling right from the start – through Piers, of course. He was the love of her life – and it hurts even now that he still was, all these

124

years later. It never bothered her being on the wrong side of the law – she said once that bringing in ciggies and booze was the same as running in brandy when Robert Burns was an exciseman.

'There was other stuff too, she said, but by then the money had got her – it always does, I suppose. She was working for a big firm and they paid her well. She liked the expensive things in life and she didn't let her conscience trouble her too much – it was only the taxman you were cheating.'

'The "other stuff"?' Strang prompted.

Angus shook his head. 'Didn't say. But then they started doing things that did bother her. Again, she never exactly told me in so many words, but it would be my guess that the smuggling might have moved on to include people too. And there was one particular event – something went wrong, someone got into trouble. I don't know what it was, but she said to me more than once, "That's what keeps me awake at night, more than anything else."

'It was after that she decided she had to get out. Somehow she managed it, but I know she was always afraid her old sins would catch up with her.' Angus's head dropped again. 'And they did,' he said gruffly.

'Thank you,' Strang said. 'I know that wasn't easy for you. Can I ask you to search your mind for any detail you haven't told me – anything specific?'

He thought for a long time, then shook his head. 'We talked a lot about how she felt, but not much about what she did.' Then he straightened his shoulders and met Strang's eyes squarely. 'I don't care what she did. I always loved her,

125

and I still do.' For a man of his age and background, it was a dramatically emotional statement.

'I can see that,' Strang said gently.

After Angus Mackenzie had gone, Strang reflected that open as he had been, difficult as it had obviously been for him, his information had proved disappointing. It just confirmed what he knew already and had been an interesting insight into Flora's character and frame of mind, but there wasn't anything concrete to feed to the Met.

Unless the lawyer was hoarding a treasure trove of incriminating evidence, he'd had a wasted journey up here, and Flora's family in Glasgow sounded unlikely to have been her confidants. Still, at least he'd be able to get back to Edinburgh tonight.

Ishbel Duncan put two mugs of coffee and a plate of biscuits on a tray and carried it through to the sitting room at Auchinglass House where she knew Shirley Reagan would be waiting in eager anticipation.

One of the mugs was for her. She and Shirley got on fine and it was a pleasant habit that when she'd cleared the breakfast things and tidied up the kitchen, she'd go in to give her all the craic. The poor woman never got anything out of her family and she did love to know what was going on in the parish now she couldn't get about very easily – and Ishbel did love being the one with a story to tell. It was annoying that she hadn't actually heard about the car fire before she came in yesterday and by now it wouldn't be news to Shirley, but she'd probably know more than the locals did, what with Sean arriving right on the spot when it happened.

'Here we are, Shirley!' she said. 'Chocolate digestives today – they're your favourites, aren't they?'

With the plate on the table by her elbow, Shirley said hopefully, 'Well, what's the news today?'

Ishbel settled in the chair opposite. 'Oh, they're all talking about the fire, of course.'

'Fire?' Shirley looked an inquiry.

'Gracious me! Did you not hear about it? The explosion on Sunday night? Around midnight?'

'On Sunday? Oh, now you mention it, I think I did hear a bang. I was just going to sleep – yes, that's right. I sat up, but I didn't hear anything else and to tell you the truth I thought I might have dreamed it. What was it?'

'You know that girl Maitland – her that inherited the croft from Flora?'

'Danni? Well, I don't know her but I've heard all about her.'

'Aye, you would. She's that sort of lassie. She'd this wee car – yellow, bit of a daft colour – and it suddenly went on fire and exploded with this great big bang. But I'm surprised you don't know about it because your Sean was nearly the first to get there and rescue her. She'd been hurt, seemingly, and he drove her down to the fish farm to stay with the Sinclairs. Did he not say anything about it?'

'No, he didn't,' Shirley said. 'Was she badly hurt?'

She could reassure her about that, and add consolingly that Sean was maybe embarrassed about being a hero, but she didn't seem to want to discuss it much. So, disappointingly, there wasn't anything new Ishbel would be able to add to what everyone knew already. Shirley seemed more interested in the row that two of the committee had been having over the community hall coffee morning and when Ishbel finished her coffee and got up, she was feeling that this had been one of their less satisfactory chats. A shame, when she'd thought she had such good material to chat over today. They hadn't even got on to the finer points of how the fire might have happened and how anyone's car could just blow up at any moment.

Just as she reached the door, Shirley suddenly said, 'Ishbel, have you heard any talk around the place about Sean's rewilding project?'

Ishbel stopped, struck with embarrassment. Of course there was talk; everyone was saying that Sean had a wolf running free out in the wilds of the estate and there were several farmers claiming they'd had sheep mauled – one said he'd even scared a wolf away and had to put down his poor beast – and they were all furious about it. She couldn't exactly say that to his mother.

'Well,' she said, playing for time, 'most people think more trees would help with the climate and of course it's brought jobs – that's a big thing around here.'

She was dreading the next question. Shirley looked as if she was getting ready to ask it, but then she didn't, just said, 'Oh, that's good. Thanks, Ishbel.'

Ishbel whisked herself out of the door before Shirley could change her mind.

She'd bottled it. Oh, Shirley could read between the lines as well as anyone, and she was particularly shrewd when it came to knowing what her son was thinking. She'd marked the slight shiftiness when he'd talked that time about no one even knowing if a wolf was out there, and she could see Ishbel was stalling just now. But she still couldn't bring herself to ask if there were any rumours that would confirm her fear.

The car fire – that was something new to worry about. She'd seen Sean at breakfast yesterday and he'd been preoccupied, definitely, and eaten quickly, gulping his coffee and finishing just as Maia had come downstairs. He'd said he was in a hurry; they were expecting a shipload of tree slips that had been delayed by the storm and he'd have to postpone the planned operation to bring them down for planting and find something else to keep the volunteers busy. He was certainly fretting about it being well into autumn when there could be a frost and it was important to get them bedded in before that happened.

It was true that while he often talked his problems through with his mother, it never occurred to him that she might like to be kept up to date with local gossip. He wasn't remotely interested, himself; he was so exclusively focused on his mission. The worry about the planting being delayed might have meant that the car fire slipped his mind.

It was odd, though. Certainly, cars did go on fire; you saw them every so often by the side of the motorway. But did they go on fire when they were just outside your house, sitting quietly, minding their own business? Maybe they did – she didn't know. It would be nice to think so.

But Shirley was ever a realist. Sean had been talking to her just the other day about ways of trying to get Danni Maitland to move on. Was it possible that he had decided to scare her out? She was of course sure he wouldn't deliberately harm anyone, and she would like to believe he wouldn't do this either, but the cold feeling in her gut was evidence that she was thinking it just might be possible.

Of course, Sean wasn't the only person with an interest in winkling Danni out. Ranald Sinclair was fighting Sean every inch of the way to persuade the girl to sell the croft to him. It would probably come down to money in the end – most things did – in which case Sean was in a good position, unless Ranald had a lot more stashed away than she reckoned he did.

Shirley knew the Sinclairs quite well. They'd often come round for a drink or a meal, especially at the time when Sean thought he was going to be able to persuade Ranald to sell up. It was like that famous review of A Star is Born – 'Loved him, hated her' – only it was the other way about. Hattie was the kind of person you couldn't help liking – a bit scatty, carrying an extra pound or two but good fun and kind-hearted. She'd always made a point of coming to talk to Shirley when there was a crowd in and most of them had better things to do that sit down beside an old lady and risk getting trapped. Ranald, on the other hand . . .

He was good-looking enough, the clean-cut type with a soldier's bearing, and he looked as if he took pride in never gaining weight. Shirley distrusted that in a man; vain, that said to her, and it was a bit too obvious that the jokes he made about his wife had a nasty edge, even if she always seemed ready to think they were funny. He'd never had a one-to-one conversation with Shirley herself and of course she knew why – she was old, so she was boring.

It was one of the few, very few, benefits of being old that people like him paid no attention to you, unaware they were constantly giving themselves away. Ranald Sinclair wasn't a nice man. She could easily picture him ruthlessly deciding that Danni had to be moved on.

She had no idea what would happen now. Would the police be calling round to question everyone? Or would it just be a question of claiming insurance? Maybe Maia would know. And had Sean told her what had happened on Sunday night? She certainly hadn't said anything about it at breakfast after Sean had left but then Maia's preferred state was silence. Shirley often wondered what went on inside that perfectly-groomed little head.

Donald Mackay was intrigued by what he had been told about his first appointment this morning. He had three more booked in the course of the day – a will, a power of attorney and a property agreement, all standard stuff. A visit from a detective chief inspector all the way from Edinburgh, relating to the death of his late client Flora Maitland, was very much out of the ordinary.

DCI Kelso Strang looked the part, somehow – quite tall, quite nice-looking, but with a very noticeable scar on the right side of his face that somehow suggested a man with more important things to worry about than his appearance. He had a good smile, that went to his eyes even when he was only giving a polite greeting. Mackay prided himself on being a good judge of character – a useful skill for a lawyer – and that was something he always made a point of noticing.

'I need to make it clear for a start that this isn't in any sense a formal interview,' Strang began as he came into the office. 'Just a chat.'

'Right,' Mackay said. 'Then why don't you take a comfortable seat by the table over there and I'll get some coffee.'

'Thanks, but not for me. I drink too much as it is.'

'That goes for me too. So – what can I do for you?'

'I think my assistant told you I was trying to find out a bit more concerning Flora Maitland or Reith, who was, I'm told, a client of yours?'

'Yes. Both of them were, really.'

'Both?' Strang said.

'Let me explain. When I first met her, she was Flora Reith – a very poised, sophisticated woman living in London. She was her father's only heir and I have to say her older brother was far from pleased about that.'

'Was there some reason behind it?'

Mackay laughed. 'This is an informal chat, right, and I won't be quoted? He was quite a wise old bird, Willie Maitland, with a trenchant turn of phrase. He summed up his son as "a great, fat, greedy sumph" and from everything I've seen of the man, he wasn't far wrong. His daughter was the black sheep – I think she'd one or two brushes with the law, but that didn't seem to bother him.'

'It's the brushes with the law I'm interested in. Do you know anything about them?'

''Fraid not. I heard there was a bit of gossip after her accident, but I don't know the details. You'd have to ask some of the older locals up at Inverbeg – they could probably tell you.'

132

From Strang's lack of reaction Mackay guessed that he'd spoken to them already. He nodded, then said, 'And your second client, Flora Maitland?'

'When she made the appointment, I didn't realise this was the Flora Reith I'd dealt with over Willie's estate. I suppose that had been about five years before and I made an embarrassing gaffe by completely failing to recognise her. She'd let her hair go grey and she didn't look as if she'd seen a hairdresser in months. She was wearing a scruffy old padded jacket and very battered hiking boots instead of the smart city suit. Fortunately, she laughed – she'd a good sense of humour, like Willie himself. She said she was just a shepherdess now and she was a lot happier.'

'So you've been dealing with her estate?'

Mackay groaned. 'Still am. You wouldn't believe how long it's taken to get everything completed. HMRC demands the inheritance tax money up front then drags its heels. Flora had a lot of investments and getting them disentangled takes time.'

'So, Danielle Maitland will have inherited quite a good sum?'

'Yes, absolutely. Her father was beside himself when he missed out the second time – he'll never forgive Flora and I doubt if he's forgiven Danni either. His sister was a very savvy lady, and then of course, there's the croft – with two bidders heading for a price war the sky's the limit.'

Mackay was expecting a follow-up question that didn't come – something else the chief inspector knew already?

Strang said, 'Presumably you are holding papers relating to Ms Maitland's estate?'

Ah! So that was why he was here. With lawyerly caution he said, 'Yes, some.'

'Can I ask whether there are papers relating to her personal life as well as her financial affairs?'

Mackay hesitated. 'This isn't for the record?' When Strang confirmed it, he said, 'I am subject to the rules of client confidentiality, but unofficially I can say that they exist. They are now of course Danielle Maitland's property and since she has not actually appointed me her solicitor, I really have no locus in the matter.'

'I see.' Strang frowned for a moment, then said, 'If she agreed, I could see them without having to apply for a warrant?'

'If she was my client, I would strongly advise against it, but it would be up to her.'

'Are you able to contact her?'

'I have her mobile number, yes.' Mackay got up and went to the phone on his desk. He listened, then left a message asking her to phone back. 'I did actually leave a message yesterday – I needed some information, but she hasn't returned the call. I'd have to say she's not very good about responding – I always have to try a few times and hope to catch her in.'

'Right,' Strang said thoughtfully. Then he stood up. 'Thanks very much, Mr Mackay. I've appreciated that. You've been very helpful and I won't take up any more of your time.' As he walked to the door he added, 'You may be getting a more formal request before too long.'

Unsurprised by that, Mackay saw his visitor out. Then he went back to his office and somewhat reprehensibly went to a cupboard and took down a box file marked 'Estate of Flora Maitland or Reith'. As the deceased's lawyer, satisfying his own curiosity wasn't actually a crime.

As Strang walked to his car he was cautioning himself not to read too much into what Donald Mackay had said. The 'personal papers' might be no more than the ordinary records people never get round to throwing away, but at least he had a direction to indicate if the Met wanted to pursue it further, which made his trip more worthwhile than he'd thought it would be.

And, it suddenly occurred to him, he actually knew where the elusive Danni Maitland could be found. Hattie Sinclair had said she was staying with them meantime, and even if they'd managed, as she'd been hoping, to get Danni to move on, she was likely to know where the girl was now. He could phone her and ask, without disclosing his whereabouts. He'd have to think up a reason for asking – perhaps he could be checking up details about the car fire?

But he didn't need to. When Hattie answered the phone, she said, 'Oh Kelso, I'm so glad you rang. I was just debating whether I should bother you with this, but really, I'm so worried.'

'Something's wrong?' he said sharply.

'I don't know what's happened to Danni. She left here after breakfast yesterday and I asked around yesterday afternoon, but no one had seen her. When she didn't come back last night I thought she might be with that boy she had the row with, but I managed to speak to him today and he hadn't seen her. You should see the weather here! It's

diabolical and if she got lost somehow and was out in it . . .'
She gave a little anxious sob.

Strang felt the hairs on the back of his neck rise. The aunt. The niece? He would have to admit where he was and go round there. And getting back to Edinburgh today certainly wasn't looking promising.

With a noise like an express train, the gale was lashing the pine trees into a frenzy. A stand of three ancient giants, linked together by their roots, moaned in agony as they were torn from the ground and their weight began to topple them, creaking, creaking, until with a final shudder they crashed to the ground.

Their canopy had sheltered the ground below from the full force of the rain but now it unleashed its fury into the open space where Danni Maitland lay dead amid a deep bed of bracken, her eyes staring, her limbs flung wide, and rainwater starting to fill her open mouth – and the ragged wound that gaped like a second red mouth across her throat.

CHAPTER NINE

DCI Strang was on principle truthful, but with operational demands sometimes making that hard, he'd become adept at the misleading statement – equally unethical, perhaps, but it somehow felt better. Now, when Hattie said blankly, 'But you can't have driven up this morning! Why didn't you come here last night? You know there's always a bed,' he said, 'Of course I know! You've been endlessly hospitable. But yesterday I wasn't sure when I'd be able get away – my boss wasn't in her office when I arrived to speak to her. And, of course, with the weather I was going to be very late, so they found me a B&B in Lochinver. I needed to tell Angus Mackenzie that there wasn't any reason for reopening the enquiry into Flora Maitland's death, and I was phoning you to arrange to speak to Danni too.'

All of that was technically true, but if Hattie had thought about it she'd have realised that a DCI driving across Scotland out of consideration for an elderly gentleman's feelings wouldn't happen. But she only said, distractedly, 'I can't tell you what a relief it is to know that you're nearby. Can you come over now?'

'No problem. I'm on my way.'

But there was a problem. A big problem. As he drove along the twisting road to Inverbeg through the battering storm, Strang was trying to work out the best way to tackle it. After all, Danni Maitland was a grown woman; she might merely have decided to take herself off without bothering to tell anyone. Hattie had asked around, but she couldn't know everyone Danni knew and if Ranald was annoying her she might well have decided to walk out in a huff and find somewhere more congenial to stay.

By now, though, the news that Hattie was looking for Danni would have spread; small places seemed able to get information out there faster than Twitter. Someone, surely, would have come forward if they'd seen her. If she wasn't safe in someone else's house in this sort of weather, she could easily have come to harm – even a minor accident that happened with no one around to help could mean death from hypothermia. And right now, no one would be going out unless they had to.

But could she just have headed home to her parents, scared by what was going on here? She wasn't the type to worry about the social obligation to tell her hostess. He had their details, so that at least was easy enough to check.

Then it struck him. She didn't have a car now. There was no public transport. So she was almost certainly still here, somewhere – here where there had been a nasty accident with the car going on fire, where her aunt too had, allegedly, suffered a fatal accident. The sooner they got out search parties the better. If only the storm would let up!

Strang parked as close to the mud room door as he could and Hattie, her face drawn with worry, had it open for him before he'd got out of the car. As he splashed through the puddles that had formed in the yard and followed her through to the kitchen, she was apologising.

'I feel it's taking advantage of the friendship,' she said, but he interrupted her.

'Not at all. It'll let us take prompt action. Do you have the number for the police station?'

Hattie's eyes widened. 'Do you – do you think something's happened to her?'

'Not necessarily, but it wouldn't do any harm to get people out looking.'

She rummaged round in a pile of papers on a desk in the corner of the kitchen and brought the number over to him. 'This is the one they gave Ran when he wanted to speak to someone about Danni's car. And it's Tuesday; there might actually be someone at the station in Lochinver.'

But when he called, it was an answering service. Strang identified himself, explained that he happened to be in the area, that there was a young woman who seemed to be missing and that on his own authority he was calling out Mountain Rescue.

By the time he finished, Hattie had the information to hand. 'They're great, these guys. And I'm sure people in Inverbeg will come out too. I can get Ran to go round knocking on the doors to tell them and see if he can get a squad together – he's good at organising, as you know!'

'Yes, of course,' Strang agreed, but with a distinct qualm. If what had happened to Danni did turn out to be the sort of 'accident' that had happened to her aunt, Ranald Sinclair would be one of the principal suspects and his own position, as his friend, would be deeply invidious.

Waves were breaking dramatically over the pier in the little harbour on the coast of the Auchinglass Estate. Used to ship the kelp harvest at one time, it had fallen into disrepair, along with the huddle of houses beside it, until the tree planting on the estate had given it a new lease of life. Instead of lorries and tractors struggling first with bad roads and then with awkward terrain, this was not only sound ecology but by far the most efficient way to bring in rewilding materials.

The ship that had brought in the young trees had made a smart about-turn to run ahead of the storm and its cargo, hastily unloaded the day before, was still lying in piles. A couple of jeeps towing trailers were parked ready beside the surfaced road that had been blasted through a couple of years before, ready to take shipments down to the lower part of the estate. With the aid of the volunteers added to the estate workforce, this had been laboriously cleared of the ubiquitous rhododendron and the odd commercial plantation of Norway spruce so that the rewilding process to restore the Caledonian Forest could be established, with the native trees like Scots pine, ash, birch, rowan and alder.

With the storm and the delay, the volunteers had been occupied the previous day with indoor jobs and having a lecture from Sean Reynolds. It was unappealing outside work today as well, but it had to be done. Even the estate workers' heavy-duty wet-weather gear couldn't do a lot against the driving wind, the blown spray and the relentless downpour. The smart ski jackets worn by a couple of the young volunteers had soaked through after ten minutes.

'Might as well wear a frilly nightie,' Sean Reynolds said unsympathetically. 'Anyway, doesn't matter how wet you get. You take a shower every day, don't you? You won't need one tonight, unless to get the mud off. We have to get the saplings in the ground as quickly as possible, so let's get on with it.'

His motley troop, shivering and moving with resignation rather than enthusiasm, set to work, casting envious looks at the drivers of the jeeps who were under cover at least. Reynolds mucked in with them, heaving the bundles on to the trailers, responding to queries, sorting out problems and driving them on with ruthless energy.

When his phone rang, he jumped into the shelter of his Discovery to take the call. He seized a cloth to wipe his wet face and hands and glanced at the name. It wasn't often that Maia called him at work.

'Yes?'

The connection was poor; he had to strain to hear what she was saying. 'Sean, have you seen Danni Maitland, yesterday or today?'

'Danni Maitland? No, why?'

'She hasn't been seen for two days. They're organising a search for her – Ranald Sinclair called round.'

'Sinclair?' Reynolds said sharply. 'What's it got to do with him?'

'She was staying with them, remember? They're obviously anxious. Is Joe Dundas there?'

'Joe? Why him?'

'She was friendly with him. Maybe he'll know. You can ask the other staff as well, and the kids too.'

'Right. I'll call you back if I get anything.'

Reynolds jumped out of the car, looking about him. Joe Dundas had taken over the supervision and was busy rearranging some careless stacking on one of the trailers. 'Joe!' he called. The man came across obediently. 'Have you seen Danni Maitland yesterday or today?'

A sullen look came over Dundas's face. 'No. Why should I?'

'Thought she was a mate of yours.'

'Was.' There was bitterness in his tone.

'They seem to think she's gone missing and they're looking for her.'

Dundas laughed. 'They needn't bother. She'll have left. She said she was going, so likely that's what she's done.'

'Right,' Reynolds said. 'That's helpful.' He turned and shouted to the rest of the workers. 'Any of you seen Danni Maitland the last couple of days?'

'Not since the pub on Saturday,' one of them said slyly and Dundas's face turned a bright red.

'I saw her yesterday morning,' one of them offered. 'I went into the store yesterday morning before your lecture and she was walking away from the fish farm.'

'OK,' Reynolds said. 'That would figure, if Joe's right.' He got back in the car and called Maia. 'Joe says she'll just have gone – that's what she was planning to do. Seen first thing yesterday walking away from the Sinclairs'. Nothing else useful.'

'Thanks, Sean. I'll get that passed on to the chief inspector.' She rang off, leaving Sean frowning. What chief

142

inspector? How could they have got a chief inspector on the scene when as far as he knew no one had said anything about Danni being missing till now?

Reynolds went back to work. They'd all worked hard; no one was still shivering with cold and the first trailer, full, was being driven off along the road. It would only take another ten minutes to get the rest of the shipment on the second trailer and at last the rain was slackening; though the wind was still strong it was gusting rather than blowing hard all the time. At last he was able to say, 'Right, guys, that's it. Thanks for your hard work. Perch yourselves on the trailer and you'll get a lift back.'

There were some resentful glances as he climbed into his own comfortable car and drove back behind them. He let them get well ahead, then turned off down an old Forestry Commission track that led into another plantation, neglected now – the foreign pines hadn't proved much of a commercial success in this bare and rugged landscape.

He drove slowly, like someone who drives past their beloved's empty house, scanning to right and to left, even though there was nothing to see apart from the low cloud tangling in the tops of the wind-lashed trees. At last he turned round, back to the road, and pushed on to catch up with the trailers that were bumping slowly along, so that they arrived at the same time.

Reynolds jumped out and was waiting for them as they clambered stiffly down. 'Great job,' he said. 'Take a couple of hours for lunch today. We'll start planting in the afternoon. And look, that's the sun struggling through.'

A pale silvery sun could indeed be glimpsed through the grey banks of cloud, but the indifferent way the workers glanced at it suggested they were far too experienced to read too much into that.

There was absolutely no way DCI Strang would be sleeping in his own bed tonight. As Hattie waited in the Sinclairs' kitchen for the Mountain Rescue team to assemble, he went through to the sitting room to sort out practical arrangements.

His first call went to Mrs Munro in Lochinver. She was delighted to book him in again, though disconcertingly she asked him if they'd found that missing lassie yet. With an inner groan, he admitted they hadn't, thanked her and put the phone down quickly. While it was good that so many people were already out looking for Danni, it did show how ruthlessly the spotlight would be trained on the operation.

His next call was to DI Rachel French. He'd no reason as yet to phone JB – and he devoutly hoped there wouldn't be one – but given that Rachel had shown signs of anxiety yesterday, it was only fair to warn her so she could prepare for the call to the SRCS that might be coming in. He'd have to break it to her, too, that if it came to that he would have to stand back. Saying that he had a friend – someone he'd actually stayed with the week before – who would be a suspect after a car had been blown up and a young woman had disappeared was embarrassing enough. Even worse, he'd have to warn her that he didn't think Ranald Sinclair's innocence was beyond question.

*　*　*

144

When she saw DCI Strang's name come up on her phone, DI Rachel French gave a tiny sigh of relief. He'd said he wouldn't be away for long and that would be him saying he was back.

She'd made a good start to settling into her role as DI here in Edinburgh; the need for efficiency and meticulous organisation played to her strengths. The SRCS, though, was completely different. She knew all about Strang's maverick style and the lack of structure there was an alarming thought; she'd been twitching all day in case a sudden summons came in to deal with a serious rural crime before he got back from Lochinver.

He wasn't back, though. 'Rachel,' he said, 'I just wanted to warn you that I'm not going to be able to make it back to Edinburgh tonight.'

She said guardedly, 'I see. Something cropped up?'

"Fraid so. I'm in Inverbeg, near Lochinver. Girl hasn't been seen for a couple of days and we're just arranging search parties to look for her. The weather's been atrocious and there's a concern that something may have happened to her.'

'That must be very worrying. Still, it's lucky that you're right there on the spot to deal with it.' She hoped he couldn't hear the relief in her voice. 'Are you going to need backup?'

'Well, not right at the moment until we check it out a bit more. But you remember the info DC Murray dug up for me, relating to Flora Maitland?'

'Yes, of course. Inverbeg was where she had the fatal accident.'

'This is the niece, Danielle. Her car went on fire and exploded outside her house on Sunday night. She left the house she stayed in after that yesterday morning and hasn't been seen since. I have to say I'm . . . very concerned.'

She got the message. The outlook wasn't good for poor Danielle. 'So what happens now?'

'Er . . . I find myself in a difficult position,' Strang said, and explained.

It was clearly an uncomfortable admission. He was sounding thoroughly awkward as she listened with a sinking heart. It wasn't hard to see where this was likely to be going. Her mouth dry, she said, 'So . . . that means . . . ?'

'If it comes to it, it will be the boss's call. But she was quite happy with the idea of you covering for me, so I guess she'll follow on with that.'

French swallowed hard. 'Obviously I'm ready to take it on, and of course we all hope they'll find the girl all right, but I'd better make my preparations just in case. Can you explain the principles?'

'Ah,' he said. 'I'm not sure there are exactly laid-down principles. We never know what we'll have to work with on the ground, and I have to say the local force here is not geared up for this sort of thing. We just have to think on our feet and we can bring in whatever we need.'

With a lightness she didn't feel, she said, 'Ah well, it's certainly going to be a steep learning curve!'

'Don't worry. Look, it's a well-oiled machine by now, and to some extent I can support at one remove, if we're careful. And listen, I know you have reservations about Livvy Murray, but she's got great hands-on experience and I would suggest that you take her with you if that's how it goes.'

She said brightly, 'I can see she could be very helpful.'

He sounded very pleased. 'Excellent! You know, you're both very able officers and I think you will make a great team.'

'I'm sure,' she said, because that's what you had to say. 'Let's hope it won't be necessary.'

'There's a possibility it may come to nothing. Danni may just have gone walkabout without telling anyone. I doubt if she'd worry about social etiquette.'

It wasn't convincing. Somehow his unease had seeped through that upbeat statement and as she switched off her phone she could feel its ripples stirring the air in her quiet office.

When DCI Strang went back to the kitchen, a couple of the rescue team had arrived – a tall, dark, young man and an older woman, stocky, with untidy greying hair. They both wore the same orange and navy jackets and rucksacks with a VHF speaker attached to a strap. Hattie Sinclair had already supplied them with coffee and biscuits and there were more mugs out on the table ready.

'We're just the advance guard,' the woman said. 'Jim here – his dad farms just along the road and I'm Jean – I live here in Inverbeg.'

'DCI Kelso Strang. How many are you expecting?'

'Another four, but they're a bit further away. There's a dog coming too.'

Hattie's black labs had been standing watching the company with polite interest. Suddenly, one of them raised her head and then they both trotted to the back door, barking.

'That'll be the dog.' Jean went to the window and peered out at a four by four that had just drawn up. 'Oh good – that's Malcolm. He's the team leader, so if you can fill in the background he'll work out what we need to do.'

Judging by his white hair and gnarled hands, Malcolm must be at least sixty, but the expression on his weather-beaten face as he greeted them hinted that he'd never lost his youthful enthusiasm. The dog now being carefully inspected by Juno and Jax wasn't, as Strang had expected, a German Shepherd or a Malinois.

His surprise must have shown on his face and Malcolm laughed. 'Didn't think a springer could be a search dog, eh? There's not a better nose for tracking than Sadie here. Now, let's sit down and you can talk me through what you know.'

'Little enough, unless something's come in recently,' Strang said, looking at Hattie.

'Not much. Ranald's still out knocking on doors – haven't heard from him, but I guess people will have started coming out to join in the search. Someone said Danni had been seen leaving here yesterday morning and Maia Reynolds phoned to say that Joe Dundas said he hadn't seen her but that she'd told him she was leaving, so she'd probably just gone. But she didn't pick up the things she has here – you'd think she'd want her toothbrush, at least.'

'Got a phone with her?' Malcolm asked.

'She hasn't left one here. I don't know the number.'

'Leave that with me,' Strang said. He could get it from the lawyer, though whether Danni would pick up was something else.

'Where was she likely to go? Surely she wouldn't go hill-walking with the weather forecast like this?'

Hattie shook her head. 'Not Danni. Yesterday it wasn't too bad, I suppose, but she definitely wasn't what I'd call the outdoor type. And I fetched the things she'd need overnight from her bedroom and there wasn't a sign of walking boots or even proper rainwear, just the sort of thing she'd wear at home in Glasgow.'

'Right. So we're talking low level here, are we? What places did she usually go, Hattie?'

'I think she went to Lochinver sometimes, but she couldn't have done that because her car burnt out on Sunday night. Apart from that – well, the pub, mostly.'

'A girl after your own heart, eh, Jim?' Malcolm said to the young man, who looked sheepish. 'Need to find her then, won't we? We can get started on the immediate area now and I'll call the others to fill in as they arrive. Jean, can you check the shoreline? I seem to remember there was an accident here when someone fell off a cliff a while ago.'

Strang froze. The other three looked at each other with identical expressions of dismay and Malcolm looked at them in puzzlement.

'What did I say? There's something I don't know about?'

'The missing girl,' Strang said. 'It was her aunt who fell off the cliff.'

'The police said it was an accident and maybe it was,' Jean said. 'Some folk thought she'd been pushed, though.' Then realising who was sitting across the table from her, she added hastily, 'Of course I'm sure they did everything they could.'

Strang couldn't think of anything to say, but fortunately Malcolm took over. He stood up, and the dog, who had been play-fighting with the younger Labrador, was at his side in an instant.

'Jean, you know the site? We'll head over there with Sadie. Chief Inspector . . . ?'

'Yes,' Strang said. 'I'll come.'

'We'll need something belonging to Danni. She's got some clothes still here, right? Can you find something, Hattie – underwear, tee-shirt, that sort of thing.'

Hattie, grim-faced, nodded and went out. Another car was drawing up outside and Malcolm went on, 'Jim, out you go now, brief them and start the search locally. From the sound of it, there's likely quite a few folk'll be starting already.'

'I'll look out for Ranald and get his lot linked in,' Jim said over his shoulder as he left.

Strang made a quick call to Donald Mackay for Danni's mobile number, but she didn't pick up. Hattie came back holding purple pyjama bottoms, a grey tee-shirt and a couple of pairs of skimpy knickers.

'She didn't have much with her. The other things haven't been worn.'

She handed them to Malcolm and then they all watched in silence as they were presented to Sadie. She sniffed all over them with intense concentration, then looked up at her owner, tail wagging.

'Right. On we go. The scents will be high today, after the rain.'

The rain had gone off at last but there was a chill wind still blowing. Strang walked behind as Jean led the way round behind the fish farm and along to where the path stopped and then on to the stony shore. The tide was out; he could smell the rafts of seaweed uprooted by the storm that were piled along the waterline. No one spoke. Sadie didn't seem to be tracking anything, trotting along at her own pace, just sniffing the air, presumably.

The ground was rising now and Strang could see a small building at the top of the hill – the Maitland croft, presumably – and he could see the cliff Flora had fallen from ahead. Could Danni, worried and depressed, have stepped off it herself? He hadn't considered that possibility.

They were rounding the corner to where they would get a clear view. Strang found he was holding his breath.

But there was nothing. No crumpled body there among the scattered rocks. Sadie's tail was still wagging, she was still trotting along, but now Malcolm stopped.

'Not picking up anything. She didn't come this way.'

There was nothing for them to do but turn round and go back. Already Strang could see groups of people moving along, past the Inverbeg Inn and fanning out across rough ground on both sides of the road leading to the Auchinglass Estate and the pods as well as the road up out of Inverbeg.

As they reached the road by the Sinclairs' house, Sadie looked as if she might be on to something, sniffing the ground enthusiastically for a few hundred yards, but then appeared to lose interest.

'Nothing here now,' Malcolm said, just as Strang looked up to see the burnt-out remains of Danni's car outside the little grey house at the top of the hill. Remains – an unfortunate word to have thought of.

'I think we should check the cottage as a priority,' he said. 'If she did change her mind and go back to it after she left the Sinclairs' there might even be some sort of trail Sadie could pick up beyond it.'

'Right,' Malcolm said, and they went on walking up the road out of Inverbeg while the others in the search party went on to join the operations behind the inn. It looped in a wide curve to reach the main road where they walked along before they reached the hardstanding with the burnt-out car. And now Sadie was going crazy, tail swinging almost in circles as she rushed ahead to the door of the cottage and then lay down beside it, pressing her nose to the crack at the bottom of the door.

Malcolm went forward, slipping the lead on and drawing her aside as he petted her. Strang, with a sick feeling in the pit of his stomach and his pulse racing, joined him.

He probably wouldn't have noticed it, there in the fresh air, if his attention hadn't been drawn by Sadie's excitement, but now he could just detect the familiar metallic taint of blood. What were they going to find on the other side of that door?

He turned the handle, but it didn't open. Locked, then. To the left there was a window with cardboard filling in for a missing pane; he pushed it through and bent to peer inside. The window was small and the room was dark. He could make out that it was a bedroom with the door standing slightly open, but there was nothing he could see to account for the smell that was pervasive now, making his stomach lurch.

He said to Malcolm, 'I'm going to kick in the door.'

It was an old, ineffectual lock and the wood, too, was soft; it splintered easily and the door swung open. Strang stepped into what looked like a slaughterhouse. Blood had dried in a pool on the floor, it had soaked into the sofa, splashed onto the table that stood beside it. There were spatters right across the room and even on one of the walls. He had to swallow hard.

He needed to get a clear view of the whole room. He edged round the perimeter, taking stock. There was a beer bottle on the table, a third full, and a few jagged shards of brown glass lay on the floor in a puddle of beer. Apart from that, there didn't look to have been a struggle. But there was no body.

Malcolm had seen too what lay inside; he was waiting at the door as Strang came out, closing the door behind him and shaking his head.

'Not here, but she has to be dead. Can you find someone to block the site till police arrive, but keep quiet on the details?'

'No problem. Natural enough to keep folk away, when it's the girl's home. Leave it with me. You'll have other things to do.'

'I'm very grateful. I'll go now to call in a forensic team.'

As Strang walked back down the hill the searchers were still strung out across the rough land beyond the village, looking for a missing girl. There was nothing to be gained at the moment by making an announcement; they'd be doing the same thing if they were looking for a body.

Danni had been having a drink with someone and that someone had then killed her. A squabble with the boyfriend she'd fought with already? Run-of-the-mill stuff, then.

But it might not be, and he couldn't take time to check it out. He'd have to tell JB the whole story and recuse himself from the investigation.

CHAPTER TEN

Strang went back and let himself into the Sinclairs' house, where Hattie had offered him the dining room as a workspace. He sat down, trying to assemble his thoughts before phoning DCS Borthwick.

No one could have survived an attack like that. But when had it happened, and what had happened afterwards?

The dog had looked as if it might have been following a scent coming away from the Sinclairs' house, but hadn't persisted. There had been a lot of rain, of course, and this morning a lot of people walking over the ground, which probably had confused any trail.

Where had Danni gone, during those missing hours? Surely she hadn't spent the time shut up alone in her dark and damaged house? It was unlikely, too, that her killer would stage such a brutal attack at a time when someone might be about and hear screaming – or a neighbour might even pop in to see how she was.

And he had to have had a car outside, to remove the body.

Conspicuous, unless it was after dark and in the middle of the storm. They'd just been having a beer – had he arranged to meet her there, with this in mind? Or was it possible that it had started out as being innocent enough, until something had happened to make him lose his temper? The broken bottle, a formidable weapon – glassings were common and too many young men had died that way. People lost their temper when they didn't get what they wanted – which led him on to such an unwelcome thought that he forced it out of his mind immediately and thought about the time of death instead. If the pathologist could be persuaded to give even the roughest possible estimate of when Danni had died – which often they wouldn't – he would put money on it being the previous night.

However, speculation wasn't going to get him anywhere at the moment. The search had already been intensified and widened: work on the Auchinglass Estate had been cancelled, more volunteers had been arriving from all round the locality and were being allocated groups and given search locations.

It was certainly being dealt with very efficiently, but Strang's heart sank at the task in front of them. There was no easy answer to where the killer might dispose of the body and, given the rugged terrain here, there was no shortage of suitable sites. With a well-chosen hiding-place it could lie undiscovered for years; it could just be left lying there and the obliging wildlife, from the tiniest maggot upwards, would take care of its disposal. And even as he sat there, he was looking out over the sea to which, weighted with stones, a body could be consigned for eternity.

A uniform from the Lochinver station at last appeared, a middle-aged man who seemed totally nonplussed by what had happened.

'We don't get that sort of thing around here,' he said, sounding faintly aggrieved, and Strang could only think that perhaps that was what had characterised the Flora Maitland investigation.

Still, he was out now securing the access to the cottage while Strang took a deep breath and made his call to DCS Borthwick. He wasn't looking forward to it. At the time, he'd been grateful that the arrival of her next appointment had cut short their interview and he hadn't had to tell her about the burnt-out car; now he really wished that he had. The way things had turned out it could look as if he'd been actively concealing something.

He briefed her on the days' events, then went on to explain his position. Borthwick listened without interruption, but when she did speak he could tell from her tone that she was put out.

'It's certainly most unfortunate. If your friend is involved, however blameless he may be, you can't head up the investigation, obviously.'

Grimacing, Strang said, 'Frankly, I'm not absolutely sure that he is. I hadn't seen him since I left the army and I wouldn't now be volunteering as a character witness. On the face of it, the jilted boyfriend has to be the main suspect for the attack, but it's not impossible Ranald Sinclair might have blown up the car, though he's not the only one who might.

'I thought I'd hold back on releasing the details until we could get a forensic team here. The search is still officially for a misper and the site's secure at the moment, so it can wait. We could probably just get them across from Inverness – until we find a body there's no question of flying in the experts, of course. It could drag on for long enough and I suppose it could be handed on with oversight from there. There's virtually no police presence in the immediate vicinity.'

'You're not in any doubt, though, that there is a body to find?'

He sighed. 'No, I'm not. And it's also at the back of my mind that there are other factors we need to take into account, like the Met's reaction when I told them about the aunt's death and the business with the car that could be some sort of warning.'

'Mmm.'

He waited, unwilling to interrupt if she was thinking. After a moment she said slowly, 'Are we talking about one investigation here, or two?'

'Linked, I suppose, but not exactly the same. Certainly, there's no urgency about digging around Flora's background to try to make sense of it, but for the current problem we need at least a small team in position right now and obviously I can't lead it.'

'And would you say DI French was the best person to take over?' Borthwick sounded uncertain. 'I like what I've seen of her, but you've shaped the SRCS to your way of working, and the position is very different from what she's used to here.'

'As far as I can see she has the qualities the job needs. She has excellent organisational skills and she's more likely to be flexible than someone with longer service who's set in a formal way of doing things. And DC Murray has a lot of SRCS experience that could be useful if you decided we should add her to the team.'

There was, Strang was pleased to notice, a smile in Borthwick's voice as she said, 'Ah, my friend Livvy.' There was nothing superior officers liked better than to have their judgement proved right.

'She's learnt a lot in the last year or two,' he said, trying not to sound defensive.

'But would DI French be able to rein her in when she gets one of her inspirations?'

He couldn't stop himself saying, 'Well, I've never managed!'

Borthwick laughed. 'Right. I'll take the recommendation. Go ahead. But you're still in charge of the SRCS, and what I have been thinking is that if we get you out of the immediate location whenever DI French gets there, you could base yourself somewhere nearby to do your "digging around" on Flora Maitland and be near enough as well to provide advice and direction to her.

'Where are you now?'

He wasn't going to say, 'In my friend's house'. He wasn't daft. 'I'm in Inverbeg just at the moment, but I'm booked into the B&B they arranged for me last night in Lochinver – that's a few miles away. I could base myself there.'

'Then get things moving. And good luck.'

He thanked her and with a brow-mopping gesture he rang off. There was no doubt about it, JB was good. For all he thought Rachel French was well capable of scaling the steep learning curve they'd talked about, he was glad to be nearby to offer support when needed. SRCS had been very much his baby and he would hate to see things go wrong.

DC Murray was on patrol duty in a squad car when the message came in from Angie Andrews that she was urgently required for an SRCS operation. Her heart leapt.

'Blues and twos,' she said firmly to her partner, who gave her a bit of a sideways glance but did it anyway.

She'd been so worried that if something big cropped up she'd be elbowed out of it by DI French, but no. She'd be working with Strang again and from the sound of it this was another homicide. As she hurried into the Fettes Avenue station and sought out Angie, Murray was already reminding herself of all the things she'd got wrong last time – the attempts to impress him by working on a separate line herself, the unwarranted conclusions she'd jumped to, the impetuous decisions that had brought Strang's wrath down on her – and vowed to get it right now. Last time they'd made a good team, in her opinion anyway – well, pretty much – but this time it would be even better.

She was beaming when she said to Angie, 'Well, where's Strang taking me this time?'

Angie gave her a pitying look. 'Not Strang,' she said. 'DI French.'

The beam faded. 'Me with DI French? I don't like her and I reckon she doesn't like me either. Is this some piddling little investigation that doesn't warrant Strang's attention?'

'Don't know yet. A misper in Inverbeg, near Lochinver. Reason to suspect the missing girl is dead. It's wild country

159

and there's a big search on, but if they find the body they'll be going for all the bells and whistles.'

Murray stared. 'But not Strang? I had to look up an address for him that was in Lochinver. Why's he not dealing with it?'

Angie shook her head. 'There's something odd. He's staying there at the moment, but French has to get across immediately and take over charge. Anyway, I'll get you the full details and then you'd better report to her. PS Erskine's assigned as well – there's not much uniform support around there. There are accommodation pods on this estate in Inverbeg and we've booked two of them—'

'Two?' Murray was horrified. 'You can't mean – I'm going to have to share with French? You're joking.'

Angie grinned. 'Unless you want to shack up with Bob Erskine, but you'd better get his wife's permission first.'

Murray's shoulders slumped. 'Oh great. I was really excited before. Now it'll have to be "Yes ma'am, I've dotted all the 'i's and crossed all the 't's just the way you like them. And once I've done that can we do some actual detective work?"'

'From what I've heard it'll probably work better if you don't get excited. And I can tell you who I'm sorry for and to be honest it isn't you.'

'Well, thanks for that. Thought you were my mate,' Murray said bitterly.

'You can drive up with Bob. French is taking her car too, unless they actually find a body and then it'll be the full works with the chopper. You'll have to drive hers across then.'

'Don't mind her car, just as long as she isn't in it,' Murray muttered and pulled a face as Angie rolled her eyes to the heavens.

Hattie Sinclair tapped on the dining-room door and opened it gingerly. 'I didn't want to interrupt you,' she said, 'but it's way past lunchtime and I thought you might like a sandwich.'

Kelso Strang was studying an Ordnance Survey map. He looked up to say, 'Oh, thank you. That's very kind. Actually, I wanted a word with you. When you were asking around yesterday if anyone had seen Danni, who did you speak to?'

Hattie put the tray down on the table. 'Only a couple, yesterday. I didn't really start getting worried until it got late at night. I called in at Auchinglass House because I thought it was quite likely she'd have gone there to tell Sean she'd sell him the croft because she was annoyed with Ran, but Maia hadn't seen her. Then I went to the pub at around six-thirty, I suppose, and Kasper said she hadn't been in by then. This morning I went out early and caught Joe Dundas on his way to work and asked if he'd seen her, but he was a bit surly – just said no, and walked on. I even went up to the cottage to see if she'd decided to go back after all, but there was no reply when I knocked on the door. Then I asked Zofia in the shop and she said Danni hadn't been in at all the day before. I bumped into a couple of people on the way there – Sally Stewart and Jock Macdonald – but they hadn't seen her.'

'Thanks, Hattie. That's useful.'

As she turned to go, Ranald Sinclair appeared in the doorway. 'How's the master sleuth getting on?' he said, with ill-timed levity, then, seeing the reaction from the other two added hastily, 'Sorry. Stupid joke. My bad. What can I help you with? Doesn't look likely we'll find her alive, does it? I was always good on logistics, you know, and that's the kind of problem you'd have with an inconvenient body to dispose of. We could pool our thinking.'

Hattie left, looking uncomfortable. Strang's nails were digging into the palms of his hand, but he managed to say coolly, 'Thanks, but at the moment we're concentrated on the work on the ground. I'm waiting for reports coming in.'

'Fine, fine. But look, there's a bed upstairs waiting for you. Doubt if Hattie's even changed the sheets and you'd be right on the spot to deal with whatever crops up.'

'Actually, I'll get out of your hair shortly. I'm not going to be handling this. DI Rachel French will be taking over as soon as she can get here.'

Sinclair looked very taken aback. 'So where will you be going?'

Fortunately, just at that moment they heard the scrabble of nails on the pine floor and Sadie appeared just ahead of her master, giving Strang the excuse not to answer.

'Malcolm!' he said. 'Any news?'

The man shook his head. 'I've walked Sadie round a bit but no reaction. None of the parties have reported anything.'

'Take a seat.' His gesture was pointedly directed at Malcolm and after hovering for a moment Sinclair left. 'What directions have you given them for this afternoon?'

'More of the same, on a widening sweep. But you're in charge.'

Strang glanced down at the map in front of him. 'I'm not sure what you've done already but I wonder if we should focus along the roadsides? Say that someone has been driving around with a body to dispose of – admittedly given a 4x4 you could go anywhere, but with all this rain you leave wheel tracks so you might feel safer staying on a metalled road. So we could get searchers looking for any sign of a car stopping on the verge in a wilderness area. Of course, he could go as far as he liked, but he might be keen to dispose of it as soon as possible. So that's the main road and the one into the village here.' He tapped the map.

'Ah,' Malcolm said, 'that one's a bit out of date. There's an old harbour on the coast of the Auchinglass Estate, with a scatter of houses round about – the kelp they harvested was collected from there and they'd likely a few wee boats for the fishing too. It was abandoned – oh, probably a hundred years ago. There'd have been some sort of rough track then, I suppose, but it was long gone. They restored the harbour a few years ago and put in a proper road – blasting through rock and everything – so they can get supplies in quicker and cheaper for the project.'

Strang thought about that for a moment. 'Is it used much by the locals?'

'Not at all. It's a private road, on Auchinglass property.'

'And it goes through pretty rough country?'

'See what you're getting at. So, something to prioritise.'

'Definitely,' Strang said. 'But however many searchers we put out, it's still going to be a long shot. In the immortal phrase, do we feel lucky?'

To his surprise, Malcolm smiled. 'If that really is the scenario, then we certainly do.'

'Really? There won't be Danni's trail for the dog to track there.'

'I don't much like the phrase,' Malcolm said, 'but Sadie's one of the best cadaver dogs in the business.'

After DCI Strang's phone call, DI Rachel French had, of course, been expecting the summons but her knees still shook a little as she went in to see DCS Jane Borthwick. The description that someone had once given of her – 'firm, fair and effing formidable' – had stuck and was part of Fettes Avenue legend now, if not always exactly in that form, and it didn't help.

Borthwick looked up and smiled as she came in. 'Oh dear, I'm sorry you've had this thrown at you so abruptly. Sit down, Rachel. How are you feeling about it?'

The tension eased. It was reassuring that this wasn't going to be ordeal by inquisition, though on the other hand Borthwick's clear, cool gaze suggested that any sort of bullshitting would be badly received.

'Nervous, if I'm honest, ma'am,' French said as she sat down. 'DCI Strang created the SRCS and his are big shoes to fill.'

'Yes,' Borthwick said drily. 'I imagine he's told you what the situation is that has brought this about?'

French lowered her eyes. 'Yes ma'am.'

'It's made things difficult – it's a weakness in the system, when Kelso could step under a bus tomorrow and local forces have less and less to offer. Oddly enough, though, there is some wiggle room. We're dealing with two cases in this general area, possibly interdependent, possibly not. With his personal connections, Kelso obviously must be removed from the ongoing search for this girl, but he can pursue the Flora Maitland set-up in detail. He would be near at hand and available for direct consultation – discreetly, of course. He's still the ultimate boss, but I'm emphasising that you'll have to front it up and the decisions are yours to make.'

'I understand, ma'am. I carry the can.'

Borthwick smiled. 'Good! Now, I'm going to detail DC Livvy Murray as one of the officers to go to Inverbeg with you. She's got direct experience of SRCS and that will be valuable.'

French had been bracing herself. She'd been well warned that Murray was a favourite and she injected as much enthusiasm as she could into her response. 'Thank you. I'm sure that will be a great help.'

To her dismay, she saw Borthwick's eyebrows go up, and she smiled. 'Not your personal choice, Rachel?'

She felt herself turning pink. She'd been right in her earlier assessment of Borthwick's shrewdness. 'I've found it a little difficult to get to know her,' she said.

'Then it will be kill or cure, won't it?' Borthwick said briskly. 'I'm sure you'll both be able to rise above any little differences. All right?'

Dismissed, French said, 'Yes, of course. Thank you, ma'am.'

Oh great, she thought as she walked down the corridor. The scale of the job itself was intimidating enough, but now she'd have to tackle it with someone on the inside who'd do her best to make it more difficult still. It wouldn't be dignified to kick the wall and anyway someone might come round the corner and see her, but there was a cushion in her living room and when she went home to pack she was going to punch the hell out of it.

Angie Andrews appeared looking anxious, her brow clearing as she saw her. 'Oh, DI French, I've been looking for you. Is it right you're going across to Inverbeg today? I've got the details for you.'

'Thanks, Angie. Yes, I've just seen DCS Borthwick. DC Murray is being assigned as well.'

'Yes, that's right, and PS Erskine. There's an estate right on-site that has those holiday pods, so we've booked a couple where you can stay. There's a small local shop and a pub . . .'

Angie went on talking, but French didn't really hear. The police force didn't squander tight budgets on pampering; she had done the calculation. Once she got back home, she wasn't going to punch that cushion. She was going to tear it apart with her teeth.

Shirley had become aware that there was a lot of coming and going this morning – the doorbell had rung several times and she'd heard the phone ringing too, but she hadn't seen either Sean or Maia since breakfast. She'd had her usual chat with Ishbel over coffee earlier, but she hadn't mentioned anything, so it looked as if something must have happened since. Not knowing was infuriating.

She looked at her watch – lunch was obviously going to be late today – and she went back to her copy of Hello with a sigh. She liked the news of celebrities, but it wasn't half as interesting as what real people were up to, and even now the doorbell rang again.

No one went to answer it and after a moment she heard a voice saying, 'Hello?'

She grabbed her stick and pressed the clever little button on the side of her chair that propelled her into an upright position and levered herself to her feet, calling, 'Hello! In here.'

She'd only made it halfway to the door when it opened and Ben Linton appeared, looking sombre. His jacket was wet through, though the rain had stopped a little while ago.

'Sorry, Shirley,' he said. 'Didn't mean to disturb you. I was just looking for Maia to see if there was any news.'

He made to withdraw and with a speed she didn't know she was capable of, Shirley reached him and grabbed his sleeve.

'News of what, Ben? I know there's something going on, but I haven't heard anything about it. You just come and sit down and tell me what's happening.'

She all but dragged him to a chair, then hobbled back to her own. He didn't look as if this was what he wanted to do, but he was too polite to refuse. She studied him as she sat down.

He was upset about something, that was for sure. She always thought he was a nice-looking man, with his fair hair and blue eyes, but today his brows were drawn into a line across his forehead and there was no sign of his usual pleasant smile.

'It's – well, it's Danni Maitland,' he said awkwardly. 'She's gone missing and we've got the rescue people and the police out looking for her.'

No wonder the poor boy was looking upset. 'Oh no! That's dreadful! Where could she have gone? In the weather we've had she'd be in real trouble if she had an accident maybe.'

'Yes, she would.'

There was something not right about the way that he said it and then she remembered – the girl's car had been set on fire too, and a cold, hollow feeling came over her.

'She's not just missing, is she?'

'We don't know. But from the way the police are reacting it looks as if they think something might have happened to her.' He bit his lip.

That was what they said when they thought someone was dead. 'Oh Ben, I'm so sorry. She was a good friend of yours, wasn't she?'

'We hadn't known each other for long, but I suppose she was. Is,' he corrected himself. 'There's a massive search going on now – people coming from Lochinver and all round. I was hoping Maia might have heard something.'

'I haven't seen her or Sean all morning. I don't know where either of them is.'

'I haven't seen Maia, but I saw Sean out with one of the search parties. I was out earlier but I was called in to deal with a maintenance problem.' He got up to go.

A door shut, and then they heard light footsteps crossing the hall.

'That's her now,' Shirley said as the sitting-room door opened.

Maia was wearing an outdoor jacket too, though hers was barely wet. Linton's eyes went to hers immediately, but she gave a little shake of the head.

'Haven't heard anything. Has Ben told you what's going on, Shirley?'

'Yes. That's just awful.'

'Yes, indeed. Actually, Ben, I'm glad I've caught you. There's police arriving from Edinburgh tonight and they've booked pods. Come with me now and I'll tell you what the arrangements are.

'All right, Shirley? I promise lunch won't be long.'

'Don't worry about that. Do me good to starve,' she said as they went out together.

She looked after them thoughtfully. She had wondered, ever since that conversation about Ben joining the board, if there could be anything going on between them. Even though she lived with Sean and Maia, she would find it hard to say what the state of their marriage really was.

And there were other things to worry about. If Danni Maitland had indeed been murdered – and it looked as if that might be what they were thinking – she knew who would feature on the list of suspects.

It was dry this afternoon, at least, with a feeble sun struggling to break through the sullen clouds. With Sadie trotting ahead, Malcolm Allan was walking up the road towards the harbour with a small group of searchers fanned out on either side, scanning the verges – Jim from his own team, a farmer from Kylesku way and three of the young Auchinglass volunteers. One, Holly, was very young, eighteen if that, and he'd already noticed her looking distressed. He'd suggested that maybe she should take a break, but her eyes had filled at the suggestion.

'How could I, when that poor girl is all by herself out here somewhere? It could be me!'

Of course, Malcolm hoped that Sadie would live up to the billing he'd given her, but right at this moment his mind was on finding an excuse to send Holly away in case Sadie did, and it was Jim who said suddenly, 'I think Sadie's got something.'

There was a forestry track off on the left and Sadie's head was up, swivelling towards it. And then she was off, not hurrying but trotting purposefully in a straight line, tail swinging. She knew where she was going.

'Jim, with me,' Malcolm snapped. 'The rest of you, stay right here.'

The two men followed a little way down the track and then Sadie veered off, scrambling up between the ranks of pines, making her way confidently across the thick carpet of sodden, browning needles that covered the knotted roots of the great trees and nosing through the rust-red sheaves of dying bracken.

As they scrambled, breathless, in her wake, Malcolm glanced at Jim. 'Awkward terrain if you were wanting to dig a hole. You thinking what I'm thinking?'

Jim gulped, nodded and glanced over his shoulder. The little group had not, as instructed, stayed on the road; the younger ones had reached the edge of the plantation now, and he shouted back with some urgency, 'Keep your distance!'

Sadie was leading them deep into the plantation. As they struggled towards her they could see a gap where a few trees, close-linked, had toppled leaving a great gash in the hillside, so raw and new that it suggested this had happened during the recent storm.

And the dog barked. The men stumbled the last few yards to where Sadie had sat down beside what was left of Danni Maitland – a bedraggled body with a great red gash right across her throat.

Grimacing, Malcolm went to release Sadie from her sit and give her the praise she was looking for. Jim, looking pale, turned and saw Holly emerging from the trees to his right. She was looking grim but determined.

'I know!' she called. 'But I wanted to be there for her, however bad it was.'

Before Jim had time to block her she had stepped forward. The colour drained from her face.

'Oh my God! They said there were wolves here – and look! They've killed her!' She dropped in a dead faint at their feet.

CHAPTER ELEVEN

No, it wasn't 'wolves', even though when DCI Strang arrived, Jim was looking white and nervous. Even Malcolm was on edge. Every inner-city policeman, though, is familiar with the hideous effect a broken bottle can have – the kind of bottle he'd seen at Danni's croft house earlier. He'd even seen an injury just like this once before – the bottle broken in a quarrel, then laid across the victim's throat with an angry backhand slash, he told them, and they looked both relieved and foolish.

He looked down at the dead girl, barely more than a child, who'd been so pert and sure of herself when last he'd seen her, playing off the two lads against each other. Poor kid – what a vile way for her adventure to end! At least it would have been quick.

Malcolm told him about Holly, who'd recovered from her faint to be helped down, sobbing hysterically, by traumatised friends. They needed to kill that story before it went viral, though Strang feared it probably already had.

'There's an incident tent in the back of my Jeep,' Malcolm said. 'It's part of the kit, in case we find someone we have to leave in place. If you can give me and Sadie a lift down, I can fetch it and we can run a roadblock too – I'll let the others know. Jim, you can hang on here meantime, can't you?'

Despite Strang's assurances, Jim was still looking a little nervously around him when they left. In the back of the car, Sadie was panting, her tongue lolling out in what looked like a grin. 'She's a clever dog,' Strang said.

Malcolm grinned broadly. 'Best in the business, like I said.' He hesitated, then said, 'Are you thinking, maybe, just a drunken quarrel or something?'

'Not really thinking anything, as yet,' Strang said. 'Not till we get a bit more information in.' It was what he always said to anyone – as it might be, like Livvy Murray – who wanted to start from a hypothesis rather than from solid evidence, but of course his mind was already running various scenarios, ranging from that to the calculated assignation with murder in mind. 'But get it round that the wolf story is rubbish, if you can.'

He dropped Malcolm, then returned to the Sinclairs' house. The sooner he got out, the better. They'd helicopter French in with all the backup immediately needed, but if the story was out on Twitter the media wouldn't be far behind – 'wolf attack', however inaccurate, would be a headline to have any editor slavering. He needed to leave with his hands ostentatiously above his head before there was any suggestion he was involved in the investigation.

He made the necessary phone calls from his car, including arranging for the parents to be told. With a sudden shock he realised he should have been driving up to their front door anyway, to talk to William Maitland about his sister. He'd been reluctant, Angie Andrews had said, but the visitors that came instead would be a lot more unwelcome.

Strang was collecting up briefcase and notes from the dining room when there was a tap on the door and Hattie's anxious face peered round.

'I heard you coming back. Have you—'

'I'm sorry. Bad news.'

Hattie's mouth wobbled. 'I was scared it would be. I couldn't think how she could just have disappeared. Was it – was it an accident?'

He could tell she didn't really expect that. 'No. There's no doubt that she was killed.' He hesitated for a moment, then went on, 'I'm afraid her throat was rather horribly cut.'

Tears came to Hattie's eyes. 'Oh no! How dreadful. She was only a kid, really, with so much to look forward to. So what happens now?'

Strang shut his briefcase. 'They're bringing in a team from Edinburgh by helicopter, with a detective inspector, so I'll let you have your dining room back.'

Hattie stared at him. 'Are you not going to be in charge? You're more senior than that, aren't you? And of course there's no need to clear out – we've plenty space. Your bedroom's there waiting for you.'

With so much on his mind, he hadn't considered how to put this. 'You're always so kind,' he said lamely, 'but I've arranged to stay in Lochinver. I've things to sort out there and I don't want to get in DI French's way.'

He didn't sound convincing, even to himself. He could almost see Hattie's mind working before understanding dawned.

'Oh God!' she said shakily. 'You can't do it, can you, because you're Ran's friend and he's going to be a suspect. Even though, of course, he didn't do it – he wouldn't hurt anyone! You know that!'

'Of course.' What else could he say?

Hattie looked at him narrowly. 'But you can tell DI French that? Just because he was annoyed Danni didn't want to sell to him, she might not realise what sort of person he is.'

'Hattie, I can't tell her anything. It's her job, and I know she'll be very professional.'

'It would just be a sort of character reference,' Hattie pleaded. 'You were brothers-in-arms, after all.'

This was even worse than he'd feared. 'If I'm in charge of a homicide investigation I don't take second-hand opinion. It's my job to make up my own mind, and that's what Rachel French will do.'

Hattie stepped back. 'I see,' she said coldly. 'That's fine. I'm just sorry—' She began to cry and hurried out of the room.

Strang picked up his briefcase with a groan and left by the front door, feeling beleaguered. He consoled himself that at least it was temporary; he only needed to stay until Rachel French arrived. Then it would be someone else's problem.

William Maitland looked at his watch again, as he had done every few minutes since three o'clock had come and gone without any sign of his expected visitor.

'That's gone quarter past now,' he pointed out to his wife, who knew already. 'You'd think the police would know the value of punctuality.'

'She only asked if we could be here at three for DCI Strang,' Moira said. 'He's maybe had other things to deal with.'

'It's me that's doing him a favour, agreeing to speak to him about Flora. And all it'll be is more trouble. I'm not wanting any more of her dirty linen getting washed in public. I've better things to do with my time.'

Moira wisely didn't say that the better things he was planning to do weren't immediately obvious. Anyway, there was a police car drawing up outside the house.

'That'll be him now,' she said.

'About time too.'

It was two uniformed officers who came up the path, though, a man and a woman, not the DCI Strang they'd been told to expect.

'What's happened to this Strang, then?' Maitland was saying as he went to open the door. 'I don't like people who can't stick to arrangements.'

'Mr Maitland?' the policeman said. They held up warrant cards. 'May we come in and have a word?'

He stood aside. 'Oh, very well. Is this to apologise for DCI Strang? I can't waste the whole afternoon, you know.'

The officers exchanged startled glances. 'Er – no. Look, could we go in and sit down?'

'Yes, I suppose so. Through here. Let's get this over with as quickly as possible.'

As they came into the sitting room Moira stood up ready to welcome them. Then she saw their faces and went very, very still.

Maitland, still oblivious, sat down and said, 'Well, what's this about?'

Moira's mouth had gone dry. 'It's bad news, isn't it?'

The policewoman was very young, round-faced and rosy-cheeked, but her expression was tragic. 'I'm afraid so.'

Moira's legs wouldn't hold her any more and she collapsed into a chair. William looked from one to the other, confused. 'What bad news?' he said.

They told them. Shorn of the usual explanations it was quite a simple message. Their daughter, Danielle, had been found dead. There were no further details as yet, but it was being 'treated as suspicious'.

Moira was crying quietly. Maitland had sat clenching his fingers into fists and releasing them again and barely spoke except to refuse the offers of help and support and usher them out as quickly as he could.

When he came back into the room Moira, her voice raw with tears, said, 'What do they mean, "suspicious"?'

'They mean she's been murdered,' Maitland said harshly. 'And you know who's done it? Flora, that's who. Old witch! I said how it would be – all that money going to Danielle before she'd the sense to know what to do with it. Oh, she's a lot to answer for, my sister!'

The pace of it all was almost shocking. One minute Rachel French was packing her bag and preparing for the long drive to Inverbeg, the next DC Livvy Murray was dropped off to do the driving while she was whisked away to the Glasgow heliport.

Now they were coming down through low cloud and she could see a big grey house below with a flat area of hardstanding behind it, ideal for a helicopter landing – of course, the owners might sometimes choose not to have to drive miles on poor roads. There were some outbuildings with various trucks and farm vehicles outside – quite an extensive operation, then – and the pods Angie had mentioned, twenty, twenty-five, perhaps, clustering in a wide circle. French had her own idea about the pod situation.

As she ducked out under the rotors, a young man was waiting and came forward.

'I'm Ben Linton. I'm the factor here and I look after the accommodation. We thought you'd want to drop your things off first. It's this way. I gather there are three of you staying, two sharing? Is that right?'

He led her off as the team got out and started unloading equipment with the speed and efficiency of experience. The light was fading already and they would want to do as much as they could before being flown back tonight.

He'd given her the ideal opportunity. 'Actually, I wanted to speak to someone about that. Police budgets are always tight but if another pod is free, could I rent it myself? Sharing is always awkward when your timetables may not be the same.' She was holding her breath.

He smiled – a very pleasant smile, she thought, or was that just because he was nodding at the same time and it didn't look as if she was going to have to be cooped up with DC Murray exuding waves of dislike?

'We're quiet at the moment, with the season winding down, and after – all this, I think a number of people will be going home.'

She could see now that strain was etched on his face. 'Of course,' she said, 'but perhaps you could put the word out that we'll need to interview everyone and they can't leave until we give them permission?'

'I'll get round them at once.' He was opening the door to a pod. 'Is this all right?'

French stepped inside. It was small and fairly spartan – a living area with two beds, chairs, a table, a hotplate and a microwave plus a bathroom – but immaculately clean and the beds looked comfortable. 'That's excellent,' she said. 'Do you know where DCI Strang is?'

'Yes, he asked me to tell you he's in the community hall. If you turn left out of here and then walk up the road, you'll see it on the left beyond the pub. All right?'

'Thanks very much.' She closed the door behind him and took stock. At least Kelso was still here; she'd had a panicky thought that perhaps he'd retreated already, but it sounded as if he'd be able to brief her properly.

She unpacked, thankful that she wasn't going to have to compete with Murray for cupboard space. Then she took a deep breath and set out to start her first SRCS investigation.

DCI Strang stood up to greet DI French when she reached the community hall. He'd managed to screen off a corner where they could sit and talk while tables and chairs for interviews were set out by the half-dozen officers they had managed to call in from nearby stations.

'We have to get the OK from the Procurator Fiscal before we begin operations – "master of the instance" as the book says, though in this case it's "mistress of the instance" – Fiona Murdoch. She's driving across from Inverness – no idea what she's like.'

'And I'll have to take her to view the body, right?'

'And view it yourself. Will that be difficult for you?'

French thought for a moment. 'I don't think so. I had a spell in Traffic, and you know what that's like.'

Those things that came at you out of the blue – they were the worst. A hideously vivid picture came to his mind: the shrieking of brakes – the lorry – his wife. He managed not to flinch, but he didn't think he could speak, so he was grateful that she went on talking.

'A murder victim – might be different? She was only young, too – and such a barbaric way to kill. But it's the job and I just have to be professionally objective.'

'Absolutely,' he managed, though his voice was a little hoarse. 'The kicker is that there's been a rumour going round. Sean Reynolds, the fat cat who owns the estate – sold a tech company or something – allegedly keeps a wolf somewhere. He's a rewilding fanatic and I guess it could be true. I heard a wolf howling myself one night, and Angus Mackenzie – I told you about him – swears he saw a wolf mauling one of his sheep.

'The problem is that one of the young volunteers, Holly someone, saw the body and thought it was a wolf attack. I've tried to set that straight, but I have a bad feeling that it'll have gone straight on the Internet.'

'Oh lord,' French said. 'Media. I had thought we might be spared, being out in the wilds.'

'They have stringers everywhere. You could try to persuade the Reynolds not to let them stay in any vacant pods – it's the only accommodation in Inverbeg.

'I'm heading to Lochinver now. I've left you the address along with the notes I've made. I know Livvy's

180

'on her way, but who's the sergeant?'

'Bob Erskine – do you know him?'

'Oh yes – you'll be fine with him.' Strang hesitated. 'It's not my place to give you advice—'

'Gratefully received,' she put in.

'Then I would suggest you let them both see the notes. Don't expect much original input from Bob, but Livvy's often got a useful contribution. Just don't let her have her head!'

'No,' she agreed, a little bleakly, he thought. 'Thanks. I'll read this while I wait for the Fiscal and rough out a plan of action to offer her.'

Strang got up. 'Sounds good. Best of luck.' He smiled at her, and got a wan smile in return.

He felt sorry for her. It was going to be tough, this one. He should be relieved he was out of it but as he drove to Lochinver he felt a pang of regret, like an old warhorse being taken back to the stable when the smell of battle is in the air.

The door to the sitting room was thrown open violently and Sean Reynolds erupted into the sitting room. His mother Shirley, sitting dozing over a magazine, jumped with a startled cry.

'Have you heard what they're saying?' he raged. 'Such lies, so ignorant!'

'No, I haven't heard. How could I have?' Shirley tried to speak very, very calmly. It was always the best way to cope with Sean in one of his rages, but it wasn't easy, with her heart racing.

'They're saying that girl has been killed by a wolf, just because they found her in the pine woods. It's total nonsense, of course, but it's pernicious – people are so stupid that they'll believe any sort of rumour someone wants to put about.'

Shirley gripped her hands together to stop them shaking. 'Are-are you telling me the girl – Danni – are you saying she's been found dead?'

'Of course that's what I'm saying. But it wasn't a wolf that killed her – I absolutely know it wasn't! How could anyone possibly think that?'

'Then why—' she began, just as Maia appeared in the doorway. Her pale face was suffused with colour and Shirley realised with astonishment that her quiet, rather bloodless daughter-in-law seemed to have been transformed into an avenging fury.

'What the hell have you done?' she shouted. 'You and your bloody stupid obsession. It's all over the Internet, apparently. Not a very good advertisement for what we've spent all this time planning. If you weren't keeping a wolf on the estate this wouldn't be happening. So where is it?'

'Maia, it's not true what they're saying. Wolves don't attack people – it's a complete myth! You know that!'

'I don't, really. Maybe they do and maybe they don't. I only know what you've told me. I asked you, where is it?'

So, Maia had suspected what he was doing, just as Shirley had, but each had chosen to pretend they hadn't. And she'd never forgive herself if this girl had been savaged to death because she'd ignored her son's infatuation with his dangerous toy.

Sean tried to bluster. 'I don't know what you mean—' But his wife's voice was like a whiplash.

'Forget that. Shall I tell you what's going to happen? The police will come with dogs and guns. It won't take them long and your precious wolf will be shot.'

He flinched as if he'd been struck. 'No!'

But she went mercilessly on, 'And then you'll be arrested and charged with manslaughter, not just keeping a lethal pet. You're such a fool.'

Shirley had often wondered what Maia really felt about her husband but she would have preferred not to witness it being spelt out quite so brutally. All those years of perfect calm, with this seething under the surface – the most dangerous volcanoes were the quiescent ones that suddenly blew off the whole top of the mountain. Sean deserved no mercy, but he was her son and she loved him, whatever he had done.

There had never been any point in trying to get him to confess to a lie. You just had to proceed as if he had. 'The best thing,' she said gently, 'would be if you got the animal under control before the police find it. Do you know where it is?'

Sean's head drooped. 'Roughly,' he muttered.

'Is there somewhere you can put it safely?'

'There's a cage that's a sort of den for them. They don't roam very far.'

Shirley's heart gave another lurch. Maia said with quiet fury, 'Dear God – a breeding pair! Were you planning on a wolf pack, that no one would notice you had?'

'If I'd got the land I'd needed, it wouldn't have been a problem,' Sean burst out, then seeing the looks on the women's faces, stopped. 'What?'

'I really, really wouldn't say that to the police, if I were you,' Maia said. 'A little decent regret over what happened to Danni might be in order. Then hand them over before they force the issue.'

Sean looked shrunken, defeated. 'All right. I'll do that. But that's just not what happened.'

He went towards the door that was still standing open just as the doorbell rang. They all stiffened, sharing the same thought, but then it opened and Ben Linton's voice called, 'Hello?' as he stepped into the hall.

'In here,' Maia called.

He came into the sitting room. 'I just wanted to tell you the police have arrived – you probably heard the chopper. DI French has rented an extra pod and I saw her in. She's at the community hall now, but the other two coming from Edinburgh will be late. I've offered to get her some supplies in before the shop closes.'

After all the high drama, it felt almost comically prosaic. No one said anything and Linton looked from one to the other, puzzled. 'Is that all right?'

'Yes, of course,' Maia said awkwardly. 'It's just, you know, Danni – such a terrible, terrible thing.'

Shirley noticed he looked tired; it must have been an effort to sound blandly professional because now his face sagged. 'Oh yes, Danni,' he said heavily. 'I can't really believe it.'

What would happen now, Shirley wondered? Would Sean apologise – and how could you apologise for your pet killing the man's girlfriend? Should she say something? Would Maia?

But Linton was going on, 'There's a team working at Danni's house. They seem to be thinking that's where she was actually killed.'

'Killed – there?' Shirley said sharply.

'Well, they don't know yet, of course.'

'But they found her in the woods, didn't they?'

'Yes, but she'd been moved, apparently.'

Maia put in, 'Have you seen stuff on the Internet about it? Something about wolves?'

Linton looked at her in dismay. 'Oh no! I thought we'd stopped that. There's one of the searchers, a silly kid who'd heard wild rumours and got the wrong end of the stick. We had a message go round all the volunteers' pods to tell them it was nonsense, but of course their little thumbs get busy within seconds. I'll ask them all to retweet the denial but it's going to mean an awful lot of bad publicity.'

'I'm so sorry all this has landed on you,' Maia said, with a pointed look at her husband.

Sean, his head coming up, suddenly looked like his old self, confident, contemptuous. 'It's so ridiculous, the ideas ignorant people get. We'll have to use the media, then, to get it across that this is rubbish.'

'Yes, I suppose so,' Linton said. 'Well, if you'll excuse me . . .'

'Of course,' Maia said warmly. 'Thanks for all you're doing, Ben. See to it you get a bit of time off – I can cope with anything that crops up.'

Was that the concern of a good boss for an employee, or was there more to it than that, Shirley wondered as Linton left. With what she'd discovered about her son's marriage, it wouldn't be surprising if Maia was looking elsewhere.

Sean said, 'I told you it was nonsense. It would save a lot of trouble if you actually listened to me sometimes.'

A full-blown domestic wouldn't help anything. Shirley said hurriedly, 'Can you catch the wolves now, even with the police around?'

Sean stared at her, and she suddenly realised that Maia wasn't with her either on this one. 'Of course not,' Sean said roughly. 'Are you daft? They've been there for a couple of months and all there's been is rumours. Keeping out of the way is what they're good at – we can leave them to it.'

Maia said more gently, 'The publicity would be really bad for the project, Shirley. We can sort things out later, when this is over.

'I'm going to go and start the supper. Sean, get your mum a drink. We'd better brace ourselves for lots of questions now the police have arrived.'

Left on her own, Shirley put her head in her hands. It hadn't been a wolf that had killed Danni. But right at the start Sean had said, 'I absolutely know it wasn't.' How could he have been so sure?

CHAPTER TWELVE

The Procurator Fiscal arrived shortly after DCI Strang had left. DI French was nervous, but while Fiona Murdoch, middle-aged and grey-haired, looked serious she had a sympathetic expression.

'Will you want to see the body first?' French said. 'It's on an old Forestry Commission plantation. I've transport waiting to take us up there, though we'll have to walk the last bit – they're checking for wheel tracks.'

'That's fine – I came equipped.' Murdoch indicated her stout walking boots. 'Fill me in as we go.' As they walked to the car, Murdoch gave her an understanding smile. 'Lousy part of the job, isn't it?'

DI French nodded fervently. As they drove up, she briefed Murdoch on the background, including the involvement of the Met with the victim's aunt.

She stared at her. 'The Met? Wow!'

French gave a short laugh. 'You don't expect that somewhere like this, do you? I think there's a lot more to this than meets the eye.'

'So – your plans?'

This was the awkward part. It was ridiculous to feel embarrassed by association as she explained the problem with Strang, especially since there wasn't, as yet, any stain on Ranald Sinclair's character. But she did.

'A close friend?' Murdoch said.

'They were friends in the army a long time ago. This was the first time they'd met since then, and he's said he has reservations now.'

'But he's right off the case?'

'Yes, I'm in charge. For the first time, actually!' she said with a nervous laugh. 'But he's following up the case the Met was interested in, so he's still in the area.'

'Not here in Inverbeg, I trust?'

'No, in Lochinver. Oh, here we are.'

They were dropped just short of the turn-off from the harbour road, where the track was barred and a constable was waiting with a clipboard, noting names and times. He indicated the lower side of the track, where a line of tapes on poles had been set up.

Murdoch seemed impressed. 'Looks efficient. Are these local officers?'

'The constable is. The organisation is all through the SRCS squad that came up with me from Edinburgh. It's routine for them. Look, there they are.' She pointed.

The light was fading fast, the livid clouds low overhead. They could hear a generator as they drew nearer and the arc lights, placed strategically around the tent, lit up the dark figures of SOCOs moving about like characters on a spotlit stage. It was hard to believe it was real, that it wasn't just a scene from a crime series; French almost expected someone to step out of the encroaching darkness to shout, 'Cut!'

Murdoch turned to glance at her as they set off up the slope. 'All right?'

French nodded. 'I think so. You must be used to it.'

'Yes, I am. It's the job. But every time . . .' She grimaced as she greeted the crime scene manager and went into the tent and French followed her, nails biting into the palm of her hand as she stepped inside, steeling herself to look at Danielle Maitland.

The glassy eyes, the waxen skin with the pierced eyebrow, the black, clotted blood at the neck like a macabre necklace, the T-shirt so stiffened with dried blood it looked like cardboard: mercifully, under the theatrical lighting she looked unreal, like some actor in Grand Guignol. The raw immediacy of accidents in Traffic had been harder to deal with – much harder – but French was glad enough to turn her attention to the pathologist instead.

He was examining the body but as yet he didn't have much to say that wasn't immediately apparent. On the way back Murdoch said, 'It's a gutter trick, that one. Any pub brawls that you know of?'

'She'd a row with a boyfriend in the pub last Saturday apparently – the story was she hit him. Top of our list at the moment.' Murdoch nodded approval and she went on, 'We can go straight to where they're working on the victim's house if you want. They've got a tent up beside it now.'

Again there was an officer taking names at the entrance. French hung back to let the Fiscal go inside; she could view the scene herself later. Murdoch didn't interrupt the workers, standing on the threshold scanning the scene with a brisk, practised appraisal.

'Nasty,' she said, pulling a face as she came out. 'Very nasty. But I've got a sense of it now. If they can rustle up a cup of coffee for us back at the hall, we could go through what you have in mind to take it on from here.'

The questions Murdoch asked as French laid out her plans were searching, but not intimidating. She put in a few suggestions of her own, then said she would have to get back to Inverness.

'I hope you haven't found that threatening,' she said. 'I know it can be hard to have someone from the outside interrogating your processes.'

'Not at all,' French said. 'I've genuinely found it very helpful – sharpened up my ideas.'

'Good. Keep in close touch.'

French waved her off regretfully. She'd felt safer with her support. Now she was on her own.

It had been a wearisome drive, particularly after darkness fell on the small and twisting roads.

It was gone eight o'clock and DC Livvy Murray was aware she should be pushing on to Inverbeg, but she was also aware of a gaping hole where her stomach used to be and what she'd heard about Inverbeg didn't suggest McDonalds would have reached it yet.

The chippie van by the side of the road in a lay-by looked like an oasis in the desert, but stinking out DI French's immaculate car wouldn't be a good way to begin what was going to be a close relationship – very close, if they were having to share a room – and she settled with a bad grace for a cold pork pie and a bar of chocolate. She'd fancied some crisps, but she didn't think she could eat them without leaving crumbs and she could imagine the look of distaste on French's face when she saw them.

At last she saw the sign to Inverbeg, pointing down a road so small that she couldn't quite see how a car could fit on to it at all, let alone pass another car. She'd been on Highland roads before, but never one like this. She gulped and then embarked on the journey from hell.

Perhaps it was lucky it was so dark; she couldn't see how deep the drops were as she rounded hairpin bends where the road clung to the edge of ravines, but she had to stop herself shutting her eyes as she crawled up slopes so steep that you had to take on trust that there was a road on the other side. The only mercy was that she drove for miles without seeing another car.

Then, just as she approached a right-angled bend, the sky lit up with headlamps. She gasped, braked, stalled, and saw a car swing round straight at her. Then, swerving into a passing-place she hadn't noticed right on the crown of the corner, it passed her without even slowing down.

It took her a moment to stop trembling enough to drive on but the worst, she found, was over now. There were lights showing from houses dotted about on either side, then a sign saying Inverbeg, and she turned off the main road into the centre of what they probably called a village – at least there was a pub and a community hall with several police cars parked outside.

As Murray got out of the car on shaking legs, her eye was drawn to a patch of bright light high on the rising ground behind. As she looked, there were odd flashes – photographing the body, maybe? She could see, too, the cluster of geodesic domes, looking bizarrely futuristic in this ancient landscape. There were lights and a tent around one of the cottages on the little hill on the other side of the road too.

There was a surprising number of young people in the hall when she went in – half a dozen grouped near the front door, three at tables talking to constables and one, a girl who looked as if she had been crying, being interviewed by DI French. Murray went to stand where French could see her, but didn't interrupt.

French registered her presence with a quick nod, then said, 'Well, Holly, I don't think there's anything else I want to ask you. Is there anything you want to tell me?'

Biting her lip, the girl shook her head.

'So you understand now, yes? And there'll be no more tweets that upset everyone unnecessarily?'

'Yes. Sorry,' Holly mumbled.

'Then you are free to have your parents fetch you whenever they can.'

The girl was on her feet before she even said, 'Thank you.'

DI French beckoned Murray forward. 'Oh dear,' she said. 'That felt cruel – as if Bambi was struggling to escape with me holding on to one leg. Come on, sit down. How was your journey?'

Holly with her big brown eyes and long skinny legs looked exactly like that. Murray couldn't help smiling, though she'd come in with her hackles ready to rise. 'Long, but no actual problems. What had Bambi done?'

French sighed. 'The victim was killed by a broken bottle slashed across her throat, but that little airhead tweeted that she'd been killed by a wolf.'

Murray looked blank. 'A wolf?'

'There's a rumour that there's a wolf loose on the estate.'

'Why?'

'Oh, DCI Strang thinks it could be true.'

Murray, a city girl through and through, was appalled. 'Just – wild? What would anyone do that for? It's crazy!'

'Well, some environmentalists want it. Wolves allegedly avoid people so you wouldn't even know they were there. Anyway, it's not relevant. I'm prioritising interviewing the kids who are volunteers on the rewilding programme – the oldest is only twenty, and I want to let them go before mums and dads scream about police brutality.

'I'll carry on here, but you'd better settle in and get something to eat first. I've ordered in some frozen stuff – there's a microwave in the pods. They're very adequate and since they'd one that wasn't taken we don't have to share.'

Murray's 'That's good!' was perhaps more heartfelt than it should have been because French said drily, 'Indeed. Then I'll see you back here. PS Erskine shouldn't be long now, so if you see him before I do pass the message on. OK?'

PS Erskine was, in fact, just getting out of his car as Murray was walking across towards the pods. She grinned.

'Bet you stopped off to get something to eat,' she said.

He was burly and grey-haired, looking as if he'd always taken care of the inner man and sounding faintly defensive as he said, 'Well, yes – chippie on the outskirts of Inverness. You didn't?'

'Just a rubbish pork pie so I don't mind having to eat another supper that French has laid on for us to microwave in our pods. You'll be stuffed.'

'Don't mind that. Long time since Inverness. Nice of her to bother – I can think of plenty DIs who wouldn't.'

'Yes, well, I suppose so,' Murray said grudgingly. 'But I bet she's chosen something terribly healthy. Something with spinach.'

In fact, it was rather a good lasagne and the pod was really cool. But as she made coffee she still felt like a cat with its fur being rubbed up the wrong way. She'd rather been counting on feeling overworked and ill-used and she'd nothing to complain about. Less than nothing, really. Apart from the fact that people who always got everything right were really hard to take.

Hattie Sinclair was in the sitting room, waiting on tenterhooks for Ranald to come in. When he appeared, he was looking worn out, his brows furrowed.

Hattie got up. 'Sit down and I'll bring your drink. You're late – did you get caught up in something?'

'You may not have noticed but I've got a business to run, and if you waste most of the day tramping round to no purpose you've got to make up the time somehow.' He sat down, saying, 'Has Kelso gone, then?'

'He's certainly left here. When I did the supper delivery to the pods there were police at the community hall, so he could be there. I heard the helicopter, so I suppose the woman who's taking over will have come with it.'

He took the glass from her and drank half of it. 'What is all that about? He was very offhand when I spoke to him this afternoon – I was a bit taken aback.'

Hattie had scooped ice cubes into her own glass and poured in gin. When he said that she topped it up a bit more, added tonic and took a swig before she sat down.

'They're not allowed to run an investigation if they know someone who's involved, Ran.'

Sinclair stared at her. 'Involved? Me? Oh, don't be ridiculous. Clearly it's the boyfriend, the "I'm-a-lumberjack" one – you saw they'd a real barney on Saturday night. Kelso would know that too. I just hope he explains that to the woman who's going to be in charge and we can get this wrapped up quickly. If she's the hysterical type she could muck our lives up for weeks.'

'I don't know what he's likely to tell her. I asked him if he could explain the sort of person you are – like a character reference, you know—'

He erupted. Hattie had a feeling that he'd been waiting for an excuse and she'd just handed it to him on a plate.

'Character witness for me? Why the hell should you think I need one? This is absolutely nothing to do with me. But you've put it into his head now, haven't you?' He glared at her, his eyes bulging with temper. 'He'll tell her there must be something suspicious I've done if you're trying to whitewash me. They'll be going through the bins to see if I've chucked out any bloodstained clothing lately. Oh, well done, sweetie! You've surpassed yourself with this.'

She'd tears in her eyes but she blinked them away fiercely. She wasn't going to back off until she'd said what needed to be said. 'Kelso wouldn't do it, anyway. He said she'd make her own mind up and wouldn't be influenced by his opinion. But you'd better realise that naturally you're going to come under suspicion – you and Sean too. You've been quarrelling like dogs over a bone about buying the croft. Danni was being difficult and it wouldn't take a great detective to work out that it could suit someone if she was out of the way. Presumably it'll go to her father now. You'd been in touch with him, hadn't you?'

Sinclair got up and went to the drinks cupboard to refill his glass. With his back to her he said, 'Well, I suppose so.'

Suddenly she felt cold. 'Oh God, Ran, you haven't got in touch with him again today?'

He swung round. 'Not "in touch" like that – not the way you mean. I just dropped him a note offering my condolences. Well, I'd met him, the girl was staying with us – perfectly appropriate.'

'I hope the police see it that way. But they'll soon find out that Danni was bidding up the price and Sean was going to top any offer you made, and it won't look good if you were trying already to go round the back.'

Sinclair's face was purple now. 'Are you suggesting it was me bumped her off? That's a nice attitude for a loyal wife. Let's just hope the police are a little more rational and objective, otherwise I'm done for.'

'I don't mean that, of course I don't,' Hattie cried. 'But with all these things going on – what happened to her aunt, and the car fire, and now this – people are going to talk.'

'That's just stirring up trouble.' He tossed back what was in the glass. 'I'm going to the pub to find someone to talk to who isn't a conspiracy theorist.'

It wouldn't do him any good to drink all night on an empty stomach. 'Have something to eat first,' she urged – to a slammed door.

When DC Murray and PS Erskine returned to the hall, most of the young volunteers had gone.

DI French was interviewing an earnest-looking youth with glasses and a bad case of acne and there were two more waiting, a boy and a girl, staring at the floor.

French saw them arrive and broke off. She switched off the little recorder lying on the table and said to them, 'You were quick. Well done. Now, if you can talk to the last two, we'll have cleared all of them to go whenever they want to.' Then she switched on the recorder and went back to the interview.

He must have something interesting to say, Murray thought, as she gestured to the girl to join her at a table. She took her name – Chloe – and age – 17 – and details, checking her out at the same time. She didn't look too traumatised by Danni's death, more excited by the fuss, and it wasn't a surprise when she said, 'I knew who she was, of course, but I didn't have much to do with her. She wasn't, like, my type, if you know what I mean.'

Chloe's 'type' was expressed in designer jeans and the sort of expensive hoodie top that suggested she was rehearsing for being the yummy mummy she would be in a few years' time. She was very assured.

'And what type was Danni?' Murray asked, with some interest.

Chloe wrinkled her neat little nose. 'She was always, kind of, causing trouble. Really, really loud and Kasper –

you know, the barman? He was forever having to shut her up – threatened to throw her out, a few times. And there were these two guys, she was always, like, goading them – you know, playing off one against the other?'

It was clearly a Neighbours-style question and she ignored it. 'Names?'

'Ben Linton and Joe Dundas. Well, Ben's fine but Joe's a real roughneck? He'd a barney with Danni on Saturday night – I think she slapped him because they'd been outside and she came back in and then he did after, with this cut on his cheek. So . . .'

Murray had not taken to her. '"So . . ." what?' she asked, unhelpfully.

The look Chloe gave her suggested that Murray wasn't her 'type' either. 'I'm not saying anything, except it's interesting. I didn't, like, see Joe prowling around, or anything?'

'Did you see Danni at all after Saturday evening?'

'No. We'd Sunday off. But nothing really happens around here, and we just sort of chilled in each other's pods, and then yesterday with the storm we'd planning meetings and a lecture about rewilding? Today we were out in all that rain doing planting stuff. Last night I was too tired even to go to the pub. It's really exhausting and my hands are wrecked.'

She held out plump little hands that did indeed show the evidence of hard work – first time in her life, probably, Murray reckoned.

'Why did you come?' she asked.

'Oh, all that eco stuff, you know? It's what you have to do, if you're young. We'll be around having to pick up the pieces after you lot have gone.'

It was a bit of a shock to realise that she was actually old, in Chloe's eyes, but the girl was breezing on, 'And my dad said I had to do it, so I had something to talk about in my interview for uni? I think it's probably pointless, all this, actually.'

'Right,' Murray said slowly. 'Now, is there anything else that you think we should know?'

Chloe thought for a moment, then shook her head. 'Can I go now? I guess no one will be finishing the second week? My dad'll be wanting some money back, I can tell you.'

That was how you got to be rich, of course. 'Yes, that's fine,' Murray said. 'I've got your contact number if we need anything more.'

The youth Erskine had been talking to was waiting for her and they went out together. Clearly he'd had even less to say than Chloe, but French was still talking. Murray went across to join Erskine.

'Get anything?' she said.

Erskine shrugged. 'Said he was sorry Danni had been killed, but that was about it.'

'That was nice of him. Chloe wasn't, as far as I could tell. Danni was the "type" you didn't have to care about.' She indicated quote marks. 'And it seems it's only to be expected that it would be a peasant like Joe Dundas that killed her. Slighted boyfriend, I gather.'

They heard French say, 'Thank you, Jonathan. That's been very helpful,' as she switched off the recording and they stood up. 'If we need this, we'll get in touch with you at your home address for a statement.'

The hall was empty after he had gone, apart from a uniform working in one corner. French came over and perched on the end of the table.

'Right. That's it for tonight. I expect you're tired – I certainly am. Did you get anything from those two?'

Erskine shook his head but Murray précised what Chloe had said, adding, 'Prejudice more than anything else, I'd guess.'

French frowned. 'It fits with what DCI Strang said, though – he was in the pub that night and Danni did have a big bust-up with Dundas. We'll have him first up for interviews tomorrow, but I think you should both pack it in. Full briefing at 08.00, right?'

'Ma'am,' they both said.

Erskine yawned hugely as they walked along to the pods. 'Thank the lord she didn't want us struggling on to the small hours. I like my bed. That's me here. Night!'

Murray walked on, seething quietly. She'd suggested that Chloe shouldn't be taken too seriously and she'd as good as got slapped down and then told to go to bed. French hadn't shared what it was that Jonathan had told her; unlike Bob, she'd have been happy to work on late into the night, just so she'd be in on the action.

She looked back over her shoulder. French had come out of the hall and was walking up the road to the cottage where they were working. She must be going to speak to the SOCOs and she'd get a report on what they'd been finding.

Curiosity was one of Murray's defining characteristics and she hated the thought of having to wait till the morning – and of not being sure how much French would decide to tell them, even then. It wasn't at all the way she'd become used to working with Strang.

* * *

Mrs Munro had welcomed DCI Strang warmly when he arrived back at the guest house, adding, 'But of course I'm really sorry about the reason – that poor wee girl!'

Inwardly cursing the efficiency of their news network, he said hastily, 'Oh, I'm not involved with that. They've brought someone in from Edinburgh.'

Mrs Munro had looked intrigued but not entirely convinced. She was clearly longing to ask more – straight from the horse's mouth was gold dust in local currency – but he must have looked forbidding enough to stop her and she said instead, 'Right. I was just wondering how long you'll be staying? I've had two other bookings come in this afternoon and I've only got the three bedrooms.'

His heart had sunk. No prizes for guessing who her new guests would be – he should have thought of that. He said quickly, 'Just this one night. I'll be getting on my way early tomorrow morning – no need to worry about breakfast.'

'Oh goodness me, you'll need something! I'll leave out a tray—'

'That's very kind, but please don't bother. There is one thing, though – could I ask you not to mention that I'm a police officer to anyone? A homicide investigation is very sensitive.'

Strang could see her disappointment but she said, 'No, of course not.' He just hoped she meant it.

He'd thanked her and gone up to his room. He needed a new plan, fast. There were – what? Half-a-dozen B&Bs in Lochinver? Even if he found one that hadn't been unexpectedly booked up, there would be prying eyes everywhere. Strang's previous cases had given him a high media profile and a number of crime journalists could probably recognise him on sight – an extra complication.

He was reluctant to leave while he still had questions to ask about Flora Maitland's death, and JB had indicated that she'd be reassured to know he was on hand. He needed accommodation where he could, if necessary, meet the team without being outed.

He called up Angie Andrews and explained the situation. 'Ideally, some small self-catering place,' he suggested. 'Anywhere nearby, as long as it's isolated.'

Angie said, as she always did, 'No problem. Leave it with me.'

He took her at her word. He'd other things to think about. It would now presumably be William Maitland's choice about authorising the release of Flora's papers. Could he go tomorrow to speak to him in Glasgow? You had to be ultra-sensitive with the newly bereaved and Maitland hadn't been keen on talking to him in the first place. On the other hand, he owed them an apology for failing to keep that appointment and they might see things differently if it could lead to justice for their daughter.

Which it might. Maybe Danni's death was just the result of a lover's quarrel, but he still wasn't convinced the two deaths weren't linked. If he could just unravel the story that lay behind Flora Maitland's death, he had a gut feeling that it would point the finger directly at whoever had killed her niece.

CHAPTER THIRTEEN

When she got back to the pod, DC Murray made coffee and settled down to check the Internet. The news channels' reports were pretty discreet but Facebook and Twitter were awash with the wolf story – ideal headlines for the tabloids, who would only report at the end of the article that the story had been denied.

It was a shock that Strang seemed to think there might be a wolf out there, though. Maybe it hadn't actually done anything, but she for one wouldn't do a Little Red Riding Hood in these woods – not that she'd have been likely to anyway, even if the most exotic wildlife she was likely to encounter was a red squirrel.

Murray clicked off her phone, thinking about French being out there, doing interesting stuff. She was feeling restless; she wasn't ready to turn in.

You didn't have to go to bed just because Nanny told you to. She'd seen the inn just along the road – it wouldn't be shut quite yet. She'd have time enough to get a quick drink and see if 'Jonathan' was there. If she could get him to tell her what he'd told French earlier, she wouldn't need to wait for the briefing to find out. Not that she'd tell French then if he did; she'd just sit there feeling one-up and smug.

Murray put on her jacket and went out. She was moving quickly, she told herself, because there was a smirr of rain, not because she was afraid French would spot her disobeying what had felt like instructions. She glanced at Erskine's pod as she passed – no lights showing. Teacher's pet!

It was late and the bar wasn't busy. There were a few folk who looked like locals, one a tall man by the bar who held himself very straight and was laying forth in a posh voice; definitely the worse for wear, she reckoned. At the far end she could see Chloe at a table in an animated conversation with a couple of boys, but it looked as if most of the youngsters she'd seen earlier had either left immediately or hadn't felt like socialising.

Murray couldn't see anyone looking like Chloe's 'roughneck', but Jonathan was sitting at the farthest corner of the room alone with a beer, reading a book. Ideal!

She paid for her lager and went over. 'Mind if I join you?'

Startled, Jonathan looked up and blinked. 'Er . . . no, of course not.'

He even half-stood up – when was the last time anyone had done that? Murray sat down and smiled encouragingly. 'I'm Livvy. I know you're Jonathan because I saw you talking to my inspector this afternoon – I'm a detective constable.'

He set aside his book politely. 'That must be very interesting.'

She hadn't time for small talk. 'Did you know Danni well? It must be hard for you.'

'Of course, I suppose . . .' He was clearly hovering between honesty and convention. 'It's horrible what happened but actually I hardly knew her. She sort of picked people out and I wasn't one of them.'

Murray homed in on the name Chloe had mentioned and French had also recognised. 'Do you know Joe Dundas?' she asked, hoping that would prompt him to repeat his evidence.

'Oh yes, he was a mate of hers. I knew him through the project, of course. He's OK.'

Wrong tack, and time was running out. 'DI French found what you had to say very helpful, didn't she?' she tried.

A faint shade of pink crept into his cheeks. 'Oh, that's good.'

And for my next trick – I will pull the tooth right out! 'We're always grateful for useful information,' she said. 'I wonder if we'll be going off tomorrow to follow up what you told her?'

'I don't think so, really,' Jonathan said. 'She said it was interesting but probably not immediately relevant at this stage.'

As if that wasn't provoking enough, the barman called, 'Time you were drinking up, ladies and gents. Closing in five minutes.'

What did she have to lose? He'd be leaving tomorrow and anyway wouldn't even think it was strange she hadn't been told, likely. 'What exactly did you say?' she said bluntly.

'Oh, it was just about Sean – you know? He runs all this. Coming back from the harbour we go past the end of the track where they found, well . . . her.' His prominent Adam's apple bobbed up and down as he swallowed. 'I've been here a couple of weeks and I've noticed him turning along there sometimes. Today it was just for a few minutes – he got back more or less as we did. That was all, really.' He stood up and finished his beer. 'We'd better go – Kasper gets stroppy if we hang about.'

Murray followed suit. 'Nice to speak to you, Jonathan. On your way home tomorrow?'

'That's right. Sean's packing in the project meantime. Thank you for your company.'

As they went their separate ways – Jonathan holding the door open for Murray – she was thinking what a pity it was that he wasn't staying longer. She'd have liked to find out more about the set-up and the personalities involved.

Probably what he'd told French wasn't very significant anyway, but it did make her wonder why 'Sean' would turn off down the track 'just for a minute'. Taking a look at something? What?

Murray got back without being spotted. The cars had mostly gone but there were lights on in the hall; French was probably still there. Then she heard the sound of the helicopter arriving – the SOCOs must be packing it in for the night.

She was still thinking about what Jonathan had said. If Sean was running the project, was he the landowner? If there really was a wolf on the estate, it could hardly be there without him knowing about it – indeed, without him having brought it in. Maybe it lived around there. Could you just check on a wolf like that? Wouldn't it move around?

But Danni hadn't been killed by a wolf, so what significance did the body being found there have? It was still on her mind as she went to bed. It would be interesting to see what French made of it in the briefing tomorrow.

It was one of those autumn days that arrives like an unexpected present. A sharp frost had made the air crisp and fresh, catching your throat as you inhaled it, and there was barely a breath of wind. The tide was rolling in lazily; the sun was barely visible, just coming up through a haze of gold, and the Suilven 'Sugar Loaf' looming up behind Lochinver was sporting a small, white cloud like a frilly mob cap on top.

What a day it would be for climbing, DCI Strang thought with a sigh, leaving Mrs Munro's at first light to be on the safe side. There were two other cars parked outside the house and as he drove through the village he noticed another B&B with three. Of course, they might only belong to tourists inspired with a sudden desire for a Highland break, but it didn't seem likely.

Angie had performed her usual magic and now he keyed the address she'd given him into the satnav. There was a code for the key box at the door, so he could go straight there now.

The views out over the water were spectacular as he drove along, the peaks a phalanx of giants shading from dark grey to palest mauve and the rough terrain lush with every possible shade of green. As he followed the A837 towards Loch Assynt there was hardly another car on the road and apart from sheep with relaxed ideas about suitable moments to cross it, there wasn't much to take his mind off the problems in hand.

He'd heard the chopper coming in the previous night, no doubt fetching poor Danni Maitland to take her second-last journey. The SOCOs would still work today but they'd be coming by road; Police Scotland had only one helicopter and its use was strictly limited.

How was Rachel French feeling, now she was in post? Nervous, he guessed, preparing for the morning briefing. Pointless to speculate on what had emerged in the initial interviews and it wasn't really his business – as if that made any difference!

And how was she getting on with Livvy? Strang hadn't always managed to convince her to share her ideas before she acted on them, and he did worry that she could be feeling she'd something to prove.

It was about seven miles further on that the satnav directed Strang off the A837 on to a single-track road for a mile before he arrived at a tiny cottage, no more than a but and ben, set back from the road and looking out over a lochan – an idyllic setting. Revamped for the holiday-letting market, it had a well-equipped kitchen at one end of the living room and the bedroom had a smart little shower room attached. Angie had triumphed again. It even had a 'welcome' pack with basic essentials and a friendly note wishing him a wonderful holiday. He read it with a wry smile.

He dropped off his bag then made himself coffee and toast. He should be safe enough to come and go here; surely media interest would die down once it was clear the wolf story was nonsense; no one was likely to link it to a death declared accidental six months before.

Now Strang had to decide if he should drive down to Glasgow unannounced. He could be there, with luck, before midday and he could be back here late afternoon. If he was on the doorstep, it would be more difficult for Maitland to refuse to see him.

He should tell Angus about the new situation and Rachel would need to know where he was. If he left that till later in the day, she'd probably tell him how things were going.

As if it was any of his business.

DI Rachel French was, indeed, feeling nervous this morning. She wasn't happy; when she'd replied to Murray's suggestion that Chloe had been prejudiced by saying that Dundas would be top of the interview list, she'd realised from her reaction that it had sounded like a snub. And then she'd suggested they go off duty and Murray had looked huffy as she left.

OK, she was way too touchy but it was French's job to make this work. She should have thought of giving them Strang's notes to read through last night; it would have saved time this morning and might have appeased Murray too, but she'd had so much to think about last night that she'd slipped up. Must try harder.

She'd been able to see inside Danni's house before the SOCOs packed up and she still felt queasy, thinking about it now. There was one thing certain; the killer had to have been bloodstained. Today when a small team came back, they'd be dismantling the drains in the shower room, but prints on the shower tap were just smudges. In the two rooms, there were so many that it was all but meaningless. They'd found her mobile but nothing on it looked significant. They'd homed in on the broken glass but it was little more than the base and they got nothing from that. There was no sign of the rest of the bottle, or the cap.

That was significant; the set-up suggested the attack could have been made in rage or frustration, but if so, the killer had calmed down afterwards to cover his tracks. On the other hand, there was nothing to say that he hadn't been cool and calm all along. Not a lot to go on.

The pathologist had sent in an interim report, which was, as usual, very vague about time of death – too many variables – and the weather had been so wretched that the forest track, where they might have hoped for tyre marks, was a sea of mud, which the Mountain Rescue jeep had churned up even more, bringing in the equipment to secure the site. They were able to say that the three trees had fallen in the storm the previous day, after the body had been placed beneath them, concealed in deep bracken.

The scientific stuff never gave you as much as you hoped it would and she was frowning as she went into the community hall. DCS Borthwick's phone call first thing this morning hadn't helped: she'd been noticeably twitchy, particularly about media coverage, and when French told her that no journalists had arrived yet, she said sharply, 'When they do, it's "no comment", Rachel, except to reinforce what was said last night. Tell them that all further statements will come from here. You can't stop them talking to locals, but it should discourage them from hanging about.'

At least French had been able to tell her she'd given all the young volunteers permission to leave, which definitely got her brownie points. She'd said, too, how helpful the Procurator Fiscal had been, though JB hadn't been much interested.

'That's good,' she said indifferently, 'but in fact we have a legal arrangement that means oversight by the Fiscal Service can be done here where they understand how the SRCS operates. Now, keep me in the picture and remember Kelso's there for support.'

Which left French feeling even more inadequate. She'd been looking forward to dealing with Fiona Murdoch who'd been so sympathetic and had left her confident that she was making a good, professional start. It would be pathetic to feel abandoned, so she didn't. Of course not.

When she walked into the community hall, PS Erskine was there already, chatting to four uniforms. French didn't recognise any of them; nearby forces must be rotating the officers being sent here, so she wouldn't be able to rely on any sort of continuity.

A sergeant came forward with a message that the SOCOs should be arriving late morning to continue investigations and hoped to have them completed that day.

French thanked him. 'And I'll want door-to-door enquiries around the local area – can you get on with that right away and then report back, please?'

'I'm not familiar with the area, ma'am, but I'll try to find someone to give us the locations of the outlying houses,' he said, going back to the others while Erskine came to join her. There was no sign of Murray as yet, but it wasn't quite eight o'clock.

They went back to the table in the corner and she picked up a file lying there and took out a pile of scribbled sheets.

'Read through this, Bob. It's the DCI's notes on the background from when he was staying here last week, and bringing us up to date on operations yesterday. It's very helpful – if you can read his writing.'

Erskine looked at it and grinned. 'Should have been a doctor,' he said, settling down to read as Murray came in.

'Morning, Livvy,' French said with what she hoped didn't sound like determined cheerfulness. 'Sleep all right?'

'Yes thanks.'

She ploughed on, 'Weather's more what we had in mind today. It's very pretty here on a day like this.'

'Mmm,' Murray said. 'What are you reading, Bob?'

'I'll give it to you when I've finished. It's notes from DCI Strang.'

'Really,' she said coldly. 'What would you like me to do, ma'am?'

'Wait patiently' probably wasn't the right response. 'Joe Dundas is at the top of the suspects list,' French said. 'He lives somewhere near Drumbeg – that's the next village. Ben Linton will have to be questioned too, but he lives right here so we can get him any time.'

'Does that mean you think it's likely to be Dundas, ma'am?' Murray said.

Annoyingly, that was right; it was exactly what she thought – indeed, fervently hoped – but it would have been more professional not to sound as if she was making an assumption.

'That's just a preliminary move, on the evidence of their quarrel,' she said, knowing she sounded defensive.

Erskine, having finished reading the notes, held them out to Murray. As Murray grabbed them and started reading, French asked Erskine what he'd made of them.

He looked a little nonplussed. 'Well – very helpful, of course.'

'Any thoughts?'

'Er . . . not really. Just, probably, interview Dundas, like you said.'

It was going to be a waste of time to keep him sitting there. Strang had been right: Erskine was not an ideas man. Reliable, though, he'd said, and now she noticed that the uniforms were in discussion about how to proceed. She heard a woman officer say, 'Surely someone must know.'

'Bob,' she said, 'Can you take over co-ordinating the door-to-door? They don't seem to know how to proceed.'

A look of relief came over his face and he got up. 'Right, boss. I'll get hold of one of the locals and get help to make some sort of map.'

Murray looked up from the notes. 'You could try this Angus Mackenzie, Bob. He seems the helpful type.'

'I'll do that. They can all report back to me and I can sort out what they've got for you, ma'am.'

'Great,' French said. Naturally she was pleased Murray had thought of that. That was the whole idea – working as a team. 'Good thought, Livvy,' she added. And she hadn't sounded patronising, really she hadn't, but she only got a cool nod in return. 'Any ideas, following on from that?'

'Quite a few. The other two the boss seems interested in are Sean Reynolds and Ranald Sinclair. They both seem to be pretty desperate to get the property – they should maybe be in the picture too. And if it was just because Danni dumped Joe, I still don't see why he would set her car on fire.'

'Revenge, maybe?' French said lightly. 'We can't really speculate at this stage. The SOCOs are going to check over the car this morning so they may have something for us later.

'Certainly we'll be interviewing everyone. Meantime . . .'

'It's funny where the body was found,' Murray went on. 'Up in the woods, you know.'

'Yes,' French agreed, but she was left with a feeling that there was more to that remark than met the eye. 'Anyway, let's make a start. We'll have to find out where Dundas lives.'

'Ma'am.' Murray got up and followed her out.

Oh, this was going to be tough. French shouldn't be having to justify herself to her junior – and that 'the boss' had rankled. Erskine had called her 'boss', which she was on this investigation. To Murray, 'the boss' could only be Kelso Strang.

Even the sunshine wasn't going to cheer Murray up. French had said nothing about the interview with Jonathan and she'd pretty much ignored the Reynolds/Sinclair angle. She was viewing the day ahead with no enthusiasm at all.

They were just leaving when an elderly man came hurrying down the hill. He was looking uncertain and they stopped to let him reach them.

'I wonder if you can help me? I've been told I should speak to Detective Inspector French.'

Murray spoke first. 'This is DI French and I'm DC Murray. Did PS Erskine send you?'

It was meant helpfully but it seemed only to make him more confused. 'PS? No, it was just that DCI Strang said I had useful information and I should bring it to you at once.'

Now it was they who were looking confused. French was even looking a little put out and she said sharply, 'DCI Strang? Is he here?'

'No, no,' the man said. 'Look, perhaps I ought to explain. I'm Angus Mackenzie—'

French said, 'Come with me. We'll go back in and find a seat. DC Murray, please can you find out Dundas's details?'

Murray said, 'Yes ma'am,' through gritted teeth. It was like French was deliberately keeping the interesting stuff to herself and though dogsbody jobs were admittedly within her job description, it wasn't the way Strang had treated her recently. She'd worked hard and gained his trust, but now she was back at square one.

She'd better get on with it, though. The only visible activity was a couple of cars being loaded with luggage – the little dears being taken home – but they weren't likely to know an estate labourer's address. Anyway, disclosing that they were interested in Dundas might not be smart. After a moment's thought she went across and walked down the drive leading to Auchinglass House. They'd presumably know where their workers lived.

There were two cars – a Discovery and a BMW 5 Series saloon – parked outside, but when she rang the bell, she got no answer. She rang again, and a half-door opened across a courtyard to one side and a man leant out. He was thickset and almost swarthy, with dark hair that looked as if he hadn't combed it for days and he was scowling as he said, 'What do you want?'

She walked towards him. Offices seemed to have been made out of what must once have been horseboxes, and he hadn't opened the bottom half of the door.

'DC Murray,' she said, showing her warrant card.

He looked at it. 'Oh,' was all he said.

'And you are . . . ?' As if she couldn't guess.

'Sean Reynolds.'

'We understand there's a worker here called Joe Dundas. Is he here?'

'No. Not working today.'

'Have an address for him?'

'Oh,' he said again, then added grudgingly, 'Yes. I'll find it for you.'

He retreated, leaving her on the doorstep with nothing to do, giving time for a subversive idea to formulate.

When he returned with an address scribbled on a scrap of paper, his hand already going to the half-door to close it, she said, 'Just a couple of other questions, if you don't mind.'

He looked pained. 'I suppose so. But I'm very busy – I hope you're not planning to drag this out.'

Oh dear! What a lot he had to learn about a police investigation! 'This is just a very preliminary enquiry,' she said. 'We'll need a lot more of your time later. First of all, how many workers do you have on your books?'

'There's a number of cleaners, three office staff and our factor, Ben Linton. Eight estate workers, including Joe. I suppose I could find a list for you.'

'I'll certainly want one, but later will do. Are they all local?'

'Within five miles, most of them. The labourers – there's two, brothers, come in from Lochinver and one from near Unapool.'

'Would any of them know Danni Maitland?'

Murray thought he flinched when she said the name, but he covered it with a shrug.

'Unlikely. They're all family men and they're off home the minute they're finished. All right?' His hand was going back to the top of the door again.

She shouldn't do it. She knew that perfectly well, but she was damned if French was the only person doing the interesting stuff.

'Mr Reynolds, I understand you're in the habit of going down the track past the woods where Ms Maitland's body was found. Can I ask what you do there?'

It caught him on the raw. His eyes widened, and the hand on the door visibly tightened its grip. She could almost read the thought: Dare I say, mind your own effing business.

Wisely, he didn't say it. He coughed, then said, 'Sorry! You took me by surprise. Obviously, I patrol the estate, checking there's nothing needing attention. The plantation's old and overgrown and I need to weigh up whether to remove it once the planting's complete at the lower levels.'

It was a disappointingly quick recovery. She hadn't gained anything, and indeed might have thrown away a chance of putting him off balance at some later stage, if that was needed. She was irritated with herself, which was perhaps why she didn't resist the temptation to say, 'That's not where the wolf is, then?'

Again, he stared at her. Then he said, in tones of disgust, 'Oh, for God's sake! If you've nothing better to do than to listen to fairy stories invented by silly little girls, I have. That's it.'

The half-door slammed shut. Feeling slightly sick, Murray turned away. She'd handled that stupidly and she was too old now to think that 'I was in a bad mood' was a reasonable excuse.

If she'd been reporting to Strang, she'd have accepted she should go and confess. But if she had he wouldn't have been judgemental, the way French seemed to be all the time. And it probably wasn't going to be relevant, anyway – French had said that herself, to Jonathan.

With any luck, she wouldn't ever need to know.

CHAPTER FOURTEEN

'He phoned me this morning,' Angus Mackenzie said. 'He wanted to explain you were to be in charge here now.'

'Oh, I see,' DI French said. It was ridiculous to feel relieved that Strang hadn't felt so unconfident that he'd risked turning up in person to check how she was managing.

'I'm sure he's happy to leave things in your capable hands,' he said, with a smile.

Was she that obvious? She said hastily, 'But there was something he thought we should know?'

'Yes. It's this – this dreadful business, of course. Poor Danni! I'm only glad her aunt isn't here to see it – she was devoted to the child, devoted!' He took out a handkerchief with shaking hands and dabbed his eyes. 'I can hardly bear to think about it. And it happened there, in her own house!'

'Yes. You're familiar with it, are you?'

'Only from when Flora lived there. Danni – well, she had parties with her own young friends, but. . .' Mackenzie's voice tailed off. 'She wasn't interested in what I could tell her about her aunt – a shame, really. But after the car went on fire – you know about that?'

French nodded.

'I heard the bang, and when I saw what had happened, I hurried along – I've a croft just along the road from here. By then Sean Reynolds had arrived and Hattie Sinclair, bless her, took Danni away – her poor feet were all cut with broken glass. I stayed to sweep it up and then another couple of neighbours arrived and between us we got cardboard to fill in the window – it was a terrible night with the storm, just terrible.

'I'd said I'd get a glazier in to fix it, so I phoned him on Monday morning. But he said he wouldn't be out this way for a day or two, so I suggested I could measure up for him and I went in to do that on Monday afternoon.'

Suddenly, French was very, very interested. 'In the house? You had a key?'

'Goodness, we never lock our doors around here! No, I just went in with my tape measure.'

But someone had locked the door – Strang had been forced to kick it open. She said carefully, 'And the house looked – normal, so far as you could tell?'

'Apart from the broken window, yes. I'd swept up the glass, as I said, and the sitting room was just as usual.'

'Can you remember what time it was?'

Mackenzie hesitated. 'I'm not good at knowing the time – it never seems to matter much, out here. But I know I forgot about doing it until quite late and then thought I better go before it got properly dark. So it would maybe be five o'clock, or a wee bit after? I was certainly back home before the six o'clock news.'

'Did you see anyone else around then? Cars parked, say?'

'Not a soul. It was such awful weather. The shop shuts at five and the pub doesn't open till six, so there'd be no reason for anyone to be around.'

This was solid gold. It had always been likely that it had happened at night but with this evidence they would only have to check movements during the hours of darkness on Monday, not throughout the whole day. It would simplify everything.

'That's been incredibly helpful, Mr Mackenzie. Thank you for coming to tell me,' she said, with real gratitude.

He stood up, shaking his head. 'Not at all, not at all. If there was more I could do, I'd be glad to.'

'As a matter of fact, I think my sergeant may be looking for you, hoping you can save us some time. The township houses are very scattered, and we don't have local officers to ask.'

'Of course. I'll go now and see if I can find him.' As he went to go, he stopped and said, 'I can only wish you every success. And maybe in finding who did this, you'll find the person who killed Flora Maitland.'

As he went out, he passed DC Murray coming in. She was looking even less cheerful and outgoing than usual, but French decided not to notice it.

'We've had a stroke of luck, Livvy,' she said. 'Mr Mackenzie visited Maitland's house late on Monday afternoon and it was normal then.'

Murray's face brightened at once. 'And the boss's notes said that Hattie Sinclair had knocked on the door but got

221

no reply early on Tuesday morning and been around the village after that. So we've got time of death pinned.'

'I'm just thankful I'll have progress to report when next I have to speak to DCS Borthwick. I'm terrified of her.'

For once, she got a good response. Murray grinned. 'I reckon that's pretty smart. But she's okay – you know, FFF?'

'Oh, I know it all right. I've been well warned. Anyway – you got that address?'

For some reason, Murray stopped smiling, but she held out the paper. 'Here it is.' Then, as they reached the car she hesitated. 'Do you want to drive, ma'am? DCI Strang prefers to.'

That felt liked a hint, and she'd tensed up – why? Then French remembered the roads round here.

'Would you rather I did?' she said. 'I've come up this way a few times hill-walking and stuff, and if you're not used to the driving it's a bit unnerving.'

Murray's face relaxed. 'Thanks, ma'am. I'll owe you one.'

French laughed. 'Wait till you see how I drive before you say that.'

As they walked to the car, French was feeling optimistic. Improvement on two fronts – maybe she'd get there eventually.

William Maitland opened his front door a bare six inches. 'If you're from the press, get stuffed. Leave us alone.'

The man was pale and his fleshy face seemed to be sagging, somehow. When DCI Strang introduced himself, it was grudgingly opened wide enough to let him in and

Maitland said, 'All right, then. You're him that was meant to come yesterday, aren't you?'

Strang admitted that he was. 'I'm very sorry for your loss,' he said as he came into the sitting room, where Moira Maitland was sitting by an electric fire, huddled into her chair. Her eyes were red and swollen and though she looked up at him blearily she said nothing, as if speaking would be an effort beyond her powers.

'I suppose you'd better take a seat.' Maitland waved him towards a sagging sofa covered by a tartan throw. 'Is there any news?'

'Have they given you a family liaison officer?' Strang asked, stalling for time.

'Oh aye, there's been a woman comes and yammers on for bit until we can get her to go away. But all she says is that enquiries are still at an early stage. Maybe you can tell me what you're doing to find out who killed my daughter.'

Moira gave a stifled sob as Strang said, 'I'm afraid she'll know a lot more than I do. I'm not a part of this investigation. Look, I can leave now if you'd prefer – you've only to say the word. As I think my assistant told you at the time, I was wanting to ask a few questions about your sister, Flora. It won't take long—'

He was interrupted by a scream from Moira. She had looked limp, but now she was on her feet. 'No! I won't sit here and listen to anyone talking about that woman! If it wasn't for her my daughter wouldn't be dead!' Sobbing, she stormed out of the room and slammed the door behind her.

In the awkward silence that followed, Strang got to his feet. 'Sorry. I'd better go . . .'

223

Maitland said wearily, 'You might as well stay. You won't go away, will you – you'll only go away just now, and then you'll come back and I'll have it all to go through again. Tell me what you want and we can get it over with.'

'I'll keep it brief. What do you know about your sister's career?'

He made a disgusted sound. 'She was into some sort of dirty stuff, Flora. Oh, it was just that one time she got in trouble with your lot but only because she was smart. She was in it along with Reith all right – and he was rotten to the core. Got what was coming to him, getting killed like that – there'd be other folks died because of him. But it never stopped her. She'd the sort of money you don't come by honestly, and she'd make a big joke of it when we asked her where it came from. Export and import, she liked to call it, but she always winked when she said it.

'Whenever Danielle was old enough she started undermining us – letting her do all the stuff we always said she wasn't old enough for, taking her places she never should have been at her age, and we knew the two of them laughed about us behind our backs. We were always scared she'd get her into real trouble and it was a relief when she wasn't around in the last few years. But now look what's happened.'

'Do you know who she was working for?' Strang asked.

'Never told us, and I didn't want to know. After my father left her the croft all I wanted was to forget about her. She'd taken what should have been mine.'

He sounded angry, but Strang could see hurt on his face too as Maitland went on, 'That's what you get for being the honest one who stuck at a job and looked after his family. She would float in and make the old fool laugh, and that was what he liked. If my mother'd still been alive, she'd have talked sense into him – she was a good, decent woman and she saw right through Flora.'

'So she never talked to you in detail about the work she did?'

Maitland gave a short laugh. 'Wouldn't have asked her. And if I had, she'd have laughed at me.'

Strang shifted in his chair. Would the man baulk when it came to authorising the lawyer to release the papers?

'Mr Maitland, you've been very helpful and I don't want to keep you any longer than necessary. But your sister's lawyer is holding some personal papers of hers that might be helpful to the continuing investigation into her death. Unless your daughter left a will, which seems unlikely, you will be the sole beneficiary. Would you be prepared to instruct Mr Mackay to allow us to see them?'

'Investigating Flora's death?' He was angry now. 'What for? She got drunk and fell over a cliff. The last thing I want is the secrets of her mucky past getting dug up to humiliate her family. She's dead now, and I can't say I'm sorry.'

Strang had been afraid he'd say that. He made one last attempt. 'If we don't need to make it an official request, there will be much less risk of publicity. And I'll tell you something in strictest confidence. It's only my personal opinion, but I think it's possible that your sister's death, and your daughter's, are linked in some way and if we can establish what that link is, it might help us bring Danielle's killer to justice – though I have to stress that it's only a suspicion.'

225

Maitland's face worked. Strang hadn't been sure about his feelings for his daughter; Donald Mackay had told him about his rage when the inheritance had gone to her instead of to him, and so far he'd seemed unemotional. Now, though, he turned away and blew his nose, hard. It seemed a long time before he spoke.

'Oh, very well. I'll speak to Mackay.' Abruptly, he stood up. 'And now you can go and leave us alone.'

Dismissed, Strang went back to his car. What he'd said hadn't, perhaps, been strictly professional, but it had been truthful. Of course, he could be entirely wrong; it was hardly unknown for young men who'd been publicly humiliated to take disproportionate revenge and even now DI French might be arresting Joe Dundas. But the deaths of the two related women living in the same house over a comparatively short period of time were a compelling reason to look more closely for some pattern that was not immediately obvious.

Ranald Sinclair came into the kitchen for the third time that morning. Hattie had been working to fill an order for the freezer in the shop and had broken off to make him coffee twice already; he didn't seem to have spent much time through in the office today.

'Are you wanting an early lunch?' she said, trying to conceal her irritation. 'I'll just need to get this pavlova into the oven and then—'

'No, no,' he said. 'I can wait. Just wanted to see if you'd had anyone in here?'

She was puzzled. 'Had anyone?'

'There's journalists around, stopping people to ask if they know anything.'

'Oh dear. Did they speak to you?'

'A couple of them tried, but of course I brushed them off. But there's plenty of people only too keen to get their names in the papers. God knows what rubbish they'll be telling them. And the police haven't been?'

'No. I went to the shop earlier and someone said they were going round all the houses, so I suppose they'll be here sometime.'

Ranald didn't say anything else, but he didn't leave either. 'They'll probably ask about our movements, though.'

Hattie looked at him, frowning. 'Well, yes, I expect they will.'

'So we should be clear about what we're going to tell them, and not stammer around looking stupid – right?'

She didn't like the sound of that. 'It's not difficult, surely? I told Kelso yesterday most of what I did after Danni disappeared.'

'Oh sure, sure. And of course I can tell them what I did on Monday – went into Lochinver to give a bollocking to Chris Peterson about getting the feed delivery wrong, came back here for lunch, worked in the office, then had to go back to Lochinver to fetch the replacement. Then, of course, remember, we were here together all evening.'

Hattie wasn't likely to forget that evening. It was when she'd realised her husband was in love with another woman. It had been hard to hold things together, not to break down and have a confrontation. She'd been grateful when he went through to the office to catch up with paperwork and she could have her cry out in peace.

'Yes, that's right. At least, you were in the office.'

He glared at her. 'That's here, isn't it?'

The conversation was getting uncomfortable. She agreed, weakly, as she put a final swirl on top of the meringue and put it into the oven.

But Ran hadn't finished. 'And no doubt they'll be going on about the car fire. Of course these things happen – the insurance company understood perfectly when I talked to them – but with Danni not taking no for an answer from the police, they may open that up now too. Futile, actually, but we should be prepared for it. We were both here, of course. I'd gone up to bed and you were just following me when you heard the bang and ran out to see what you could do. OK?'

'Well, yes,' she said hesitantly. 'There was a programme I'd been watching – started about eleven—'

Ranald pounced. 'Now you see, that's the sort of detail you needn't go into. We both know it's nothing to do with us so it would be just a distraction for them when they've enough on their plate. You don't want to go wasting police time.'

She used the excuse of ducking into the fridge for cream not to reply directly. She took her time finding it and when she came back out he was leaving, apparently satisfied.

Her heart was pounding and she collapsed onto a chair. Why would Ran be using her to construct an alibi? Why should he need one?

She'd heard all about what had happened at the cottage when she went to the shop earlier – they could talk of nothing else. She'd been feeling ill just thinking about it.

She couldn't, she wouldn't believe Ran was capable of brutality like that. He'd seen action as a soldier, of course, but even when they'd had rows, she'd never for a moment been afraid of his fists – only his tongue.

There was the car too. That hadn't actually hurt anyone, just made a big, dramatic noise. If it was done deliberately to dislodge Danni it had certainly worked. So Sean was just as likely to have done that – though why would he bother? It would surely all come down to money in the end, where Ran couldn't compete, unless Danni was ready to grab the first offer to get out of Inverbeg.

But, Hattie remembered suddenly, Ran had tried to put pressure on Danni to do just that, the following morning, after he'd done the phone calls for her. She'd thought he was just chancing his arm in a rather stupid and clumsy way. Then yesterday, he'd got in touch with Danni's father – just a condolence letter, of course, but . . .

And now she remembered, too, her last awkward conversation with Kelso, when she'd asked him to speak up for Ran's character. He hadn't said he wouldn't, just that there would be no point, but thinking it over there had been reluctance there.

Had she lived with Ran all these years and not really known him at all? It was a terrifying thought. She gave a little, frightened sob, and though Juno came over to see what was wrong, she didn't even notice her.

She hadn't realised quite how much she had been pinning her hopes on a quick solution. It was a bitter disappointment that DI French would have no neatly wrapped package to hand in to DCS Borthwick to get her gold star. She was feeling crushed as she got back into her car to drive back to Inverbeg.

Joe Dundas had been nervous. A rabbit in the headlights would have been more composed; he kept twitching, his replies to their questions were monosyllabic and he visibly flinched when Danni's name was mentioned. However, he lived at home and after working all day he had spent the evening watching TV with his parents. He didn't have a car; the estate workers were picked up in the morning in a minibus and dropped off at night. He wasn't their man.

'So,' French said, trying to sound upbeat, 'Pick ourselves up, dust ourselves off . . .'

DC Murray didn't reply. She was holding her breath, as French slid into a passing place to let the van that had looked about to hit them head on go through and drove on without stopping.

'God, how do you do that?' she said and French laughed.

'You work out whether it's a tourist or a local. If it's a tourist, you stop or they'll hit you. If it's a local van like that they'll adjust their speed and so do you. You get the hang of it if you come often enough.'

'If I never see this place again it'll be too soon. All that stuff.' Murray waved her arm at the aggressive growth, pressing close to the road, overhanging it: straggly trees, rough grasses, bracken. 'And those.' She pointed to a great grey monolith that blotted out the sky on one side. 'I really hate those – they're malevolent. Just sort of saying, "This is ours. We were here long before you and we'll be here long after you've gone. We can wait."'

'Goodness! It's really getting to you. I think that's sort of what I like about it – puts things into perspective. We're not that important.' Then she sighed. 'In a hundred years it won't matter that the obvious suspect wasn't the right one.'

'Oh, you want it with jam on, don't you?' Murray said.

It was, amazingly, a friendly joke and French laughed. 'Definitely. And I'll have the clotted cream on top, too. Now – Linton next, I suppose. Have you met him?'

'There was someone talking to parents picking up one of the kids last night, so I guess that was probably him, but I haven't spoken to him.'

'He met me coming off the chopper yesterday afternoon – very helpful. Smart, well-spoken, confident. Not at all in the same style as poor Joe. Danni must have had catholic tastes.'

'From DCI Strang's notes, she sounded more Joe's kind than Linton's, but you never know. And just suppose he's got an alibi too – what then?'

French didn't want to think about that. Yesterday she'd have made a cross-that-bridge-when-we-come-to-it remark; now she realised that would have been seen as a slapping-down.

Carefully, she said, 'Any ideas?'

Out of the corner of her eye she could see Murray giving her a look of surprise. Then she said, 'Maybe this is daft, but for me, the big story's really her and her aunt, isn't it? There's these two big men, fighting over the croft. And maybe one of them thought that as long as Flora was living there, she wouldn't sell it and shoved her off the cliff. Then if Danni looked like settling in too, neither of them would be very chuffed.'

231

Her stomach lurched at the thought of having to get a grip on all of that, but she said only, 'Well, it's a theory. Let's keep it in mind.'

They had reached Inverbeg now and as they turned down towards the community hall they could see a group waiting for them. French groaned. 'Oh dear. Well, they're going to be disappointed. We've just to repeat the statement that went out last night and tell them that all future statements will be put out from Fettes Avenue.'

'That should get rid of them,' Murray said cheerfully. 'If they've got an excuse to get back to civilisation, they'll take it.'

Shirley Reynolds was trying to doze in her chair – she'd had a bad night – but she was too worried to drop off and when she shut her eyes, pictures that she didn't want to see formed behind her closed eyelids. She knew she was just working herself into a state, but knowing what she was doing and stopping doing it were two different things.

When Maia came in, she was relieved at the diversion. Perhaps Maia's calm would soothe her jangling nerves. But it wasn't long before she realised Maia, too, was very much on edge.

She asked if the police had come in, and when told that they hadn't, stood tapping her foot. 'I'd just like to get all the nonsense over with. Goodness knows how long they'll drag it out for, and you know I'm expecting Antony any day now. I don't want to involve him in a mess like this.

'And surely it's obvious that Joe just lost his head over her, poor boy. Sean said that one of the detectives came

232

round to get his address, so maybe they're arresting him right now.'

Shirley stared at her. 'Do you think that's right?'

'Of course it's right that it was him. I'm only afraid that they'll bungle it somehow, and we won't be able to get on with the project while they stump around in their hobnailed boots.

'Anyway, I'd better go. Sorting out the bills for these kids is going to be a complete nightmare, with everyone expecting we'll waive all charges in recognition of the trauma the little dears have suffered.'

Shirley was left thinking over what she'd said. Maia seemed so very sure and she was usually right. Of course it made sense, and her own terrible thoughts were the product of an overvivid imagination. All at once, she felt better, much better.

As the reporters, disappointed at the blandness of DI French's statement, turned away PS Erskine stepped forward.

'I've been watching out for you, boss. The SOCOs are wanting a word.'

'Right,' French said. 'Anything come in from the house to house?'

'They're still out – there's houses miles off the road. But so far there's nothing. Most of the ones I spoke to didn't even know who Danni Maitland was.'

'Doesn't sound too promising. I'll go up to the cottage just now, then.' French said, turning to go. Then she turned back. 'Livvy, you'd better come too.'

Murray, all ready to resent being told to go in and write up the interview, was pleasantly surprised. Maybe French was beginning to accept she was useful after all. Progress!

There was a line of uniformed officers doing a fingertip search in a wide sweep round the house. A SOCO, standing photographing the burnt-out car, came to meet them.

'Nothing in the drains. They'll be packing up shortly,' he said. 'I'm basically finished here too. I've taken samples and the lab will be able to give you chapter and verse about the substance used, but I'll stick my neck out and say there was a planted charge, probably activated with a detonator. Someone did this deliberately.'

Then he grinned. 'Your job to find out who.'

CHAPTER FIFTEEN

DI French had decreed they should carry on as planned with the Ben Linton interview. Murray's instinct would have been to start trying immediately to find who might have a detonator, but at least if he turned out to have an alibi too, it would clear the ground.

The project office was part of Auchinglass House and Linton would be, they were told, either there or in his flat above. When they found it, the door was open on to a lobby with stairs up to it and a glass partition on the right separating off the office, a rather grand room in the Scottish baronial style kitted out with modern office furniture. Through it they could see Linton sitting at a broad desk, his head propped on his hands staring at a file that was open in front of him. He looked up as they tapped on the door, called, 'Come in!' and stood up.

He looked very weary but he smiled, invited them to sit down and said, 'How can I help you? I'm glad to be taken away from this, anyway.' He gestured to the file in front of him.

'What is it?' Murray asked.

'Oh, Maia needs the details of how long the volunteers stayed and when they left, but the problem is none of them informed me – when they were told they didn't have to stick around they just went. One or two are still here, I think, but I'll have to check that later. And I'm having to give a flea in the ear to the reporters wanting to hire a pod and squat here.'

Murray would have liked to ask more about the set-up, but he was going on, 'You're not interested in my problems. What can I do for you?'

French said, 'At the moment it's just routine questions. Danielle Maitland was a friend of yours, is that right?'

He gave a sigh. 'Yes, she was. I got to know her in the pub – it's the social centre round here, particularly on a Saturday, and occasionally I drop in through the week as well if I've time. With the kids who came on the courses joining in there was always quite a good vibe. There's not much else around. Danni was quite a live wire – we had a lot of laughs.'

'Was she your girlfriend?' French asked.

'Just a friend.'

'Did she see it that way?' Murray put in sharply.

Linton looked taken aback. 'I . . . I don't know. I never gave her reason to think anything else. Joe was more interested in her in that way, I think.'

'Right,' French said. 'Now, your movements on Monday?'

There was an appointments diary open on the desk in front of him and he gestured towards it; there was a line drawn cancelling all the Monday slots and MEETING written in block letters.

'There was a VisitScotland Conference in Ullapool. Ten-thirty start, then a break and an afternoon session. I got back here around five-thirty, I think – maybe a little later. Then I was in here, picking up a few problems that had arisen during the day. Replacing a broken loo seat – that was one of them. That happens a lot.

'So plenty of people can vouch for me till around eight, but afterwards all I did was come back here to the flat, had supper and then watched TV for a bit, so you've only my word for it. Then I just went to bed – I was tired. It had been a long day.'

French said, 'As you were working around, did you see any activity at Ms Maitland's cottage? A car parked there, say?'

Linton frowned. 'I'm trying to picture it. No, I don't think so, but then there'd be no reason for me to look up towards it. It was a filthy night and I was hurrying around with my head down, I guess.'

'Is there anything you could tell us that you did notice, then or earlier, that might help us with our enquiries?'

'I wish I could,' he said with a grimace. 'Can't bear to think about it. She was so excited about her future – she'd never had money before and she'd great plans.'

'Right. I think that's all for the moment,' French said, standing up. Then she paused, she actually paused, and turned to Murray to say, 'Unless there's anything else?'

She was starting to feel ashamed that she'd behaved so badly before. 'Just one thing that occurred to me,' she said. 'Do you ever use detonators on the estate?'

Linton looked surprised. 'Well, we have done, I think. I know there was a lot of stuff had to be blasted away when they were making the road, and no one ever throws anything out around here. You'd have to ask Sean. Maybe they need to use explosive sometimes for clearing new ground to be planted.'

'Thanks, that's very helpful. Oh, and just one more thing – do you know anything about wolves on the estate?'

Murray heard French making a small, irritated noise and knew she was pushing her luck. Strang would have pulled her up for that; it really wasn't relevant, it was just that she wasn't sure if she'd get another chance.

Linton laughed. 'Well, no one's denying Sean would love to be in a position to do it legally – wolves are his big thing – but he'd probably need a little more space than he's got if he's not to have farmers forming a lynch mob. I've certainly never seen one lurking about.'

'Thank you, Mr Linton,' French said. 'We'll leave you to your billing problems now.'

As they went out, she said to Murray, a little stiffly, 'I think it might be better to focus on one thing at a time. We can go back now and work out a plan to follow up the new information about the car in a systematic way – and I think we should leave wolves out of it. The last thing we want to do is have the press thinking we're taking that seriously.'

'Sorry, ma'am,' she said meekly.

But she wasn't sorry, not at all. Sean Reynolds was an unpleasant man. Linton had said he was daft about wolves, so he had a socking great motive for wanting to enlarge his estate. And he likely had a detonator. She didn't think hers had been an irrelevant question at all.

Just as they reached the community hall, French's phone rang and she stopped to answer it while Murray went on

238

inside. PS Erskine was waiting at a corner table but the room was surprisingly quiet.

She sat down beside him. 'Not a lot going on, is there?'

'Not a lot of people live here, I suppose. The pub's the only gathering place. A few of the regulars knew who Danni was but apart from Kasper and Zofia Novak who run that and the shop, no one else claims even to have spoken to her, apart from Angus Mackenzie and he hadn't spoken to her for a week or two. There's not a single line we could follow up.

'We haven't been to the two employers – Sinclair and Reynolds. From Strang's notes they'll have to feature as suspects, and I thought maybe the boss will want to question them in detail.'

For a moment, Murray thought he was talking about Strang, but then realised that he meant French. 'I think myself we need to spread out, not just sit working through one suspect at a time. She likes everything tidy and investigations are messy. Hope she can cope with it.'

She stopped as French appeared, putting her phone away, and came to join them. Murray looked at her enquiringly but she didn't say who she'd been talking to, just, 'Right – let's look at what we have. Anything more, Bob?'

Erskine shook his head and she went on, 'At least Dundas's alibi eliminates him. Linton – check out the tourist board meeting, Bob, but he was unlikely to be lying about that. No alibi from early evening on, so we can't strike him off the list.'

'But we still need to find out where Danni was during the day,' Murray pointed out. 'So now shouldn't we start checking out the fish farm and the Auchinglass Estate? The

Auchinglass workers are off today but if the ones on the fish farm are in, maybe someone could have a word with them before they're away home?'

French still seemed reluctant to move on from Linton. 'His is the most personal connection we've got and we've only his word for it that it was the merest friendship. The crime scene suggests two people having a beer together and then a flare-up.'

'They could be having a drink together for lots of reasons – say, if someone was wanting to buy the croft and she refused,' Murray argued.

'Yes . . . yes, maybe you're right.' She looked flustered by the idea. 'So, Bob, can you organise interviews with the fish farm staff? Livvy, we could interview the Sinclairs now – or do you think it should be Auchinglass House first?'

With a sinking heart, Murray realised that French was floundering, scared to make decisions. She seemed to have no sense of urgency, despite having viewed the crime scene and the body; though Murray hadn't, she was worryingly conscious that they had a brutal and calculating killer at liberty to plan whatever might next be in his mind.

Murray hadn't always agreed with Strang, had even taken her own line more than once, but sometimes she'd got it wrong. She didn't want to be the one making the decisions, without him at her back to sort it out if necessary. The investigation was lacking leadership.

She didn't dislike French any longer. She was a nice woman and that dislike had said a lot more about her own inadequacies than French's. But she seemed out of her depth; Murray had a dreadful feeling that this could be a complete disaster and she'd be right there in the firing line.

Answering French's question with, 'Let's toss a coin, shall we?' wouldn't be very professional. Instead, she said, 'Should we maybe pick up the pace, ma'am? The DCS likes lots of activity. We could go separately and do preliminary interviews and then report back?'

'Right, right. I'll go to Auchinglass House.'

That made Murray nervous – what if her previous encounter with Sean Reynolds came up? – but it was too late to argue. 'Fine. I'll speak to the Sinclairs,' she said.

French had been alarmingly ready just to go along with her suggestion. Admittedly, Murray had pressed the JB button deliberately, but it was unnerving to have a superior officer so lacking in initiative.

Hattie Sinclair had seen two police officers go past her window ten minutes before. She was ironing; somehow smoothing out wrinkles had seemed a soothing thing to do, but it left her mind free to fret. A friend who had popped in earlier had asked if the police had been round yet, and seemed surprised they hadn't.

'I was in the shop just now and they seem to have gone door-to-door and got round most people,' she said. 'I don't think anyone's been able to help much. I still can't believe this could happen in such a quiet wee place. It's terrifying when you think he's likely still around. I tell you, if it wasn't for the police being everywhere, I'd just be staying locked in my house till they got him.'

Hattie had agreed, feeling sick. The police hadn't come to the house, just walked on past and now, as she was folding one of Ranald's shirts, they walked back past. Why

241

hadn't they come in to speak to her, the way they had to everyone else?

The front doorbell rang. The dogs, who had been lying beside the Aga, leapt up, barking furiously. No one ever did that; everyone knew to come round the back. You wouldn't, of course, if you were a police officer. Ordering the dogs to be quiet, she went to answer it on trembling legs.

It was a young woman on her own. She was of medium height with a neat crop of very unnatural black hair and she was smiling pleasantly, holding up a warrant card. 'Mrs Sinclair? DC Murray. Could I have a word?'

'Yes, of course. Come in,' Hattie said, escorting her to the sitting room. She hoped her voice didn't sound as shaky as she felt inside. 'This is all so dreadful.'

'May I sit down?' Murray said, not waiting for permission and taking the chair with its back to the window.

'Yes, do,' Hattie said, flustered. 'Did you want my husband as well? I think he's in the office.'

'No, I'll speak to him later. Can I just ask you about Danielle Maitland? You were almost the last person to see her alive. How did she seem?'

Surely there wasn't any need to say she'd been annoyed with Ran pushing her about the croft? Hattie said carefully, 'She went off in a bit of a mood, actually. She was upset about the car and . . . well, angry really, that the police wouldn't come to see it and look again at her aunt's death. She was going on and on about that – she was completely determined, talking about negligence.'

Murray was reluctant to get involved in a discussion of the shortcomings of Police Scotland. 'I know she came here after her car went on fire, but how well did you know her before?'

Hattie sank gratefully into one of the big armchairs. Sitting, it wouldn't be so obvious that she was shaking – or at least she hoped it wouldn't be, though the young woman was studying her with unsettling intensity.

'I knew who she was, of course. We're such a small community that any new member is interesting. I took up a cake and a card when she arrived and we'd a chat then, but after that I only saw her in the pub with a group of youngsters.'

'What was she like?' Murray asked.

Hattie hesitated, a picture coming up of Danni in the midst of them, whipping up trouble. How could she be truthful without speaking ill of the poor girl?

It was as if Murray had read her mind. 'I know. You're not wanting to say anything bad because of the awful thing that happened to her. But if she's to get justice we have to know the truth, so say what you're thinking.'

'Oh dear. Well, she was always causing friction. It was as if she couldn't enjoy herself unless there was something brewing. Kasper in the pub kept threatening to throw her out. Latterly she was trying to play Ben Linton off against Joe Dundas. There was an incident last Saturday night—'

'Yes, we know about that,' Murray said. 'Tell me about Sunday night.'

Hattie's stomach lurched. Ran had rehearsed this with her; she knew what she was supposed to say. She wouldn't have to lie directly; it was all in the way that the truth was presented. But there were two considerations: the first and

243

most important was what she owed to the murdered girl; the second was that, skewered by the detective's unrelenting gaze, she wouldn't get away with papering over the crack in the timeline.

'I was in the kitchen, watching TV.'

'On your own?'

'Just with the dogs.'

'Not your husband? Where was he?'

This was the crunch moment. 'I think he'd gone up to bed. I'm more of a night owl.'

It couldn't really have been more than a moment before Murray's next question, but it felt a long time.

'You think?'

'He'd been working in the office. I was doing stuff around the house, so I don't know what time he packed it in, but he'd been in bed when I brought back Danni to sleep here.'

'I see.'

It had felt the previous question had hung in the air; this reply fell with a thud. She'd landed Ran in it. She wasn't happy, but it was the honest truth.

Murray went on, asking in detail about the events that night and the next day. It felt like being fed, very slowly, through a mangle and Hattie was exhausted by the time they came to the Monday evening.

'I was still thinking Danni might come back, but she didn't. Ran went up to bed and I watched TV as usual until my programme finished, around midnight, I suppose.'

'So you were together all evening?'

'Yes,' was a simple word to say. But somehow it came out as 'More or less'. Before Murray could ask the question, she was obviously framing, Hattie added, 'He was along in the office.'

'Did you see him there? Or when he came back to go up to bed?'

Hattie was face to face with what she'd done and now she was feeling sick. 'Well, no – I was in the sitting room mostly. But he couldn't be sure I wouldn't come through to the office looking for him – that quite often happens. If you're trying to suggest that he had supper with me then went along to kill Danni in that particularly horrible way and got back in time to be in bed and asleep before I went up, then you're totally wrong.'

She squared her shoulders as Murray studied her face for a long moment. Then she said, 'How soundly do you sleep, Mrs Sinclair?'

It sounded like a trick question, but she could only say, 'Pretty soundly, I suppose. I'm usually tired.'

'And do you have a double bed, or twins?'

That was the trap, there. 'A double bed,' she said firmly. 'So yes, I'd have known if he'd got up and gone out, if that's what you're really asking. Anyway, I was on edge about Danni. I'd have wakened if there'd been any sound.'

DC Murray nodded, then stood up, 'Thank you for your time, Mrs Sinclair. I appreciate your help. I'll send someone round sometime later to take a formal statement.'

Hattie burst out, 'I would hate you to think from anything I said that Ran might have killed her. He has a temper but he's not a violent man. We have a . . . well, I suppose you could say a combative relationship, but it's all words. I've never for a moment been frightened, however much I provoked him.'

Murray looked at her and smiled. 'I'll take that on board. Thanks for your frankness, Mrs Sinclair. I'm going to speak to him now.'

And that was all she had to cling on to until Ran came back.

Shirley had managed to doze off and when the doorbell rang she woke with a start. Maia went to answer it, then she heard her saying, 'Oh yes, of course. Come in, Inspector.'

She was sitting up, shaking her head to clear it when the detective walked into the sitting room – tall, slim and with good hair. Shirley always noticed hair: this was a thick, dark, long bob, very well cut. She'd have described her as elegant if Maia hadn't come in behind her – Maia who always made other women look clumsy.

'This is Detective Inspector French, Shirley,' Maia said. 'My mother-in-law, Shirley Reynolds.'

French smiled pleasantly. 'Er – may I sit here?'

'Yes, do,' Maia said. 'This is about poor Danni? I don't know that there's anything helpful that we could tell you, but I'm sure you'll have questions.'

'That's right,' French said. She looked towards Shirley. 'Mrs Reynolds—'

'Oh, call me Shirley, love. If you say Mrs Reynolds, there's two of us and we'll get in a right old fankle. She's Maia.'

'Shirley, then, can you tell me about your movements last Monday?'

'Movements – well, I don't move much now, not really. I was a right little mover in my day, you know, but mostly

I'm just sat here in my chair. If it wasn't for my ejector seat,' – she pressed a button and the chair tilted her upright, then back, to French's obvious surprise – 'I'd never move at all. I take a few wee walks through to the kitchen just to keep me from seizing up altogether, but really that's it till bedtime.'

French gave her a reassuring smile. 'I think that's all I need from you. Maia—'

It was only now that Shirley realised, with some surprise, that Maia seemed a bit tense.

'Can I ask how the investigation's going, Inspector? Can we hope for an early arrest?'

French's face went blank. 'I'm afraid I can't comment, at this stage. Can you tell me about your own movements on Monday?'

Shirley could read the text behind that. No, they weren't expecting an early arrest. Maia's confident assertion about Joe Dundas had been whistling in the dark and all her previous fears returned.

Maia recited, in minute detail, what she'd done on Monday – made breakfast, gone into the Lochinver Spar shop for a few things, came back, spoken to Ishbel the cleaner, worked in the office until lunchtime, made lunch, office again. 'Oh, and Hattie Sinclair popped in briefly to ask if Danni had been in, which she hadn't. Then I phoned my son Oliver at boarding school, made family supper, and did some household chores before bed. All right?'

French said, 'Thank you. That's a very full description. And your husband – he was with you for supper?'

'Yes,' Maia said. Just yes.

It wasn't a lie; Sean had appeared at supper time, for all of five minutes, spurning Maia's casserole for a cheese sandwich, saying there was a flooding problem in one of the outhouses, what with all the rain.

'And did you see anyone while you were in your office?'

Maia stared at her, then gave a little laugh. 'Do I have an alibi do you mean? Oh – I hadn't thought I'd need one. No, I don't think so. I made one or two phone calls, but to be honest I couldn't tell you who it was to, though you could find out from the phone company, if you felt I was a sufficiently important suspect.'

Maia's expression was bland, but French reddened. 'No, I'm not of course suggesting that.'

'Usually, I'd have seen Ben Linton two or three times and he could have spoken for me, but he was away all day. Oh, though I do remember now – I went to close up the office just before I went to bed and there was something I wanted to ask him. His flat's just along the corridor and I popped in. Does that help?'

For some reason the inspector looked taken aback. 'He was in his flat?'

'Yes, watching TV. Actually, I think he was just on his way to bed – he was in his dressing gown.'

French hesitated for a moment. Then she said, 'Thank you. I think that's all I need. Now, could I speak to Mr Reynolds?'

Maia laughed. 'If you can find him! I've no idea where he is – could be somewhere round the estate, could have gone in to Lochinver. I can call him if you like, but the signal's a bit iffy round here.'

She made the call and Shirley heard it ringing, then the artificial voice of the answer service. Maia rang off, saying, 'Sorry, no luck. I'll tell him when he gets back.'

The inspector thanked them both and left. Maia looked after her, then shrugged. As she was going to the door herself, the mobile she was holding rang. Glancing at the name, her face lit up.

'Antony! Where are you?' she said, then, 'No, of course not. I've just been given the third degree so they won't bother us tomorrow. What time?'

She spoke for a minute or two then rang off. 'That was Antony,' she said, cheeks flushed, eyes very bright. 'He's coming tomorrow. That'll be a bit of a lift, after all this. I'll tell Ishbel to get the spare room ready – he'll be here mid-afternoon.'

She left Shirley feeling profoundly depressed. She'd witnessed yesterday the worrying state of her son's marriage, but it wasn't because Mia was carrying on with Ranald Sinclair, or even Ben Linton. All those times she'd gone off to London recently to 'see her father'! That explained why she wanted to put Ben on the board – to allow her to have still more of those visits. And when she'd so unusually asked for her mother-in-law's opinion, she'd been preparing the ground.

Shirley was pretty sure Sean had no idea this was going on. But she wasn't sure, either, whether if he did find out, he'd care.

249

CHAPTER SIXTEEN

DCI Strang wasn't happy after his phone call with DI French. He'd stopped for petrol a couple of hours short of Lochinver and decided to phone her then, hoping for good news. But her voice was brittle; he wondered if Livvy was causing problems, but she'd volunteered that they were getting on surprisingly well. But she'd sounded downbeat, as if Joe Dundas's alibi had come as more of a blow than it should have done. Ben Linton, though she said he was still in the picture, didn't sound promising to Strang.

He'd told her where he was staying and said, in what he hoped was an unintrusive way, that she'd be welcome to come any time. She'd jumped at the offer, sounding a bit too grateful, and said she'd take him up on it whenever she could and rang off.

The start of an investigation was the exciting point, when you were still confident you'd get your man. Almost invariably that confidence soon got shaken, but to him, this was what kept you going through the bleak and sordid realities. But Rachel wasn't excited. She sounded scared, and now he was wondering if he'd made a bad mistake.

The free-flowing SRCS could simply be wrong for her. Flair, imagination – you needed those, and he'd an uneasy feeling she didn't have them. Livvy did, though she still lacked judgement. That could be developed through experience; imagination – not so much.

He would mind very much indeed if a failed investigation tarnished the SRCS's reputation. Perhaps he could coach Rachel through it. If she'd let him.

DC Murray saw DI French leaving Auchinglass House and hailed her. 'Hello, ma'am!' She held up the bag she was carrying. 'I just broke off to go to the shop before it closes – I'm starving already and by tomorrow morning my belly would have been touching my backbone. I've spoken to Harriet Sinclair, though, and I'm just about to see Ranald. Did you have any luck with the Reynolds?'

'Sean Reynolds wasn't there and the women hadn't much to offer except that Maia saw Ben Linton in the flat in his dressing gown that evening.' She looked very down as she said that.

'Didn't think it would be him anyway,' Murray said cheerfully. 'Couldn't see what was in it for him. Wasn't really into her, was he, and he'd hardly have a fit of jealous rage about Dundas after Danni had publicly humiliated him. And the car, too – why?'

French sighed. 'I suppose that's right. How was Mrs Sinclair?'

'Oh, sticking up for her man. But there's gaps, definitely. Are you coming to speak to him as well?'

She must have looked unenthusiastic since French said hastily, 'I'll just come and sit in while you carry on.'

Murray had never seen a fish farm. She wrinkled her nose as they walked past the back of the house, the office and the fish farm buildings then along the shore beyond. There were a couple of round fish tanks close in, but they were empty.

'Pooh! They stink!' she said, peering in. 'That's not much room for a big fish like a salmon that's used to swimming round the ocean. How many do you think would live in these?'

'They won't live in them at all.' French pointed to the squares of nets right out in the sea loch. 'They'll be brought in from there when they're expecting a refrigerated lorry to collect an order.'

Murray pulled a face. 'Poor things. Not that I like fish, anyway.'

'The wild salmon tastes better. But this is a lot cheaper and more people can afford it. And it's good for you!'

'That's it, right there, then. I don't like things that are good for you. See me – I'll be the one having the sausage supper at the chippie,' she said, and French laughed.

As they walked back towards Sinclair's office, she waited for French to suggest the line they should be taking, but she seemed content to leave it to Murray.

It was getting dark now. The outer door of the office was closed but there were lights on inside and when they rang the bell she could see someone getting up and walking past a couple of small windows. A moment later an outside light came on, but the door opened on to an unlit corridor and they could only see a man's outline – a tall shape with broad shoulders.

'Yes?' he said.

'Mr Sinclair?' They pulled out their warrant cards. 'DC Murray and DI French. Could we have a word?'

'Yes of course. I was expecting a visit.'

The room he took them into was small, with a low ceiling and a desk, office chair and computer as well as shelves of box files and a couple of filing cabinets, all very neat. There were pegs on one wall where a yellow oilskin suit hung with seaboots on the floor underneath.

Beyond it was a larger room, but this was very different – a sort of man-cave. It had an open fire that was dying to ashes with an oriental rug in front of it, two worn leather armchairs and a desk with an old wooden revolving chair beside it. There were untidy piles of paper as well as an open laptop, showing the weather forecast.

He sat down at the desk. 'Sorry, I'm afraid I'm not very tidy. Take a seat.'

Murray could see now that he was wearing what was almost the uniform of posh folk – dark red cord trousers and a navy Aran sweater over a dark blue shirt. He was quite fit in a rigid sort of way, if you liked that, which she didn't. He was the man she'd seen holding forth in the pub the previous night.

'This has been a terrible shock to everyone,' he said. 'Poor little Danni – only a child, really. Naturally I'm ready to do anything I can to help, Inspector.'

Murray said, 'Just the routine questions, sir. Can I ask you to take us through your movements, Monday morning to Tuesday morning, please?'

'Monday. Right. I was working during the day. In the evening I was at home with my wife.'

He'd addressed his answer to French and looked surprised that it was Murray who said, 'All evening, sir?'

He didn't like that. 'Yes – well, most of it. Oh, I probably popped through here to do a bit of work. I often do.'

'So how much time did you actually spend in your wife's presence?'

She could almost see the penny drop. His lips tightened and he said, 'I couldn't tell you, exactly. You'd have to ask her that.'

'Yes, I have. As far as I can make out, you had supper together, you then came through here to work and from there went straight up to bed. She joined you when her programme finished around midnight.'

His face flared in temper. 'That's what she told you, is it? And now you think that with my wife next door, I popped out to perform a brief act of butchery on that girl, then came back for a quick shower to wash off the bloodstains before I popped into bed? This is an absolutely outrageous accusation!'

'It's not an accusation, Mr Sinclair. I'm trying to establish exactly what your movements were on the night after Danielle Maitland disappeared.'

She became aware French was shifting in her seat and that Sinclair had realised this.

'Perhaps I could ask you, Inspector,' he said, 'if you are going to let your attack dog treat an innocent civilian in this way?'

French said, 'I think you're jumping to the wrong conclusion – DC Murray isn't attacking you, sir. But I think she's probably finished with that line of questioning.'

254

Strang would have pulled her up on that too. She'd let it sound belligerent, which wasn't good – that way you could get an official complaint. And in fact, she didn't really believe he could have done it either, but it might make him more vulnerable when it came to the next stage.

'Can we move on, then?'

Sinclair's lips tightened. He looked at French and said, 'Perhaps you might like to ask the questions? I've rather taken against your sidekick.'

To Murray's surprise, French wasn't going to let him shoehorn her into the 'good cop' role. Her reply was sharp. 'I don't appreciate offensive remarks about an officer doing her duty, sir. Carry on, DC Murray.'

'Ma'am. Do you have a detonator, Mr Sinclair?'

He actually flinched. Bullseye! 'A–a detonator?'

'Yes. You know, the sort of thing you use to set off a charge from a distance.'

'Of course I know,' he snapped. 'I spent years in the army, as you probably know – along with your DCI Strang, in fact. But I've no need for one here.'

'Would you have any objection to your premises being searched?'

His face cleared – he must have thought of that. If he'd had one, it was now presumably somewhere at the bottom of a fish pool. 'None at all,' he said smoothly. 'Be my guest.'

'Thank you, sir. Now, Danielle Maitland's car exploded on Sunday night. Can you tell us what you were doing that day?'

'Let me see. I went into Lochinver to pick up the Sunday papers, came back here, took the boat out to check the pens. In the afternoon I took the dogs for a walk. Then I had supper – I'm sure my wife will at least vouch for me on that.' There was bitterness in his tone. 'Afterwards, since I can't get peace and quiet during the day when everything's going on, I was working in the office here as I often do. All by myself.

'So, of course, that immediately makes me what nowadays they call the prime suspect. Or are you old-fashioned – bring out the handcuffs first and evidence later? Which you won't find, because it was nothing to do with me. And I'm sure DCI Strang will tell you what a fine upright fellow I am.'

He was blustering, nervousness showing through. Murray paused for a long moment to allow the nerves to build, then turned to French. 'I think I'm finished for the moment, ma'am. Unless . . . ?'

'No,' French said, getting up. 'I think that's all. Thank you, Constable.'

Sinclair looked taken aback. 'That's all?'

'Thank you, Mr Sinclair,' Murray said, then, 'For the moment.'

He didn't move. He was still looking after them as they left the room.

Walking back to the community hall, Murray said, 'I feel a bit guilty. He's going to be absolutely livid with his wife. You could tell he was expecting a rock-solid alibi and he didn't get it.'

'Right,' French said. 'Let's see if anything else has come in and then you can brief me on the interview with her.'

They saw no one in the street on the way to the hall. You wouldn't really be tempted to hang around with a brutal murderer on the loose, Murray reflected, and again the hall was all but empty. There was a PC working at the computer in one corner, another sitting looking bored at a table, ready for non-existent witnesses. PS Erskine, sitting looking at his phone, jumped up when they came in.

'Any reports?' French said.

'You saw the SOCOs' report on the crime scene, didn't you, and the autopsy results. What else were you expecting, boss?'

'Nothing special. Just – something might have come in.'

Murray saw with dismay that French was looking nonplussed. She wanted to shout at her, 'Nothing will come in unless you've commissioned it!' She should have been ordering checks on backgrounds and records, setting up lists of people to vet and people to talk to about the community's life. Interviews were all very well, but they weren't enough.

French said, 'My visit to Auchinglass House didn't yield anything except confirmation that Linton was actually watching TV that evening, Bob. Reynolds was out, Mrs Reynolds senior is all but immobile and Mrs Reynolds junior was to and fro between the house and the office all evening. Livvy, you can brief Bob on the interview with Ranald Sinclair later, but what did you get from Harriet?'

'She'd make a great witness. Very straightforward, despite being uncomfortable about leaving gaps in the alibi her husband was obviously expecting to have. At the relevant times she didn't set eyes on him for hours on end and she wasn't prepared to lie and say she had. On the Monday night, the gap after their supper was roughly four hours, possibly a little less.'

French said eagerly, 'So he could have killed her?'

Much too eagerly, Murray thought. 'He'd have to be pretty cold-blooded and well organised to meet Danni, kill her, hide the body in the woods, clean up and be back in bed by the time his wife joined him. She was adamant that she'd have wakened if he'd got up later on – she'd had half an ear open hoping Danni would come back.'

'Yes, of course. I see that.' French looked disappointed. 'But the car fire . . . ?'

'That's different. He was in the army, he'd know what to do, and if you ask me, Harriet thinks he did it. Proving it – not so easy.'

'But it's something to follow up.' French was looking brighter. 'I can tell DCS Borthwick we've a strong lead to follow. Bob, tomorrow can you organise questioning again of his employees, with that as the focus, and start a search of Sinclair's outbuildings – he's agreed, so no warrant needed. Forensics should give us the explosive used and get someone on to tracking down suppliers – he may even have needed to clear ground along the shore there for those fish tanks.

'Livvy – a report on the interviews, please, and perhaps construct a timeline to fit together all the information about their movements. I'll add a brief summary of Maia Reynolds' interview so we're up to date.

'Then pack it in for tonight. We've a clear plan for the morning, so we've done quite well. Thanks, Livvy – great contribution today.'

She said goodnight and went out, leaving Erskine and Murray looking at each other. He spoke first.

'That's what she's good at, isn't it? Once she's been

shown where to look, she'll organise but she'll not be coming up with an idea in the first place.'

Murray nodded. 'She's not taking an overview. She's focusing on one thing at a time, but not doing any background digging. She's not good on interviews, either – when we were speaking to Sinclair, she didn't have a single question. Of course, it's usually a DC's job, but Strang's always liked being hands-on. God, I miss him! He always had a grip on things. Right now, I feel I'm doing stuff that's way above my pay grade and it's seriously scary.'

'What did you get from Sinclair?'

'Bluster, mostly. I think he's scared. Anyway, I'd better get on with the report. What are you going to do?'

Erskine glanced round the room. 'Have a word with these guys and then send them home. I'll detail the new shift tomorrow to get on with her list. I'll be in the pub later – chat up some of the locals.'

'What do you suppose French is doing?'

He grinned. 'I saw her through the window just now, driving off somewhere, and if you want me to bet, she's gone to see Strang.'

'What! Where is he?'

'Just down the road, apparently. Angus Mackenzie said he was staying there to look into the Flora Maitland case. He's a nice old boy – knows everything there is to know about this place, I reckon.'

'Where does he live?'

'He's got a croft that backs on to the hall here. In fact, you can see his house if you look out of the back window –

it's just to the left when you reach the main road.'

Murray stood up and craned to see where he was pointing. It was a solid white-harled house, a lot bigger than the Maitland cottage, up across rough ground where she could see a few sheep browsing. She sat down again.

'Oh, right. See you later,' she said vaguely as Erskine collected his things and went over to talk to the uniforms.

She hoped she hadn't shown how furious she was. They both needed a meeting together with someone who knew what should be done. Instead of that, French had gone by herself for a cosy little session with Strang. She hadn't properly involved Murray right from the start, despite looking to her to produce the ideas. She'd shut her out of the conversation with Angus Mackenzie and hadn't shared the information she'd got from the young volunteer, which had led Murray to have that stupid confrontation with Sean Reynolds. She accepted that she'd no one to blame but herself for handling it badly, but the warm feeling she'd been developing towards her inspector had evaporated. She'd better write up the report first, but then she was going to go and see Mackenzie. It was about time to fill in the background.

Hattie Sinclair was trying to concentrate on preparing a supper that she wasn't sure anyone would eat. She couldn't imagine being able to swallow a mouthful and Ran had stalked past the window just after she'd seen the two detectives leaving.

She'd expected him to erupt in, raging because she hadn't repeated the lines he'd coached her to repeat. She'd been working out her response, because however angry he was, she wasn't going to apologise. She was going to take him on, the way she always had when the chips were down.

But he hadn't given her the chance. He'd gone to the pub, presumably, since his car was still parked outside. Unless he'd gone to see Maia? Hattie choked a little on that thought, but surely at supper time she'd be at home with her husband and mother-in-law?

She could go the pub too, of course, but the last thing she wanted was the sort of epic row they were heading for providing entertainment for their neighbours that would be enshrined in local legend. Anyway, the dogs were milling around her feet, looking for their supper. She fed them, then took them out for a run on the shore.

When they came back, he was there. The dogs greeted him; he snapped, 'Basket,' and they instantly complied. To her he said, 'Gin?' in much the same tone and she followed him to the sitting room.

She could tell he'd been drinking but he wasn't drunk – that at least was good. She sat down, studying him as he silently made the drinks. His face was pale and grim, his mouth a thin, angry line. She'd expected the explosion that was usual when he didn't get his way; this cold anger was more alarming.

'Did you go to the pub?' she said, trying to keep her voice steady.

He sat down opposite her. 'Yes. Are you going to ask me why?'

'Why?'

'First of all, I wanted to establish that the police had been making a perfectly routine call since we were the last people to see the girl. I didn't want any stories to start.' He stopped and took a swig from the glass he'd half-filled with whisky.

'And . . . ?' she prompted.

'And quite honestly, I was afraid I would break the habit of a lifetime and hit a woman. You know what you've done, you stupid bitch? You've promoted me to top of the list of suspects. You know I didn't kill her, you know I didn't blow up her stupid car—'

He was turning red; Hattie could see the rigid control starting to slip. It was going to take courage to speak out, but she was a soldier's daughter. She took a deep breath.

'No, I don't know,' she said. 'I don't believe you would kill her and I can't see that you'd have had the time to do it anyway – I said that to the detective. But I do believe you blew up the car. You did, didn't you?'

It was as if she'd struck him. He recoiled, and then turned ashen pale. 'I-I don't know what you mean,' he stammered.

'I mean that it couldn't be anyone else. OK, Sean wanted Danni out of there, but he knew he could up the price until she couldn't say no. You wanted to scare her into taking an immediate offer from you – you actually even tried emotional blackmail on her that morning. Then you started the chatting-up process with that letter to her father yesterday. If I can work it out, so can the police.

'They obviously know already it wasn't an accident. If I'd given you the sort of alibi you wanted me to produce for Sunday night when the car blew up, the police wouldn't believe what I told them about Monday night, and you'd be in an even worse mess than you're in now.'

Ranald looked at her, dumbstruck, as she went on,

'There are two ways to do the next bit. You can go on pretending you didn't do it while they turn the screws, question everybody, ransack the house and the yard. They'll find the evidence and end up charging you, anyway. Or you can plead guilty, pay a good lawyer and hope for the best.'

He collapsed, slumping forward in his chair and covering his face. 'Oh God, what have I done! I don't know why I did it, except that I couldn't bear losing to that bastard. And we need the space, if we're to expand—'

'But did we need to expand? We were doing fine as we are. It had just got to be a sort of macho struggle with Sean, hadn't it?'

This wasn't the moment to mention Maia, but his sigh that was almost a groan told her that he was thinking about her too.

'If he gets the croft, we'll be encircled – he'll do everything he can to close us down. We'll be finished here—' Then he stopped, a stricken look on his face.

'Yes,' she said. 'We're finished here anyway, aren't we? A shame – I love this place.'

There were tears in her eyes.

'I'm sorry, I'm sorry! What am I going to do?'

Hattie wiped the corners of her eyes with her finger. 'Why don't you phone Kelso? He'll know the best way to go about it.'

'You're right, of course.' Ranald had finished his whisky and stood up. 'Another?'

'No,' she said. 'Your mind needs to be clear. Come and have supper while we work out just what you're going to say.'

He nodded obediently. As they both stood up, there was the wailing sound of a police car in a hurry.

'What the hell—' he said.

'Oh dear God,' Hattie cried. 'Whatever now?'

263

CHAPTER SEVENTEEN

'Come on in,' DCI Strang said. 'I've got the kettle boiling for coffee, and I have Hobnobs.'

'That might just save my life – I'm starving. Nice little pad you've got here,' DI French said, looking around. 'Cut above the usual. A little boat too – got in any fishing yet?'

Strang smiled. 'No such luck. I've just been to see Danni Maitland's parents.'

'Oh, poor things. How are they?'

'Not good – she's in a state of collapse, both blaming Aunt Flora.'

'Mmm. Fair enough, in that if the brother had inherited it wouldn't have happened.'

'William Maitland believes Flora was a thoroughly bad influence, taking Danni to the unsuitable places teenagers think are cool and encouraging her to rebel. More than that – who knows? Does it look as if there's anything she'd actually got Danni involved in?'

French looked awkward. 'I suppose we should be looking into it. I'm not sure where to begin, though.'

Strang was taken aback. She'd known the Maitland story from the start; surely it was an obvious line of enquiry, along with all the others? He brought coffee and biscuits and sat down. 'Well, background checks I suppose – who were her friends, where did she work, her phone records. . .'

'And I can just ask Glasgow to do that?'

'Yes, of course. Ask for whatever resources you need, and you'll have priority to get them. You could run police checks on the locals too. Bob Erskine can fix that.'

'You did tell me that. It's just. . .' She took a sip of coffee, then burst out, 'Oh, I'd so hoped it would be straightforward. Danni's row with Joe Dundas, the way it looked at the cottage – them just having a drink, him losing his temper – I thought we'd only have to lean on him and he'd confess.'

'More than one reason for having a drink,' Strang said. 'And easy to stage that scenario afterwards.'

'I didn't think it through. Didn't want to, I suppose. It opens up so much, I just feel lost. And, well, I don't think the DCS is very impressed.'

Strang's heart sank. Recommending her didn't seem to have been his smartest move and JB had very exacting standards. She must have been sharp with French; she was blinking away tears.

'What did you say?'

'It looks as if Sinclair couldn't have killed Danni, but I could tell her he probably had blown up the car.'

'Really? Any proof?'

'She said that. But there isn't, as yet, and she said "probably" wasn't good enough and wanted an action plan. Livvy's only starting one now, so I just said we'd be searching the property. Then she asked about progress on the homicide and I had to say "not much". Didn't go down well.'

It wouldn't. Strang could almost hear JB's exasperation at second-hand. 'So . . . ?'

'Then she asked how Murray was doing and I said very well, really. She's got good ideas, Kelso, and she gets more out of people at interviews than I do.'

'That's her job as a DC, of course.'

'Yes, and I wasn't a DC very long – got my sergeant's stripes very quickly. And since then, I've been behind a desk, analysing reports and actioning further investigations.'

'This is a very different ballgame, isn't it?'

'You could say. She suggested I talked to you and brought Livvy for a brain-storming session but I wanted your advice first. I should be directing her but she's taking the lead. Oh, it's my fault, probably, but . . . What should I do?'

He could hardly say 'Do what the lady says, for heaven's sake!' He said instead, 'Good idea, probably – throwing ideas around, planning strategy . . .'

'That would be brilliant! We've been getting on OK, except she's always ready to bristle.'

And if she discovered French had ignored JB's suggestion, she'd bristle even more. Oh dear.

'We'll try to smooth things over. Now, tomorrow I'm seeing Flora's lawyer. William's consented to let me have the personal papers that he still holds. I've no idea what they might be – probably just marriage licence and income tax records, but you never know. I'd like to have it tidy to hand over to the Met, but that should be finished in the next twenty-four hours and then I can't hang round enjoying a little holiday at the taxpayers' expense.'

She looked alarmed at that, but she thanked him for his help, apologising for eating all his biscuits, and when she left seemed to be more confident about what to do. As he cleared up, Strang thought about the evening.

He liked Rachel, and he was feeling guilty that he'd jumped at what looked like an easy solution to the problem his Sinclair connection had created. She'd built up a good reputation in post, but even then he'd sensed a lack of underlying confidence and now he'd put her in a position that could damage it more.

And the investigation seemed to be rudderless; JB was worried and he'd be surprised if he didn't get a call tomorrow asking what could be done. But pulling French out would put another big dent in her self-esteem, and there was no guarantee that whoever came instead wouldn't find it equally hard to adopt a maverick approach.

On the other hand . . . What she'd said about Ranald hadn't surprised him, and if he couldn't have killed the girl but had blown up the car, it could be a game-changer. If Ranald was no longer under suspicion, there would be no real problem about his discreetly taking over. JB would be happy, Livvy would be happy and he didn't think Rachel would object in any way.

* * *

DC Livvy Murray finished her report and the timeline plotting the movements of the people interviewed. PS Bob Erskine had given her the info from door-to-door, but she couldn't see anything useful. No one here spent much time just walking around – if they'd shopping to do, they'd go to Lochinver. Maybe they could get a photo of Danni and pass it round there?

But that was for tomorrow. Now, she wanted to talk to Angus Mackenzie. He might be down the pub but when Murray stepped outside she could see lights on in his house, so he was probably at home. She glanced over at the community hall, but it was shut up with no cars parked outside. If DI French had come back from her little tête-à-tête with Strang, she hadn't returned to work.

It was dark, but very cold and clear. The sky was thick with stars and the moon was almost full so that even beyond the light spilling out around the pods and the pub it was easy to see where you were going. She'd planned to walk up to the main road and then along it to the house, but then she saw there was a path across the rough ground that was more direct – probably well-worn by years of Angus Mackenzie going to the shop and the pub.

Murray set off up it, disturbing a sleeping sheep that jumped up with an indignant baa and ran off. She wasn't sure when she reached the house if she should go round to the front, but there was an outside light burning over a door to the back and she decided to try there.

Angus Mackenzie looked an enquiry as he opened the door, but before she could show her card, he said, 'Ah! You're one of the detectives. I saw you this morning.'

'Yes, that's right. DC Livvy Murray.'

'And what can I do for you? Come in, anyway.'

He was in his seventies, Murray guessed, but he was lean and wiry, with a shock of fluffy white hair, and he was fit-looking. Healthy life, farming.

The door opened straight on to the kitchen, a fairly basic room with old and shabby fittings. An unwashed pan, a plate, a glass and a knife and fork stood on the wooden draining board beside the chipped porcelain sink.

'Come ben the front room,' he said. 'I've a fire on there. It's a chilly night – there'll be a hard frost by the morning. Sit yourself down.'

It was a room that looked as if it had happened, rather than been designed, with unmatched chairs and a sofa. A collie on the hearthrug raised its head to look at her, decided no action was required and dropped it again with a sigh. The recliner chair nearest the fire was extended and the TV was on; he'd been watching a football game, but he switched it off and returned the chair to its upright position as he sat down.

'Oh, please don't let me interrupt your match,' Murray said hastily. 'It's not an official visit.'

'Och, I don't mind!' he said. 'The wrong side was winning anyway. Fire away!'

'If it's really all right, I just wanted to pick your brains about Inverbeg and the people here – background stuff, you know? It would be helpful from our point of view to know a bit more about it.'

He settled back into his chair. 'You've certainly come to the right place. I was born here, and though I did have a career that took me away, I came right back whenever they paid me to retire. It hadn't changed much and that's suited me fine. You get good craic in the pub and the sheep keep me busy. If I need anything there's a dozen people I could ask for help – and they'd probably have offered before I did. What's happened – it's hard to believe it, really. It all went wrong from the time Flora Maitland died.'

Murray nodded sympathetically. She knew from Strang's notes what the situation was there, but she didn't want to go over it. 'Tell me about the Sinclairs,' she said. 'Did they start up the fish farm?'

'No, they bought it as a more or less going concern from the previous owners – well, pretty much a barely hanging-on concern, but Ranald's done a good job sorting it out. Very able fellow – runs a tight ship. Not universally popular, but he's giving employment and that counts. And Hattie, of course – well, that's a good girl. Involved in everything locally and always a smile for everyone. Not sure he appreciates her as much as he should.'

Murray realised, with joy, that he liked to gossip. 'Really?' she said. 'Is that what they say?'

'He always makes a bit too much of a beeline for Maia Reynolds – you know, Auchinglass House? – and there's talk. She's the slinky type – makes all the right noises, sweet as you like, but you never know what she's thinking. Hattie's worth two of her, if you ask me.'

'I've met Sean,' she said. 'What sort of reputation does he have?'

'Oh, fancies himself as a bit of a rough diamond. People are kind of careful what they say – he's a big employer round here. He's made himself unpopular with the crofting community with this nonsense about the wolves.'

'Is it really true? Ben Linton said it was just a silly rumour.'

Mackenzie snorted. 'It's no rumour. There was one attacking one of my own sheep and I had to scare it off – and I'm not the only one that's had to do that. But all Reynolds says is it's just someone's dog out of control. Oh, there's going to be trouble and claims before very long, but money's no object, anyway.'

She'd wondered about that earlier. 'Where has it come from?'

'Ah, now that I don't know. They came here while I was still living in Edinburgh, not long before I retired. The story is he sold an Internet company for millions, but I couldn't vouch for that. And of course they've got on this rewilding bandwagon and the government's always giving them wee presents with our money. Nice little business too, with the volunteers paying for the privilege of working as farm labourers – oh, they're not daft.'

'Who owned it before?'

An expression she couldn't read passed over Mackenzie's face. 'I can tell you who owned it when I was young – a man called Reith. An evil lot, that family. But the son was killed and shortly afterwards I heard the parents had divorced, so I can't tell you what happened then. I'd the impression it was an absentee landlord before the Reynolds came, but you'd have to ask around.'

She got the idea somehow that he didn't like talking about it and said quickly, 'And who else is there that I should know about?'

'Hard to say, really. We're a douce lot, mostly, just getting on with life and minding our own business. Kasper and Zofia, at the pub – now, they've made a name for themselves around here. Work all the hours God made, put some heart into Inverbeg again. Mind you,' he gave a sigh, 'it'll be quieter now with Danni gone, poor wee soul. There was hardly a night she was there that she didn't cause some sort of fuss and some of the folk who just liked a quiet drink actually stopped coming. Kasper will have an easier time now.'

Murray tried not to show that her ears had pricked up but Mackenzie noticed. Looking annoyed with himself, he said, 'Now I wouldn't want you to make anything of what I said. Kasper's a good man. And I'm maybe starting to talk out of turn. Was there anything else you wanted?'

Murray took the hint and got up. 'No, that's all. You've been a great help, Mr Mackenzie. It's difficult when you come into a place like this without knowing anything about it. I'll let you get back to the football – maybe your side's doing a bit better now.'

'They'll need to! Glad if I've been useful. Er . . . I don't suppose you can tell me how it's going?'

'I don't know myself,' she said. 'We're just at the beginning.'

As she set off back down the path it was Kasper she was thinking about. You could have a row with someone who was making your life more difficult, day in day out, lose your temper—suddenly there were sheep jumping up round about her, running with agitated bleats. Startled, she looked around and realised there was one, not very far from her, that wasn't running. It was lying on its side with a bloody wound showing up on the white fleece and there was a dog, tearing at it. Long legs, a great ruff, sharply pricked ears, fur showing silvery under the moonlight—Murray froze. Surely not – but could it really be a wolf? And now it had noticed her and was lifting its head.

Not a dog. There was was no doubt about it now. This was the creature of the darker fairy tales and the hairs rose at the back of her neck in atavistic fear. She was ready to run – but would that only tempt it to chase her? And there was the poor sheep, so pitiful in its silent agony . . .

She had to do something to drive it off. They were timid, afraid of people, she'd been told, and Angus Mackenzie had done it. She began yelling, waving her arms, making as if to come towards it.

That stopped the attack, but it didn't run. Showing no sign at all of timidity it turned towards her, baring its teeth with a snarl.

She wasn't afraid. This was way, way, beyond fear – she was terrified, panic-stricken, sweat coming out on her brow as adrenalin coursed through her, with its message of fight or flight – futile, when she could do neither.

It had moved away from the sheep, and begun a wide, circling approach. She could smell it now, a rank, feral smell, see the red gums, the row of pointed teeth. She was screaming now, but that made no difference. It moved steadily closer, closer. It would leap into an attack at any moment and there was nothing she could do. Except die.

Then she heard the frantic barking of a dog and for a moment the wolf paused, looking round to assess the new threat, then dismissed it. It was coming again—

A shot rang out. With a howl, the animal leapt in a sort of convulsion then collapsed to the ground in a heap. A moment later Angus Mackenzie's collie was at her side, dancing round her in circles barking furiously and Angus himself, holding a shotgun, was hurrying towards her.

'Are you all right, lass?' he called.

Murray was trembling so that she could hardly stand. 'Thank you,' she gasped. 'It was going to attack me! I thought I could save your poor sheep . . .'

Mackenzie looked grimly at the victim. 'I'll need another shot for her too. You don't need to see that. Away you go in and sit before you fall down.'

She heard the other shot as she went inside, but didn't turn, going instead to huddle by the sitting-room fire. When Mackenzie came in he was carrying two glasses.

'Brandy,' he said. 'I think we both need it.'

Her teeth chattered against the edge of the glass. 'That was just so horrible! It would have killed me. I thought they were meant to be afraid of people! And you'd managed to scare one off before . . .'

'I had a big stick and a dog, and even then it was touch and go. Once they have a taste of meat, they'll defend their prey. Still, that one's had his last lamb and Sean Reynolds can't spout his rubbish about me not knowing what a wolf looks like. He's in big trouble now.'

He was picking up the phone as he spoke. 'Police,' he said.

The Sinclairs came back into the house. The drama was more or less over, a couple more police cars had arrived and people were drifting away from the gathering in the street now that everyone had claimed their turn to say they'd known there was a wolf there all along.

'Well, that will fix the bastard,' Ranald said with some satisfaction as he walked in behind Hattie, smiling. 'It could even land him in jail, with luck.'

Hattie stopped dead, turning to look at him, and Ranald turned red. 'Yeah, I suppose . . .'

'I don't think it's funny that a beautiful creature has been needlessly killed and for some reason I'm feeling a bit sensitive over jokes about jail,' she said stiffly. 'What we need to do now is decide what we're going to do about your own particular problem.'

Subdued, he followed her into the kitchen. 'I'm going to make coffee. Want some?'

She shook her head wearily as she sat down at the table, absent-mindedly patting the dogs who were greeting her. 'I've drunk so much coffee already that I won't sleep for a week if I have any more. We've agreed we need to contact Kelso, right?'

Ranald gave a sigh that was almost a groan. 'Yes, right. But I think it would be better if you called him. He was very short with me the last time we spoke, and he'll be more sympathetic towards you. He'll realise that it will affect you too and that you don't deserve that, even if I do. It's not just that I'm hiding behind your skirts.'

Hattie thought he was, in fact; Ran had never been into humiliating acknowledgements of his mistakes and if one had to be made it would be more comfortable at one remove. Even so, she didn't trust him not to get stiff-necked about it and she would be more likely to strike a better tone – for what good that might do.

'Oh, very well,' she said, then, reluctantly, 'Might as well be now, I suppose. I can say I've called to tell him about the wolf, and work round to it.'

'He's probably heard already, but you might as well.' He sat down at the table and propped his head on his hands as Hattie made the call.

He hadn't heard, in fact. There was no need for anyone to have informed him, and Strang was suitably astonished, and anxious.

'Is the detective all right?'

'It must have been a terrible experience for her, but apparently she's pretty much OK. It's certainly been a shock to us all.'

'I can imagine. Well – thanks for letting me know, Hattie.'

He was puzzled that she'd bothered; she wouldn't know either that he had worked very closely with 'the detective' or that he was nearby. It only became clear that it had been an excuse when Hattie said, 'Actually, Kelso, can I sound you out about something?' It wasn't hard, then, to guess what was coming.

'I don't want to take advantage of our friendship,' she began, and he cut in.

'Hattie, if this is to do with the investigation, I can't be involved.'

She said, 'I know. But it's only indirect, it's only asking for a friend's advice, in the abstract. If a friend of yours was going to admit to doing something that was – well, wrong, what would be the best way to go about it?'

His heart gave a little leap. Yes! But he said, very gravely, 'I'm a police officer, Hattie, even when I'm not on duty. The best advice I can give is that the admission should be made at the earliest opportunity to whoever is handling the investigation. There are considerable advantages to be gained from an unforced confession. All I'm able to do, as a friend, is to suggest that your friend gets the best possible lawyer as soon as he can.'

He heard the defeated note in her voice as she said, 'Yes, I see. Thanks, anyway,' and put down the phone.

It was Hattie he was truly sorry for. Ranald – well, he deserved what was coming to him. But Hattie, who had worked so hard at making a satisfying life here, was going to lose it. They couldn't go on living here, after what he'd done.

And there was going to be drama too, with Sean Reynolds and his wolf. He'd joked to Hattie that they lived life on the edge out there in Inverbeg but he'd never imagined anything like this.

His brain was whizzing with ideas, but he'd have to wait patiently for the summons that would only come once Ranald Sinclair had made his confession. As long as he didn't change his mind.

CHAPTER EIGHTEEN

Shirley Reynolds had gone up to bed early. She was tired and stressed and Maia, normally the personification of serenity, had been jittering around all evening, making arrangements for Antony Stanton coming, and it had started to get to her. Maia was a married woman, married to Shirley's own son, for heaven's sake, and here she was behaving like a love-struck teenager. It was when she had fluttered, 'It's so difficult to know how to make sure all this doesn't spoil Antony's visit,' that Shirley decided she'd had enough.

'I'm going to bed,' she had said abruptly, knowing that in another minute she'd have found herself giving Maia her character, which wouldn't be constructive.

Now she was theoretically watching TV, though if anyone had asked her what the programme was about she'd have been hard-pushed to tell them. She couldn't even have told them what she was thinking in any coherent way, as different worries crashed around in her head.

When she heard the police sirens – three, at intervals –

her heart began pounding so that she thought she might be having a heart attack. If only she knew what was happening! But no one came to tell her and no one rang the doorbell – as surely they would if it was anything to do with them? – and eventually she felt calmer and even a bit sleepy. No doubt she'd hear about it in the morning.

She had just turned the TV off when her bedroom door burst open and Sean lurched in. He looked distraught; he was sobbing as he staggered over to throw himself on his knees by the bed and buried his face in the covers.

'Oh Mum, I've done this terrible, terrible thing! It's all my fault! I so believed it would be all right, but now this has happened!'

Was it still possible to speak when your heart has stopped? Through stiff lips, she said, 'What have you done, Sean?'

'He's dead!' He looked up at her from swollen eyes. 'Lying there, limp, broken – that noble, majestic creature! And his silver ruff, clotted with blood—'

Struggling to make sense of it, she said, 'Ruff? Sean, are you talking about a wolf?'

'Yes of course! Akela – I can't bear it!'

'And are you telling me you killed him?'

'Killed him? No, of course not! Except that I did, I suppose, in a way.' He was still shuddering with sobs, but he had sat back on his heels, wiping his nose with the back of his hand.

Summoning up the voice she would have used to him when he was still a child, Shirley said, 'Sean, you're going to get up and fetch the tissues from the dressing-table and then sit in that chair and blow your nose and tell me exactly what's happened.'

He did as he was told, becoming gradually calmer. 'It was that idiot policewoman. She thought it would be a good idea to drive him off when he was eating a sheep, but naturally he was going to defend his kill—'

Her voice sharp with horror, Shirley said, 'Did he attack her? Is she hurt?'

'Oh no, perfectly all right. But that bastard Mackenzie – he could just have fired to scare him off. Oh, I'll go after him for that! He'd no right to shoot to kill.'

She'd been moved by his distress, but now sympathy evaporated. 'Oh, I think you'll find he had every right,' she said acidly. 'A farmer's entitled to kill any animal worrying sheep and a wild animal that shouldn't be roaming free at all, and was about to attack a woman – thank God he did, that's all I can say! And you should be grateful too.'

'Well, I'm not.'

He was glaring at her. He wasn't used to her speaking to him like that; she should have done it a lot more often, challenged him rather than choosing to keep things pleasant.

'Can I ask what's happening now?'

His shoulders drooped again. 'Now I'm going to have to work out what to do for Raksha. He was her mate, after all – she'll be confused, frightened . . .'

'I can't say I'm too bothered about her feelings. What has happened with the police? They've spoken to you?'

'Oh, they've spoken to me all right. Arrested me, in fact. I'm to go to the police station tomorrow to be charged, despite the fact that the government and everyone agrees that wolves and lynx belong in their original habitat—'

'Not everyone, actually. There's one right here in this room who doesn't. Sean, you must take this seriously. What are the police going to do about the female?'

He looked sulky. 'Nothing. They don't know she's there.'

Shirley stared at him. 'Sean, I can't believe this. You're in serious trouble. Why make it worse?'

'Oh, I'll go up and leave food to tempt her into the cage. And then, all right, if it makes you happy, I'll find some zoo where the poor girl can drag out the rest of her life in captivity.'

Suddenly she was very angry, very angry indeed. 'No, it doesn't "make me happy". Bringing them here at all was disgustingly selfish, and now you've made both those poor creatures suffer. And I don't suppose Angus enjoyed having to kill it either, and I don't suppose the sheep came very well out of it, never mind the policewoman. I blame myself too; I had a feeling that this was what you were doing and it was cowardly of me not to take you on.'

Sean stood up, bristling with hostility. 'Oh, thanks a whole heap! I'm sorry to have bothered you. I was naive enough to think that my mother would understand my pain and sympathise, even if my wife doesn't. It's apparently more important to see to it that nothing messes up Stanton's visit than to help me cope with all this. Well, sod him, frankly! And sod her, too.'

He went out and slammed the door. Shirley sank back onto her pillows and closed her eyes, still shaking with the intensity of her anger. How dare he behave so badly! He was her son, she'd brought him up, as she thought, to have proper standards. She'd obviously failed.

And now she was left to ask herself, if he was capable of that level of callousness, could she be sure that a more dreadful crime couldn't be laid at his door?

There were two police patrol cars, their lights flashing, outside the community hall when DI French arrived back from her visit to DCI Strang. With a touch of panic, she stepped out of the car to hear the siren of another car approaching. What in God's name had been going on while she was away?

PS Erskine spotted her coming into the community hall and hurried over. 'Bit of a drama, ma'am. There's cars arriving from miles round about, but we're not needing them – we've got it under control.'

'What happened?'

'Mr Reynolds has been keeping a wolf loose on the estate. Livvy found it attacking a sheep and tried to scare it off – maybe not very smart, but you know what she's like! Mr McKenzie had to shoot it.'

'Good grief!' French looked round and saw Murray, still looking shaken, sitting talking to a woman PC, and went over.

'Livvy – are you all right? What a dreadful thing!'

Murray produced a grin. 'Oh, never laid a tooth on me! I'll be fine.'

French was far from convinced – the grin had a very wobbly edge – but Murray wanted to tell her about it and she sat down to listen.

It was a long story and Murray was visibly flagging by the time she reached the final act of the drama. 'And then they brought in Sean Reynolds. He was going radge – you'd have thought Angus Mackenzie had killed his granny, yelling away about how he should just have given it a wee fright when it looked as if it was going to come for me too, and then let it get on with finishing its snack. He's unhinged!'

'I think he must be.' French turned to Erskine. 'So where is he now, Bob?'

'We've said he can come in tomorrow to the Lochinver station to be charged. Not going to do a runner, is he?'

She agreed. 'Wouldn't be worth it. Hefty fine, at most, but with all this emphasis on the environment, my guess is they'll make allowances.'

'I wouldn't,' Murray said with some feeling. 'But whatever they do, his real punishment will be the wolf being killed.'

Suddenly she gave a huge yawn and French said, 'You need to go to bed, Livvy – you're shattered. Don't hurry in the morning.'

Murray nodded and got up. She was still looking shaky, but she said, 'Did you see the boss, ma'am?'

French hadn't realised she knew that. 'Er . . . yes, he's in a cottage not far from here. He's suggested we get together for a session, just to pool our ideas.'

'That would be good. Sooner the better, with all this stuff now. Night, everyone.'

Watching her go, Erskine said, 'You have to hand it to her – she's tough. Mackenzie heard the sheep bleating first and it was lucky his gun cupboard's by the back door. It would only have been seconds before the wolf attacked – her life must have flashed before her eyes.'

'What worries me is what will happen when she closes them tonight. I wouldn't like to have the nightmares she'll be having.'

And French was having a few herself now, about what JB would say about what had happened on her watch.

DCI Strang arrived at Donald Mackay's office promptly at nine-thirty. He had hoped to have heard from DI French by then; he was on tenterhooks about Ranald Sinclair. Confessing would be a hard thing for a proud man to do. Of course, she'd have plenty to keep her busy this morning – the media would be thrilled at this second chance for 'WOLF!' headlines.

Mackay welcomed him in and they sat down at the desk. There was a file lying there – a disappointingly slender file.

'Yes,' Mackay said, noticing his expression. 'Not a lot there, I'm afraid. Deeds for the house, details of her bank account, investments and so on. She was very efficient, very precise.' He pushed the file across to Strang.

'No personal stuff like medical records and so on?' he said, opening it.

'No. Must have kept them at her house, I suppose, and there she wasn't organised at all. The cottage had a mess of papers all over the place. We had to send people in to clear them up before Danni arrived.'

Strang looked up. 'Odd to be so messy at home, when she was so precise otherwise.'

Mackay didn't seem struck by that. 'Oh, a lot of people are more careful when they're dealing with a lawyer – time is money, you know.'

The first item was a copy of the will of Flora Maitland or Reith. Stripped of the usual legal terminology, it was brief and straightforward: a bequest to Angus Mackenzie of £5,000, a bequest to Cameron Christie of £10,000 and the rest to Danielle Maitland.

Strang raised his eyebrows. 'Cameron Christie?'

'Yes. Can't really help you there – no idea who that is. Didn't mean anything to the Maitlands and Flora didn't comment, just gave me the name and address, but he isn't there. It's a block of flats in London and tenants move to and fro all the time. We're pursuing it but no luck so far.'

'Right,' he said. 'Send me what you have and I'll pass it on to the Met. If this is someone of interest, they'll track him down.

'Now – what's this?'

'This' was a plastic envelope and Strang pulled out the papers inside and riffled through them – about fifty, probably. They seemed to be lists of names and numbers.

'Doesn't mean anything to me,' he said.

'Nor me.' Mackay hesitated. 'I'm not sure if this is breaking a client's confidence – I've wrestled with it, but in the circumstances I feel I should tell you. When she gave me that, she said to keep it safe for her but that once she was dead I could just chuck it out. I was going to do that once we'd wound up the estate, but the tax department isn't exactly quick on its feet.'

'So I can take this, then?'

'William Maitland's exact words were that you could take what you effing well liked as long as he didn't hear any more about it.'

'I'm not able to promise that, but I think if a case were to be brought it would be more London-centred – and once I get this to the Met and they start digging it just might give us an insight into what's been going on here.'

He got up. 'Many thanks for your time. If they find this Cameron Christie, I'll make sure you get the address.'

'That would be kind. We've a duty to pay it out and I'd been puzzling about what to do next. A private detective seemed – well, a bit too Sam Spade for around here.'

Strang laughed, though recent events in Inverbeg had rather knocked its 'peaceful backwater' image, and he went back to the car with plenty to think about. Mackay hadn't seemed to think it strange that the highly efficient Flora Maitland would have left papers 'all over the place' in her own home, but to him it suggested that someone who'd been searching for something had been forced to do it hastily.

Perhaps, just perhaps, the file he was holding was what they'd hoped to find. From what Flora had said to Mackay, it sounded almost like her insurance policy. If he was right, it was going to make DCI Jason Dryden of the Metropolitan Police a very happy man.

And Cameron Christie – could the legacy be conscience money for Flora Maitland's undisclosed sin? Perhaps Angus Mackenzie might recognise the name.

The phone rang as he got back into his car and his pulse rate rose just a little as he picked it up and said, 'Strang.'

DC Livvy Murray had tried to take a lie-in but she woke at half-past six, feeling as if she'd been on the lash the night before. It wasn't fair to have a pounding headache after just one wee glass of brandy taken for medicinal reasons.

It was probably lucky she couldn't remember her dreams in detail, but she had a vague feeling of having been constantly pursued and getting lost. She was actually grateful to escape from sleep and got up without trying to doze off again. A long shower helped and after that she dressed and went out, keen to see what the day would bring.

The community hall was open already and DI French was sitting at a computer looking wan, as if she'd been staring at it for some time. She looked up as Murray came in.

'Livvy! How are you? After last night I thought you might sleep in.'

Murray pulled a face. 'Better being busy. What's on for this morning?'

'Sean Reynolds is being lifted at eight o'clock and taken in to the Lochinver station to be charged under the Dangerous Wild Animals Act. The advantage of that is, when the media turn up I can say that the matter is now sub judice and I've drafted the barest possible statement. I'll clear it with DCS Borthwick once she gets into her office, but that should be all right.

'I'm just ordering investigations in Glasgow to find out more about Danni's background, and when Bob arrives I'm going to have him run police checks for local names – not that I'm expecting much, though you never know. I've put in for a search team to check out Sinclair's yard, and I think too that you could push him a bit harder today – he was definitely on edge yesterday. All right?'

Hallelujah! French's little chat with the boss must have galvanised her and at last there seemed to be signs of action. 'Yes, of course, ma'am,' she said. 'Shall I head round there right now?'

'Why not? Sooner the better. You might get him before he's properly awake.'

'Right.' She hesitated, then said, 'Is there a plan for the meeting with DCI Strang? I wouldn't want to miss it this time.'

She'd chanced her arm with the last two words and French gave her a cool look. 'Not right now. But I'll certainly see that you're included.'

Murray wasn't really feeling jealous – of course not! But she was getting the nasty feeling that French wanted to keep Strang to herself, maybe even because she didn't want Murray to spot that she needed him to feed her ideas. If so, it was way too late for that – it had been obvious right from the start that she'd none of her own. She'd said there was going to be a session, though, and Murray wasn't going to let her forget it.

There was no one around and after a frosty start it was raining, the sort of soft rain that couldn't quite decide whether to do it properly and soak you at once or just drizzle away all day. She put up her hood anyway and squelched though the puddles to the Sinclairs' house.

The lights were on, so she wouldn't be dragging Sinclair out of bed – a pity, that. She would bet he'd have properly posh pyjamas and seeing what those looked like would be a chance unlikely to be repeated. She rang the front doorbell.

It was Harriet Sinclair who opened it, heavy-eyed and pale. 'Oh! You're – you're very early.' She sounded dismayed.

'Sorry to disturb you, but I wanted another word with your husband.'

'I suppose . . .' she said, then, 'Yes. Yes of course. Come in. He's in the kitchen.'

Sinclair was sitting at the table with a mug of coffee in front of him. It was a cosy, domestic scene: the Aga, the pretty china arranged on the dresser, the dogs trotting forward to greet her and the smell of toast in the air – as long as you didn't notice Sinclair's hunted look and the hands that shook as he set down his mug.

'Oh God, you!' he said, with marked distaste. 'It would have to be you, of course.'

She knew he didn't like her but she didn't quite understand the tone. 'I'm sorry, sir?' she said at the same time as Hattie said warningly, 'Ranald—'

He got up. 'I haven't many options but I'm damned if I'm going to give you the satisfaction. Where's your inspector?'

'DI French? At the community hall, I think.'

'I'll go there, then.' He headed for the back door and when Hattie made to follow him said roughly, 'No, don't come. The loss of dignity is bad enough and being humiliated in front of my wife would be intolerable.'

She burst into tears. The dogs swirled round her, fussing, and Murray, feeling there was nothing she could say that wouldn't make things worse, quietly let herself out.

Now she understood what was happening, she should have been feeling triumphant. But somehow all she could feel was sadness at the wrecking of two lives, all over something as stupid as a few acres of crappy farmland.

But it wasn't only their lives. Yes, Ranald Sinclair might be feeling mortified, but it was Danni Maitland who had been the real victim of the struggle and there was nothing dignified about lying in a pull-out drawer in a morgue with an identity tag round your big toe.

It took Shirley Reynolds a long time to get out of bed. She'd been so tense that she'd slept badly and it felt as if every individual joint had to be coaxed back into functioning before she could even stand up. She took her pills and creaked around, washing and getting dressed, and by the time she sat down at her dressing table they were at least starting to take effect.

The face that looked back at her out of the mirror was a horror show. Beige and baggy were the words that came to mind. Oh, she'd never been a beauty, but she'd always kept up her standards and you could get a long way too with vivacity and a great smile. She couldn't conjure one up this morning, though, and her hand shook as she tried to pencil in her brows and outline her mouth with one of her morale-boosting red lipsticks.

She was wearing her favourite wrap dress in that same red after giving it a lot of thought – what, after all, she'd wondered with a flash of sardonic amusement, does one wear for one's son's arrest and the visit of one's daughter-in-law's lover? – and now she fastened a double string of pearls round her neck, got her stick and stood up, as ready to face the day as she ever would be.

Shirley had no idea what would be waiting for her as she walked along from her ground floor bedroom to the kitchen. She could hear Ishbel hoovering upstairs but there was no one else around and she didn't know whether that was a good sign or a bad one. She could smell something cooking so presumably Maia was still preparing for her visitor.

It was a very smart kitchen, the sort you could see featured in women's magazines – all pale ash-grey wood and cream paint with the appliances concealed behind their own little doors. It wasn't very welcoming on a dull, dreich morning, though. Maia was chopping vegetables with what Shirley thought was unnecessary vigour and when she said good morning the look Maia gave her over her shoulder was cool to say the least.

'Good morning, Shirley. Would you like some tea?'

'Yes please. And toast, if it's not too much trouble.' She sat down at the table that had been set for breakfast; there were two dirty mugs, she noticed, but it didn't look as if anyone had eaten much.

Maia didn't assure her that it was no trouble. She left the vegetables, made a pot of tea from the boiling water tap and put bread in the toaster, then went back to them, her mouth in a thin straight line.

Sooner or later Shirley had to say something. 'Is Sean all right? He was in a bit of a state last night.'

Maia whipped round. 'Do you know, I don't really care how your son is. At the moment he's at the police station – they came to get him at eight o'clock. He's totally screwed up with his obsession with his bloody wolves. I was so anxious that despite everything else we could make this a good day for Antony – and it's a big day for Ben

291

too. Provided Antony is with me about appointing him to the board, we'll be having a dinner tonight to celebrate, whether Sean's back here or rotting in jail.' She took a deep breath, then said in a milder tone, 'I'm sorry, Shirley, but I'm frightened when I think of all the damage he has managed to do.'

Shirley bent her head. 'I can't defend him. I can't defend myself either – I knew, as you did, what he was doing and neither of us put a stop to it.'

'I thought he'd get away with it! There's all those deer they're supposed to eat – I wasn't to know they'd leave the forest and come down here. If he'd got the extra land, he'd probably have got permission to fence it off and the wolves would keep people from just wandering about all over the place.

'Still, I've put a stop to it now. I told the police about the female this morning, so they'll be out after her today, no doubt. Hopefully with a gun.'

Shirley gasped at the callousness. She was angry with Sean, yes, but she knew what it would do to him to be responsible for that death too. Maia had just put the toast on to a plate for her, but she realised she couldn't eat it. She levered herself to her feet.

'Sorry to have bothered you – I'm not hungry, after all.'

'Fine,' Maia said indifferently. 'I'll get Ishbel to bring you through coffee later.'

There were tears in Shirley's eyes as she went through to the sitting room. She'd been grateful to her son and his wife for giving her a home when age and infirmity had taken away her independence, and she had learnt that when you were a parasite the opinions you had always expressed so freely in the past were only welcome if they were asked for. She had bridled her tongue and she despised herself now, when she realised she had been determinedly ignoring the quagmire shaking beneath her feet.

CHAPTER NINETEEN

'I'm looking to you to take a grip on this,' DCS Borthwick said. 'At least we have Sinclair's confession to announce – makes it look like progress, even if it's tangential. But I have a distinct feeling that the homicide investigation is drifting.'

Strang didn't want to dump DI French in it but not being able to deny that he'd come to the same conclusion, he told her the result of his meeting with Donald Mackay by way of diversion.

'I'm pleased we have something to hand to the Met,' he said, 'but I also think it offers us a fresh angle on the situation here.'

'You said that before,' Borthwick said, 'but I get the impression French is looking in Danielle Maitland's social circle. The two most likely suspects have alibis, but she mentioned checks on her Glasgow background and police checks on local people?'

He smiled inwardly; French had clearly implemented his recommendations right away. 'Sounds a good idea – we need to keep an open mind. But I'm keen myself to home in on Sean Reynolds, who's been very elusive so far. There's a story there we need to know.

'I'm going to meet French and Murray whenever they've got Sinclair taken off to Inverness. He'd hate to see me watching and we don't want any sort of scene – there'll be reporters following up the wolf story any time now.'

Borthwick made an impatient noise. 'Oh, that really was seriously unfortunate. It was what drew all the interest in the first place, and this will crank it up again – by now we could have hoped for a small report on an inside page. Murray's humanitarian instincts were no doubt laudable but it's not helpful and we need to keep her out of it if at all possible. It will come out in court, but meantime just give them the story about the sheep being attacked and hope that stalls them.'

'I think we have to accept it will be all round the neighbourhood by now, but I can certainly see that Murray plays it down.' Then he paused. 'Now, what about French?' He'd hate to see her packed off unceremoniously whenever he arrived.

'Do you need her?'

'Initially, at least. I'll need a full debrief anyway, and she could concentrate on coordinating backup evidence for the cases with Sinclair and Reynolds. There's precious little local support, and that would give me space to assess things and work out how much longer we need to stay – hopefully, just a couple more days before we hand on to Inverness.'

Money was always the bottom line and he could almost hear JB calculating. 'Right,' she said at last. 'But send her back whenever you can, and keep it tight yourself – we really don't have the budget to cover your Highland holidays.' There was a smile in her voice.

'I promise to resist the temptation to drag my feet, even though it's very appealing here, when it isn't raining.'

'Which it more or less always is, as I understand it. Edinburgh's bad enough – sun and sand for me when it comes to holidays. Anyway, keep me posted.'

Strang was amused. He'd never really thought of JB as a sun-worshipper, more a sort of Italian-cities-and-galleries-wearing-a-floppy-hat type. It seemed almost insubordination to think of her wearing a bikini and he'd plenty more to think about as he set off for Inverbeg.

The events of the last twenty-four hours had changed the whole investigation. It almost felt as if undergrowth was being cleared away so that you could at last see the pattern it had been covering.

DC Murray found herself at a bit of a loose end. She hadn't been detailed to do anything except interview Ranald Sinclair; since he was now presumably in the community hall talking to DI French, it wouldn't be helpful to upset him by turning up to cheer on the sidelines, considering what he'd said.

She went back to her pod and checked on her phone to see if anything had come in overnight but there didn't seem to be anything useful. She checked the news website and stiffened when she saw the headline, 'Wolf shot in Highland village.'

My God, they'd got on to that quickly! And there would be stringers locally retained by the main newspapers who would be on their way – might be outside even now. She didn't need to be told not to share her experience, but she'd seen the crowd in the street last night and there'd be folk here who'd sell their granny for a mention in the local paper, let alone the Scottish Sun.

Still, she couldn't stay hiding in here all day, and then she remembered – Kasper Novak! Danni's killing could have happened in a moment of blind rage – say if he'd come round to tell her to keep away and she'd defied him. She could picture it, in lurid detail.

She didn't really think it was likely, but the door-to-door checks had only been for useful information, not checking personal movements; Hattie Sinclair had mentioned the animosity that existed, so even though Angus Mackenzie had bridled at the notion, Novak should at least be properly questioned. And it would give her something to say she'd checked out on her own initiative when it came to show-and-tell at the Strang meeting.

There was no one who might be a journalist hanging around when she emerged. The pub itself was shut but she saw someone coming out of the shop at the other end and headed for it. It was quite busy, for Inverbeg: there were four women and one older man gathered at the counter and Zofia Novak was talking when she came in.

'I had the call from her this morning – no more frozen meals from today. She goes away, she says.'

'Saw him going into the hall earlier,' the man said. 'Wonder what he wanted, this time of day?'

Zofia noticed Murray and smiled. She was a plump, pretty woman with big dark eyes and rosy cheeks. 'Sorry – we were just chatting. I can do something for you?'

She held up her warrant card. 'DC Murray. I was wondering if I could have a word with your husband?'

They didn't actually shrink from her, but she felt as if they had. There was suddenly a chill in the atmosphere and Zofia said, 'Very well, I will see. He is in the bar.'

She disappeared through a door and Murray was left in an uncomfortable silence. At last, one of the women said, 'All right, are you, after last night?'

'Oh, fine,' she said and added firmly, 'It wasn't as dramatic as it looked, you know.'

Unconvinced, the woman shrugged. 'Not what I heard,' she said as Zofia came back and said, 'You can speak with him now. Through here.'

As she shut the door behind her, Murray could hear the conversation starting again. Kasper Novak was waiting for her, polishing one of the beer taps.

'You want to see me for something?'

She went through the usual routine – introduction, just standard questions, grateful for your help – but he was looking at her with coldly suspicious eyes.

'You say this, but a detective doesn't come to ask these "standard questions" to everyone, do you?'

'We're getting round everyone whom we think has some sort of acquaintance with Danielle Maitland and I think you knew her quite well.'

'She came to the pub, yes. Not otherwise. There are many others who knew her the same or better.'

He was interestingly defensive. Did he have reason to be? She wasn't there to argue and dance around the fact that his attitude to Danni had been hostile. 'You didn't like

298

her much, did you, sir? She was a considerable nuisance to you.'

She couldn't tell what he was thinking, but he was stressed; his jaw had tightened into a rigid line. 'I am a publican. We are used to dealing with difficult customers. If it is a problem, I can ban them. You cannot say I kill her, just for this!'

'Of course not, sir,' she said. But he was almost visibly twitching, and she persisted, 'Did you ever meet her outside the pub?'

'No! Never!' Novak raised his voice and Murray became aware that the conversation next door had stopped and that he was gripping the bar counter so hard his knuckles had gone white.

All at once there was a cold feeling in the pit of her stomach. It wasn't because he was guilty he was acting like this. He was just plain frightened. And perhaps, if you were an immigrant, you might be. She'd done it again, followed gut instinct instead of straightforward procedure.

'Right. Thank you, sir,' she said as soothingly as she could. 'That's very helpful. Now, can you just tell me what you did on Monday? Did Danni come in that day?'

He looked round wildly. 'Monday? The day before she is found? Well, I am here. In the morning I prepare the bar and help my wife with shop things. I am open after twelve and we are here till we close. The girl did not come. Then my wife and I go to bed and the next day, we do it all again.'

Murray pasted on a sickly grin. 'That's a very full account. I don't think we need to bother you any more. If anything occurs to you, will you let us know?'

The tension went out of him so abruptly that he noticeably sagged. 'So far I do not think of anything, but if I do, naturally I will.'

Murray thanked him again, ran the gauntlet of silent disapproval in the shop and stepped out into the street. She'd got above herself, what with her success over Sinclair and the feeling that she had to direct operations because French wasn't taking the lead, and she'd done exactly what Strang constantly told her not to do – thought of a motive and looked for the evidence to fit it. She wasn't going to be boasting about this to him. More hoping he wouldn't find out.

At least the police car that had been sitting outside had gone, presumably taking Ranald Sinclair with it, so she could go back to the community hall to find out what was happening. As she walked up the road, a voice hailed her. 'Excuse me! You're the detective who was attacked by the wolf, aren't you?'

She turned. There was a man in jeans and a hoodie that was already soaked through, holding a small recorder.

'No,' she said, without stopping. 'I wasn't, nor was anyone else.'

'I was told—' he began.

'Then you were told wrong,' she said. Just as she went into the hall, a Land Rover swept past her with Harriet Sinclair at the wheel, looking fixedly straight ahead, and with the two dogs in the back.

Murray gave a sigh as she closed the door firmly behind her.

* * *

300

Ishbel had brought Shirley Reynolds' coffee but they hadn't had their usual chat. She'd asked sympathetically how Shirley was feeling but avoided the hottest topic, only saying that Maia seemed to be pushing the boat out with supper for her visitor. 'Smoked salmon and venison – nothing but the best!'

'Do you know when he's expected?' Shirley asked.

'Mid-afternoon sometime. It's just to be a sandwich for your lunch – will you go through to the kitchen or would you like me to bring it here?'

'Yes please,' Shirley said wearily. 'I don't want to get in the way.'

'Oh, she's in a bit of a stushie, right enough. Who is he, anyway?'

'He's on the board of Maia's father's London company. He's been here before, once or twice.'

When Ishbel had gone she thought back to Antony Stanton's previous visits. She hadn't paid him much attention at the time; there'd been a dinner party once and a drinks party when next he came, so she'd only retained a vague impression of someone older and very much the London businessman, wearing the sort of expensive tweeds that were expected at shooting parties. Tonight it seemed the entertaining was to be more domestic, with only Ben Linton added to the family party.

She hadn't seen Sean at all this morning, didn't even know if he'd come back from the police station, didn't know whether there was an official marksman out even now stalking the female wolf. Its death would be devastating for Sean and, whatever he had done, he was still her son and he'd get no comfort from his wife. And if he realised the situation with Stanton, it would be another blow to his pride. Her heart ached for him.

He appeared carrying sandwiches and mugs of soup at lunchtime. He had dark circles under his eyes and his hair was a stranger to the comb, but he looked calmer than he had the previous night and though his manner towards her was stiff, it seemed she was more or less forgiven.

'Maia told them about Raksha, you know. I told them I'd get her into the cage and they let me pick up some tranquilliser from the vet. Got a nice lamb gigot from the butcher and put it up there in the cage. I'll have to keep checking, of course, but I think she'll smell it, as long as some damned fox doesn't get there first. I'm pretty sure she's around there – the cage has basically been their den. Anyway, they've agreed to come and collect her once she's safe.'

'Well, that's a relief,' Shirley said. 'What did they say at the police station?'

'Not a lot. Nor did I. My lawyer told me to say "No comment" until he could get here,' he said, biting into a ham sandwich.

He seemed unworried by it, impervious to her own tension, and there clearly wasn't any point in asking anything more. Instead, she said, 'It seems it's going to be quite a fancy dinner tonight. Maia's been working flat out all morning.'

She was eyeing him closely. He didn't react, but she thought he sounded a little acid when he said, 'Ah well, have to keep him sweet. He's the one who sends the cheques, isn't he?'

She didn't know that. 'I thought it was Maia's dad,' she blurted out.

'Only sort of. Lucas is chairman, Stanton's the CEO. Have a sandwich.'

Shirley took it, wondering what exactly that meant. She'd never really known what the financial situation was and she didn't want to know. She'd more than enough worries at the moment; she'd no need to go looking for new ones.

The conference area that had been marked out in the community hall wasn't ideal; a few screens round the coffee table didn't give much privacy. Still, it would have to do and there were only three uniforms around anyway, including PS Erskine, who broke off his conversation when he saw the chief inspector.

'Hello, Bob,' Strang said, handing him the plastic envelope he was holding. 'Could you get this scanned for me and sent off to DCI Jason Dryden at the Met? I've emailed him, so he'll be expecting it. Thanks.'

Erskine was looking pleased to have him back. 'No problem, sir. Good to see you.'

Behind the screens he found French sitting, tapping at a laptop on her knee. She jumped up when he appeared, looking awkward.

'Hello, Kelso. Look, I don't know what the form is here. Do I vanish immediately now?'

He sat down. 'No, no. We've got a breathing space for a debrief and so that you can tie up what we need for Sinclair and Reynolds. As much corroboration as you can find – confessions have been withdrawn before now.'

She brightened. 'I'm on to that now, in fact.'

'Great. How is Livvy after her horrible experience?'

'Very brave throughout, but she has to be feeling shaken. Sinclair refused to speak to her this morning, and I think she's just keeping out of the way.'

'OK.' He opened up his laptop and was signing in just as Murray appeared through the screen, grinning when she saw him.

'Hello, Livvy. Are you all right?'

'Sure, boss. Not a scratch on me.'

'Thank goodness for that. We'll try to keep it quiet, OK?'

'I just told a reporter no one had been attacked. True, thanks to Angus.'

'Yes, played a blinder, didn't he? Now, Auchinglass House. Rachel – your interview with the two Mrs Reynolds. Can you flesh it out a bit for me?'

Her report had been disappointing. It was bald – no doubt accurate, but without any observation of reactions or sensitivities.

'I suppose I'd have to say Maia Reynolds was cooperative.'

Strang glanced at the report on his screen. 'She certainly gave you a very meticulous account of her movements that day.'

'Yes, sort of,' French said. Then she burst out, 'To tell you the truth, I felt she was taking the piss.'

Surprised, Strang and Murray stared at her as she went on, 'It was as if she was emphasising how utterly dumb it was that I would even need to ask her the questions. And on a purely practical level, I suppose it was – Danni wasn't what you'd call slight . . .'

'She wasn't,' Strang agreed.

'So she couldn't have transported the body. I just felt she was sneering at me the whole time, as if people like her shouldn't be subjected to such an intrusion. The only thing that threw her was that Joe Dundas hadn't been arrested; it was almost as if she'd been assuming he would.'

'Interesting,' Strang said. 'And the mother – Shirley?'

'Quite jolly, very ready to be helpful in theory, but nothing to add. They made an odd pairing. You could imagine her behind the bar of an old-fashioned local and the wife is so tasteful she's practically invisible.'

'Great description,' Strang said. 'Tensions there?'

French thought for a moment. 'Not that I could see.'

'And what about Reynolds himself? Did he just happen to be out or is he avoiding us?'

'She called him on her mobile and it went to answerphone, so I think it was genuine enough.'

Strang nodded. 'So no one's managed to speak to him yet?'

'Er . . .' Murray cleared her throat. 'Well, I have, sort of.'

French looked surprised. 'I didn't know that. Is there a report I haven't seen?'

'Um, no,' Murray said, looking uncomfortable. 'Not yet. It wasn't really an interview, actually.'

Strang frowned. 'What was it, then?'

'It was when you were talking to Angus, ma'am. I went to get address details for Mr Reynolds' workforce so we could go on and interview Joe Dundas. That was all, really.'

It wasn't all. Strang could tell that from the look on her face and he was disappointed; he thought Murray had got past that stage. She caught his expression.

'And, well, I did ask him why he sometimes went down that track that led to the tree plantation where they found Danni's body.'

'How did you know that?' French said sharply.

'Talked to Jonathan in the pub.' Murray sounded defensive.

There was a subtext here that Strang didn't understand. He'd been worried before that there might be friction, and this was it, right here. He stepped in swiftly.

'Am I to assume that you both knew this, but didn't communicate?' Neither woman spoke. He waited, then said, 'If we want the investigation to be successful, information needs to be shared. Livvy, perhaps you could report now.'

Murray gulped. 'Jonathan was one of the volunteers and he'd happened to notice because the track was a dead end. Reynolds didn't like being asked about it – he looked really taken aback, but then all he said was that he checked on all parts of the estate.'

She didn't meet his eyes. 'And . . . ?' Strang said.

Murray's face had gone red. 'There was just . . . well, I asked him about the wolf rumour and he was very rude and aggressive. Told me it was a fairy story and slammed the door in my face.'

'I see.' Then he turned to French. 'And you knew about this too?'

It was her turn to look embarrassed. 'It came up when I questioned the volunteers. I taped Jonathan's statement but I didn't feel it was immediately relevant. Joe Dundas was still chief suspect at the time.'

As he had thought before, this was what had been going wrong – too narrow a focus.

'Right. Let's move on, then. The DCI was delighted about Ranald Sinclair's confession – well done to you both.'

'Mainly Livvy,' French said. 'She was the one who got him pinned down,' and Murray murmured, 'Thanks, ma'am,' without looking at her.

'Obviously Reynolds can't be allowed to go on avoiding us. Interviewing him has to be a top priority. But I want to take a step back and look at what we've assembled is telling us.

'The crime scene evidence: Danni was having a drink with someone and something happened to make her assailant smash the bottle to use as a weapon. It's not unreasonable to read it as a sudden eruption of rage – there's no indication it was planned. She hadn't been assaulted or restrained, yet she disappeared on Monday morning – why, if she wasn't being confined somewhere? We want to know where she went, who she was with. We haven't yet been able to place anyone at the scene. No leads, am I right?'

Both women shook their heads. 'Any ideas?' he said.

Murray said, 'We've got round the locals, but I wonder if there was maybe a delivery that day? Or a lorry picking up from the fish farm?'

'Worth checking out, certainly. Pass that on to Bob. Anyway, the next step has to be speaking to Reynolds – Rachel, I want you with me on that, if you don't mind. Given that you've had a bit of a run-in with him already, Livvy, not to mention that you were nearly a victim of his folly, it wouldn't be appropriate. So get on with the backup on Sinclair, could you please?'

Looking crestfallen, Murray muttered, 'Yes, boss,' as the others left.

As they walked to Auchinglass House, French said, 'I want to apologise, Kelso. I feel I've been very unprofessional.'

His patience had been sorely tried. He took a sideways glance at her, then said bluntly, 'Quite honestly, you've both been a pain in the neck. Your agenda has been fear of losing authority, hers has been fear of losing her place in the team. It's actually the same problem. Talk to each other about it – or preferably, concentrate on just getting on with the job.'

They reached the front door. The woman who opened it was wearing a pink overall and told them Sean Reynolds had come in for his lunch and gone back out again. On her suggestion they went across to the old stable block where he had his office, but he wasn't there either.

To say that Maia Reynolds didn't look pleased to see them when they returned was a serious understatement. Through tightened lips, she said, 'I have no idea where he is. I'll give you his mobile number, then you can call him yourself.'

Strang entered it on his phone, then they had to step back smartly as she slammed the door shut.

Miserably, DC Murray opened up the file and settled down to pick up where the inspector had left off. Fair enough, she'd known that when she talked to Sean Reynolds she'd screwed up, but she'd hardly chosen to be 'nearly a victim'. So being stuck here felt like unfair punishment, especially when she knew French wouldn't have lots of ideas to offer in an interview – though maybe, now she thought of it, Strang would prefer it that way. She settled down to work gloomily, but at least she hadn't been forced to admit she'd screwed up with Kasper Novak too. He was unlikely to complain.

She was proud, though, that she'd made Sinclair realise confessing was his best option. And it was thanks to those interviews, too, that they'd been able to get Strang back on the job; she'd managed to show that there'd not been time that evening for Sinclair to go out, kill Danni and be back for bedtime.

Making notes on the Harriet Sinclair interview she took pride too in the way she'd managed to manoeuvre her into admissions she didn't want to make, working on the woman's honesty – much better than the aggressive tone she'd taken with her husband. She marked it down as a lesson to be learnt, even if it had got a confession from Sinclair.

Murray went on, marking up the important points. Suddenly she stopped. She reread it, and felt a chill run up her spine. There was a gap. She hadn't noticed it and nor had French.

The bus for the workers would go at – what – five, quarter past? Time enough there for Sinclair to decide he'd try to talk to Danni again, find she was no more ready to listen than she had been before and explode into uncontrollable fury.

The artery would go on pumping after it was severed and there would be a fine spray of blood – even if he leapt back instantly there had to be at least some on his hands, on his clothes, even. But it would have been dark by then; it would only have taken him minutes to get back to his office. Even on fabric, salt water removes fresh bloodstains and the sea was right there, in front of him. There would have been time for drying off in front of the fire before he went to the house for supper.

And he'd been wearing dark clothes when they interviewed him. She felt suddenly sick: had he been sitting there in front of her wearing clothes that might still hold traces of Danni's blood that had only been sponged away?

Surely he would have shown signs of stress when he went home? But then Sinclair obviously wasn't an even-tempered man anyway, and his wife would be used to ignoring his moods. After they'd eaten, he'd have had plenty of time to 'go back to work' and plan the disposal – find plastic sheeting or something. Then park his car at the cottage, drive up to the forest, clean up again in his office and back in plenty of time to be in bed and asleep – or if not actually asleep, to do some artistic snoring when Hattie came up to bed.

Murray leant forward, putting her head in her hands. What this meant was that it had been unsafe to conclude that Sinclair was only guilty of the car fire. Not only that, it meant that Strang shouldn't be back. His personal connection could affect the integrity of the whole investigation.

It was only a theory, though. It might not be right – and if it wasn't and he had to withdraw, she had no confidence at all that Danni would get the justice she deserved. French certainly hadn't spotted that gap.

So what was she going to do?

CHAPTER TWENTY

As DCI Strang and DI French walked back towards the community hall, the man who had approached DC Murray called to them, 'You're police, right? Kevin Muir.' He waved a press pass. 'What's the story with the wolf attack last night?'

They stopped and Strang said pleasantly, 'A sheep was attacked and the wolf had to be shot by the farmer. We'll be issuing a full statement later.'

Muir persisted. He was holding a notebook and he read from it, '"The wolf was attacking one of the polis when it got shot." That's what this lady said. Can you comment?'

'If that's what she told you she can't have been an eye-witness. As I said, there'll be a statement issued later through the Edinburgh HQ. Thanks.'

The man annoyed, said something else but he didn't wait to hear what it was. He'd turned away, anyway; hopefully he'd realised there was nothing more to hang about for. As they came into the hall PS Erskine came over.

'One of the lads who took Reynolds in this morning says there's another wolf up there. Reynolds is claiming he'll get it into a sort of cage they've got with drugged meat, but they've sent out for a vet and someone to track it. No word of when they'll manage to get here.'

'But it's still on the loose? That's all we need,' Strang said grimly. 'Let's just hope it's not general knowledge before that stringer gives up and goes home. Anyway, I'm going to summon Reynolds now, and if he isn't answering this time, we'll get people out looking.' He dialled the number.

It was answered immediately. 'Oh, I was expecting to hear from you. I suppose you want to speak to me.'

'Yes, we do, sir. At your earliest convenience.'

'I'm out on the estate at the moment. I can be back in quarter of an hour. You'd better come to the office. My wife's not happy about more police visits today – she's expecting a guest.'

'Quarter of an hour. Right,' Strang ended the call. 'That'll give me time to prepare JB. I usually try to find some good news to give her along with the bad, but I can't for the life of me think of any.'

He went back into the conference area where Murray was bent industriously over her laptop. She didn't look up when he came in until he asked her how it was going.

'Just logging the calls Sinclair says he made to the insurance company and the police on Danni's behalf, boss.'

French went over. 'That's good. I was planning to do that, and then to check from the other end what he actually said.'

'I'll chase that up next,' Murray said.

Strang glanced at her. She seemed very meek; he'd rather expected a chilly reaction to being passed over. Perhaps French wasn't the only one who was feeling guilty. Good!

He squirmed his way through the call to JB. 'So, do we come clean now,' he said at last, 'and tell everyone to stay inside until they track the beast, or do we assume that since the wolves have been there for some considerable time and they seem only to have a taste for mutton and the occasional detective, we just wait?' He'd said that with a smile in Murray's direction, but she didn't seem to have heard him.

DCS Borthwick said, as he had feared she would, 'You're on the spot, Kelso. What's your gut feeling?'

Strang hesitated. 'There was a reporter here, but I choked him off and if he's gone away I'm inclined to wait. I know it's a big risk, but you have to take those sometimes and just hope it all doesn't blow up in your face.'

'Comes down to that, doesn't it?' Borthwick said. 'If you're feeling lucky, Kelso, run with it.'

It hadn't exactly covered his back, but he hadn't thought it would. Switching off his phone, he noticed Murray looking at him with an expression he couldn't quite read. He hadn't time, though, to stop and try to work it out. Sean Reynolds should be waiting for them in the office by now.

As they walked along, a silver Range Rover drove past them and up to the parking area beside Auchinglass House.

'That must be Mrs Reynolds' visitor,' French said. 'I wonder who it is. Someone important?'

The man who was getting out was tall – six-one or six-two, with well-cut grey hair, wearing an expensive-looking green tweed sporting jacket.

'Looks the part, anyway,' Strang said. 'Now, for our Mr Reynolds. I'll lead the interview, but I'd like you to come in on the wolf question while I observe.'

Shirley Reynolds was having a little after-lunch nap when the sitting-room door opened and Ben Linton came in. He hesitated on the doorstep, looking tentative.

'Sorry – Maia said just to come straight in.'

She struggled upright. 'No, you're all right, love! Come and sit down. Only resting my eyes for a minute.' Now she looked at him, he wasn't just being tentative, he was looking nervous. He was never untidy but today he was looking particularly smart, as if he'd made a special effort, and as he sat down, he rearranged the collar of his shirt to make sure it was neat.

'Antony Stanton's texted Maia to say he'll be here any time now. She wanted me to come to greet him.'

Shirley looked at him shrewdly. 'Are you a bit nervous? He's the big man, isn't he?'

Ben gave a slightly shaky laugh. 'Just a bit. I don't really know what it's about, but I've got the feeling I'm going to be under scrutiny.'

He was right about that, anyway, she thought, remembering the conversation she'd had with Maia. 'I don't think you've any need to worry. I know they're dead chuffed with what you've been doing here. Anyway, I'm glad to have your company. How's things going out there? No one tells me anything.'

Ben looked hunted. 'To tell you the truth, I've no idea myself. The police come and go but I've no idea how they're thinking. The rumour is that Ranald Sinclair has been arrested for causing the car fire, but I don't know if that's right.'

'Goodness me!' If it was true, it could lift the weight of misery she was carrying. 'And the killing too?'

'Hopefully,' he said. 'But I haven't heard that yet. Hattie's left, though – told Zofia she won't be doing the frozen meals any more. That'll be a big headache for us when we have the next batch of volunteers and—' He broke off and stood up, looking out of the window. 'I think that's the car now.'

Oh dear, poor boy, he did look worried! Maia had obviously scared him, and Shirley thought that for all she was excited about Antony's visit, she was nervous too. She could hear Maia's footsteps going across the hall; the front door opening; her voice, higher than usual; a deeper voice, replying, then a short silence and laughter.

'Here he is!' Maia said gaily as she opened the door. 'You made very good time, Antony!'

Shirley had tried to remember what sort of impression he'd made before, but she hadn't really paid much attention. She did now, and as the man came in it felt almost as if she and Ben were supporting characters on a stage, waiting for the star's entrance. Everything about him – the silver-grey hair, the light tan that he certainly hadn't got in London, the faint tang of expensive cologne as he came across to kiss her on both cheeks – seemed perfectly calculated to exude power.

'Shirley, my dear! Good to see you – and looking younger than ever! You'll have to tell me your secret.'

315

Her flesh crawled. She said tartly, 'Tell the truth and shame the devil, as my gran used to say. She'd have the soap ready to wash out your mouth.'

She could see Maia looking horrified but Antony gave a delighted roar of laughter. 'Isn't she great!' he said. 'And now, this must be young Ben. Heard a lot about you from this lady.' He turned to smile at Maia over his shoulder as he went to shake Ben's hand.

Oh dear God, she was actually simpering. And now Ben was turning pink. 'How do you do, sir,' he said.

'Trying to make me feel old? Antony, of course.' He looked round. 'And where's the master of the house?'

'I'm not sure,' Maia said. 'There's been a bit of a fuss. He was crazy enough to import a couple of wolves before he'd got permission and the police are getting a bit stroppy with him.'

Antony had been smiling but suddenly his lips tightened. 'Oh?' was all he said, but somehow the temperature in the room dropped.

'The male's been shot and they're going to track down the female and deal with her,' Maia said hastily. 'Not a problem, really. Now, I'll bring through some tea and then Ben and I will take you up to the office and you can tell us where we've been going wrong and slap us about a bit.' She gave him a coy glance under her lashes, biting her lip like a little girl.

Shirley pressed what she called her ejector button and was gratified to see Stanton jump. 'No tea for me, thanks, Maia. I'm just going along to my room for a bit.'

'Fine,' Maia said, without really looking at her. 'Drinks around six-thirty, all right?'

As she left, she heard Maia say, with a note in her voice she'd never heard before, 'Antony, I can't really believe you're actually here at last. It's all that has been keeping me going.'

How Shirley would be able to cope with the evening, she didn't know – she'd left abruptly just now because she was afraid she'd have thrown up if she'd stayed.

And tonight, even if Sean was still obsessing about his blasted wolf, Maia was so blatant he couldn't possibly miss what was going on.

There was something of the sulky schoolboy about Sean Reynolds, DCI Strang thought, as he greeted them with a surly grunt. 'Don't need to introduce yourself,' he said. 'Saw you in the pub with the Sinclairs the other night.' He waved them to a padded bench on one side of a low table while he sat on one of the chairs opposite.

It was quite a small office, a sort of glass box partitioned off from a long room that still showed architectural signs of the stable it had once been, where a woman was working at one of three desks.

Reynolds' own desk was in a corner in front of a tier of bookshelves. There were several volumes out on the surface, a couple of them open as if he'd been consulting them. Strang didn't have time to see what they were before he had to sit down.

'You don't need to tell me I've been a naughty boy,' Reynolds said, echoing Strang's thought. 'They've given me smacked fingers already today, so you can skip that bit. I know I shouldn't have brought the wolves in yet, but I thought I'd just get them quietly established so that when I got the rest of the land I needed we'd be off and running. It's their right to live here – they were here before we were, after all.' He scowled. 'We'd have got away with just paying compensation for sheep, if that stupid woman—'

'I'm sorry, sir – can I just take you back on that? When you got the rest of the land you needed?'

'Oh, there's stupid regulations. The powers-that-be are keen on rewilding but it could be on the small side to be considered for enclosure once the political decision's made.'

'And how were you planning to get it?' Strang asked.

He gave him a truculent look. 'Well, Danni Maitland's croft, obviously. For a start.'

'And she had agreed?'

'Oh well, she hadn't, but she would've. She knew I'd top anything Sinclair could offer, no problem.'

'But the croft's acreage would make the difference?'

'Pretty much, I reckon, and it marches with the estate. And of course now,' his face brightened, 'I reckon Sinclair will be happy enough to sell his. Won't be able to set foot here again after what he's done.'

'Let's just return to the question of the croft. This was something you were counting on? You would be very upset if Ms Maitland did refuse to sell and it fell through?'

Reynolds' eyes narrowed. 'Hang on – are you trying to fit me up for this?'

'Certainly not, sir,' Strang said smoothly. 'But it would be helpful if you could tell us your movements on Monday?'

'Monday? Oh, for God's sake, I don't know! I hardly notice the days of the week here. Oh, it was then there was a delayed shipment came in and I'd to deal with it. After that, yes, I went in to Lochinver quite early on, I think – that's right, the garage. Took in a tyre with a puncture. Then I was around the estate – did a lecture to the volunteers – came in for lunch – worked here – fetched the tyre – had supper. And I remember I went out then because with all the rain one of the buildings was flooded. That's about it. Will that do?'

'For the moment. You could write that down and try to remember who you spoke to and at what time and it will be followed up.'

Reynolds looked as if he was about to argue, but French, with a glance at Strang, said, 'I want to ask you about the wolves. You said there was a cage. Where is it?'

Reynolds didn't like that question, did he? He squared his shoulders as if bracing himself. 'It's up the hill at the coastal edge of the estate – rough ground and a tree plantation. The sort of country where there's a bit of cover for them, and the deer like it too. That's why they're needed, you see – to stop the bastards killing off all the new trees.'

Strang and French exchanged glances. 'Do you mean it's near where Ms Maitland's body was discovered?' she said.

'Not near,' he said, but he looked uncomfortable. 'Away up near the coast, like I told you.'

'I see,' French said.

That was all, so Strang followed up. 'But it could be accessed from the track you were seen making visits to before?'

Reynolds was briefly startled, then said with a sneer, 'Oh that's right. That girl – Murray, was it? – seemed to have found someone who'd been spying on me. No, it couldn't.'

It was a pity the question hadn't taken him by surprise, but it probably wouldn't have made that much difference. 'So what were you doing on the track?' Strang went on.

Oddly, Reynolds was looking embarrassed now. 'If you must know, they sometimes hang around in that area and I like to watch for them. That's all.'

French said, 'So how do you get to this cage?'

'There's another disused track that leads round from the harbour. It's well out of the way and I put a bit of food in from time to time to keep them away from the crofting land. They'll see it as a den if they have pups.'

'The trouble is,' Strang said, 'it hasn't really kept them away, has it, sir? There's been trouble already, even before last night. So what's the position now? Is the female back in the cage?'

That didn't please Reynolds. 'Give me a break, OK? If she's in the area she should have smelt the doped lamb by now but me watching her has probably spooked her. I'll back off for a bit, wait till it gets a bit darker, when she'd naturally think about hunting. But if you sods get there first, I don't know what they'll do.'

Their level best to avoid killing it was the answer, but Strang didn't give it. It would do Reynolds good to sweat for a bit. 'I'm afraid I can't really say, sir,' Strang said then, glancing at French, 'I think that will do for the moment.'

French nodded and as they got up to go he added, 'Please keep us in touch about the situation with the wolf, and we will be looking for clearer details about your movements on Monday. Thank you for your cooperation.'

He stole a glance at the books on the desk as he went past and saw that the top one was open at a picture of a wolf opposite the chapter heading, 'Feeding habits.' The bookshelves behind looked like a reference library for rewilding projects.

As they walked away Strang said, 'Well, what did you make of that?'

'Obsessed to the point where he can't see straight,' French said. 'He got defensive when you challenged him but Danni Maitland's murder was an irrelevance, as far as he was concerned. He went right back to the wolves immediately.'

'You're right, of course. Do you think he might feel killing was justified in the service of a higher cause? Is the indifference innocence or just a lack of guilt?'

French thought for a moment. 'I see what you mean. He was sneering at us, rather the way his wife did. I think he feels entitled, that he's got the moral high ground on conservation so nothing he does can be questioned.'

She might not be a natural interrogator, but that was a good analysis. They were nearing the community hall when he stopped abruptly; he hadn't closed down the wolf story, after all. A small group of waiting journalists gathered round to shout questions as he arrived.

He muttered, 'Hold that thought,' to French, then stopped to repeat to them what he'd said earlier. They were still focusing on the wolf, so it didn't look as if Edinburgh had released a statement about Sinclair yet. That would provoke another flurry, so once inside the hall, he said, 'There's a lot we need to discuss arising from that. Livvy!'

DC Murray looked round hopefully. 'Yes, boss?'

'I think a strategic retreat to my cottage is called for. Grab what you need and we'll go now.'

As they left, the reporters hurried forward but they were away before anyone could follow.

Shirley Reynolds left it until quarter to seven before she walked slowly along to the sitting room. She'd tried to time it so that she couldn't find herself with just Antony oozing what he no doubt thought of as charm but which left her feeling as if she had slimy snail tracks all over her. She could hear voices and laughter now, so it was safe enough.

As she opened the door, Maia said, 'Oh for goodness' sake, Sean, give that to Antony! We'll have it all over the carpet if you open it like that.' She was wearing a silk dress with a softly layered cowl neck in a rich goldy cream, expensive-looking, flattering.

Sean was holding a bottle of champagne; he put it into Antony Stanton's outstretched hand. 'Oh, no doubt you get a lot more experience than we do out here in the sticks.'

'You can certainly say that again!' Maia said, laughing. 'I'm deprived, Antony!'

Depraved, more like, Shirley thought acidly as she made her way in. She could only hope that Sean, who had turned to greet her, hadn't seen that significant look.

'Shirley! Now the party can really get going,' Antony said, easing the cork out of the bottle with barely a whisper of sound. The shirt he was wearing – subtle pink – fitted so perfectly that it had to be tailored. 'Now, the first glass must be for you, but let's get you installed on your throne before you start.'

She gave him a straight-lipped smile and went to sit down, while Ben Linton brought over her glass. He was beaming, so things must have gone well. While Antony went on pouring she said quietly, 'You're looking a lot happier now!'

He started laughing. 'Better than I could ever have dreamt! I can't believe it! I'd no idea that Sean and Maia had this in mind. I don't need champagne – I feel high enough already.'

Sean had collected his glass and came over. 'Couldn't afford to lose you and she's got you tied down now. Got you trussed like a chicken, boy.'

Shirley saw a flash of anger in Ben's face at the contemptuous tone, but he managed to force a smile as Sean went on, 'Made you the offer you couldn't refuse, right? Maia spelt it out: she needs more freedom and she thinks I'm useless – can't be trusted on my own, you see?' He took a sip of champagne. 'Probably right.'

He hadn't changed for dinner; his shirt was crumpled and he looked downcast, drained of the energy that was so typical of him, and now he came closer Shirley could smell that there was drink on his breath already. Something to do with the wolf, no doubt, Shirley guessed, though he'd surely be more upset if they'd actually shot it. The wretched animal was most likely still out there, ready to cause more trouble.

'A toast!' Antony cried. 'Ben, congratulations on your promotion to the Auchinglass board. Well-deserved, lad, from what Maia tells me and what I could see of the work you've been doing. Ben Linton!'

'Ben Linton!' they all echoed, and Maia added, 'And to you, Antony, for confirming my judgement – oh, and Shirley as well. She recommended you too, Ben.'

True, she had. She'd been surprised at Maia asking for her advice, but it was clear that getting her blessing had been to blunt any suspicions Shirley might have had about her daughter-in-law's motives.

Ben tilted his glass to her. 'Thank you – I'm grateful.'

'I speak as I find,' she said. 'You've earned it.'

He made a little self-deprecating grimace. 'I'm still very grateful.'

As Antony and Maia clinked glasses, she gave him another of those long looks under her lashes and Shirley tensed. Sean had noticed, she was sure he had.

Sean raised his glass. 'And now, a toast to me since no one else is proposing it. To Sean, who's only useful for – well, I don't know what I'm useful for, really. Except having brilliant ideas that can save the planet, only they're not allowed to work.'

Maia and Antony exchanged worried glances. 'Nonsense, Sean!' Antony said. 'You're the one Maia relies on – you're the one who does the vision thing. You know that!'

'Do I? I don't think I do.' He was turning belligerent. 'I think she has . . . other interests now.'

With a sinking heart, Shirley realised that she'd been wrong; it wasn't a surprise to him.

He'd known well before this – even before Shirley had noticed, possibly – but absorbed in the wolf dream he was converting into reality he hadn't felt it mattered that much.

Before he could say anything more, she said, 'I was just wondering about Raksha. Has she come back to the cage? I know you've been worried.'

At least it distracted him. 'No,' he said heavily. 'No, she

hasn't. I went up there once it started getting dark and I think the meat had been moved but she hadn't eaten any. Maybe she could smell it was drugged, or too many people had handled it. She's still out there and I don't know when the bastards are going to get their killing squad here.'

'What are you going to do about it, then?' Maia said. Her voice was harsh, and as she spoke she gave an anxious glance at Antony, whose lips had tightened again.

Sean had gone to the drinks table to top up his glass. 'Go out tomorrow once it's light and get some stuff for her – rabbits or something. Lay a trail to finish in the cage. I reckon she's hungry – she wouldn't try for deer without her mate. Then I can hover around and get the gate shut.'

'I only hope you're right,' Maia said. 'Anyway, it's time we ate.' She went to the door. 'Shirley, can you do the sheepdog bit and get them to the dining room while I serve up?'

Thank goodness for that, Shirley thought. If Sean got something to eat it might help soak up the alcohol. But of course the first thing he did was pick up one of the decanters of red wine that was breathing in a coaster on the polished table.

He went round to his usual seat and was ready to fill up his glass when Maia said sharply, 'Sean, we always seat Antony at the head of the table as our honoured guest – remember? And perhaps he'd prefer white with the smoked salmon – there's a nice white burgundy, Antony.'

Antony, to be fair, looked uncomfortable and said hastily, 'No, no, old boy. No ceremony tonight.'

But Sean, looking thunderous and still clutching the

325

decanter, had gone to the other end of the table and sat down. He drank half a glass, then topped it up again.

Maia, her colour heightened, said, 'Shirley, you come and sit beside Antony. I'll sit here and Ben, you come on my left. And you could do the honours since the host seems to have abdicated.'

Shirley looked down at her plate, at the delicately sliced salmon, the lemon quarter tucked in muslin, the pretty salad of frilly lettuce and the plump, glistening mound of home-made mayonnaise and wondered how she would manage to eat a mouthful, let alone the whole plate, and the smell of the rich venison casserole floating through from the kitchen was a threat of what was to follow.

Perhaps she could have a dizzy turn. But the atmosphere was so toxic that she was afraid of what might happen if she did leave; she had Sean on her other side and as long as she was here, she might manage to divert his attention while the others were talking about the improvements made to the harbour since Antony's last visit.

'You must come up and see it tomorrow,' Maia said, and Ben added earnestly that it could mean much greater efficiency in bringing in supplies of all kinds.

'If we got a big speedboat, we could get all our supplies delivered to Lochinver and fetch it by water much more economically than going there or having it come here by road. It's what they did in the old days.'

Antony beamed at him. 'That's good thinking, Ben! Well done for finding him, Maia my darling!'

It was the sort of casual endearment anyone might have used but she raised her glass to him with her heart in her eyes.

Shirley was just about to tell Sean she was sure the police would come with a tranquilliser gun when he rose unsteadily.

'It's bad enough having to pimp out my wife to you because you hold the future of everything I care about in your grasping hands, but I'm damned if I'll sit here and watch you making love to her before my eyes.'

He picked up the wine glass and hurled it straight at Antony. It was a wild throw: it didn't hit him, but the crystal splintered on the table and the red wine splashed right up the front of the expensive pink shirt and sprayed red spots all over the gold silk dress.

Sean lurched to the door and slammed it behind him.

DCI Strang arrived at the cottage by the lochan ahead of the other two and went round switching on lights and the coffee machine and lit the wood-burning stove. His phone chirruped and he looked to see the text that was waiting.

It was from DCI Jason Dryden. He wouldn't have got back to him this quickly unless he had something to tell him, would he? He opened it with some eagerness.

CHAPTER TWENTY-ONE

DC Livvy Murray was very quiet as DI French drove them back along the single-track road to join the main road that led to Lochinver. French didn't talk much either, apart from mentioning there were all sorts of question marks over Sean Reynolds. She seemed lost in thought too, or perhaps she was concentrating on the road. It was dark and there were more cars than there had been the previous time, perhaps people returning home from work – what passed for a local rush hour. There were two or three occasions when her own braking foot slammed down but the driver seemed impressively unfazed.

She'd been really looking forward to having a brainstorming session with Strang but now guilt was mucking everything up. It sounded like they might be on to something with Reynolds, but suppose he was innocent and they went in hard, and then it was found out that they had written off the DCI's friend – the mess would be horrific.

She could confess what she'd missed to Strang. Correction, what she and French had missed, but then he'd be implicated in what the press would make sure was presented as a cover-up for a friend. It would be curtains for him, however unfair it might be.

For herself, it would only be something she'd failed to pick up on. She might get a reprimand but that was all. Of course, if Sinclair had killed Danni it was possible he might kill again, but she consoled herself with the thought that right at the moment he was very probably waiting in a cell somewhere to hear the result of his submission for bail.

And even if it was theoretically possible that he could have done it, there was no proof. As they reached Lochinver and turned on to the A837 Murray told herself she just had to keep quiet. As Strang had said himself on the phone to JB, sometimes it was worth taking a risk.

And if she had to lie – well, she was good at it. You got to be ace at lying when your mother would clatter you if she found out the truth.

It was a great cottage. Someone had given a lot of thought to making it welcoming. Definitely a cut above the spartan arrangements in the pod.

Strang saw Murray's expression and grinned. 'You're thinking "jammy beggar", aren't you?'

'We both are,' French said as they sat down. 'We don't have downlighters and uplighters and task lighting in the kitchen area, which in our case is a microwave and a sink.'

'Not set up for working, though – too much emphasis on mood music. Now – coffee? You'll be happy to know I've bought in a fresh supply of biscuits.'

French laughed. 'Oh dear – put them at the far end, away from me.'

Murray hadn't said a word since they came in. They were sharing a joke that didn't include her and she was feeling resentful now as well as miserable. Two's company, three's a crowd . . . She noticed Strang giving her a quizzical look as he set down the coffee mugs and hastily produced a smile, of sorts.

'How did the interview with Reynolds go then, boss?' she said.

Strang pulled a face. 'He's slippery – we'll have trouble piecing together what he actually did. His world is the wolves and nothing else features – he pretty much waved Danni's killing aside. I couldn't be sure he has any sort of standard morality.'

'Like wolves were kind of a religion?' Murray said. 'What we've done to them, like driving them out – that's what wickedness really is. He's got a temper too.'

'I'm not sure what his motive would be, though,' French said. 'He's got all this money and he was quite sure he could buy her out.'

Murray noticed Strang shifting in his seat. He never liked speculation about motives: it led to confirmation bias and looking for the evidence to fit. Now he said, 'I think we can leave that side of it meanwhile. What we did find out, Livvy, was that the pine forest where the body was found isn't far from the place where the wolves' cage is. Can we kick that around?'

After waiting for a moment to see if French, who'd had time to think about it, had something to say, Murray said, 'I suppose you have to look at it two ways. Say it wasn't Reynolds. Did the killer just pick somewhere the body

330

might never be found but was reasonably easy to get to, or did he know Reynolds went there, and that other people knew he did? So if the body was found, he'd get suspected.'

'OK,' Strang said. 'Go on, Livvy. And if it was Reynolds?'

She said slowly, thinking it out as she went, 'If he put it there, he knew the wolves were nearby. Did he do that because he thought – oh God—' The smell, the teeth, the terrible yellow eyes – and the fear. She was there again for a moment and she choked, unable to go on.

'Livvy, are you all right?' French said anxiously. 'Take it easy – you had a dreadful experience. I don't know how you've coped.' Strang was on his feet, fetching a glass of water.

'I'm fine, I'm fine,' Murray managed, but she was grateful for the water that gave her time to get control. She despised herself for having let it get to her. 'I wasn't expecting that – all I got was a fright, after all. But I'm all right now.'

Strang gave her a doubtful look but sat down again and she went on as if determined to prove she could hack it, 'After all, that's why killers leave bodies unburied in woodland – they're relying on nature to do its bit. Wolves – quicker and more efficient, I suppose.'

'It's a pretty sick idea,' French said. 'But that argument would apply to anyone else as well, if they'd known they were there.'

Strang nodded. 'Let's mark that down for further questioning: who knew about them? Was it actually common knowledge? But let's move on now.

'What I want to consider is, where was Danni from the last sighting on Monday around 9 a.m. until she arrived back at the cottage sometime after 5 p.m.? No one has come forward to say she spent time with them, there are no signs she was in any way constrained. The weather was dreadful and nothing suggests she was at all inclined to outdoor pursuits. So . . . ?' He spread his hands, inviting response.

'Somewhere she'd gone of her own free will,' French said. 'What did she like doing?'

Murray was quick with her answer. 'Going to the pub, as far as I can make out, but she wasn't there on Monday. I spoke to Kasper Novak and he said Danni hadn't been in.' As she spoke, she remembered that she hadn't planned to mention that particular little initiative and she hurried on before French could pick her up on it. 'There'd been that fuss with Joe Dundas on Saturday night. She could have gone into Lochinver to look for a different pub.'

'That's an interesting idea,' Strang said. 'You said before there could have been a delivery or something, and she could have hitched a lift. And now I think about it, the tracker dog found her scent near the fish farm and followed it for a few yards before it lost interest. I put it down to too many people passing around there, but it could have been that it had just disappeared when she stepped into a vehicle.'

'And Reynolds said he'd gone into Lochinver on Monday morning. I can follow that up,' French offered. 'Find out when he came back. And I can task Bob with finding out which of the men saw him here through the day and try to pinpoint times.'

'Excellent. Livvy, there's a photo her parents provided on file. You could flash it around in Lochinver – the store, cafes, bars. You know the routine.'

'Sure, boss.' She was feeling better all the time. The net was definitely closing round Reynolds and she didn't feel she had to worry about Ranald Sinclair any more. It was possible he might have heard the rumours about the wolf – obviously most of the locals had – but if he'd known where they were, she'd put money on him ratting to the police, so there'd be a black mark against Reynolds' name with the authorities he was getting all those nice fat cheques from.

'Let's see what emerges from that,' Strang said. 'And I think I'll speak to our friend Sean again – nothing formal, just a friendly little general chat about the basis of the whole operation. Where exactly the money comes from and so on.

'There's one other thing that's come in. As you know, I've been digging a bit into Flora Maitland's background. There was an unexplained legacy left to a Cameron Christie and I passed it to the Met for investigation. Unfortunately, it was a dead end – literally. A woman, actually – died four years ago. I'll request more detail but I'm afraid even if Flora Maitland was murdered, there's nothing we can do about it.

'Anything else? No? Thanks – a good meeting. Hope we have a quiet night and I'll see you tomorrow.'

As they drove back, French gave Murray a sideways glance. 'Are you really all right, Livvy? An experience like that – it's not something you can just shrug off.'

'Oh, you can if you're from Glasgow. They breed us tough, you know.'

It was kind of French to ask, she supposed, but the less she talked about it the better. She was proud of the way she'd managed to carry on back there, but she still felt shivery inside and she was afraid that when she went to sleep, the wolf dream she'd so far managed to escape would appear.

When she got back to the pod, it looked bleak after the cosiness of Strang's posh pad and the bed looked almost as if it was waiting for her, ready to inflict more horrors. She'd been going to take off her jacket; now she zipped it up again and went along to the pub.

Kasper took her order for white wine politely, but she'd have had to be insensitive not to notice the frosty atmosphere. It was quite busy and there were people standing around the bar in animated conversation, but no one spoke to her; she'd be a marked woman by now and if you were polis, you got used to being a pariah. When she got her drink, she took it to an empty table beside one of the most animated groups. Even if no one would talk to her, they couldn't stop her listening.

As she sat down, they fell frustratingly silent for a moment and when the conversation resumed it was in lowered voices, but it is hard for people talking together to keep the volume down and after a few minutes she could hear what was being said. She took out her mobile and pretended to be absorbed.

One woman was holding the floor. 'She was sent home early,' she was saying. 'She'd been meant to stay on to clear up after the dinner, but Maia came through with her dress all stained, up to high doh – said it was someone dropped a glass of red wine and it'd made a mess so they'd go through to the other room while Ishbel cleaned up the table. But she told her just to go when she'd done that – not to wait. So she didn't know what happened after that.'

'And did she know who dropped it?' a man asked.

'Not dropped it, according to Ishbel. One of those heavy, crystal glasses, she said, and it wouldn't get broken that way. There'd been shouting and then this great crash, so "thrown" was more like it.'

'So who was it, shouting?'

He was doing her job for her, Murray thought, tapping out nonsense with her thumbs.

'Oh, Sean, of course. Ishbel reckons there's something going on with Maia and this visitor, the way she's been carrying on.'

'Always thought she was too sweet to be wholesome. You can't trust those quiet types,' another woman put in. 'She's had a lot to put up with, though. He's a bad-tempered sod. And poor Hattie Sinclair, too. See men!'

There was a ritual protest from the two men at the table and the conversation moved on to speculating about how much more Ranald Sinclair might be being held responsible for.

It was the last thing she wanted to hear, just when she'd put him out of her mind. Murray finished her wine and got up, concentrating on what she'd heard about Reynolds instead. Violent rage – that fitted with the pattern of the crime. And if the power of his money hadn't brought Danni into line as it ought to – if she'd said she wasn't going to sell at all, say, what would his reaction be?

She was tired enough to be ready for bed, after all. And she had very useful info to pass on at the morning briefing.

* * *

335

The next morning Shirley Reynolds opened the door of her bedroom and stood listening. She'd considered just staying in bed, but after a bad night she'd stiffened up so much that she needed to get moving. Anyway, having had no supper she was hungry.

After Sean's dramatic exit, there had been a stunned silence when nobody moved. Then Maia leapt to her feet. 'Oh Antony, I'm so sorry about that! Are you all right?'

'Yes, of course.' He gestured towards his shirt. 'It's wine, not blood.' He spoke lightly, but his face was a mask of cold fury.

Ben Linton, looking painfully embarrassed, said, 'I'll get a cloth, shall I?' and bent forward to pick up a shard of glass.

'Don't touch it!' Maia screamed. 'Oh, sorry, I didn't mean to shout. I just didn't want you to cut yourself. Ishbel can deal with it. Antony, you'll probably want to change and so will I. Ben, if you could go through to the sitting room with Shirley . . .'

Shirley felt the chill as Maia's icy look slid over her. She groped for her stick then stood up. 'No, I'll just go to my room. I'm feeling a bit upset.'

She could almost hear the words, 'So well you might be,' as she had limped out. She'd been so angry – angry at Sean's lack of control, and angry with the treacherous Maia, and angriest of all with Antony Stanton, the puppeteer who was pulling all the strings from above.

Shirley wasn't angry this morning, she was just infinitely sad and very worried indeed. She couldn't begin to see where they would go from here: even if Ranald Sinclair was arrested for Danni's murder and the police went away, how could Sean go on living in the same house as Maia – Maia's house, of course – and what would she do herself?

She could hear someone clattering dishes in the kitchen – Ishbel, probably. Antony Stanton wouldn't be expected to sit through that so breakfast would be in the dining room. She'd better get it over with. She took a deep breath and went across the hall.

There was a tablecloth spread at one end of the table, with four places set. Maia and Antony were sitting in the places they had occupied the previous night, Antony spreading marmalade on toast and Maia cradling a coffee mug. He rose politely when he saw her.

'Good morning, Shirley! How are you today? Can I fetch you a cup of coffee?'

'Thank you, Antony. That would be very kind,' she said as she went to sit on his other side. She could see that the plate and mug set at the fourth place hadn't been used.

'No, no, Antony, sit down. I'll get it. Do you want toast, Shirley? Or granola?'

Again, Maia had spoken without actually looking at her, but clearly they were meant to play nicely. 'Not cereal, thanks,' Shirley said. 'But I could do with some toast.'

'I'm sure you could. Better make it two slices, Maia,' Antony called after her, 'the poor lady didn't get her supper last night.' He smiled at Shirley. 'One of these occasions when it was the demon drink talking and we all just forget about it the next morning – isn't that right?'

'Oh yes,' she said feebly. She certainly wouldn't forget it and she didn't think for a second that he would either, but she had to be grateful to have initial awkwardness smoothed over. 'What are you going to do today?' she asked.

'I'm driving up to a shoot in Scourie later, but Maia's going to walk me up to the harbour first to see what they've done there. When last I was here there was only a track, but I hear it's a surfaced road now. Such a beautiful morning for a walk, too.'

The sun was indeed streaming in and though the leaves were disappearing fast, a few of the trees in the garden were still showing the rich reds and golds of autumn. 'Beautiful,' she echoed, but in her present mood the bare branches spoke of decay and darkness.

And where was Sean? Sleeping off his hangover – or more likely up checking on his wolf. She didn't like to ask, but she heard the phone ring and when Maia came back with her breakfast she said, 'That was the police to say the tracker should be here this morning. I haven't seen Sean, but I guess he'll be trying to get the creature cooped up first. At least it means that one way and another the nonsense will be over, Antony.'

She smiled nervously at Antony, who said, 'Good,' but didn't smile. He stood up. 'I'll just go and pack up my things. Set out in half an hour, say? Would that suit you?'

'Of course,' Maia said. 'But you'll stay to lunch?'

Shirley knew she'd been planning on that, and the disappointment showed as Antony said smoothly, 'I think not, this time. If you're going to have to deal with all the fuss with dogs and policemen you don't want me here getting under your feet.'

And being around when Sean, stricken and further enraged, came back would not be a good idea, he didn't

338

say. But Shirley could see that even Maia recognised that it made sense.

'What a shame – I've got a lovely fish pie in the fridge. But I'll pop it in the freezer and you can drop in on the way south.'

'Excellent idea,' he said heartily, but Shirley was fairly sure there'd be another excuse. Antony was plainly someone who liked to steer clear of trouble. He turned to her. 'Shirley, dear lady, I'll take my leave. As always, it's been a delight to see you.'

She realised as he came across that he was planning to kiss her hand, so she grabbed his firmly and shook it with vigour. 'Enjoy your walk. You certainly couldn't have a better day for it.'

He looked a little put out at having his gallantry sidestepped, but he smiled and said, 'Au revoir!'

Shirley gave him a gracious nod, thinking childishly, 'Not if I see you first,' as he went out.

There hadn't been any more wolf problems overnight and they'd informed DCI Strang this morning that a vet and a tracker dog were on the way now, so the risk he'd taken had paid off – a considerable relief. Not only that, he'd drawn up a press statement about Ranald Sinclair's arrest after Murray and French had left the previous night and submitted it to Edinburgh; the authorisation had come through this morning as well, so before he drove to Inverbeg he could get PS Erskine to distribute it to any reporters and tell them that was all they would be getting before he arrived.

It looked like being a purposeful day. By now DC Murray should be showing round Danni Maitland's photo in Lochinver. First, he'd get hold of Sean Reynolds and if at the same time French got somewhere with establishing exactly what he did last Monday they might be able to put real pressure on him. It was perhaps too much to hope that there would be enough progress on both fronts for an arrest on suspicion, but at least the news of Ranald Sinclair's arrest must have taken some of the heat off them.

To his surprise, Murray was not in Lochinver. She was waiting for him at the community hall to report on her eavesdropping in the pub the night before.

'I thought you should know before you saw Reynolds, boss. Maybe not strictly relevant, but it's a wee glimpse behind the scenes.'

'It certainly is,' he said – and, of course, it chimed with his own impression that Ran hadn't much of a chance with the very cool Mrs Reynolds, who clearly had bigger ideas. 'Well done. Great use of initiative.' He said it straight-faced, and saw Murray grin. He hadn't always appreciated her using her initiative, but there was no doubt she was developing a fine instinct for investigation.

French had been working on her laptop and came forward to report on progress. 'I've written up our talk with Reynolds and given a note of his workforce to Bob so he can organise working on that, along with a list of general questions about the wolves. I'm hoping I can get strands of information to put together to give us a clearer picture of his activities that day. And there's feedback from Glasgow this morning about Danni Maitland's background – I've never known a response come back so quickly!'

Strang laughed. 'Ah, that's the top priority status JB wangled for SRCS. So?'

French shook her head. 'A few casual labour jobs, bar work, receptionist – that sort of thing. She's got one mate with a breach of the peace recorded, after an Old Firm match. No known association with master criminals, I'm afraid.'

'Too much to hope for. Nothing else?'

'I've been pursuing the other lines we've talked about, but nothing of interest so far.'

'Great,' he said. 'I'll just get off now to find Reynolds and have a go at squeezing him till the pips squeak.'

French was a good officer too, he thought as he left the hall. Her talents just lay in a different direction and without giving it enough thought he'd pitchforked her into a situation that needed skills she didn't have. It must have dented her self-confidence – and he could only hope that the case against Danni's killer hadn't been seriously damaged too. The words, mea culpa, mea maxima culpa, were running through his head as he reached Auchinglass House.

There were two cars parked outside: the silver Range Rover the visitor had arrived in yesterday and a BMW 5 series, but the Discovery he had noticed yesterday in passing wasn't there. Damn – it probably meant Reynolds was out. He went across to the stable office to check, but the woman working there hadn't seen him, had no idea when he would be back. He could ask at the house, but he wasn't hopeful.

The door was opened by a woman in a pink overall – the 'Ishbel' Murray had mentioned, presumably. No, Mr Reynolds wasn't in, and Mrs Reynolds had just gone out. Chancing his arm, he said, 'I heard there was some sort of trouble here last night?'

For a moment, she hesitated. Then, perhaps making a rapid calculation about the possible cost of disloyalty, she shook her head. 'Wouldn't know about that.'

She'd been tempted, though. She had the look of a natural talker and he tried again with, 'I expect Mr Reynolds has been very upset about his wolf.'

This was safer ground. 'Oh, he's been just beside himself! It's the other wolf, you see – it's like they were pets!' She glared at him. 'It's not nice if the police go and kill the poor beast – it's not its fault!'

'I can promise you they'll bring a tranquilliser dart. But what's he planning to do about it?'

'Well, Maia said he was away out early with his gun to lay a trail of rabbits to get it back into its cage. So that'll be what he's doing now.'

'Right,' Strang said. In fact, he'd heard a couple of distant gunshots this morning; in a country place like this, it wasn't unusual someone shooting a rabbit or two for the pot, or even one of the legally protected – and loathed – crows and ravens.

'When will he be back?'

'Don't know about him. Maia'll likely be back for lunch with her visitor.'

'Can you tell me who he is?'

Ishbel looked cautious. 'I suppose that's all right. It's Mr Stanton – he's the heid bummer, I think.'

That was a surprise. 'The head of what?' Strang asked.

That was going too far. 'Don't exactly know. Sorry – I'm needing to get on with my work now.'

The door was politely but firmly shut. She must have been warned about talking to policemen.

When he called Reynolds' mobile there was no answer. He now had the interesting question of what organisation 'Mr Stanton' might be in charge of to consider, but apart from that he'd nothing to show yet for his 'purposeful day'. The only consolation was that there was an air-conditioned van parked outside the community hall that told him the tracker dog had arrived.

CHAPTER TWENTY-TWO

Maia Reynolds had pictured this walk with Antony Stanton so often, so vividly: the two of them walking in golden autumn sunshine, a blue sky with not a cloud to be seen and perhaps the tiniest edge of frost in the air to prickle the back of the throat like the bubbles in champagne as they scuffed through the fallen leaves, laughing like children.

The weather, for once, had obliged, but the sodden leaves that carpeted the drive of Auchinglass House had been trodden into a squelchy, soggy mulch and thunderclouds gathering overhead would have been more mood-appropriate.

Her dreams had been all she'd had to keep her going between London visits and it was going to have been exciting too, to show Antony what she'd achieved since the last time he was here. In her imagination this was when they would be on their own and could say the romantic things they couldn't say when anyone might overhear.

The way she'd planned it, he would have come to her room last night; it was more than a year since Sean had been banished to one right at the back of the house, and the guest room allocated to Antony was conveniently to hand. But by the end of the evening, when only Ben Linton's presence had stopped Antony giving vent to his rigidly controlled fury, there wasn't a chance.

At least Ben had been a success. He'd shown he had the right ideas, like the one about bringing in supplies through the harbour – Antony had liked that – and now she would have the freedom she wanted for visits to London and even exotic holidays, if he could find an excuse to join her. He hadn't been keen before on her leaving Inverbeg in the hands of a secretary and she could understand that: Sean wasn't fit to take over if anything went wrong, but how much longer could she bear living in this hell of little people with their pathetic little concerns, measuring out her life in coffee mornings? She'd served her sentence, surely. Now, just when she had her escape plans in place, Sean had buggered it up.

As she and Antony set off from the house, they heard a gunshot, and then another one. Antony said coldly, 'If that's Sean, it presumably means he's trying to get his stupid rabbits and the blasted animal's still on the loose. And is it safe to go on walking here if he's going around with a shotgun?'

'That was a long way away. You won't find rabbits in woodland and that's all there is up this way,' she said.

'I'll take your word for it. But what on earth possessed him, Maia?'

She could read the implication: why didn't you stop him? 'I hadn't the faintest idea he was doing this,' she

345

said, though it wasn't quite true. With all the rumours going round, she'd suspected it, and Shirley had too. 'The infuriating thing is that he'd only to wait. We'd explained it to him quite clearly – the wolves were an important part of the enclosure plan.'

'Enclosure, right. The sort of rewilding everyone's in favour of, the sort that brings in pats on the back, not the sort of nonsense that brings the police sniffing around, and no more cheques from the government. What part of that didn't he understand?'

'He doesn't understand anything that isn't totally wolf-centred. It's an obsession – there's no reasoning with him.'

Antony was walking so fast she was having difficulty keeping up. 'Either that or he's completely lost the plot. So what happens now?'

'I don't know. Quite honestly, after last night I don't see how I can go on living with him in the same house, now this has erupted into the open.'

Antony stopped. 'Oh no, Maia. No, no. We need him. He's the guy who speaks the eco-maniacs language. OK, he lost it last night and we had a big bust-up. People do. It happens. But this puts all our plans back. We'll have to shut down everything until the police lose interest. Stay out of contact for a bit.'

Maia gasped. 'But – we've just got Ben put in place! I was planning to spend quite a bit more time in London now.'

He walked on. 'Better not for the moment.'

It was as if he'd stabbed her. She'd never fooled herself that she meant as much to him as he did to her; there were no doubt other women, not to mention his wife, but she'd believed she was special. 'Beauty and brains – the winning combination' was what he always said.

'You mean we can't meet?'

He heard the hurt in her voice and swung round. 'My darling, that will be a huge sacrifice for me too. You know how I absolutely live for your visits!' With a quick glance round about, he held out his arms. 'Come and let me show you how much this means to me.'

She allowed herself to be convinced by the velvety assurance of his voice and came to be kissed. Those doubts might return later, but surely somehow they'd get round it. She'd have to go down to see her father, after all.

It was as if he'd read her thoughts. He said, as he released her, 'I know Lucas will be disappointed – he's been really looking forward to seeing you more often. But he'll understand.'

Yes, he would, Maia thought bitterly. The business had always taken precedence over everything else, but she couldn't really complain – like father, like daughter.

'Not far now,' she said brightly as they climbed the steep hill up to the harbour. But it was Sean's Discovery they saw first, parked at the entrance to a rough, narrow path leading into the trees.

She stared at it. 'So is this where he's got the cage? It's quite an extensive plantation, in fact – they put it in when Nordic pines were to be the big cash crop, but now it's all about native woodland so it's been neglected since. I had it down for felling and selling off, then getting a grant for replanting but Sean would never discuss it – that must be why. He was constantly out checking yesterday to see if the wretched creature had come back.'

They both peered along the path but couldn't see anything and after a moment Maia turned away. 'The police will take care of it. And now, look! This is what we've done.' She gestured proudly. 'Do you remember what it was like before?'

'Vividly – and the road too! You've done a fantastic job, sweetheart.'

The sea was very calm, grey-blue and glinting in the sunlight, the tide just on the turn as they reached the harbour. The row of long-abandoned, crumbling houses was still there but a lot of work had been done to create a good loading area on the quay, with the restored pier curving round to shelter the harbour basin and jutting out into a little bay given its own protection by rugged promontories on either side, angled like encircling arms.

He was beaming. 'It really couldn't be better, could it? The farthest outpost of our empire!' He strode off along the pier.

Maia watched, amused. 'Monarch of all you survey,' she called. 'There's a couple of cottages here that have been combined to be a store. I'll open it up to let you see it.'

There was a sudden very loud bang – a gunshot, nearby. If that was Sean, he was too damn close. She ducked automatically, yelling a warning to Antony.

When she turned round, he wasn't there. He'd probably hit the deck – but where was he? Not on the pier, not on the cobbles of the quay. He couldn't have moved fast enough, surely, to take cover in one of the ruins?

Then Maia noticed there was something in the sea beside the pier, gently moving with the sway of the waves – a raft of greenish brown wrack? And was that a patch of red dulse in the middle?

No, it wasn't. It was a jacket – lovat green tweed. Antony's jacket. And those were his hands, outspread as he floated face down, and there was a great raw red patch on it, spilling blood into the water.

'Antony!' she cried. She had to do something, rescue him, but the horror – the horror! Somehow she couldn't move – and even as she watched he was pulled further out on the retreating tide. She wasn't a strong swimmer and he was a big man. Her legs were buckling and she heard someone screaming. Even when she realised it was her she didn't know how to stop.

She had no idea how long it was before Sean appeared out of the trees, his shotgun broken over his arm – two minutes, five minutes, ten – but when he did, he was in a furious rage.

'Shut up, you stupid woman! If Raksha was anywhere near, you'll have scared her away by now. What's the problem? You're hysterical! Look, calm down or I'll have to slap you.'

Somehow she managed to get her breath. 'Antony – you have to get him out.'

Sean looked bewildered. 'Antony? Where is he?'

'You've killed him!' she shrieked. 'Look – there!' She pointed.

Sean walked across to look and turned a sickly grey. 'But – I haven't done anything! I heard a shot, but—'

Maia went very still. 'Are you going to kill me now too?'

'No, of course I'm not. I didn't kill him, I told you!'

A current had caught Antony's body, moving faster now, further out into the bay and drifting on, sinking lower and ever lower in the water. Sean bent his head and covered his eyes.

Maia started to cry convulsively. 'Help – have to get help.'

With a shuddering gasp, Sean put his hand into his jacket pocket and got out his phone. 'He's been trying to get me all morning,' he said, then, 'Strang?'

When it came to efficiency as a tracker, DCI Strang would be the first to say that Malcolm's excitable Sadie had done him proud, but the German Shepherd was more the classic image of what one should be. Siegfried got out of the van looking as if he took the job very seriously, standing calm and dignified beside PC Anderson, his handler, and taking no interest in what was going on around him.

John Maxwell, the vet, was carrying a rifle and a case, which he patted. 'Tranquilliser darts,' he said. 'But I've bullets too, if needed. Just hope they're not – I get enough of seeing animals punished for the stupidity of their owners.'

'How do you get started?' Strang asked. 'It's not as if you can give Siegfried something with the scent on.'

'No,' Anderson agreed. 'But I believe there's some sort of cage? The scent'll be there and he'll pick up from that.'

'The wolf may come to take a look at him first,' Maxwell said. 'They tend to be curious about dogs and if she's used to having humans around, we probably won't worry her too much.'

'Good luck, anyway. My information is that if you follow the road there up to the top, there's another track that brings you near to the cage. I've been trying to get Reynolds on the phone, but he's eluded me so far. When I get hold of him, I'll send him to show you where it is – but I warn you, he's not rational about wolves.'

'Like them myself,' Maxwell said gruffly. 'It'd be good to see them back in their place if they were introduced properly.'

'Not sure if you'd get the local crofters to agree with you,' Strang said. 'In fact, I'm bloody sure you wouldn't. Anyway, I'll let you get on. Good hunting, Siegfried.'

At the sound of his name the dog turned his head to regard him with profound indifference. Strang laughed and went into the community hall.

As he came in, DI French got up and came over; she'd obviously been looking out for him. 'Something here you might like to see,' she said. 'Could be interesting.'

Strang's ears pricked up. 'Oh?' he said, just as his mobile rang. He looked at the number. 'Sorry – it's Reynolds,' he said.

'Yes, Mr Reynolds? I've been trying to contact you— What?'

He listened, barely able to take in what he was hearing. French looked at him sharply and the nearby conversations stopped.

'Right,' he said at last. 'Stay where you are. There'll be a police officer there in a few minutes. Explain to him and I'll be with you once I've contacted the lifeboat.'

'The lifeboat?' French said as he rang off.

'Put everything else on hold,' Strang said. 'Contact the coastguard and get hold of Bob Erskine and send him up to the harbour. Their visitor's been shot and he's fallen into the sea. Reynolds claims it was an accident. I'll get on up there now.'

DC Livvy Murray's morning hadn't proved as fruitful as she had hoped. It had been her idea that Danni might have gone to Lochinver and she'd hoped to come back with new lines to pursue. There weren't many shops, cafes and bars in the village but it had been slow going, checking them all and getting only blank faces when she showed Danni's photo, apart from one woman who'd been in the Inverbeg Inn when Danni and Joe had their row and she hadn't seen her since.

She drove back feeling crestfallen. A dead waste of time. And unless Strang had persuaded Reynolds to condemn himself out of his own mouth, the work ahead would be slow and painstaking, a lot more French's style than hers – and always at the back of her mind was that lingering worry about Ranald Sinclair.

The sound of a police siren alerted her to a badged car that was coming up fast behind her. She was on the single-track road; there was no way they could get past and she had to drive faster than was comfortable until she reached a passing-place and could duck aside.

Something had happened, and she hadn't been there. French was no doubt right in the middle of it, and the pang of jealousy that took her as she turned off into Inverbeg was so sharp she actually winced.

When she arrived, the badged car had stopped in front of the hall and there was a coastguard jeep too, oddly enough. She drove along to park near the pods and walking back she could see people talking busily in the street outside the shop.

At that moment her mobile rang and when she snatched it up French's voice said, 'Livvy, where are you?'

'Just outside. Hang on.'

There was quite a crowd of people she didn't know when she went into the hall. French was talking to two uniforms – the ones who'd overtaken her, she guessed – and she chatted to a couple of other PCs for a moment until French broke off to speak to her. 'I hoped to catch you before you left Lochinver. You're needed back there. The man staying at Auchinglass House has been shot and they've arrested Sean Reynolds on suspicion. Kelso's going to interview him in the station at Lochinver, so he wants you there.'

Murray gawped at her. 'He's shot him?'

'He denies it, but he was found holding a shotgun. And after the row you heard about last night you would have to wonder.'

'Too right. But what are the coastguard doing here?'

'Victim fell into the water. The lifeboat's out trying to bring him in.'

'Dead, then?

'Very, as I understand it. Bob says the guy's name is Antony Stanton, so I'm just going to run a search on him and then I'll be going to Auchinglass House. Maia Reynolds saw it happen and I'm to speak to her, if possible, though it seems she's distraught.'

353

'Right. I'm on my way.'

As Murray drove out it did occur to her to worry that she might meet another police car coming in a hurry, though with the shortage of manpower in the area it wasn't all that likely. And she had a warm glow inside as she thought that Strang had wanted her there, right at the business end.

It had been a wretchedly long morning. Shirley Reynolds had sat there, trying, and failing, to find something to distract her from the interminable, circular thoughts tormenting her. She couldn't bear the phony hilarity and false matiness of TV and radio and ended up flicking through a pile of old magazines, but that didn't help either.

She'd heard the doorbell go once, and when Ishbel had come in with her coffee she'd said it was the police just wanting to see Sean, but she obviously didn't want to chat. Shirley could feel hot waves of embarrassment sweeping up her neck.

It was quite a lot later that Shirley heard the sirens and her heart started up the pounding that was becoming familiar. She'd thought that Maia and Antony would have been back by now, with him planning to leave before lunch, but there'd been no sign of them. Sean hadn't appeared either and now her tormented mind settled into a whole new cycle of fears. What might all this mean?

Then she heard footsteps, and a moment later there was a tap on the door and Ben Linton appeared, looking surprised to see her on her own.

'Sorry I'm late. I was working upstairs in the office, and then I realised it was past time to report for lunch and I thought everyone would be waiting. Do you know what's happening? I heard sirens.'

Shirley had brightened up when she saw him, but it seemed as if he didn't know any more than she did. 'Oh, I've no idea, Ben,' she said wearily. 'I've just been sitting here worrying myself silly, even though I can't be sure what it is that I'm worrying about.' She always prided herself on being tough, but to her annoyance tears had come to her eyes. She blew her nose fiercely.

Ben sat down on the chair beside her. 'Look, I'm sure everything's fine,' he said awkwardly. 'It's probably something to do with the wolf. Sean will be keen to make sure the police don't hurt it. I thought Maia and Antony would be here, though.'

'So did I, but I can tell you there won't be a posh lunch. Antony's going straight on up to Scourie so the fish pie's in the freezer. Sorry about that!'

Ben laughed and pulled a face. 'So am I. Have to be fish fingers back at my flat, then. Do you want me to get something for you? Ishbel's probably in the kitchen . . .'

She was too worried to feel hungry. 'No, no, I'm sure Maia will be back shortly.'

'Sure?' he said. 'Well, I'll leave you, then, if you're really all right.'

Poor boy – he shouldn't have to cope with a weepy old woman. 'I'm fine. But if you find out what's going on I'd be really grateful to know.'

'Of course,' he said, and left.

So now Shirley was on her own again, and the longer this went on, the worse it felt.

When he was arrested, Sean Reynolds admitted he had been near the harbour at the time the shot was fired and he had been carrying a gun, but he denied vehemently that he had killed Antony Stanton. Well, he would, DCI Strang thought as he drove along to Lochinver, still feeling stunned at the pace of events.

His day hadn't been improved, either, by hearing that Ranald Sinclair had come back home the previous day. It would have been surprising if he'd been refused bail, but this could make Strang's own position now more tricky. He'd rather hoped that he wouldn't have returned until the furore died down and that before then his own work here would have been finished, one way or another, and he could have gone back to Edinburgh. Fat chance of that, now.

He'd called JB to warn her what was about to hit them, but she was in some meeting and couldn't be disturbed, so he'd had to leave a message. He'd hoped to break the news before the media did; he knew she'd been on edge already and he'd been trying to work out the best way to present it – if there was one.

The Lochinver police station was a low, whitewashed building with little more than an entrance hall, an office, a lock-up and an interview room where Sean Reynolds would be waiting for him. Strang stopped to talk to PS Erskine and the other officer who had brought him in.

'Anything from the coastguard, Bob?'

He pulled a face. 'Nothing so far, boss.'

They both knew that was seriously bad news: if they hadn't found Stanton's body by now, it would mean waiting till it was washed ashore, and given the miles of unpopulated coastline around here it could be days or weeks until it was found. Or even never.

He'd hoped French might have managed to contact Murray before she left Lochinver, but apparently not. This was going to be tricky. They hadn't the evidence for a charge of homicide and Reynolds was entitled to legal representation, which could mean 'No comment' and getting no further forward. Strang wanted to persuade him into self-justification, and Murray might rile him enough to do that, and not sit silent until his brief arrived.

The little room was overheated and the fetid atmosphere was familiar from many other rooms like this; Strang always thought of it as the smell of fear. Reynolds had been waiting some time and his skin had a greasy sheen.

'For God's sake, can we get on with this?' he burst out as the door opened. 'I've said I didn't do it, you seem to think I did. What do we do now?'

Strang nodded to Erskine, who set up the recording. 'You've been arrested already, Mr Reynolds. You were informed of your rights at the time. We haven't charged you yet. Do you want to be represented?'

'Too bloody right. You're not going to fit me up for this. But first I want to know if they've killed my wolf?'

It was hard to believe, in the circumstances. 'I'm afraid I don't know,' Strang said.

Reynolds scowled. 'Then let's make a deal. Why don't you phone them and find out, then I'll phone the lawyer?'

'It doesn't work that way, but you are entitled to the phone call,' Strang was saying as DC Murray arrived, hurriedly identifying herself as PS Erskine made way for her to take his place.

Sean, still scowling, took the phone Erskine held out to him and had a terse conversation with the person at the other end.

Strang murmured to Murray, 'Whatever he's being told, see if you can needle him into talking.' She nodded, quick to understand. You didn't have to spell it out for Murray.

Reynolds rang off. 'He'll be here when he can.' He turned his attention to Murray. 'Have you heard if they've killed the wolf?'

Surprised in her turn, Murray said no.

Sean glowered at her, sat back in his chair and folded his arms. 'You'd better find out, then. Otherwise I'm not going to say anything till my lawyer gets here. It could take him some time.'

CHAPTER TWENTY-THREE

It was a pity she hadn't had the chance to speak to Strang before he went off, DI French thought as she walked across to Auchinglass House. Still, time enough later, and if she got the details from Maia Reynolds now it would prepare the ground for a formal statement to be taken tomorrow.

But the woman who opened the front door was emphatic. Mrs Reynolds was definitely not to be disturbed.

'I'm DI French. It's very important – I must talk to her as soon as possible. I spoke to her before – perhaps if you explained—'

'Wouldn't do any good.'

She looked as if she'd like to say more, though. French said, 'Your name is . . . ?'

'Ishbel Wilson. I look after the house for them, and I do what I'm told or I'd lose my job.'

'Did Mrs Reynolds tell you what had happened?'

She hesitated, then gave in to temptation. 'Not really, no. She came back with one of your lot – oh, just in an awful state! Walked straight past me and away up the stairs. Then she turned and just said, "I'm seeing no one. No one at all."

'Well, you don't argue, do you – not with Herself. Me and the policeman, we just looked at each other and shrugged. But that's all I'm telling you.'

Remembering her last visit, French said, 'What about Mrs Reynolds Senior? Could I speak to her?'

Ishbel looked doubtful. 'Don't think she knows what's happened yet. I haven't had the heart to break the news to her about her Sean getting taken away.'

'So you know about that, do you?'

She gave her a pitying look. 'All over the village,' she said. 'Well, you'd maybe be the best person to tell her. I'll see if she wants to speak to you.' As French made a move to follow her, she said firmly, 'You stay there.'

Waiting meekly on the doorstep, she heard her phone buzz.

'Rachel? Get anything on Stanton?'

'Yes. You know that firm you asked me to look into, Transco? He's the chief executive.'

There was silence for a moment, then Strang said, 'I see. At least I think I do, partly. Thanks.'

'There was something else—' she said, but he had rung off.

Ishbel came back. 'You can come in if you want. She says she doesn't know how she could help you, but she'd be glad to talk to anyone. Don't you go bullying her, now.'

French remembered the impression she'd had of Shirley Reynolds – a robust, cheerful soul despite her physical infirmities. What she saw now was a broken woman, looking ten years older with shaking hands and a trembling mouth. You would have to be cruel indeed to want to make things worse for her than they were already.

She sat down beside her. 'Are you happy to talk to me? I'm not going to annoy you with questions if you don't feel up to answering them.'

Shirley's voice was shaky but she was perfectly clear. 'For any favour, tell me what the bloody hell is happening. I know it's something awful, I just don't know what it is.'

'Yes,' French said heavily. 'I'm afraid it isn't good. Antony Stanton has been shot.'

Shirley's eyes widened and she grasped the arms of her chair as if she was afraid she might fall off it. 'Is he dead?'

'Yes.'

She bowed her head. She could even have been praying, and French waited quietly until Shirley looked up again and said, with infinite pain, 'And my son killed him?'

'We don't know that,' French said. 'He denies it, but he was at the scene with a shotgun and he has been arrested.'

'I don't know what to say.' She put her hand up to wipe away tears. 'I live in the house but I don't know what's going on here. They've been married for years, but I couldn't see what she saw in him, right from the start. Oh, he's good-looking, if you like that type, and they met through this green movement thing, so I suppose they shared the rewilding dream, but . . .' She gave a heavy sigh.

'What did he see in her?' French asked.

Shirley thought for a moment. 'I'm ashamed to say I've always wondered if it was the estate he really fancied, not her. He's had this thing about wolves ever since he was a wee boy and it was to give him his big chance.'

French was puzzled. 'I thought the estate belonged to him – that he'd sold an Internet company, or something?'

'Is that what they're saying in the village? No, Sean's not the brainy type. The whole place belongs to Maia's father, in London. It was let out for years and years and they only came to live here at the start of the project. Oliver was just a wee thing at the time, and I was able to help with him then, but he's nine now – away at school.

'Lucas is the chairman of the firm where Antony's chief executive, as far as I know. Auchinglass is expensive to run so it gets a lot of money from the company – and of course there are the grants from the government and all the fees from the young people, and Maia's very shrewd, I think.'

The hairs were standing up on the back of French's neck as she recognised what she was hearing described. 'That's . . . very interesting,' she managed to say.

'But then there was Sean's nonsense with the wolves,' Shirley went on, 'and it was like how it is before a thunderstorm – the tension just building and building, till I knew it was bound to break. And last night – do you know about last night?'

'Yes, we know.'

'I suppose everyone does.' For the first time there was a touch of bitterness in her tone. 'Ishbel's a kindly enough soul but her tongue's hung in the middle and flaps at both ends. What was a real pity was that it spoilt Ben's evening – Ben Linton, you know?'

'Oh yes. It was a special evening for him, was it?'

'They'd put him on to the board and he was so delighted. He's done a brilliant job running things since he came and he's a nice lad – the sort that takes the trouble to speak to boring old ladies, you know?'

French smiled. 'I know what you mean, though I don't think you'd be boring. And this was to celebrate?'

'Champagne and everything,' she said. 'And then Sean threw the glass—'

Thus far, Shirley had managed to control herself but now she broke down. 'I'm-I'm sorry, but it's too much. I can't go on like this, I can't stay here. I'm going to phone my sister to come and get me and leave tomorrow.'

French got up at once. 'I'm not going to trouble you any further. I'll ask Ishbel to bring you a cup of tea.'

It was all she could think of to do for poor Shirley. And anyway, she couldn't wait to get back to tell Strang what she had discovered.

DCI Strang stood up. 'We don't play games,' he said to the scowling Reynolds.

You could chip enough ice for a couple of gin and tonics off his tone, DC Murray thought as she scrabbled to her feet. Reynolds was looking now as if one had suddenly been thrown in his face.

Strang turned to Erskine. 'Check that the lock-up is prepared and make whatever arrangements will be needed. Mr Reynolds, you'll hear from us when we have reviewed the situation. PS Erskine will fetch you when he's ready.'

She had to work hard not to laugh at his astonished face as she followed Strang out of the police station. 'What do we do now, boss?' she said when they were standing by the cars.

He smiled. 'We could just stand and wait for the olive branch to arrive. I don't think it'll be long. On the other hand, I was planning to go up and take a proper look at the harbour. There was too much going on earlier and I wanted to get the layout clearer in my head. Leaving him in a cell for a bit will turn the screw.'

'Meet you there, shall I?' She put it in the most positive form to make it harder for him to say no, and he said, 'Fine,' and got into his car.

Murray had spent a lot of time in the car today and it had given her an unwanted opportunity to think. Her theory about Reynolds taking Danni to Lochinver having collapsed, she'd been considerably cheered to hear he'd been arrested. But he hadn't been charged, and in the brief minutes she'd spent in the community hall today one of the lads had mentioned that Ranald Sinclair had come back and she'd felt her stomach lurch.

Of course. Why shouldn't he come back? He'd a business to run. But she'd have been happier if he hadn't until they'd put the cuffs on Reynolds. That he'd come back the day before someone else was killed was unnerving.

Murray had never been beyond the pods. The road was surprisingly good and the harbour itself and the area round about was so impressively well maintained that it looked oddly out of place beside the ruins of some old village. Strang had parked on a loading area; she drew in beside him and they stood looking back down to Inverbeg.

'The dog van's gone,' he said. 'The path that leads to the cage is about a hundred yards down there on the right, in the trees. Do you suppose that means they've got it, or they've given up?'

'I can find out for you,' Murray said, taking out her phone.

'No, don't do that. When Reynolds asks me again, I can say I don't know with perfect truth.'

She put it away. It wouldn't have bothered her to say whatever suited her, but she sort of admired his scruples, like you'd admire some old vase you saw in a museum without wanting to take it home.

The brightness of the morning had gone. There was a grey veil of cloud now, and a fresh little wind was getting up, ruffling the surface of the bay. Murray hadn't brought a jacket and she shivered as she followed Strang along to the end of the pier.

'The lifeboat will still be out there searching,' he said, 'but eventually they'll have to be stood down. I'm not optimistic. When I arrived this morning, the body was just a speck out in the bay.'

'What did Maia Reynolds say happened?'

'Incoherent. Stanton had fallen off the pier and was in the water with a great hole blown in his back. Then Reynolds came out of the trees down there carrying a gun and she was quite sure he'd killed him, but she was too frantic for me to ask any more questions.'

Murray was looking out to sea. 'It's a great place this,' she said. 'Good shelter for the boats, look, and you could just load everything on to trucks – one of the witnesses said it's how they bring in the saplings from Scandinavia. You could even use lorries, with a good road like this.'

He didn't immediately reply and she glanced at him. He had turned round and was standing absolutely still, again looking back down towards Inverbeg. Then, 'Yes,' he said slowly. 'You could.'

She turned to follow his gaze, but Strang was definitely seeing something she didn't. 'Right,' he said abruptly. 'I think we should see if our Mr Reynolds is in a more cooperative mood.'

As, yet again, she drove back along the too-familiar road she was puzzling away. It was irritating her like an itch she couldn't scratch that she couldn't think what it was that he'd been looking at.

DCI Strang's brain was buzzing as he drove to Lochinver. At last he could see why the investigation had been going so badly – they'd been looking through a microscope to study a culture when they should have been using binoculars to scan the wider terrain.

And what he was seeing now was alarming. Certainly, he'd had this unsettling thought at the back of his mind ever since his conversations with Angus Mackenzie and DCI Dryden, but they'd got distracted by the intricate workings of relationships within the community and allowed them to form the focus of their investigation. They'd been directing their attention to the sheep while the wolves were circling round – and they weren't the ones Sean Reynolds had let loose in the forest.

Standing there on the pier, he had found himself reading the story the layout told him. A sheltered harbour in a remote place, a good road out. A plan that could thwart Scotland's inconvenient 'right to roam' legislation, as Ranald had said, and that would ultimately give you almost total control over who came and went – and when. An invaluable property for an 'import–export' business.

And now he knew, too, what he wanted to ask Reynolds.

When Strang arrived he got a broad grin from PS Erskine. 'He'll be pleased to see you, sir. He's been asking when you'd be coming back. Still going on about the wolf. Actually, they've—'

'Stop right there,' Strang said. 'Don't tell me.'

'Like when you've recorded the Big Match?' Erskine said, grinning, but Strang barely heard him. Murray's car was drawing up and Strang said, 'We'll get set up, then bring him in.'

When Reynolds was brought through, he was looking more anxious than belligerent.

'Well?' he said.

'Sean Reynolds has just entered the interview room,' Murray said for the benefit of the tape, but Reynolds looked at her as if she was mad.

'What the hell is that for? Some sort of joke? Look, I know I was stupid to take you on. You're holding all the cards. You know what I need to know. It's driving me crazy – I feel sick, dizzy. For God's sake, tell me what's happened.'

Indeed, he was looking positively ill, but it was amazing how homicide hardened your heart. Once Strang might have been moved by so much abject misery, but he was long past that now.

'As I told you, I don't know. There are more important things on my mind – like a man being killed.'

'Yeah, well – I told you, I didn't kill him.'

'So tell me what happened, then.'

'My lawyer told me to say nothing.' He crossed his arms again.

Murray stepped in. 'Good advice, that,' she said. 'If you're guilty, that is. And by all accounts, from what I heard about last night you were really up for it. Not nice, to have someone mucking about with your wife, is it?'

Reynolds reacted to the provocation exactly as Strang had hoped he would, looking at her with angry contempt. 'Wouldn't have killed him for it, though. Don't care that much about her, to be honest – she's a cold fish. I was angry last night – they were out to humiliate me and I was crazy anyway, about Raksha. And drunk. I lost my temper. That was all.'

Suddenly he looked at Murray as if he'd just remembered who she was. 'It was your fault, wasn't it?' he snarled. 'If you threaten an animal's prey they'll defend it – you should know that. If you'd left him alone, it wouldn't have happened, all this.'

Seeing the look on Murray's face Strang said hastily, 'We'll leave that. So, you got drunk. And you woke up with a hangover, I guess. What did you do then?'

Was he going to clam up again? It could go either way, but after a moment his shoulders sagged as if he hadn't the strength to go on battling.

'I haven't anything to hide. I drove up there whenever I could see straight. Raksha still wasn't in the cage, so I walked back down to open ground to see if I could get a few rabbits to tempt her with. There weren't many around anyway and I'm not a great shot – only potted one, but then realised time was running out. I reckoned if I was there, I could do something to prevent you bastards from killing her, so I walked back up through the woods and laid down the rabbit near the cage.

'Then – oh, I don't know. There was just all this screaming, and all I could think was, if she had smelt the rabbit and was coming, it would scare her away. So I came out and told Maia to shut up.'

The single-mindedness was truly astonishing. A woman screaming, and his only thought was that it might disturb the animal. Strang was having doubts anyway, and this was almost enough to make him believe Reynolds was telling the truth.

Murray gasped. 'You told your frantic wife to shut up?'

He did look a little awkward. 'Well – it was Raksha, you see. But then she told me what had happened and accused me of doing it – I told her I hadn't, that she'd seen me herself coming out of the woods and I'd my gun broken over my arm. I don't think a twelve-gauge shotgun could do that, even if I'd tried.'

Strang hadn't seen the gun himself. Reynolds had been disarmed by PC Anderson by the time he got there, and he had been directing his attention to Maia. A 12 gauge, at that range – if you got hit, it was unlikely to kill you. It certainly wouldn't blast the sort of hole in your back that Maia had described to him between hysterical sobs.

It was time to ask the big question. 'When you saw Antony Stanton's body in the water, which side was it on – the bay side or the harbour side?'

There was at last emotion in Reynolds' face. 'I was . . . pretty shocked. I didn't know what to do. He was sinking deeper and deeper in the water and then a current picked him up and started moving him along. So I suppose it must have been on the bay side – if he'd gone in the harbour he'd have drifted into the wall first.'

Strang could picture the pier as he said that – the gentle curve at its end, sheltering the harbour entrance. Stanton had been shot in the back; if he'd been shot from the woods he'd have fallen into the harbour. The tumbledown houses on the other side of the road would provide the perfect place for an assassin to lurk.

He got up abruptly. 'Thank you, Mr Reynolds. That's all for the moment.'

Reynolds' face changed. 'You mean I can go?'

'I'm afraid not, right at the moment. We are allowed to keep you for questioning for twenty-four hours, but it may not be as long as that.' Then, as Reynolds gave a cry of misery he said, 'But I feel sure Sergeant Erskine can find out for you what the situation is with the wolf if you ask him nicely.'

Erskine, waiting outside, came forward and Strang said, 'We're holding him meantime. And you can tell me now – have they got his blasted Raksha?'

'Not so far, boss. The dog found a trail but they didn't get a sight of her. They're going to come back tomorrow with a couple of traps and night-vision cameras.'

'Not ideal,' Strang said. 'We just have to hope all the activity will have kept her avoiding people for the next bit.'

As they walked to their cars, Strang said to Murray, 'I'm going get a progress report from Rachel. Depending on what she says, I'll go there to talk to Maia Reynolds or I'll go back to the cottage.

'I'm going to order fingertip searches up at the harbour and in the woods tomorrow, but I'd like you to go back there before it's completely dark and check around to see if there's any sign of someone having been there – too much to hope for hard evidence, I suppose, but you never know.

'After that, I want to have a briefing at the cottage. Rachel will bring you out. OK?'

'Yes, boss,' she said.

'Thanks, Livvy.' He got into his car without noticing the effort Murray was making to sound bright and upbeat.

When he called French, the message wasn't encouraging.

'Ishbel's doing her jobsworth act,' French told him. 'Maia's said she's not to be disturbed.'

'Tomorrow will do. I'm inclined to think we'll be letting him out with nothing more than a charge of keeping a dangerous animal, but a period of quiet reflection won't do him any harm.'

'Shirley Reynolds was interesting, though. She innocently described what seemed to me the ideal set-up for a money-laundering business for Transco.'

'Well, well, well!' he said. 'And the harbour's the perfect layout for landing goods that you didn't want to attract attention. We're looking at quite an operation here.'

Before the briefing, he had to talk to JB, however reluctantly. There'd been no message from her so the meeting must have gone on a bit.

It had just finished and she sounded tired, and not pleased at the latest development. 'Of course I understand the circumstances, but please tell me that you've got some sort of handle on this?'

'It's becoming clearer,' he said, 'but I can't be sure where it's going from here. We need to establish who it was that was shot – the man playing around with another man's wife or the chief executive of Transco?'

Maia Reynolds lay on her bed until she had sobbed herself to a standstill. Then the pictures started playing in her head: the bright day, the sudden, gut-wrenching horror. Sean, the gun that had killed Antony over his arm, coming out from the trees shouting, threatening to hit her . . .

She sat up. Sean, coming out from the trees. He couldn't have shot Antony in the back from there. So who had?

A wave of nausea took her and she lay down again, struggling to control it. Sean had a temper – but killing in cold blood? And she knew her world. Antony was a powerful man and powerful men had enemies.

Her father must be told, but she had to get herself calm first – Lucas didn't know about her and Antony. He would have been angry, and Maia had never in her life taken him on.

You didn't. He was in his nineties now, but he still scared everyone. She got up cautiously and went to the bathroom to splash her face with cold water.

Even so, Lucas knew immediately there was something wrong and his voice was sharp as he said, 'Something's happened?'

Once she started, Maia couldn't stop. It all poured out, and she ended by saying, 'And the thing is, I don't see how Sean could have done it.'

'Oh, I think you'll find that he could have,' he said with the softly inexorable tone he always adopted when he was determined Maia would accept that black was white. 'Things are . . . difficult just now and we don't want too many questions being asked, do we?'

Greatly daring, Maia said, 'Do you know something about this?'

'No. But there's trouble coming and we're circling the wagons. If we don't want to lose everything we've worked for all these years, we have to keep things tight. Antony got across quite a lot of people, you know, and I'm not as surprised as I might be.

'Tell the police you're still in shock. You've told them already you believed Sean had killed him. Leave it at that.'

Maia put down the phone and slumped onto the bed again. What else could she do? Her own hands weren't clean. She had been cradled in evil and she had never asked the difficult questions. She had seen what happened to those who did.

CHAPTER TWENTY-FOUR

It wasn't quite dark, but the sky was heavy with clouds that had a strange, greenish tinge, creating the sort of twilight that you could believe would tempt predators to come out – at least you could believe it if you were DC Livvy Murray, who gave an involuntary shudder as she got out of her car beside the harbour. The scent of pine was heavy in the damp air and the woods to her left were in deep shadow; she could almost think that they'd crept closer since her last visit.

It hadn't occurred to Strang that she'd be nervous about being sent to poke around here just after she'd been told the wolf was still at large. It was all very well for people to say they were shy, retiring creatures, but she had reason to know that they weren't always. She looked round fearfully, but there was nothing moving.

Of course there wasn't. And the sooner she got on and did what she had come to do, the sooner she could get out of here. And if she sang loudly, maybe it would scare it off.

Her singing, according to her music teacher at school, was bad enough to scare anyone and feeling ridiculously self-conscious she began a rendition of 'Who's Afraid of the Big Bad Wolf?' as she went in and out of the abandoned cottages.

Here and there she saw an old pot, a rusted spade, a broken cup – even a worm-eaten and broken chair. If it hadn't been so wet recently, she might have hoped for footprints in the dust but the cracked stone floors told no tales, except about a community of people long dead.

Murray stood in one for a moment looking towards the pier, wondering who might have stood this morning exactly where she was standing now. And it looked as if it couldn't have been Reynolds after all, so where did that leave them?

She couldn't think why Ranald Sinclair would have wanted to kill this man, but then Strang was always warning her not to start with motive – and he'd come back here yesterday when you'd have thought he wouldn't, until things calmed down. Was it time she told Strang what she'd noticed, or dare she go on hoping that it wouldn't come to that?

One way and another, a bad day at the office. Still, she'd done what she'd come to do now and she could leave. She hadn't been able to keep singing – she felt idiotic – and as she walked back to the car she became very conscious of how quiet it was. She could hear the waves rushing on the shore, but there was a weird kind of heavy silence beneath that.

Silence – and a feeling at the back of her neck that someone was watching her. She swung round. If there were luminous yellow eyes looking back at her from the darkness of the trees she was going to faint.

There were only shadows. But even so there were chills going up and down her spine as she sprinted to the car and bundled herself in.

When she got back, French was ready to set out for the cottage where Strang was waiting for them.

'We've lots to talk about. First – get anything up at the harbour?' he asked Murray.

She shook her head. 'Nothing except a creepy feeling that I was being watched by big yellow eyes – don't laugh!'

He looked conscience-stricken. 'I won't laugh – that's why you never look at a target. But I am sorry – are you all right?'

'Oh, sure I am,' she said, not adding, 'now, in this nice warm room.' He could send French next time. 'But any of the cottages on the opposite side to the woods would put you in perfect position for a shot.'

'And with the perfect means of disposal for the body right there,' Strang said. 'Very – well, professional, you might say.'

Murray stared at him. 'Do you mean – a hit man?'

French was nodding. 'I think it's quite likely there are big guys involved in this. The whole rewilding scheme offers the ideal money-laundering opportunity.'

'And with their own private port being developed up here,' Strang said.

So that's what he'd been looking at. 'And if you'd wolves roaming around, people wouldn't be too keen to wander in when they weren't wanted,' Murray said hollowly.

'That brings me on to a phone call I just had. I managed to speak to DCI Dryden and what I got from Flora Maitland's lawyer has meant they're starting to close in. When I told him what had happened here his response was, "Somebody's rattled, then." So – where do we go from here?'

For a moment no one spoke. Then Murray said, 'I suppose I can sort of believe it. If you were a pro you could come in, do it and get right out again. No evidence. Look at that banker in Nairn all these years ago, shot on his doorstep, and they've still never got anyone.'

'And what about Flora Maitland?' French said. 'Nothing to say it wasn't an accident, but—'

'Indeed,' Strang said. 'The link is certainly there. But we need to look closer to home before assuming it's an outside job. What do we know about Ben Linton?'

French shook her head. 'Solid alibi for Danni's killing. No record. And I got employment details from Reynolds' office and it was a couple of weeks after Flora Maitland died that he started work.'

Strang said slowly, 'What's on my mind, you see, is that Flora's death and Antony's could both be professional, and they were both heavily involved in Transco—'

French interrupted. 'Oh, I've been meaning to tell you! It came up on the background check that Cameron Christie, the woman who died, was a Transco employee too.'

'Really!' Strang said. 'Points in the same direction, doesn't it? Danni, on the other hand, wasn't one. And the method there could hardly have been less professional.'

Murray couldn't tell if her face had actually gone pale, but she felt as if the blood had drained from her head.

She'd told herself that it wasn't likely that Ranald Sinclair would have any reason to kill Antony Stanton, but he sure as hell did for killing Danni Maitland. Perhaps this was the moment to confess . . .

But French was saying, 'I think we need to look again at Reynolds' movements last Monday. Bob was making a start on checking them before this happened and he has the profile – given to rages and no scruples when his wolves are involved,' and Strang was nodding agreement.

'We've got him where he can't do any harm at the moment. And Dryden is digging around – when a company scents trouble splits develop as they all try to find scapegoats. So let's proceed on that basis, yes?'

The moment had passed. Murray nodded, feebly.

As they got up to go, Strang said, 'You've been very quiet.' He was looking anxious. 'It was really thoughtless to send you up to the harbour like that. It must still be on your mind.'

She didn't actually say, 'Oh, that?' She said 'No, no, I'm not bothering about it now,' which was true. The wolf wasn't going to come back and bite her as hard as disclosing what she had been concealing probably would.

'Who gave the order?' Maia Reynolds said.

Ben Linton looked up from the computer. 'Sorry?' he said blankly.

The Auchinglass House Ltd office was on the first floor of the main house and she had walked along the corridor from her bedroom. He was working at her own desk and she went to sit down on the chair in front of it, her legs so shaky that she was afraid they wouldn't hold her up.

'Who told you to kill him?'

'What are you talking about? Sean killed him. You know that – everyone knows that!'

'He couldn't have. I was confused, at first, but the wound was' – she caught her breath on a sob – 'it was in his back. Couldn't have come from the woods.'

Linton clicked to shut the file and sat back. 'Tell me about this – what did you see?'

'Nothing! I was in shock.'

'So they sent someone good,' he said. 'I wonder why.'

She looked at him, unconvinced. He went on, 'Have you spoken to your father?'

'Oh yes,' she said bitterly. 'I've to stick to the story.'

'Then that's what you'd better do, isn't it? He's not exactly the kind of guy you argue with.'

'Oh no, he isn't. I'm not to rock any boats – there's something happening, apparently. Everything has to be smoothed over, even if I've to spend the rest of my life incarcerated in this mausoleum.'

He looked at her with sudden interest. 'Something's happening? Do you know what?'

'Oh, he doesn't tell me things, he just tells me what I'm to do.'

'Very wise, probably. You don't really want to know too much, do you?'

Maia gave a long sigh. 'No, I suppose I don't. So . . . I just hold firm?'

'Oh yes,' he said gently. 'I think you really should.'

She got up and dragged herself back to her bedroom, while Linton returned to the computer and clicked on the file again.

* * *

Livvy Murray had always had the enviable talent of being able to fall asleep whenever her head hit the pillow. She was tired tonight, tired of the torment inside her head, and she did indeed crash out, but then the nightmares started – a confused jumble of images where she was tormented by threats that she couldn't see closing in, first from one side, then another. She came awake, gasping in terror, and sat bolt upright to wake herself up.

She tried lying down again, but her nerves were still too jangled. Cup of tea – that might help. She turned on the light and went to switch on the kettle. But now she was awake all the worries came awake too, and after that brief nap she wouldn't be tired enough to fall asleep quickly – even if she wanted to risk it.

She might as well work. With her mug of tea, she sat down, opened her laptop and signed in. She ran her eye down the files and stopped at 'witness statements'. It would probably only make her feel worse to read her report on Sinclair's interview but like someone prodding a bruise to make sure it still hurts, she couldn't resist.

And it did. Still, she told herself, there wasn't actual proof there, and there were others whose statements should be looked at more closely too.

There wasn't much point in wasting time over Reynolds' because it was so incomplete, but she paused at Angus Mackenzie's. His was the evidence they'd worked from to assess time of death, but was there anything else to back it up? He could have killed Danni earlier, upset that she'd shown no interest in Flora who had left her everything, but he seemed such a nice old guy that she couldn't imagine him inflicting that sort of savagery on anyone. It made her think, though: she could construct a scenario that implicated him, just the way she had for Sinclair.

So maybe she didn't need to tell the boss about that just yet, which comforted her a little. Maybe once she finished her tea she could get back to sleep, after all. She flipped on to Joe Dundas – no, she couldn't build anything on that. And Ben Linton—The alibi was there, and it had been checked. But then it hit her. She'd been out looking in the wrong place. This wasn't just possible, it was bloody well likely.

Livvy drained her mug and went to set her alarm for six o'clock. She'd get into trouble if this didn't come to anything but if it did, she'd be forgiven. She could leave a note for Bob Erskine and take the badged car. She got back into bed, put out the light and then the alarm went off and it was morning.

Strang had an early phone call with DCI Dryden, and then another with DCS Borthwick.

'He has a couple of names to follow up there in London,' he told her, 'and I'm going to liaise with Glasgow CID. They'll be able to finger a few – maybe even supply a mugshot or two to try around here. The problem is—'

'Oh, you don't have to tell me the problem,' she said wearily. 'How much does putting out a contract cost these days? Couple of hundred, maybe? The chances of nailing him are pretty slim. It's going to be messy, isn't it?'

''Fraid so. Not much more we can do from here, but I'd like to keep the operation going for a couple more days. It's hard to see why they'd needed to get rid of Danni Maitland – there was all the money she could possibly want on offer. The method there looks more like a straightforward case of someone losing their temper and lashing out and Sean Reynolds is in the front line there.'

'The wolf man?' Borthwick said. 'You've still got him in custody, haven't you?'

'Yes. There's evidence of furious temper and irrationality. He was familiar with the woods where the body was found – it stretches right up to the coast and there was a cage for the wolves near there.'

'And he could reckon that the evidence would, shall we say, disappear promptly? I like it, Kelso. If we could get that pinned down, we can see Flora Maitland's case doesn't get another airing, and then talk about internal politics when it comes to Stanton. Is Dryden making progress there?'

'Good progress, he tells me. They're starting to sweat.'

'Excellent! It's brightened up my morning. Makes a pleasant change. I often wonder why I wanted to do this job.'

Oh dear, Strang thought as she rang off, it must have been a difficult meeting yesterday. He never ceased to be happy that he hadn't had to settle for an office job.

It looked like being a stormy day as he set out for Inverbeg. There was a shepherd's warning sky – roiling clouds in violent shades of red and orange and even purple, hanging low, and he could hear the droning of a rising wind as he got into the car. Apocalyptic – but of course it wasn't! He was a rational being, for goodness' sake. It was just that it felt that way.

When he arrived, PS Erskine was in an animated conversation with DI French that broke off whenever they saw him.

'Problems?' he said.

They both looked self-conscious. 'Morning!' French said. 'No, not really. I've phoned Auchinglass House and Maia Reynolds feels able to see you now.'

Erskine greeted him too, but he was clearly not happy. Strang looked round the room.

'That's good, Rachel,' he said. 'And a very neat change of subject. I don't see Livvy this morning – off somewhere, is she?'

The other two exchanged glances like schoolchildren in front of the teacher. French's face flushed. 'She's gone to check something out.'

Strang's heart sank. Murray had done it again – would he never break her indulging in private enterprise? 'Something?'

'She didn't actually say,' French said.

'Look, loyalty's all very well, but there's a problem,' he said irritably. 'What is it?'

After a pause, Erskine said, 'She's got the patrol car. She said she'd be back by now, and it's holding me up with checking on Reynolds' movements.'

'Have you called her?'

'Left a message. She could be out of range – the signal's not reliable.'

French said quickly, 'It's not a big problem. Bob can take my car.'

'Fine,' Strang said, tight-lipped. 'Anyway, I'll go and speak to Maia Reynolds now. You'd better come with me.'

He didn't say anything as they walked across. It was Murray he'd wanted in on this; French would listen and do a calmly efficient report but she wouldn't contribute much. He was fuming, not least because it was his own fault; Murray had got away with a slap on the wrist too often. It was going on her record this time.

Ishbel was more welcoming today. 'She's waiting for you,' she said, leading them through the hall to a small room looking on to the garden. The rain was starting now; great, heavy drops were lashing against the pane and the trees were swaying in the wind.

Maia rose to greet them. She looked like a little, red-eyed ghost, her pinched face sunk into the wrap she huddled round her as she sank back into her chair as if she was feeling cold, though the room was comfortably warm.

He made the usual soothing remarks; she thanked him in a faint voice that sounded rough from tears.

'Can you think of any reason why Mr Stanton should have enemies?' he said.

She hadn't expected that. She sat upright, and her voice was much stronger as she said, 'Apart from my husband, you mean? No.'

'No business problems, say?'

'Certainly not! Why should there be?'

He ignored that. 'Now I know it's hard, but this is important. Could you tell me exactly what you remember about yesterday?'

She was looking at him warily but said, 'Of course, I know I have to. For Antony.'

As she said the name her voice shook. 'I-I was showing

him the harbour. He had walked out on to the pier and I'd gone over to open the lock-up. I heard a shot nearby and I screamed with fright. We'd heard Sean shooting earlier and I thought he'd not noticed us and was trying to kill something for that damned wolf. I turned to warn Antony and he had . . . gone.'

She stopped, her eyes brimming. She picked up a tissue from the table beside her, dabbed at them and blew her nose.

He wasn't going to let her stop. 'And did you see your husband?'

'Yes. Came out of the woods with his gun. And he started yelling at me, as if it was my fault.' She paused, then said with a change of tone, 'Look, I'm not saying he did it deliberately. I think he fired without checking – he's not a very good shot. And this terrible thing was what happened.'

'You saw no sign of anyone else there at the time?'

Her reply cracked back. 'No, of course not! What on earth do you mean?'

'Just a routine question. And when Mr Stanton was in the water, was he in the bay or the harbour?'

She frowned. 'Well, the bay. He was face down, floating there . . .' She started to cry.

'I think we can leave it there,' Strang said. 'Thank you. You've been very helpful.'

He made to get up, but to his surprise French said, 'I just wanted to ask you if you could think back over the statement you gave me about your husband's movements on Monday – is there anything you would want to change, or add?'

The tears dried. 'No,' Maia said crisply. 'I think I gave you a very full account.' She got up. 'Unless there's anything else . . .'

'No, that's fine,' French said. 'Thank you. We can let ourselves out.'

'So what did you make of that?' Strang said as they walked back. 'Piece of work, if you ask me.'

'Wouldn't argue. There's a lot going on there – some of the tears looked genuine, but the rest . . .'

'Crocodile,' Strang agreed. 'At the moment we can't push her but when it's decent to do it, she can be taken over everything she said about Sean in detail. She didn't seem keen on that line of questioning – well done, Rachel.'

Perhaps she was learning. But back at the hall, there was no sign of the patrol car and his lips tightened once more.

She'd miscalculated, not only on how long it took to drive to Ullapool, but how reluctant people were to get going in the morning. When DC Murray arrived, barely a shop was open apart from a Spar and a baker. She showed Danni's photograph, but not hopefully. The only result was a bacon roll she munched as she walked along.

Even so, she was convinced she'd got it right. On a dreich October day the place didn't look very inviting but it had an awful lot more to offer than Lochinver. With its fishing port and the bustling fish market and all the lorries taking shellfish to go off to the Continent, as well as its thriving tourist industry, it had plenty of cafes and bars as well as lots of little shops that a bored young woman could spend time browsing through while her escort went about his business – a meeting that gave him any number of impeccable witnesses to his alibi.

Why, though, should Linton have wanted to kill her? A crime of passion was unlikely, but maybe they had a row, he lost it and slashed her? But there she was, getting hung up on motive again.

Her phone buzzed and she gave a guilty start. Erskine had phoned twice already; this could be Strang demanding to know where she was. She ignored it. The signal round here was iffy, after all, and she didn't want to tell him until she'd some justification.

It was ten o'clock now and at last shops were opening and cafes filling with depressed-looking tourists keen to get out of the rain – heavy now, with a wind whipping up the waves in the harbour. At least now she'd work to do, but she'd no luck. One waitress thought she might have seen Danni having a coffee one day, but couldn't say when.

Murray was starting to lose confidence. With so many tourists no one noticed individuals but, lacking proof, her belief that this was what Danni had done on her last day on earth was pointless. She began to wish she'd just mentioned her idea, instead of dashing off.

She'd covered the high street now – maybe she should just cut her losses. But coming to a crossroads she saw a long, low white restaurant up at the far end. It looked inviting, the sort of place she'd choose to go herself. Worth one last throw of the dice, anyway.

It was busy, but staff were ready to be helpful, passing round Danni's photo among themselves. There were a couple of tentative maybes but nothing definite until a dark-haired young waiter looked, then lingered over it.

'I think perhaps, yes.' He was foreign, French or Spanish maybe.

Chancing her arm, Murray said, 'Could have been with a man – fair hair, blue-eyes, five foot ten or so . . .' The man's face cleared. 'That is right! I noticed them because he is good-looking, she not so much. Just – very loud.'

It wouldn't do to embrace him, so she only said, 'That's well helpful. And – do you know what day it was?' She held her breath.

'Monday,' he said confidently. 'I have had days off – this was the last day I was in. It is in the book, I think.' He went back to the desk and opened the bookings list to the right page. 'There,' he said, pointing.

There was no doubt about it. 'Twelve-thirty, 2, Linton.'

There was still no sign of Murray and she still wasn't picking up her phone. With an irritated sigh, Strang said to French, 'We'd better go and talk to Ben Linton now. I don't know what he'll be able to tell us, but—'

Just then, the door to the community hall opened and Ben Linton appeared. He was carrying a laptop and he looked around, seeming very nervous. When he saw Strang he came across.

'Chief Inspector Strang, can I talk to you in confidence? I've something very important to say. Important and urgent.'

CHAPTER TWENTY-FIVE

The hall was quiet, with only one uniform working at a computer near the door. Strang beckoned Linton into the screened-off area and they sat down at the coffee table. Linton looked askance at French as she joined them but didn't say anything, just setting the case down on the table and giving it a light push in Strang's direction.

'This is terribly difficult for me,' he said. 'I-I really wish I didn't have to do it. I was so excited – I'd never dreamt of being invited on to the board. I was truly, truly honoured.' His blue eyes met Strang's squarely. 'I had no idea what was going on until I started going through the computer, after Antony was shot. And then I realised – I must have been very naive.' His eyes dropped. 'Money-laundering. It's what this whole set-up is about.'

Nicely done, was Strang's first thought. Just the right amount of regret – and now, just a soupçon of guilt, perhaps?

'The awful thing is, it's such a betrayal of the trust they placed in me. I feel bad about that, but it's nasty stuff.'

'Guns or people?' Strang said bluntly.

Linton jumped. 'Well, both probably, I think. I haven't had time to investigate properly but I've spent the day copying everything I could onto this laptop.' He patted it.

Strang couldn't resist pulling it towards him. 'Passwords?'

'No, I've set it up so you can access direct. The thing is, whenever they realise what I've done, they'll come after me. You saw what happened to Antony. I need to get away. Can I leave now?'

He wanted to refuse. He didn't believe that there wasn't a lot more Linton could tell them, but he had no power to detain him, and if this was genuine – possibly even a case of thieves falling out – his life might, indeed, be in danger.

'We'll want to talk to you again,' Strang said. 'Where will we find you?'

Linton got up. 'Yes, of course. I'll be at my parents' house.' He gave a clever little sigh. 'Such a shame. They were so pleased to see me settled into a good job – planning to come up and visit me, too. They'd love it here.'

French handed him a pad and he scribbled on it. 'All right? Am I free to go now?'

She escorted him out and Strang was frowning at the laptop when she returned. 'Can't make anything of it. But if it's genuine, I know a man who can.'

French picked up the pad again and went to the constable by the door. 'Can you check this out, please? An address in Surrey, Mr and Mrs James Linton. And a postcode and all.'

The woman typed for a moment, then shook her head. 'Sorry, ma'am, doesn't exist.'

'Thank you,' French said. 'I had a feeling it might not.'

She went back to tell Strang. 'Classic example of the narcissist – thinks he could perform that charade and we'd believe every word. How deep in is he, do you think?'

'Oh, very deep. Look, get on to Bob now and make sure Linton doesn't leave. Arrest him for obstruction, if necessary.' He closed the laptop and handed it to her. 'And give this to the constable – tell her to forward as many files as she can to the Met address immediately.'

The door of the hall opened, so violently that it swung back on its hinges, and Murray came in. She was obviously bursting with information and before Strang could begin on the speech about insubordination and irresponsibility, she said, 'Linton took Danni to Ullapool on Monday. I've a witness who can identify her and I think him too.' She looked at him expectantly.

'There was some reason why you couldn't have mentioned your idea and done it in the orthodox way?' he said icily, and saw her face fall.

Maia had gone upstairs to the office after Strang and French had left. She didn't know what to do with herself, really. There was a great hole where her heart should be; she'd known what Antony was but she'd loved him, and that was linked, too, with the promise of a life that didn't mean permanent incarceration here. Being allowed to appoint Ben as a stand-in had been Lucas's reward for all these years of obedience.

But everything was going wrong, and she was scared. Had Ben told her the truth – that this time, he hadn't been the assassin? If they'd sent someone up, it was frightening evidence of fractures inside the organisation. Of course, he could have been lying to stop her turning on him – he was a good liar. As she was.

There was another door in the study, the one that led into Ben's flat and down to the project office, and she could hear him moving around behind it. She should update him that she'd stayed solid in her statement to the police. She gave a token knock and went in.

The door to his bedroom was open, there were clothes all over the bed and he was kneeling with a pile of shirts in his hand, packing a suitcase. He looked up, startled.

'What are you doing, Ben?' she exclaimed.

He laid the shirts carefully in the case and stood up. 'Ah,' he said. 'I was rather hoping you wouldn't come in until after I'd gone.' He smiled, giving her the full big, blue, honest eyes treatment.

Maia froze. 'Why, Ben?'

'Well, the more distance I can put between me and your lot, the happier I shall be. They'll be coming after me when they discover that I've given the police access to all the accounts.'

She couldn't believe what she was hearing. 'The accounts? But . . . but I've covered for you! Now I'll tell them what you've done, and they'll be after you too – Darren.'

He smirked. 'Ben, if you don't mind. Of course they will, but I'm well prepared to disappear.' He picked up a pile of trousers.

'But why?' Her mouth had gone dry. 'We've done everything for you since you came out of jail. You owe us.'

Linton sneered at her. 'And how did I get in jail, in the first place? And do you, by any chance, remember a girl called Cameron?'

Oh, she remembered Cameron. It had been a bad business, that whole operation. 'The girl who went to jail too?'

'My girl,' he said savagely. 'Cammie – the one who slit her wrists and died in prison in a bath of blood. You didn't hear that part, did you? Oh, they made sure no one did. And it was Flora Maitland who should have taken the rap, not us, but you closed ranks to protect her. I started looking for her the day they let me out. It wasn't difficult – she'd talked to Cammie about the croft where she spent her holidays as a child – first place I checked. She was right back under your noses here.'

'I never knew her,' Maia said faintly.

'No, but you knew the word was out for her. Lucas was well chuffed when I offered to take care of her, then she spotted me in the pub and I knew I'd have only that one chance. Neat and efficient, if I say it myself – Lucas was impressed. That was why I got this job, and you owe me for that, too.'

'But – Antony . . . ?'

Linton laughed. 'That's what I've been waiting for. He led the cover-ups. He was . . . unfinished business. I'd have settled for just that. But then, I couldn't believe it!' He laughed again. 'You actually invited the fox into the henhouse, and any minute now all the chickens will be lying with their heads bitten off. Oh yes, even the evil old rooster himself.'

He lifted the last of the clothes into the suitcase and closed it. 'If you take my advice, Maia, you'll just play the innocent who's been manipulated by your father, who had no idea what was going on. Lay it on thick – they're not very bright, the plods.'

Maia was feeling sick with panic. What to do – phone her father and tell him what had happened on her watch? She might as well just kill herself now. She ran back to the office, slamming the door behind her.

DC Murray sat by the coffee table, her head in her hands. She'd really blown it this time. Sure, she knew Strang would rage as usual, but he'd always given her credit when it worked out. This time, there was going to be a black mark on her record and worse, he'd take DI French next time instead of her. Still, thank God she hadn't confessed what she'd been concealing about Sinclair – with this as well, she'd probably have been on a charge.

He'd taken French now; Murray was alone, and something had happened. He hadn't even told her what it was, only said to French, 'That gives us legitimacy to act now. Livvy, would you please tell Lochinver to charge Reynolds under the Dangerous Wild Animals Act and release him. Let's get across there, Rachel.' He hadn't thanked her.

She always hated being out of the loop. But if she was honest, it was more than that. She was just plain jealous.

She'd been trying not to admit it, but it had been building ever since she got here. She'd been so proud that Kelso had come seeing her as a valued colleague; now she'd ruined everything. Rachel might be a lousy leader but as a second-in-command she had all the virtues – good at detail, conscientious, clever. All the things Livvy wasn't. Not only that, she'd heard them more than once chatting like friends;

she and Strang only talked about work, but they liked the same things – mountains, for instance. Given a bulldozer, Livvy would have levelled the lot.

Well, it had been years since his wife had died – he was probably starting to look around for the next one, and French would tick all the right boxes. She'd be the sort he could take home to tea to meet his father, Sir General Wotsit. Good luck to her!

But the pain was so sharp she nearly cried out. And she still didn't know what was going on at Auchinglass House.

The door to the project office was open. DCI Strang posted PS Erskine and a PC at the foot of the stairs while he and DI French went up to Linton's flat. That door was unlocked too, and they walked in.

There was a suitcase standing in the corridor. Linton's voice called sharply, 'Hello? Who's there?'

They went towards the sound and Linton appeared in a doorway a little further down. He looked alarmed and none too pleased to see them.

'What is it now?' he said. 'I told you, I need to get away quickly.'

'If we could just have a word,' Strang said, moving towards him so that Linton had to admit them to the large square room overlooking the front garden – cream-coloured walls, neutrally furnished with an oatmeal tweed suite, a wide-screen TV, a coffee table. An impersonal room.

Linton retreated to the far end. Putting his back to the wall, Strang thought wryly. 'Can you tell us precisely what you did on Monday?' he said.

'I told her,' he said, pointing at French. 'Surely there's no need to go over it all again, when I'm in danger every minute I stay here?'

'Indulge me,' Strang said. 'On Monday morning, you set out for a 10.30 meeting in Ullapool—' He stopped abruptly.

He was standing on the other side of the open door and he'd heard nothing. It was the frozen look on French's face as she stood opposite with her back to the window that alerted him. Then he saw that Linton had gone white.

Maia Reynolds' voice said, 'First you – then her – then me.' She moved forward into Strang's line of sight. There was a gun in her hand – a Springfield, he registered automatically, small but deadly, trained on Linton. And she knew what she was doing – two-handed, feet braced.

There was no time to think, no time to worry where a deflected bullet might go, only the fraction of a second before she'd notice him. He launched himself at her, striking the gun down at the same time.

It went off. The noise of the explosion left him almost stunned, his ears ringing as he lay pinning Maia to the floor. She made no attempt to struggle, lying as if dazed herself.

He eased himself up to see that French had crumpled, clutching her leg with a hand that was red with blood. Linton had slid down the wall, half-fainting. And then, thank God, he heard the sound of feet charging up the stairs and PS Erskine and the constable appeared.

It was only when DC Murray heard the sound of sirens and first one, then another patrol car swept past, with officers leaping out and sprinting across to Auchinglass House that she realised there was an incident, and by then it was all over. She rushed out, in time to see DI French coming from Auchinglass House, limping and bloodstained.

She was protesting that she was fine, but Murray grabbed her arm. 'There's a first-aid pack in my bathroom. Come on, we'll go there.'

'It's just a flesh wound, honestly. It's made a real mess of these trousers, though,' French said ruefully. They were, indeed, ripped and bloodstained.

'Sit on the bed,' Murray instructed her. 'I'm making you tea – you're probably in shock. What in God's name's going on?'

Once French started it came spilling out, her teeth chattering on the edge of the mug. Murray listened intently to the horrifying story. 'Sort of like a thunderbolt coming from nowhere, wasn't it?' she said.

'We knew by then what he was,' French said, 'but her . . . it was weird, unreal, somehow. She'd have done it, though, if Kelso hadn't—' She broke off.

Murray had fetched a bowl of warm water and was swabbing the wound. The bullet had grooved a shallow furrow in the calf and she said, 'He took quite a risk, but I suppose he'd no alternative. You won't die from this, right enough, but you'd probably better get it seen to properly if you don't want the scar as a souvenir.'

'Like Kelso's,' French said. 'Do you know why he hasn't had it fixed? Plastic surgery's brilliant these days.'

Murray sighed, getting out another pad. 'It happened when his wife was killed in a car crash. I think it's sort of like a black armband.'

'Not very healthy, though, I'd say. You're quite close, you two, aren't—ouch!'

'Sorry,' Murray said. 'It's the disinfectant, it stings a bit. He's a brilliant boss, but I'm really in the doghouse now. And don't tell me – I know it was dumb. I just get an idea, and then . . .' She sighed.

'It was thanks to you we'd the excuse to arrest him today. If we hadn't, he'd have been dead and she would too. He ought to give you credit for that.'

Oh, she was a generous woman and that only made Murray feel worse for resenting her.

'Yeah, well,' she said, knowing that she sounded ungracious. As she got out a bandage she said, 'So what happened after all the drama?'

'Maia just lay there – pretending she was dead, I think. Kelso charged her with attempted homicide and Bob had to lift her up bodily. She's there now, handcuffed and waiting to be taken to Inverness. They'll have to put her on suicide watch – she looked fully prepared to kill herself after she'd taken care of us. Then he arrested Linton on suspicion of obstruction initially, and he's been taken to Lochinver. Kelso's going to interview him when he's tied things up with the local guys.'

Murray stuck a plaster across the bandage to hold it in place and stood up. 'There you go. So . . . do we all get to go home now?'

'Yes, I suppose so. We're assuming he was part of the Transco set-up, even possibly a paid hitman, but I still don't understand why he needed to kill Danni. OK, he lost his temper with her, but so violent? What could she have done? He struck me more as the calculating type.'

'Oh, the boss would tell you it's not about motive, just about proof. But I was sitting here while you were all having fun and I remembered something Hattie Sinclair had said to me. It was about Danni being determined to get the enquiry into Flora's death opened up again. If Linton killed her, he'd see that as an existential threat, wouldn't he?'

French was impressed. 'You could be right.'

There was a knock on the door and Strang came in. 'How are you doing?' he said to French.

'Oh, Livvy's done a cracking job here.' She held out her leg.

'Well done, Livvy,' he said, but he didn't look at her. With her heart sinking Murray realised that he still hadn't forgiven her.

French said, 'Livvy says Danni Maitland was trying to get Flora's case reopened and that would make her dangerous to Linton. It would explain how she was involved, wouldn't it?'

It was kindly meant, no doubt. But Strang said only, 'I'll keep that in mind. Rachel, they're sending the chopper to take Maia Reynolds to Inverness, and they can take you back with them afterwards. I don't think you're fit to drive and there's no reason to stay here.'

'I'm sure I could, but it is stiffening up a bit. I won't say no to first-class travel. I'd just better get out of these and put on something a bit less draughty!' She held out the rags of her trousers.

He laughed. 'Good idea! Livvy, you could drive Rachel's car back, couldn't you?'

'Yes, boss. Of course.'

Then they both left. He hadn't asked her to join the Linton interview. Murray had never been a crier, but she sobbed until she began to feel ashamed of herself. She usually felt a terrific buzz at the close of a case but today she was too burdened by her own failures and it looked very much as if she wouldn't be getting another chance.

The arrogant ones were easy when they still thought they could blag their way out. Ben Linton – not his real name – had begun by waving away a lawyer, talking about 'misunderstandings' with a confident smile, which faded as Strang, with Erskine observing, outlined the case they were building against him for Danni Maitland's murder. He emphasised that there was a forensics team already analysing her clothing and would be going over his car, that there was considerable advantage in tendering an early plea and finished by reminding him that his alibi for the evening hinged on Maia Reynolds' testimony.

'I doubt if she'll stick by it now,' Strang said, and he could see Linton's eyes narrow – making a rapid calculation of the odds?

Then his hand went up to his brow in a dramatic gesture. 'Oh God, oh God! It was the most terrible thing that has ever happened. I have a temper, you see. My mother always said it'd be the ruin of me.'

'That would be Mrs James Linton of Surrey?'

Again, he could see calculation – did they know it was fake, or not? Wisely, Linton said, 'It was only so I could get away quickly. You saw the kind of people they are, this afternoon.'

'Let's not talk about that. Let's talk about how you killed Danni.'

Linton gulped loudly. 'The thing was, she was leading me on. That night – she laughed at me, mocked me for being a gold-digger – me! And the red mist came down – we were having a drink in her house and before I knew what I was doing I had broken the bottle and just lashed out. I didn't mean to kill her. And the blood—' He shuddered. 'It brought me to my senses, but it was too late.

'Then I panicked. The only thing I could think of was get back to my flat and clean myself up and Maia saw me. She said I had to get rid of the body, and it was her idea to take it up to the woods. It was a good hiding place, she said, easy to get to, and with luck it wouldn't be found for years, even.

'I know I shouldn't have listened. I should have phoned you and confessed right then, but I was so scared! A moment's loss of control – I'm paying for it now. I'm haunted by that poor girl! I'll have to live with the guilt all my life.' He bent forward, his hands curled over his head.

Strang waited for a moment. 'I see. So it wasn't because Danni was determined to make us reopen the enquiry into her aunt's death?'

He caught a flash of panic, then became rigidly controlled. 'I've no idea what you're talking about,' Linton said. 'I never met the woman – I only started work here after she had died.'

'Yes, we know that. But we've checked your fingerprints and we now know who you really are. Your name is Darren Thomson and you were an employee of Transco until you were jailed for weapons offences. They seem to have looked after you when you came out – I suspect you did a big favour for them by eliminating Flora Maitland, who knew too much. We haven't proof yet, but we'll keep digging.

'I don't know why you handed over the files, or why you killed Antony Stanton – internal politics, at a guess – but you were arrogant enough to believe you could drive away with the rifle you used to kill him still in the boot of your car. Oh, I admit I'm speculating there – we haven't actually done the tests, but I'd be very surprised if it didn't match up when we find Mr Stanton's body, wouldn't you?'

Darren Thomson's face looked as if it had been cast in granite. 'I want a lawyer,' he said.

'I think that's a good idea.' Strang got up. 'I'm having you kept here until we see what we can charge you with. But don't count on being out in time to take up that flight to Tunis you booked for tomorrow.'

EPILOGUE

Detective Chief Superintendent Borthwick was beaming when DCI Strang came in.

'Well, you did stir up a hornets' nest, didn't you Kelso? I've just had a very complimentary call from the Chief Commissioner of the Met. They've had their eye on this Lucas Reith for a very long time. Have you worked out how it all fits together? Coffee?'

'Thank you.' Not only coffee, but chocolate biscuits. Oh, he was the wee boy, all right! 'Mostly. We've had help from an unexpected source. Of course, with Maia Reynolds on a charge we can't question her, but she's insisted on giving us a full statement. She's out for revenge on Darren Thomson and she's setting herself up as the innocent victim of her wicked father's crimes too. That's Lucas Reith – his son Piers was killed years ago trying to outrun the coastguards on a suspected smuggling run, but the boat sank, so there was no further action.

'He divorced a couple of years later and Maia is his second wife's child. Auchinglass House had a long-term tenancy until Sean Reynolds with his wolf obsession appeared on the scene and it didn't take Reith long to see the potential of the rewilding scheme – all that money neatly laundered through grants and fees paid by the volunteers.

'Maia claims Thomson killed Flora, then Danni had to die because she was demanding a new investigation. She's refuting his claim that she helped dispose of the body.'

'But then she would, wouldn't she?' Borthwick said.

'Choose which liar you fancy. Now forensics have DNA evidence from Danni's body and with Antony Stanton's body having been washed ashore they should be able to establish that the rifling on the barrel of the gun Thomson was dumb enough to leave in his car matches the bullet that killed him, so we've got him all tied up.'

'Why, though?' Borthwick said. 'He was in a good position, all set to make big money.'

Strang shook his head. 'She clammed up about that. Thomson killed Stanton just because Thomson was a bad person, and of course she would never have actually fired her own gun at anyone. So my only answer to "why" is what Flora Maitland's friend said, that she was haunted by something bad she'd done, and she left money – conscience money? – to a woman she didn't know had killed herself in jail. Could this somehow be payback?'

'And it was Danni who had to pay. The sins of the fathers – or the aunt, in this case. Poor child.'

Strang sighed. 'Old sins cast long shadows, as the saying goes.'

'Still, a good result. Oh, and the wolf. What's happened about that?'

'They managed to trap her. She's joined the pack at Edinburgh Zoo.'

'Best place for her. And how did my friend Livvy do?'

'Don't ask,' Strang said. 'This time it's a reprimand – insubordinate behaviour, which is annoying because she came up with some excellent stuff.'

'Oh dear,' Borthwick said. 'Completely blotted her copybook, has she? How about Rachel French? Seemed a bit vague and timid when she spoke to me.'

'You have to remember you're kind of scary,' he said, smiling. 'Square peg, I'm afraid. In her own way she's first rate, but not a leader.'

The phone on Borthwick's desk buzzed and she raised her eyebrows. 'Finished?'

He nodded and got up, swallowing the last bite of his KitKat.

'Going to forgive Livvy?' she said, picking up the phone. 'Borthwick here.'

He pulled a face, then walked back down to his office. He was feeling the low you feel when you've been in a state of high tension and the adrenaline fades. He could take the rest of the day off, but he wasn't sure what he would do with it and for once going back to the peace of the fisherman's cottage wasn't appealing.

He hadn't seen Rachel French since she left Inverbeg, though he'd checked that she was all right, of course. But he liked her, and if he wasn't going to live like a hermit for the rest of his life, he'd have to make an effort sometime. Asking how the leg was getting on was a good excuse to phone her.

She greeted him warmly, and for a few minutes they talked shop. Then he said, 'I still feel guilty about landing you in a situation you just weren't prepared for, not to mention getting you damaged! Could I take you out for a meal by way of apology?'

It obviously took her by surprise. 'Oh!' she said, then, 'That's very kind of you. Quite unnecessary, of course – if it wasn't for your quick action, I'd have been dead.'

'Self-interest came into it as well, of course. Do you like Italian?'

'Doesn't everyone?'

He rang off feeling buoyant. It was probably long past time he rejoined normal life.

The evening went well. The conversation flowed easily: a bit of work talk – including her plea for leniency towards the infuriating Livvy – and then general chat about interests they shared. He'd almost forgotten how pleasant it was to sit talking to a woman over dinner.

Afterwards, as they waited for her taxi to come, she said again, 'That was very kind, Kelso. Thank you so much – I enjoyed myself.'

'So did I. You know, there's a play by the Royal Shakespeare Company coming next week – I could get tickets, if you like.'

He suddenly realised she was embarrassed. 'Oh, Kelso – I didn't realise you didn't know I had a partner. I'm sorry.'

He felt a fool. He'd been thinking this was the tentative start of a relationship; she was seeing it as a work outing. He was grateful that it was dark He felt the sort of frantic blush he hadn't experienced since he was a teenager sweep up his face and out until his ears were burning.

'No, no, it's not your fault. Gauche of me not to find out beforehand,' he said with an awkward laugh. 'My apologies to your partner.'

'Jane would love to meet you,' Rachel said. 'She's really grateful to you for saving my life. Will you come round to supper soon?'

'That would be lovely. Here's your cab now.' He gave her a peck on the cheek and waved her off.

He didn't hail another cab immediately. It was cold but clear tonight, with a full moon looking as if it had been specially placed to spotlight the elegance of the New Town and he walked on along George Street to Charlotte Square, where he and Alexa had liked to pretend they'd heard a nightingale. That seemed a long time ago now.

The summons she'd been dreading came and DC Murray's legs were shaking as she reached DCI Strang's office. She'd never known him be so coldly angry and she had small expectation that she could just blag her way through this time.

He waved her to a seat. 'Livvy, we need a serious talk.'

She looked down. 'Yes, boss.'

'Do you know why I'm so annoyed with you?'

'Yes, boss. I shouldn't just have gone off on my own.'

'No, you shouldn't have. It's your besetting sin. I keep hoping you've learnt a lesson, but no. Do you know why I am so particularly angry about this?'

She shook her head dumbly.

'It's not because you took away a car that was needed, annoying though that was. It's that on previous occasions when you've struck out on your own it's been because you thought, rightly or wrongly, that I'd stop you doing something. Did you really think if you told me, I'd prevent you going to Ullapool to check out your idea?'

'No, boss,' she muttered.

'I want you to consider why you did that.'

This was worse even than she had feared. She knew why: she'd been feeling threatened by Rachel French and she'd wanted to showcase her own more brilliant detective skills in a way Strang couldn't ignore. But how did you present that in a less humiliating way?

'No, Livvy, don't even try to bullshit me,' he said.

She forced back the tears that were forming. 'Jealous, I suppose,' she said.

'Yes. Not impressive. You and Rachel have different, not competing skills. And otherwise, you did well. It's been a good result, and I'm giving you some credit for that.'

At least she'd managed to cover up some of the things she'd handled badly – and actually, did he but know it, he owed her for not sharing her fears about Ranald Sinclair when that could have messed everything up.

But he was going on. 'I'm afraid this is going on your record. You've been well warned.'

She'd still hoped for forgiveness. The lump in her throat felt like a boulder and her eyes were really stinging now. 'Not much point in going for my stripes now, is there?' she said gruffly.

'Don't be dramatic, Livvy. Get your head down and study this time and don't get any more bad marks.'

'Sir,' she said, with a surreptitious sniff. Then she asked the question she needed to ask, despite not being sure she wanted the answer. 'Does – does that rule me out from future SCRS investigations?'

Strang sighed. 'No, Livvy, I hope not. You're a good detective and I would miss your insights. Just take the lesson on board this time, all right?'

'Yes, sir. I'm really sorry.'

She felt more cheerful as she left. He'd said he'd miss her – but then a nasty little inner voice pointed out he hadn't said he'd miss her, just her insights. It was better than nothing, but as she sneaked back into her favourite spot behind the filing cabinet in the CID room and took out her textbook, the heavy sigh wasn't only because she hated studying, but also because of the dull ache somewhere near where she thought her heart must be.

Acknowledgements

My grateful thanks go, as always, to my agent Jane Conway-Gordon, my publisher Susie Dunlop and all at Allison and Busby, especially Claire Browne and Felicity Bage.

ALINE TEMPLETON grew up in the fishing village of Anstruther, in the East Neuk of Fife. She has worked in education and broadcasting and was a Justice of the Peace for ten years. She has been a Chair of the Society of Authors in Scotland and a director of the Crime Writers' Association. Married, with a son and a daughter and four grandchildren, she lived in Edinburgh for many years but now lives in Kent.

alinetempleton.co.uk   @Aline Templeton